P9-CDN-925

CONSIDER THE LILIES
OF THE FIELD

THE MACMILLAN COMPANY
NEW YORK · BOSTON · CHICAGO · DALLAS
ATLANTA · SAN FRANCISCO

MACMILLAN AND CO., Limited
LONDON · BOMBAY · CALCUTTA · MADRAS
MELBOURNE

THE MACMILLAN COMPANY
OF CANADA, Limited
TORONTO

Consider the Lilies of the Field

A Novel

By ERICO VERISSIMO

Translated from the Portuguese
By Jean Neel Karnoff

THE MACMILLAN COMPANY

NEW YORK 1947

PART ONE

Chapter 1

The doctor closed the door of Room 122 behind him and began quietly to address the nun who was waiting in the corridor.

"Sister Isolda, I'm afraid you'd better notify Dr. Eugenio. There seems to be no hope for her. It will be a matter of hours, perhaps only minutes. She knows she is going to die."

Silence. . . . A gust of wind blew across the corridor, followed by the dry sound of a door closing. The Sister of Charity felt her blood chill, as she remembered the dawn when the paralytic in Room 103 had died. The horrified woman orderly had told her afterward how she had sensed the cold spirit of Death stealing into the sick man's room.

"Is he at the family's home, doctor?"

"No. You can probably reach him by phoning his father-in-law's country place in Santa Margarida. Tell him Olivia wants to see him, that he may still get here in time." The doctor shrugged his shoulders pessimistically and lit a cigarette with hands which trembled slightly.

Sister Isolda walked to the far end of the corridor, to the telephone booth. She entered and began to dial nervously.

"Hello! Hello! This is Metropolitan Hospital calling. We have a very urgent case. Give me long distance, please." Tears were streaming down her face.

3

". . . and there was a hemorrhage . . ."

At the sound of the veiled, far-away voice Eugenio's heart for a moment failed him, as though it, and not his brain, had received the first shock of the terrible news. Its beats became far-spaced and hollow.

"Dr. Teixeira Torres says there is no hope. . . . She knows she is going to die. . . . She asked for you . . ."

Eugenio felt each word reverberate painfully throughout his body, but the dull agony which settled in his chest was like the heavy blow of a club. His hand fell limply from the telephone. He was aware of only two things—of irrevocable disaster, and of the desperate pressure of his heart, which seemed at every beat to grow, to swell suffocatingly. His breathing was painful and uneven; his mouth burned, and his chest ached. Upon his body there seemed to have fallen suddenly all the weariness of a long and furious race. Automatically he replaced the telephone on its hook, his mind torn by a confused, unreasoning hope that the voice had been no more than an evil dream, an illusion.

Outside, the afternoon sun flooded the meadows with gold, and the irrigation reservoir gleamed yellowly at the edge of the eucalyptus grove. But Eugenio saw nothing of this. He saw Olivia lying pale and still on an operating table, her body covered with bloodstained cloths.

She knows she is going to die. . . . She asked for you . . .

He must go. He must go immediately.

A childish voice vibrated through the afternoon silence. A little boy was driving a spotted cow to drink, switching her to the edge of the reservoir, where animal and child were mirrored in the still water. Peace, thought Eugenio, God's great peace, about which Olivia spoke so often . . .

4

Silence followed the boy's cry, a silence filled for Eugenio with remorse, with the realization that this day brought him to the beginning of his just retribution. His eyes filled with tears. Little by little his breathing became more normal; but his body was weak with the tremulous weakness of a man recovering from a long, grave illness.

Suddenly, he was seized by a wildly excited hope, which seemed to be born of the peace of the sunny fields and of the thought of God. Olivia might be saved! It would be too cruel for her to die now. He had heard strange, miraculous stories. He snatched up his hat and hurried toward the stairway.

On the landing he paused abruptly, as though his descent had been barred by an unexpected obstacle. Fear, his immense, constant fear, loomed overwhelmingly before him, blinding him, holding him back at a moment when he should forget all else and hurry to Olivia. For an instant he stood transfixed, kneading his hat in his nervous fingers, thinking of his wife down in the garden, of the possibility that now she might discover the truth. He must invent an excuse for his sudden trip. Olivia was dying. How brutal it would be to let her go without one loving word, without at least asking her forgiveness! But he knew that his own exaggerated pride and cowardice would never allow him one gesture of humility before strangers.

My God, I must go, at any cost!

Slowly he began to descend the stairs. He imagined that he was in the hospital. There was Olivia, with Dr. Teixeira Torres at her bedside, explaining coldly, technically. There were the others, too, with their smug looks and their whispers. *Who? Lovers. . . . Ah! He's Eugenio Fontes, married to the daughter of that old moneybag, Cintra. Do you know him?*

Eugenio's fingers grasped the stair railing convulsively, and his heart pounded with desperate fury. Hot tears streamed down his cheeks, and he wiped them away, trembling in all his body. He walked unsteadily toward the garden, shouting, "Honorio!" Then, as the chauffeur appeared: "Get the car out! We're going to town immediately! Hurry!"

Eunice was reading in the garden, in the shade of a wide red and blue beach umbrella.

"I have to go to town right away," said Eugenio, making an effort to control his voice.

Eunice raised her eyes indifferently from her book and stared at her husband.

"What's wrong with you? You're pale."

"Nothing. Some news I just received." He hesitated and looked away. Then he lied. "About Ernesto."

A cold light shone in Eunice's eyes. They seemed to pierce the mask of his deceit. "You needn't explain." There was a pause, and for an instant they gazed at each other like strangers. "Of course you're not coming back today."

Eugenio looked at his watch. "It's almost six. I'll get to the city at nine or a little after. I don't think I can be back before tomorrow morning."

"You know I insist on not interfering in your affairs." Eunice tossed her head back lightly and seemed to address the clouds. "Do as you please. In any case, thank you for letting me know."

"Your father is coming in a little while, so you won't be alone all night."

"Oh, don't worry about me. I can take care of myself. Besides, you know, I like to be alone. Solitude invites one to examine one's conscience." She laughed. "You, by the way, must be needing to examine yours."

6

Eugenio felt his face grow crimson. Eunice lowered her eyes to her book. He stood for a moment looking at her, aware of a cold, tenuous anger.

"Until tomorrow," he said, and hurried away, as though he were fleeing.

"Until tomorrow," murmured Eunice, without raising her eyes from her book.

The automobile rolled forward, past the big gateway of the estate, into the highway.

"Hurry, Honorio!"

"When we get to the cement stretch we can do sixty," the chauffeur answered, without turning his head.

The afternoon light was gentle and sad. Cattle were grazing in the fields; a quero-quero called stridently, and in the distance a dog barked.

Eugenio felt an impulse to leap into the front seat and confide his anguish and his secrets to the chauffeur. In his heart he knew that he belonged more to Honorio's class than to that of his wife. He had never been able to treat the man with the superiority which Eunice and his father-in-law used toward him, as if he were made of commoner material, as if he had been born exclusively to obey.

"We must get to the city in less than three hours, Honorio. It's a case of life and death."

Eugenio closed his eyes and saw Olivia lying white and still among the sheets, dead.

Chapter 2

It was in the school yard, at recess time. Eugenio was bending down to pick up the rag ball, when suddenly someone shouted behind him:

"Genoca's got a hole in the seat of his pants!"

The boys surrounded him in a screeching chorus, shoving, jostling, and kicking him, punching with their elbows, screaming and laughing. They were like blind chickens all running at once to peck at the same fistful of corn. In the center of the group, red-faced and bewildered, Eugenio stood covering his torn pants with both hands. He felt an intense burning in his face; it seemed as though a thousand fiery ants were crawling over his flesh. The boys broke out in frantic hooting:

"Hole in his pa-yunts! Hole in his pa-yunts! Hole in his pa-yunts!"

They shouted in an even cadence, clapping their hands. Eugenio's eyes filled with tears. He stammered words of weak protest, which were swallowed up in the deafening chorus:

"Hole in his pa-yunts! Right in the sea-eat! Looky at Genoca! Hole in his pa-yunts!"

From the other side of the school yard the little girls were watching curiously. They were amused, and they hopped up and down, laughing. Soon they too began to shout, their voices mingling in a strident chorus, like an excited flock of crows.

The morning wind which stirred the cypresses in the yard carried the sharp young voices on its cold breath, spreading them through all the city, announcing to everyone that the little boy Eugenio's pants were torn, right in the seat. Tears slid down the child's face, and he allowed them to run freely, let them stripe his cheeks, enter his mouth and drip from his chin, for both his hands were placed like a shield over his buttocks.

The boys joined hands now to form a great circle, which gyrated and pulled from side to side as they screeched incessantly, "Hole in his pa-yunts! Hole in his pa-yunts!"

Eugenio closed his eyes, as though he could bear no longer to look upon his shame.

Then the bell rang, and the recess hour was over.

In class Eugenio felt humiliated, like a criminal. When the time came for the arithmetic tables the teacher would move her pointer to indicate the numbers on the blackboard, while the students shouted in unison, "Two and two are fo-wer, three and three are si-ix." And the rhythm of that chorus reminded Eugenio of the taunting voices at recess time: *Hole in his pa-yunts!*

What awful shame! Eugenio's father owed the money from last month, and the teacher had demanded payment loudly, in front of the whole class. He was poor and badly dressed, and because he was quiet the other boys mistreated him and played tricks on him. Sometimes they pinned paper tails to the back of his trousers. Last Saturday he had had to stand in disgrace with his foot in a corner, because his fingernails were dirty. But the worst part of all was the little girls. If only there were just boys in the class . . .

Oh, Lordy, how awful, how shameful it was to be poor! Nelson wrote with an amber pen that had gold rings around it, and Heitor had a leather case to carry his schoolbooks. At the parties at the end of the year it was Tancredo who made the speeches for the teacher, because he was always clean and well dressed, and he smelled of perfume.

9

"Eight and eight are six-teen." *Hole in his pa-yunts!*

"Eugenio, tell your father to come pay the bill for last month."

"Yes, senhora, I'll tell him."

Pay. Horrid word. Pay. Pants. Torn pants. Eugenio could see his father shake his head, complaining, "Just to send the boys to school costs me the eyes in my head."

A face on the front bench turned around to look at Eugenio. It was Ernesto, his little brother. He too had helped make fun of him. *Good for nothing! I'll make you pay for that!*

When it was time to go home, Eugenio lingered deliberately and was the last to leave the schoolhouse. Even so, he did not escape another siege of hooting. A group of six boys lay in wait for him on a corner and, as he passed, they broke out again:

"Hole in his pa-yunts! Hey, a speckled chicken! Hole in his pa-yunts! Hole in his pa-yunts!"

Eugenio walked on, followed closely by the derisive chorus. Again tears came to his eyes. Ernesto whispered:

"Don't be stupid. Crying only makes it worse. Pretend you don't care."

When the band had left him alone, trooping off in another direction, Eugenio walked on, his head low.

The wind was sweeping the street, shaking the leafless trees, lifting bits of straw, fragments of paper, grains of dust.

Eugenio was ashamed to look at the people who passed. Surely they all *knew*. Fortunately now his old black overcoat, green with age, covered the tear in his pants; but it could not make him forget the humiliation of that mocking refrain. At his side his little brother walked in silence, smiling with the corner of his mouth. Through the holes in the bottoms of his shoes Eugenio could feel the pene-trating cold of the flagstone sidewalk.

Suddenly Ernesto began to hum, marking the rhythm of their steps:

> One, two, beans with rice,
> One, two, beans with rice.

Unconsciously Eugenio began to accompany the rhythm, adjusting his steps to its beat. He began to whistle softly, to drive away the anger, the hate, the bitterness. But never, not if he lived a thousand years, would he forget the sound of those mocking voices.

Ernesto stopped humming, pulled from his pocket a cigarette butt, placed it in his mouth, and lighted it.

"You had a cigarette in class!"

Ernesto shrugged his shoulders, blew a cloud of smoke from his mouth and threw away the burned match.

" 'At's none of your business."

"If the teacher catches you, you'll be sorry!"

"She's not my mother."

"But Mamma and Papa don't like you to smoke."

"Well, I like to, so there!"

When they came within sight of the house, Ernesto threw away the cigarette butt and spat with an expe-rienced, hardened air. Eugenio wiped away his tears with the back of his hand.

"Ernesto, come wash your feet before dinner!"

Eugenio was already drying his own with the coarse, hard towel made from a manioc flour sack. From the tin basin, from the water whitened with soap, there arose an almost invisible vapor.

Dona Alzira seated her younger son in the chair and placed his feet forcibly in the water.

"Genoca's water's got a crust on it!" protested Ernesto.

"Don't be so persnickety. It's your feet that's got a crust. I don't know where these children get so dirty. A body'd never tell they wore shoes."

As Eugenio put on his wool socks he looked at his father, who sat curved over a pair of trousers, sewing. He was a silent, wilted old man, although he had not reached the age of forty. His face was expressionless, the light long quenched in his dull eyes, which had an almost bovine air of resignation. He wore glasses, for his vision was already short. (*This accursed black cloth, this dim light.*) He coughed more often than he spoke, and when he spoke it was to complain about life. He complained without bitterness or anger.

Eugenio felt very sorry for his father, but he could not love him. He knew that children should love their parents. The teacher talked in class about "filial love," and she illustrated what she meant with stories and examples. But, as much as he tried, Eugenio could feel no more than pity for his father. He pitied him because he coughed, because he sighed, because he complained, and because his name was Angelo . . . Angelo was the name of an unhappy man, the name of a murdered man. Eugenio could not look at his father without thinking of the seventh lesson in his second reader. He had been so greatly moved when he read it for the first time that he had remained a whole day under its tragic spell:

Angelo was an old farmer, very industrious and honorable, who lived near a small village in Portugal. One day he journeyed toward the hamlet with a heavy load of grain, the product of his labor, to sell it at the public fair, which was held there monthly. Having made a good sale, he was returning to his little house, with cloths and other things needed by his beloved family.

A highwayman, who had followed him around at the fair and had seen him sell his grain, lay in wait for him on the mountain road, in order to kill and rob him. As the poor old man went contentedly along the road to his hut, the evil man descended suddenly upon him and pierced him with his dagger. Angelo could speak only these words, as he breathed his last breath: "Criminal! He who strikes with steel, by steel shall be stricken!"

In vain the officers of the law sought to identify Angelo's murderer. No witness could be found, and the crime remained unpunished.

Scarcely a year afterward, the highwayman, being at the same fair, provoked a fight and received a dagger thrust. Recognizing that he was about to die, he confessed that he had killed poor Angelo and said, "How truly did he exclaim in the hour of his death, *He who strikes with steel, by steel shall be stricken!*"

The story had awakened mysterious echoes in Eugenio. Always as he reread it he saw the murdered man's body with his father's face. Angelo had been poor as they were poor; surely he had had a hole in his trousers in that certain place. Eugenio felt the pain of the dagger wound in his own flesh.

Slowly a desire for justice was born in the little boy's consciousness, and he began to ask himself questions which he could not answer. Why did people kill one another? Why were there evil men in the world? Eugenio could never bear to scratch a classmate or throw stones at dogs. He could harm neither animals nor people, for he pitied all creatures. It pained him to see others suffer, and the sight of blood horrified him. How was it then that there were people in the world who could stab upright farmers like poor Angelo? The boy pictured the sorrow of the "beloved family," which must surely have come to a miserable end. He imagined the little donkey trotting helplessly along the road, or standing beside his dead master, licking his face affectionately. *He who strikes with steel, by steel shall be stricken.* These words recalled to the boy's mind his mother's familiar admonishment, "God punishes."

One day lightning had struck the house of old Galvão, killing him and injuring his daughter. Mamma had said: "God punished them. They were very wicked." Was there then, besides the teacher's punishment, besides the punishment of one's parents, still a greater, a much greater one—the punishment of God?

Eugenio feared this God whom his mother tried in vain to make him love. When he prayed at night, "Our Father, which art in heaven," he prayed to a God in human form, but who was terrible, mysterious and implacable. He was invisible, but He was everywhere, even in one's thoughts.

It was then that the idea of sin began to worry Eugenio. He studied his lessons and behaved himself well in class, because he feared the teacher's punishment. He did not smoke, did not say bad words or "do awful things in private," because he feared his mother's punishment. He banished wicked thoughts and did not do anything naughty even secretly, because God was everywhere and saw everything.

One day, in enumerating a list of the principal sins, someone had told him, "It's a sin not to love your parents." Then Eugenio was sinning! As much as he tried, he could not love the father who never lifted his hand to strike him, who did not so much as raise his voice to scold.

At school the other boys boasted of the advantages and prowess of members of their families. "My pop's been to Rio de Janeiro. Has yours?" "My uncle knocked a nigger down with one sock." "I've got a brother who's a rower in the Barroso Club."

Humiliated, Eugenio would stand listening in envious silence. He had nothing to tell. His father was only poor Angelo.

Shivering with cold, Eugenio put on his slippers and went to look for old magazines to thumb through while he waited for dinner.

"Don't get your feet on the floor, child!" Dona Alzira called to Ernesto. "You'll catch cold."

Angelo raised his tired eyes. "All we need now is for one of the children to get sick in bed."

Dona Alzira seized Ernesto by the waist, seated him on the table, and began to pull on his socks. Angelo lifted his needle against the light and, with one eye shut, tried to push the black thread through.

Eugenio moistened the tip of his forefinger against his tongue and began to leaf through the magazines. They were old copies of *L'Illustration*, which he had picked up in the garbage of a near-by Belgian engineer's house. How many times had his eyes passed over those pictures? A hundred? A thousand? He never grew tired of looking, for they had a powerful, mysterious fascination. He especially liked the ones which showed odd sailboats on the rivers of Indo-China, Annamese with conical hats, and Europeans dressed in white, with cork helmets on their heads. He always thought of those men as "valiant explorers," for he knew that people who went to hunt wild animals in India and Africa wore that funny-looking kind of hat. The legends which described the pictures were written in a language which he did not understand. Seu Florismart said it was French. It must be nice to know French, German, English, African . . .

Eugenio looked at the coolie on the edge of a river, carrying across his shoulders a pole with heavy baskets, his shadow reflected in the water. It was sad. It almost brought tears to his eyes, although he did not know exactly why. The Chinese, poor Angelo in the story, Papa—they were dreary figures which mingled with one another.

Eugenio looked again at his father. Angelo was bent over his work—bent as if at that very instant some evildoer had stabbed him in the back. Poor Angelo . . . He lived in constant flight from his creditors. When they knocked at the door he would tremble and rise swiftly, trying immediately to hide or to escape into the rear of the house. It might be someone trying to collect money . . .

Eugenio could not forget what had happened a few days ago. Seu Jango from the grocery store had come in person to collect the unpaid bill.

"Say I'm not home, Alzira. Say I went to the town hall," Angelo had whispered in alarm.

Dona Alzira had delivered the message: "Look, Seu Jango, can't you see Angelo's not home?"

Behind the bedroom door Angelo had listened, biting his lip. Heavy steps had sounded in the hall, and Dona Alzira's voice, more hurried now, had had an anxious, fearful note.

"But, Seu Jango—I told you Angelo's gone—"

Suddenly Jango had entered the dining room. He was a big man, strong and dark, with very white teeth. When Ernesto saw him come in, in his shirtsleeves, with his muscular, hairy arms showing, he whispered into Eugenio's ear, "Golly, he looks like Tarzan!"

Strange . . . On seeing Seu Jango, Eugenio had thought immediately of Destiny. Always, when anything unpleasant happened to the family, Dona Alzira would say, "It was Destiny." Destiny was a cruel being, all-powerful and inexorable. Seu Jango was Destiny.

There had been nothing for Angelo to do but to appear. He had come out of his hiding place, cowering, his head low.

"Well, Seu Angelo, fooling a body, eh? You think I'm stupid? I guess I know my customers pretty well."

"Now, Seu Jango," Angelo had mumbled, scarcely daring to face the creditor. "I didn't mean any harm. A man's ashamed to have to owe money."

"That's easy enough to say. If you're so ashamed, then why don't you pay me? I don't live on air. I made a sale, and I want my money."

"Be patient—" Dona Alzira had intervened timidly.

"I'm just going to deliver a suit to a customer," Angelo had said, as if to reinforce her words. "I'll get about eight-five milreis for it, and then—"

"That's an old song," Seu Jango had scoffed. "Everybody's going to get money, but nobody pays. What you need, Seu Angelo, is a little more shame on that face of yours, you hear?"

Angelo had been pale. Eugenio had heard him murmur imploringly: "Seu Jango, please. The children can hear—"

"Well, let them hear! Let them know their father's a goddam chiseler!" The grocer had gone out stamping his feet, and he had slammed the door.

Some day, thought Eugenio, someone will go to Seu Jango's house and say all those things he said to Papa.

He who strikes with steel, by steel shall be stricken. Someone had to avenge poor Angelo. Maybe God would do it.
Or then . . . For the first time Eugenio thought of growing
up, of studying to become a doctor and earning money to
free his family from that poverty, from that shame.

Dona Alzira clapped her hands. "Come on and eat now!
Hurry, or dinner'll get cold!"

They sat down around the table, in the center of which
steamed a platter of rice with a stew of jerked beef.

They began to eat in silence. The first to speak was
Ernesto.

"At school today they booed Eugenio because he had a
hole in his pants." He doubled over completely, represent-
ing his laughter, and his little eyes shone with cunning.

Eugenio's face was aflame. Dona Alzira shook her head
slowly and looked at her elder son.

"Didn't I tell you not to put on them striped pants?
Why didn't you put on the black ones?"

Eugenio lowered his eyes to his plate and said nothing.
Angelo served himself more rice.

"It don't seem true," he said thoughtfully. "A tailor's
son with a hole in his pants . . ."

They could hear the *minuano*, the cold southwest wind,
howling outside.

"A sad thing, the winter!" sighed Dona Alzira.

Eugenio looked at his mother. She was pretty. Yes,
much prettier than lots of rich women he had seen. She
always said that some day they would be happy and comfortable. "No one escapes from Destiny," were her words,
"and I think that if he's brought us so many bad things
some day he can bring us some good."

Angelo had already crossed his knife and fork on his

empty plate when they heard a knock at the door. Husband and wife exchanged questioning looks.

"Must be Florismart," said Angelo.

"Go and open it, son," Dona Alzira told Eugenio. Then she added swiftly: "No, let me go. You might get in a draught and catch pneumonia."

Florismart . . . For Eugenio that name held a secret enchantment. The man who bore it appeared at their house almost every evening. He would arrive very calmly, smoking his two-for-a-nickel cigar; and as soon as he entered he would sit down in the only rocking chair. He was a short man with thin hair—almost bald, and his heavy beard always a bluish shadow on his plump, round face, even when he shaved very closely. His teeth were small and dark. He had, however, a gentle voice and a statesmanlike dignity; he was of a conciliatory nature, and he boasted of his ability as a smooth talker. "I was born to be a lawyer," he would say. "If I had had a little more sense when I was young . . ." His voice would trail off, and he would turn his head to one side, knock the ash from his cigar, and assume a dreamy attitude. Surely, thought Eugenio, Dr. Florismart was reviewing his past, his mistakes, his lost career. Or perhaps he was only thinking of the effect which his words and that suggestive posture might be producing in his audience.

It was true that Florismart's friends and acquaintances always called on him to render verdicts, to solve problems. They said the little man arranged cases for clientless lawyers and earned fat commissions for his trouble. Lots of important men tipped their hats to him in the street. He even made political speeches, and for this reason all his friends called him *Dr.* Florismart. At first they spoke the title with a touch of sarcasm. But Florismart, both flattered and amused, accepted it with a smile; and, as time went by, his friends who were fondest of him forgot the joke and came to believe in "Dr." Florismart.

That night the little man entered with a serious expression.

"Things are black in Europe," he began immediately, even before he said good evening.

All eyes in the room were fixed on him. He sat down in the rocking chair, lit a small cigar, and, like a chief of state addressing a council of ministers, said deliberately, gravely:

"Germany has invaded Belgium."

Husband and wife looked at each other in a mute consultation. They did not read newspapers, but they had heard that in Europe things were not going well.

"Then there's really going to be a war?" asked Angelo.

Dr. Florismart cocked his head to one side and made a gesture as if to rid himself of all responsibility for the catastrophe.

"It's inevitable. The Kaiser wants it."

For a moment no one spoke. Angelo sat looking at his friend, aghast.

"August, month of disaster," murmured Dona Alzira, getting up to clear the table and wash the dishes. The war was far away in Europe, and, in any event, it could never be great enough to alter the rhythm of life in her small household.

"But what do you think, Dr. Florismart?" Angelo called on his friend, as if the little man in the rocking chair sucking his thin cigar held the fate of the entire world in his chubby, well groomed, and almost effeminate hands.

Dr. Florismart smoothed his thin hair affectionately. In a soft, slightly cautious voice, he gave his opinion:

"What I think, my friend Angelo, is this. First of all, Germany will crush Belgium. Then she will attack France. Of course, England will never stand by and watch France take a beating, so she'll be the next one in. It will be some war. Things may even go so far I'd hate to try and guess what will happen. I don't know who Italy and Holland will side up with." He had a great admiration for Holland. "I'm a little worried about the Dutch. What wonderful people!" He sat for a moment silent and motionless, his thoughts far away.

At length Angelo spoke, shaking his head. "But without any help the Kaiser can't hold out against all that."

"Oh, he'll hold out, Seu Angelo, he'll hold out. Did you know the Germans invented the death ray? No? Well, they did. A terrible invention. It can kill miles away. And the worst part is, it's absolutely invisible. A hideous thing . . ."

"Just think!" Angelo shook his head again, rolling a cigarette in a piece of straw.

Eugenio listened. He understood. There was going to be a war in Europe. The Kaiser wanted war. He knew the Kaiser from a picture in *L'Illustration*. He was a stern man with an iron helmet and a hard, twisted mustache.

The word "war," with its connotations of suffering and disaster, brought to Eugenio's mind the story of poor Angelo. He had seen some colored pictures in a book about the Russo-Japanese War. They were terrifying scenes of bearded Cossacks charging fiercely and Japanese with bayonets drawn to kill. There were bloody corpses on the ground, a soldier without a head, and others with their arms and legs cut off, their bellies open . . . Kaiser. A fearful word. More fearful, he thought, because it was spelled with a *k*. "Crime" should be spelled *krime*. The

Kaiser was Destiny, too. The Kaiser appeared to Eugenio confusedly now as the murderer of poor Angelo.

Dr. Florismart was making prophecies, painting a dark and bloody picture for Europe and the world. But in the picture of sorrow and destruction he left one crevice through which a minute, timid ray of hope might enter:

"If I were the President of the United States of America, I would prevent this hecatomb."

The last word filled the mouth of Dr. Florismart completely. Everyone sensed in it a mysterious, enormous significance. Dona Alzira, who was carrying a stack of dishes to the kitchen, paused for an instant in the middle of the dining room. She looked at Dr. Florismart and stood waiting for him to save the world. Dr. Florismart began to expound his plan for peace. Everything in the world could be arranged with a little maneuvering . . .

Eugenio listened, his mouth slightly open, his breath suspended. How he admired Dr. Florismart! There was a man who knew everything. He must have traveled and studied a great deal.

"Come here, Seu Genoca. Tell me who Florismart was." The little man asked that same question every time he came. And, without understanding what he was saying, Eugenio had to repeat correctly the words which that wonderful friend of Papa's had taught him:

"He was one of the Twelve Peers of France!"

Dr. Florismart smiled contentedly, chewing the thin cigar with his tiny, dark teeth.

That night Eugenio went to bed greatly impressed. He prayed "Our Father, which art in heaven," imagining that God, the Kaiser, and Destiny were one and the same person. The three were powerful, invisible, and unpitying. God was master of the world, the Kaiser wanted to conquer the world, and Destiny was to blame for all the evil things which happened there.

Under the covers, with his legs doubled up (as a precaution against a possible attack by the souls-from-the-other-world), Eugenio lay for some time with his attention divided between his own thoughts and the zumzum of the conversation in the dining room. Outside, the wind was still wailing, rattling the tiles, shaking the grove of trees, causing the window panes to shiver.

Dona Alzira entered the bedroom noiselessly and placed a hot brick between the feet of the two little boys. She left as silently as she had come.

Again Eugenio heard the jeering of his classmates—faintly now, from the depths of his memory, and blurred by the more vivid voice of Dr. Florismart: *Hole in his pa-yunts! Hole in his pa-yunts!* The Kaiser was also in the group which gyrated around him, screaming and leaping; the boy could see his iron helmet, his rigid mustache. *Hole in his pa-yunts!* The little girls were shouting and laughing, too. Oh, how shameful!

Eugenio fell asleep to the sound of the mocking voices. He dreamed that he was rich. He awoke a little later, however, when his parents were getting ready for bed. Their double bed was in the same room with that of the two children, for there were only three rooms in the whole house. Angelo coughed, groaned, sighed.

"You ought to stop smoking," whispered his wife.

On the back of his neck Eugenio could feel the warm breath of his little brother, sleeping soundly. He listened to his parents' conversation, which was interspersed with long silences, with sighs and stifled moans. Once his father said:

"Please God that war don't come here!"

23

"The Lord knows what He's about," said his wife. After a few seconds she spoke again. "Are your feet still cold?"

"Like ice."

"Do you want a hot brick?"

"You needn't bother."

Silence. . . . And then, after who knows what thoughts had passed through his mind, poor Angelo's doleful voice echoed tremulously, almost sobbingly, in the cold, dark, silent room:

"Oh! How can they call this living, Alzira?"

To Eugenio the pathos of his father's words was like physical pain. He was still thinking of them when he fell asleep.

Minutes went by, and the automobile glided rapidly and serenely over the cement ribbon of highway.

Eugenio took off his hat and ran his fingers back over his hair. Through his mind there passed a disturbing succession of images of the people who had been sacrificed to his own ambition. Their sad, dead eyes haunted him. He had never thought of them when they had been alive. There had been no time.

Yet how selflessly they had loved him! There was his father, meek, obscure, humiliated . . . There was his mother, who had devoted her youth to her husband, to her sons, to her home . . . Now both were dead. He would never see them again. It was just as well: Eugenio thought with regret that, if he were given the opportunity to live again the years of his childhood and adolescence, he would not be able to change them. He had not succeeded, and he would never succeed, in loving his parents as they had deserved to be loved.

And Olivia . . . Olivia had given him everything. How

24

blind, how unfeeling he had been! It had taken him years to understand Olivia. His desire for success, his preoccupation with his own interests had blinded him. He had wanted to rise. Mediocrity had stifled him, and poverty had smelled of death . . .

His career had been that of a sacred elephant trampling a human carpet. How many souls had been crushed by his brutal feet!

And now his ambition was dissolved like dust, like coarse ashes which escaped between his fingers, leaving only a bitter, empty remembrance.

What was he, after so much cruelty, so much effort, so much struggle? He was no one. He was only a mediocre person who, having sought and attained success through a wealthy marriage, found in it at last only the familiar worries and uncertainties, the old, joyless sensation of inferiority which had pursued him in the days of his poverty. He was only the man who had married Vicente Cintra's daughter.

And Olivia was dying. She was dying now, just as he was beginning to live. She was dying before he could make reparation for the wrong he had done her.

The automobile sped on. Two more hours! And if Olivia should be dead already?

He loosened the knot in his tie and unfastened his collar. Where was God, Olivia's God? Must He reveal Himself only in the form of a cruel retribution?

Eugenio looked out of the window of the speeding automobile. He saw a broad-beaked colheireiro with rose-colored wings flying low over the innocent greenness of a rice field.

Chapter 3

It was September and early spring in Brazil. On that Sunday morning, as he sat on the threshold of the front door of the boarding school, Eugenio felt as never before the changes which had taken place in his body and in his life since he had become fifteen years old. There was not the slightest doubt: he was becoming a man.

He had acquired the habit of looking at himself frequently in the mirror, from far away, from close up, sidewise, with all the obstinate fury of a research analyst. He found himself ugly and crude, and the knowledge of his unattractiveness tortured him. God could very well have given him a different appearance, since He had not made him rich. Pimples broke out on his face, neck, and shoulders. His soft, youthful mustache pushed up darkly, shadowing his upper lip. It was springtime in Eugenio's poor, adolescent body. A cloud of strangeness and wild distrust lurked in his eyes, which could look neither long nor steadily into the faces of other people. They appeared nearly always half closed and were darkly sullen, giving to his features at times an almost imbecilic expression. In mute anger he would stare at his reflection in the mirror. He seemed to stand before an enemy, a dangerous enemy who knew all his secrets and all his sins, even the most sordid and hidden.

Worst of all, however, was his voice. Its usual tone was thick and hoarse, and it had a way of descending unexpectedly to the lowest notes, only to leap suddenly upward in tuneless squeaks. Then it would return almost without warning to the deep tone which at the end of every sentence disintegrated into a snort. His voice was one of his greatest sources of anxiety and shame. He suffered whenever he was called upon to read aloud in class. His schoolmates laughed at him, and even the teachers were often unable to maintain a serious expression. As a result, Eugenio became more reticent than ever.

Why, he asked himself, was everything about him so disagreeable? Why was everything which pertained to him awkward and unattractive, from the poor clothes his father made him, to the body which God had given him?

Eugenio longed intensely for beauty. It was perhaps this very longing which made his passion for Miss Margaret, the daughter of the rector of the school, so great, so unhappy, so hopeless.

Yes, he thought, he was becoming a man. He was aware of his body as never before, and he tried to discover what mysterious relation the spring might have to his desires and to his unrest. He recalled an incident whch had occurred at home during his last vacation. Mamma had complained to Dr. Seixas: "Look, doctor, I feel something here, in my liver. It don't rightly hurt. It's *something* . . ." And the doctor had replied, "When you can feel some organ, it's because that organ is sick."

Eugenio was aware of his genital organs in a way that was simultaneously painful and pleasant. They seemed to be the center of his whole life, attracting nearly all his thoughts, drawing them irresistibly away from other subjects. He was filled with both anxiety and disgust, because Dr. Parker's sermons, the Old Testament, and the ever-present mystery which veiled things pertaining to sex, all cried out to him at once that *that* particular portion of his body was the source of the most loathsome sins. Could his feeling be natural, or was it the consequence of some illness? Eugenio was astute enough to conclude that it was natural. He knew that for the majority of the boys at the

27

boarding school sex held no mystery. Nearly all the older students had already known women. As for him, that which he had desired before merely curiously and with premature longing he had come to crave now ardently, with all his body. His craving became a torture, for the idea of sin mingled with his desire and made it even more intense and painful. Between his body and the object of his fiery dreams there arose the fear of punishment by his teachers and, even more terrifying, the fear of punishment by God.

The fact remained, however, that none of these thoughts could appease his desires. He satisfied them solitarily, in the privacy of his room, filled with fear, shame, and a tremulous, anxious pleasure. Afterward, he was confronted by tremendous struggles with his conscience. The teachers circulated among the students books on sex education, in which there were fearsome threats to those who yielded to such lonely and sinful gratification. Nature punished those who transgressed her wise laws. Eugenio read and reread the dark menaces and considered himself already lost, already on his way to idiocy, unfit for his studies and for life. He looked in the mirror and saw purplish spots around his eyes. He felt his head now empty, now heavy as lead. His back ached, and his memory was poor. There was no doubt of it. They were the symptoms in the book . . .

He buried himself then in his studies and tried to dispel his immoral thoughts by fleeing from magazines which contained suggestive illustrations, by avoiding those of his classmates who delighted in discussing obscenities. But he could not escape from his desires, from his body.

This morning Eugenio felt his body as never before in his life. It pulsated under his light, crisp clothing. It was alive and filling slowly with a force so great, so warm and strange that he began to believe that he might really be ill. From the playground, where some boys were batting a ball, shouts were borne to him on the wind, on the perfumed breeze, which caused his flesh to prickle, which licked his face and awakened in him erotic thoughts.

In order to escape from the sinful visions which rose in his mind, he forced himself to think of Margaret. The love which he felt for her was different. He even *wanted* it to be different. He had been in love with her since the preceding year, and he had spent his three months of holidays from the boarding school wanting to return, reflecting on the girl with a strange longing, which was tempered with hope, distrust, fear, and something of despair. Margaret would never know about his love. She was delicate and fair. She had a doll's blue eyes, a soft little voice, and the charm of a picture. Yes, a picture. He could find no better comparison, however much he tried. Margaret was not exactly real. She was a painting, like that of the rosy-faced girl on the Ross soap advertisements . . .

Eugenio sighed. He leaned his head back against a pillar of the doorway and looked up at the sky. Margaret was as far from him as that crow flying up near the clouds. She was pretty; he was ugly. She was delicate; he was rough. She was pure and good; he was a pig.

He pulled a blade of grass from the ground and bit it furiously. Why did he want suddenly to bite the trees, to bite the leaves, to bite the flesh of his own hands?

Just then a boy in white shorts and a red shirt ran by. "Want to play ball, Genoca?" he shouted, and ran on without waiting for an answer.

Eugenio was still thinking about Margaret. His secret love was the finest thing in his whole life. It was like a romance, a romance which he was writing with his imagination, with his desire, since life had refused to give him a real adventure.

In the silence of certain nights, when the moonlight entered the windows of his room, he would lie in bed with his eyes closed, thinking of Margaret. He would imagine a rendezvous at night, under the trees in the garden. At such times he was no longer timid, for the moonlight seemed possessed of a magic power, which cleansed the blemishes from his face and the sins from his soul, which performed even the miracle of making his voice suave, manly, and pleasant. In his dreams the two lovers would stand looking at each other in silence. Her hair shone like silver in the moonlight, and his own was like bronze. A mysterious organist played sweet music in the chapel, while Margaret told him stories about the days when her family had lived in China, where her father had been a missionary. In return, Eugenio described to her his dreams, the great plans he had made for his life. He intended to study more and more each day, and some day he would receive his degree in engineering. Engineering? No, in medicine. He would become a doctor, in order to cure his father of the sickness in his chest and help poor people, the way Dr. Seixas did. He would become rich and famous. He would no longer be called by his childish nickname, Genoca. People would address him as "Dr. Eugenio Fontes," and they would respect him. They would tip their hats to him in the streets: *How do you do, doctor?*

And then, one bright, sunshiny day, Dr. Eugenio would come to ask for Margaret's hand in marriage, and Reverend Dr. Parker himself would marry them in the school chapel. Afterward they would walk out arm in arm under the avenue of plantains, which stretched from the door of the chapel to the big main gateway. It would be spring, and there would be plum and peach trees covered with flowers. Eugenio saw the newlyweds walking, very close together, among the ranks of trees and people, heard the whispers of admiration which rose as they passed. *Who is the girl, my dear? . . . Don't you know? She's Miss Margaret Parker . . . And the tall young man? . . . He's Dr. Eugenio Fontes, the doctor who saved her family. He's rich and famous . . .*

Suddenly the dream would disappear, and Eugenio would find himself again in the bare little room of the boarding school, with its iron beds and washstand, the little wooden table, the trunk and the vivid, familiar smell of linseed oil. A few steps from his bed Mario, his roommate, would be sleeping peacefully.

Never before had Eugenio felt so acutely the changes in his body and in his life as on that morning. For what was he waiting, as he sat there? He himself did not know with certainty. Perhaps he was waiting for the end of the English language service which was being held in the chapel. Margaret was in the chapel. How excited he had been as he watched her enter, dressed all in blue, carrying in her hands a yellow straw hat with an enormous, floppy brim! He imagined how she must be standing just then beside the organ, the sunlight filtering through the tricolored rose window in the back of the church, painting her hair with shimmering gold.

The church bells began to ring, and the musical sound filled the air, adding somehow to its luminosity. Eugenio felt the chimes reverberating through his body, and at each stroke he trembled, continuing to vibrate as the sound died away. He thought of other bells, of other churches, in past days. He could see and hear the bells of the first school he

31

had ever attended. His memory was filled with sad echoes of their tolling the day one of his schoolmates had died of typhus. Suddenly he felt like weeping. The bells reminded him of so many things . . . His father used to tell him how as a child he had been a sacristan, and the priest ordered him to pull the cord of a hoarse-voiced, old bell. His mother used to sing a mournful, slow song about the evening bells. Bell . . . Fire . . . Procession . . . Mass . . . Burial . . .

Was it joy or despair, this feeling which gripped him? Eugenio pressed his lips tightly together and closed his eyes. The bells sang in his ears, in his brain. Their echoes spread deep beneath his skin and imbedded themselves in his nerves.

"I must be sick," he murmured to himself.

An automobile drew up before the front gate, and a man and a woman got out. Eugenio opened his eyes and saw in a glance that both were blond and slender, that they were dressed in light colors, and that they must be English. For a second he glimpsed the flushed, smiling face of the woman, illumined by the sun and projected against the deep blue background of the sky. Automatically he arose, and when the strangers had passed he felt oddly as though he were a beggar at the door of a church and the man were going to turn and throw a coin into his hat. He felt the hot blood rise to his temples. Why did he feel so inferior in the presence of those people? Was it because they had passed without noticing him, as if he had been a stone, an ant, a splinter?

Eugenio sat down again. The couple disappeared down the avenue of trees, in the direction of the chapel.

Soon a group of men and women approached the gate, conversing animatedly in English. Eugenio saw them as a confused blur of sunburned faces and wind-blown hair that was auburn, white, bronzed, and blond. Again, without thinking, he got to his feet, and he wanted to run away. He felt ill at ease in the presence of people like that, while at the same time he admired them. They had everything he dreamed of, everything he did not have. They had pleasing personalities, attractive faces and bodies, clean, elegant clothes, money and position.

The group passed, and Eugenio seated himself once more. The bells had stopped ringing. A cloud, which had arisen from behind the hills, was now high in the sky. It was shredding finely, carried by the wind. The grove of trees was whispering, and Eugenio thought the murmur of the sea on calm days must be like its sound. He felt a nostalgia for the sea, which in reality he had never seen. The sea . . . marine . . . Margaret . . . He thought of getting up and going to the church door to hear her sing. She was a soloist in the choir.

Suddenly he turned his head, attracted by the sound of barking. He saw a tall, auburn-haired man, in a tobacco-colored jacket and creamy flannel trousers, leading a dog on a silver chain. The man entered the gate hurriedly, walked a few steps past Eugenio, then turned.

"Eh, boy!" he called.

Eugenio got up and walked toward him. The stranger extended the hand which held the chain.

"Hold this dog!"

He spoke in a dry, authoritative, voice, and Eugenio obeyed without thinking. The man made a swift half-turn and directed his long strides toward the chapel.

The dog barked and leaped frantically, tugging at the chain in a vain attempt to follow its master. Eugenio looked at the animal stupidly. The beating of his heart had

33

accelerated, and his face was aflame. Everything had happened so swiftly that he had not felt the slightest hesitation. He had merely obeyed. It was a disgrace. It was an insult. He looked with hate after the man in the brown coat and cream-colored trousers, who was now entering the chapel. *Hold this dog!* It had been a command, as if Eugenio were a servant. Eugenio's shame was so great that he wanted to hide, and he began to look about for a refuge. He found it between the body of the building and one of the huge columns of the portico.

As he walked toward the sheltered spot and stooped to sit down on the granite step, his thoughts were in a turmoil. He and the dog, the two central figures in the whole world at that moment. . . . The dog was handsomer, better cared for, and happier than he. Eugenio Fontes, less than a dog . . . Poor folks . . . The life of a dog . . . *My father and I, with our dogs' eyes, with our eyes of a beaten dog . . . The English think we Brazilians are dogs . . .* Eugenio had read stories of the war in the Transvaal, stories written by men who said that the English thought God put other men on earth expressly to serve Englishmen. The English and the Americans, he knew, hated the Negro. He had been treated like a Negro. He was a nobody. He was worth less than the ants crawling over the flagstones, carrying leaves and tiny bits of wood, less than the ants which the Englishman's dog was trying to lick up with his red, wet tongue.

Curled up in the corner, holding the chain tight in his hand, Eugenio reflected on the circumstances of his life. He could afford the luxury of an exclusive boarding school because his mother paid his tuition and living expenses by washing the linen at Columbia Academy. Every Monday poor Angelo came to check the list with the housekeeper in the linen room. On those occasions Eugenio would hide, in order not to see his father cross the garden, very humbly, smiling servilely at those he met, at the teachers, who scarcely acknowledged his presence, at the students, who laughed at him and sometimes played cruel tricks on him. The poor man tolerated their mockery with a patient smile, with the air of one who, after all, must ask their forgiveness for his very existence.

One day, as he was passing the open window of the linen room, Eugenio had heard the dictatorial voice of the housekeeper say, "Sheets, sixty-five," and his father's gentle, crushed reply, "Check." That word had lodged in Eugenio's mind for many days. Through it he could see all his father's life of subservience. *Check.* Even if the number of sheets were incorrect he would not have the courage to protest. *Check.* Angelo always agreed with everything. He was resigned, and his resignation caused Eugenio to pity him, while at the same time it infuriated him. It infuriated him, for it was that very lack of self-assertion which had caused his father's failure in life. Angelo should have bequeathed to his sons a good name, a comfortable and decent position in the world, but, no, he preferred to go on saying "Check" submissively, without courage to resist his fate.

Eugenio glowered darkly at the dog. He wanted to kick it, to kill it. Immediately he repented of his thought. He must be sick to think of such things. Warm compassion replaced the ugly impulse, and the look which he next directed toward the animal was one of pity.

After all, he reasoned, he could not escape reality. He was a poor devil. The other boys knew how things were with him. Eugenio detected scorn, condescension, in the manner in which most of his schoolmates treated him. In sports he had proved a failure. He had been tried out on the first football team and had shown himself a bad player, lacking altogether in aggressiveness, preoccupied with trying not to bruise or injure his fellows. The other boys misinterpreted his attitude and classified him immediately: "Genoca's a girl."

He did not associate himself with any group, nor did he mingle with the gang which, every day, after every meal, met behind the classroom annex to smoke cigarettes and discuss forbidden topics. For this reason he was called a sissy. He made every effort to enter into the noisy fun of the free hours, into the rollicking spirit of the dances which the boys improvised in the big gymnasium. But it was no use. One day in the midst of the uproar he had forced himself to scream like the other boys; during the remainder of the festivities he had been haunted by the echo of that scream without grace, without gayety, without spontaneity, without youth. He had felt ashamed.

At the same time, he saw how the fifth-year boys sought Margaret's company. They were invited to weekly teas and monthly luncheons at the rector's house, and the mere thought of them sitting around the table, a short distance from Margaret, caused Eugenio to suffer. The fifth-year students were older than he; some were handsome, big fellows. All of them knew how to talk with a girl, and they dressed with a simple, natural elegance.

For compensation, Eugenio had to turn to his books. He studied diligently and distinguished himself in his class, taking the highest honors and winning for himself, as a consequence, fresh enmities which pushed him deeper and more inextricably into his solitude. His sensitive mind registered with exaggerated precision the blows which others deliberately or inadvertently directed toward him.

36

His idea of the world became increasingly distorted, and the humiliations to which he was subjected began to incrust themselves in his personality and cripple it.

The chain burned Eugenio's hand. If Margaret should come out of the church then and see him with the dog, he would die of shame. If the boys discovered him, they would make fun of him. Why was he such a coward? Why didn't he let the animal go? Why didn't he send the Englishman to the devil?

Instinctively he arose and walked swiftly toward the trees in the little park behind the big annex of the school. He would hide there in the cool, bluish shade, and when the bell rang again to announce the end of the service, he would get up and return the dog to that despicable person.

Seated under a plantain tree, pressing his back against the hard trunk, Eugenio fought to regain his peace. He wanted to be calm and happy like other people. Why couldn't he? Was he somehow incapacitated? Was he perhaps different from the other boys?

The wind shook the plantain leaves, and Eugenio felt sifting down over his head, face and hands a green powder that was acrid of smell and exciting. He breathed deeply of the perfumed air, detecting in it the fragrance of sap. There sprang to his mind the thought of a nude woman, and a disturbing warmth flowed through his body. Why did the trees, the wind, and all nature suggest such thoughts to him? What did the springtime have to do with his desires? The fine green dust which sifted through the air around him must, he thought, come from the plantain. It reminded him of pollen. He thought of his botany teacher standing before the class with a pencil in his hand, his spectacles glittering. "Today we will discuss how fertilization may occur from a distance." Yes, Eugenio was

37

breathing pollen. The birds which kissed the flowers carried pollen on their beaks. Pollen was also carried by the wind. If he were a flower now he would become pregnant!

He despised himself for harboring such a thought. He could not, however, escape thinking about pregnancy. There passed through his mind the figure of his mother, her abdomen swollen with her third pregnancy, the child which had been born dead. Eugenio recalled having known that she was pregnant, even before he understood clearly how children are born.

A second vision blotted out the first: he saw Margaret, pregnant. Horrible! His face contracted involuntarily with disgust at the repulsive thought. And then, for the first time, painfully, Eugenio desired Margaret with his flesh. It was a revelation. His heart began to beat faster. The focal center of his body, of his life, seemed to grow suddenly, pulsating, threatening to become the very center of the universe.

It was the spring which caused all this, Eugenio explained to himself. The trees were bursting with green buds. The wind lifted the skirt of a woman who was passing far away in the road. He hated Nature. She had no modesty about making love openly, about voicing her sensuous thoughts loudly in the bright sunlight. Eugenio tried to withdraw his attention from Nature, as though looking away from a too voluptuous picture. But his body went on as before, throbbing. *I must be sick*, he thought.

The stranger's dog was barking ferociously at a black cat which was walking at that moment along the roof of the rector's house.

Eugenio awoke suddenly in the middle of the night. Passing from the darkness of a dreamless sleep to the darkness of his bedroom, he was for a few moments only a creature without memory. The dissociation of sleep continued to becloud his consciousness, arousing in him sensations of distress and bewilderment which, he felt, must be very like insanity. For a brief instant he was aware only of an unbearable torment, of a sharp anxiety, a heavy pressure in his chest, a hot, crawling sensation throughout his body, a desperate need for light and air. He was possessed of an eerie sense of suspension, a feeling that this moment might be the end of the world.

Lying on his back in bed, Eugenio struggled to vanquish the darkness, the mist, and the anguish. During rapid seconds he asked himself who and where he was. He stretched out an arm and felt on the back of his hand the cold hardness of the iron bed. Slowly he began to understand. He was in his room at Columbia Academy. How long had he been asleep? Had it been hours or only minutes? He could remember vaguely a conversation he had had with Mario before going to bed.

Outside, he could hear the howling of the wind, and the lonely sound augmented his misery. In his body he felt the storm which was about to break outside. It was always like this. Night after night he would awake suddenly, as if shaken by an occult warning. Then there would come that itching desire to leap out of bed, to wake his schoolmates, to scream for light, to open the windows and breathe in all the air in the world.

With a blind, almost frenzied gesture, he threw off the bedcovers, for the heat which coursed through his body was suffocating him. What could he do? He thought of calling to his roommate, but he knew that Mario would not awaken. Or, if he did, it would only be to call him an angry name and fall asleep once more.

If only the wind would stop! It was the incessant moaning of the wind which made him feel worse. No, it was the lack of air. He unbuttoned the top of his pajamas with such fierce eagerness that one of the buttons, torn loose, was flung far away and fell on the floor with a dry snap. He tossed in his bed. He turned over on his stomach and pressed his heart against the pillow, clenching his fists. He felt somewhat relieved in this position. He must have heart trouble, he thought. What he felt could not be natural. How could the others sleep on a stormy night?

For a time sleep seemed to come to him. He dozed. Then abruptly, without knowing how, he was again awake and wondering whether he had actually been asleep. His discomfort returned, much stronger now. The wind was blowing violently. It seemed to him that he could actually see the wind hurling despair through the night. As time went by the heat in the little room became more oppressive.

Suddenly he had the distinct impression that he saw lightning flash outside. He saw it in spite of the closed shutters and the darkness of the room.

He was going to die of suffocation. Long ago he had read a horrible story, which had filled him with an unreasonable fear of being buried alive. At the funeral of a classmate the year before he had been terrified at seeing the coffin lowered into the grave. Poor Eduardo! Without air, in the darkness, alone and forever . . . The people sealed up in the cemetery must certainly hear the howling of the wind on stormy nights. Now he too was sealed up. If the windows were not opened he would die . . .

Eugenio sprang from his bed and began to grope blindly in the direction of his roommate's bed. He shook him lightly.

"Mario . . . Mario . . ."

There was a sound of bedsprings creaking and, after a moment, a voice:

"Hm?"

"It's me—Eugenio."

"What is it?"

Mario's voice was a consolation, a support, a hope. Eugenio felt tears in his eyes. In a tone of utter misery, he pleaded:

"Do you mind if I open the shutters?"

Again the bed creaked, and Eugenio sensed that his companion had turned on his side toward the wall. Mario was immersed once more in sleep. How good it was to have no heart! He would have envied Mario, had he not been afraid. He was afraid, because he was going to be alone again . . . Eugenio made a desperate effort to call himself to reason, to convince himself that there was nothing wrong. He had behind him the experience of other, similar occasions. Next morning he would laugh at tonight's distress. The world was not going to end. In the dormitory there was enough air for all the students to breathe all night long. He was not buried. That idea was absurd, it was insane. Yes, insane . . . He might go insane. He was afraid of going insane. If the wind did not stop he would lose his mind. If he did not get light and air he might run screaming out through the hall, in the direction of the stairs, the door, the open air . . .

He took a few steps forward, searching for the window. Suddenly, he was lost in the darkness. He did not know where his bed was, where Mario's bed was, nor the door, nor the window. He knelt, placed the palms of his hands on the floor and began to creep slowly. The vague consciousness of his ridiculous position mingled with his

41

anxiety to find the window. Meanwhile, there was the wailing of the wind, the beating of his heart and the burning, itching sensation, like hosts of swarming insects, in his body.

Eugenio's hand encountered a hard, cold object. By the feel he made out its shape. It was the iron washstand. The window must be near! He moved his palms a few more inches ahead. Joyfully he reached the wall and, raising himself, the window.

Outside, the darkness was intense. Then the dirty, poor light of a lightning flash crossed the gloom, and for one swift instant Eugenio saw the outline of the distant hills. It seemed that the world had not existed until suddenly that fleeting, magic light appeared, creating a whole landscape. It was a landscape of mystery and terror. Eugenio felt that the mountains, too, were tortured, that they suffered as he suffered. Even outside the window he could find no salvation. There was another flash, and he glimpsed the slaty sky, the burdened clouds which were about to bury the world. He wanted to raise the window pane and let the wind freshen his face, his hands, his body, and his aching heart. He was afraid, afraid because everything was going to be worse, now that he could find no salvation in the world outside. Oh, if only it would rain, if only the clouds would spill their heavy contents! If only that pressure, that weight, that anguish would go, would leave his poor, tired body in peace! Then he would be able to sleep. How good it would be to sleep!

He ran back to his bed and plunged his head into the pillow. From time to time flashes of lightning brightened the room. Eugenio longed for the morning to come, for the bell to ring, for the other students to awaken, so that he could be sure that he was alive, that he was saved.

He started up involuntarily. Someone had spoken. Yes, he had heard a human voice. He held his breath, not daring to open his eyes. Again he heard the voice.

"Oh, Genoca! . . . Genoca!"

It was Mario. Eugenio turned over on his side. A flash of lightning illumined the room, and in the livid glare he saw his companion sitting up in bed.

"Go close the shutters," begged Mario.

Eugenio did not move.

"Close that thing!"

Mario leaped out of bed, and Eugenio heard the soft, muffled sounds of his bare feet on the floor, the slam of the wooden shutters. His uneasiness mounted. Darkness engulfed him once more. He tried to think of pleasant things, of Margaret, as a sailor in the midst of a storm at sea might think of the patron saint of his ship. His eyelids began to ache with sleep. He pressed his chest against the mattress and imagined that he was strolling down the avenue of plantains arm in arm with Margaret. They were walking, walking, walking, and there was no end to the avenue. It was a limitless perspective, and the two figures became ever smaller, smaller . . .

He slept. How long? Suddenly he was awake again and aware, painfully, that morning had not yet come. He wished that he knew the time. The murmuring of the wind had ceased, but the heat in the little room was growing again, and his torment was returning. He must have light.

He rose, went to his companion's bed and shook him violently.

"Mario."

"Huh?"

"Do you have a candle?"

There was a pause, a snort of impatience, at last a reply:

43

"Yes. In the table drawer. A match too. What's wrong with you?"

Eugenio did not answer. He groped for the table, opened the drawer, took out the candle and the matches, and lit the wick.

"Careful with that candle," warned Mario.

Eugenio sat down at the table, picked up a magazine, opened it, and propped it up behind the candle, trying to keep the light from shining up over the half-wall which separated the room from the hall outside He gaped senselessly at the pages of the magazine. His thoughts were confused, his eyelids heavy. If sleep would only come! It was fortunate that the wind had ceased. He opened a book, *Elements of Physics:*

"This is known as atmospheric air, or, more simply, air—"

Suddenly a tremendous clap of thunder ripped through the night, shook the building, and was followed by a violent peal, which sent long echoes rolling into the distance. *Thunderbolt!* The word flashed through Eugenio's terrified mind. Involuntarily, he began to mutter a prayer which he had forgotten long ago. Once again he saw his mother kneeling in the center of their house, mumbling, "St. Barbara, St. Jerome . . ."

Mario was sitting up in bed, his feet thrust outside the covers. When the thunder died far away in a vague, stifled roll, he muttered, forcing himself to appear brave:

"I wish the whole damn world would fall in!" In his voice there was a slight tremor.

Eugenio looked at the clock. In the silence now he could hear its rhythmical ticking. He watched the second hand travel across its broad face. But how slow, how invisible was the movement of the big hand!

44

If only it would rain! The atmosphere would be less oppressive, less—

Suddenly a sharp report rang out, like the crack of a gigantic metal whip, followed by the crashing of the thunder. The two boys looked at each other. Mario smiled weakly. Eugenio merely looked. He was thinking of little six-year-old Eugenio, explaining the cause of the thunder to Ernesto: *It's moving day up in heaven. That noise is St. Peter dragging the furniture around* . . .

When the thunder died away, they heard a desperate human scream. They held their breath for an instant, consulting each other mutely, with their eyes. The scream had come from the dormitory itself. It was the scream of a murdered man, a scream of terror. Mario blew out the candle in a gesture of defense, and the two boys sat listening in the dark.

"Must be 'Old Shellshock'," whispered Mario.

Yes, it must be Mr. Tearle. He was the youngest and newest teacher in the school. He had come from the United States less than a year ago, bringing with him the scars of the war. He had gone to Europe with the first American troops and had returned from the trenches with his nerves in shreds. Through a member of the Episcopal Church, a man who had been a college friend of his father, he had been given a position at Columbia Academy. They had hoped the weather and the even tenor of life in a peaceful country with a good climate would cure the young man. But here in the boarding school poor Mr. Tearle had become an object of ridicule. Never before had the students seen the remains of human cannon fodder, and they did not understand. They laughed at him, and none thought to pity the aged creature who was not yet thirty, who had been stripped of his youth and could find

45

no peace, who gestured brusquely and would walk off aimlessly and alone, with a look of insanity on his face. Sometimes, stirred by no one knew what hideous dream, he would scream piercingly in the middle of the night. Many times the boys came upon him talking to himself in English.

One night, when it had been his duty to supervise the noisy study period, Mr. Tearle's patience had snapped suddenly. His eyes flashing and his mouth twisted in a grin of hate, he had pulled a revolver from his waist and had placed it with nervous calm on the desk before him, hissing between his teeth, "I'll put a bullet in the head of the first one who says another word!" His action had been followed by a deathlike silence in the study room. Later, when one of the older boys complained to the rector, Mr. Tearle had been reprimanded for his behavior. The incident had even caused Dr. Parker to call a special session of the Academy, in order to explain in his kind way that Mr. Tearle was "ill," that he suffered from "shell shock." The boys must be patient, like good Christians, and act sometimes as nurses to help cure the poor young man. The rector cited passages from the Bible, invoked the spirit of Christ and cursed war, and ended by affirming his unshakable confidence in the boys of Columbia Academy. At the end of the speech the boys applauded enthusiastically. But two days later, in the morning study period, one of the boys in the intermediate class burst an envelope full of air against the palm of his hand. *Bang!* Mr. Tearle, who was sitting at his desk on the dais, jumped to his feet, his face distorted by insane terror. In his eyes there was at first dread, then hate. He was a tall, strong man, and he stood then bent half forward, his big shoulders drawn up so that his head was sunk slightly between them. He looked

46

like an orangutan, and his breathing was like the panting of a wounded beast. He stood a few seconds in that position, and then he began to pound on the desk with his clenched fists, shrieking, "Stupid—stupid-stupid!" through tight lips, pronouncing the Portuguese word oddly in his strange American accent. "Stupid! Stupid! Stupid!" The desk shook, and every student in the room was silent. Mr. Tearle sat down, passed his hand over his head, sighed, and said in English, "Sorry, boys!" He frowned and went on reading as if nothing had happened.

Now Eugenio and Mario ran to their door. Yes, the scream of terror had come from "Old Shellshock." They almost always heard him on stormy nights when there was thunder. He must be remembering the war, imagining himself deep in a trench, immobilized by the bombing.

Down the corridor came his footsteps, growing louder. Standing with their faces pressed almost flat against the door, the two boys felt Mr. Tearle go by. They were horrified to hear his breathing, which was almost like the panting of a hunted animal, almost like the hoarse rattle from a dying man's throat. The footsteps faded away. They seemed to hurry somewhat on the stairs. There was a brief silence before the boys heard the front door slam.

Mario crossed the room and flung open the shutters of the window.

"Come see, Genoca."

Eugenio obeyed. He looked out, over his friend's shoulder.

"Where?"

"Close to the gate."

When the first flash of lightning whitened the sky, Eugenio caught a glimpse of Mr. Tearle opening the gate. Another flash revealed the American crossing the street, and by the glare of a third bolt Eugenio could see him running in the direction of the ball field. He imagined that he saw the teacher in the uniform of an American soldier, such as he had seen in movies about war. Mr. Tearle's helmet glittered as the lightning flashed, and he ran with his bayonet bared for the attack. It was his last charge. He was all alone, running across the battlefield. His enemy this time was the thunder, the storm.

"I hope the lightning strikes that old crackpot," said Mario.

Eugenio said nothing. He liked Mr. Tearle and felt sorry for him. The American had few friends among the students. Like Eugenio, he was humiliated. He was scarcely tolerated in the boarding school. He was there by a favor.

It had not taken Mr. Tearle long to understand the boy's sympathy for him. One night in a mood of profound depression, he had confided his "secret" while the two of them sat on the steps of the portico. Something had happened to him which he could never forget. He was haunted by a ghost which pursued him both night and day, when he was awake and when he slept. He could not escape from the vision of the German he had killed. Oh, yes, undoubtedly he had killed innumerable Germans—from a distance, without seeing their faces. *This* one had been different. . . . It had been a bayonet charge. . . . On the night before he revealed his secret, the man he had "murdered" had appeared to him in dreams, so that now he was afraid to sleep; and he told Eugenio, as he went back to his room for his pipe and a tin of tobacco, that he meant to pass the night walking and smoking.

A bolt of lightning tore the sky. By its light Eugenio looked in vain for the American.

At that moment it began to rain. Immense drops began

to fall, splattering on the window pane. Eugenio forgot "Old Shellshock" and stood listening to their magic sound. Gradually a feeling of relief and well-being invaded his body. He stretched himself out the length of his bed, thinking of Margaret. He imagined that she lay by his side, and he fell asleep dreaming that he was kissing her hair. The sound of the rain was as fresh and sweet as the girl he loved.

The first to discover the body next day was the colored gardener, Bernardo. Mr. Tearle's corpse lay face down in the middle of the ball field, half covered by water and cold. His revolver and a spent shell were found near his right hand. The bullet had gone through his chest, and the doctor who examined the body said that his death must have been instantaneous.

The school buzzed with excitement. Dr. Parker was overcome. The suicide, besides being a horrible act in itself and a violation of God's divine law, might in some way darken the school's reputation.

A service was held for Mark Tearle in the grand reception hall at Columbia Academy.

Eugenio saw the body sealed into a grave in the cemetery. But he knew, strangely, that the American would not find peace there, that he would remember the war on nights when the heavens crashed with thunder. And many nights during the months which followed Eugenio saw Mr. Tearle's ghost in his dreams.

Eugenio glanced out of the automobile window at the landscape flying by. He saw haystacks at the edge of the road; mountains turning blue in the distance; a lagoon; a eucalyptus plantation; a rose-colored bungalow with a woman at the window, a man wearing striped pajamas and a straw hat watering the flowers in the garden . . . Everything so swift, so fleeting . . .

His thoughts were of Eunice now.

After more than three years they had discovered the grave error of their marriage. How little they had in common! Marriage to her had offered him a means of escape—escape from struggle, from anonymity, from the shabby black bag and the endless row on row of destitute frame houses. He had not wanted to become a poor man's doctor. He had wanted an office in a fashionable building downtown; he had wanted an automobile and a library filled with fine books. He had loved comfort, had sought peace and freedom from the poverty which had shadowed the lives of all his family. And Eunice had been attractive. Marriage to her, he had considered, would be no sacrifice. He had even succeeded in deceiving himself for a time into thinking he loved her. But what had seemed to be love had been no more than curiosity—curiosity and the simple animal desire to possess her.

The automobile sped past huge signboards, road markers, an enormous truck, a bridge . . .

Olivia. . . . And at her side now a child, a little girl who smiled confidently at him—Anamaria! Why had he not thought of her before?

"My daughter," he stammered weakly. If Olivia should die, what would become of Anamaria?

Eugenio drew his hand across his face. It was drenched with cold perspiration.

Chapter 4

Eugenio was supremely happy when one afternoon, just as he was leaving the medical school, Alcibiades came up to him and took his arm intimately. He was proud of his friendship with Alcibiades, who was one of the most admired and envied boys in the school. He was the son of the Secretary of the Interior, and he had a car of his own, race horses, and a collection of more than forty beautiful neckties.

"Looks like we'll have to walk today," said Alcibiades. "My car's in the garage. You know what, Genoca, I'm thinking about touching the old man for a '24 Cadillac."

"But the one you have now is almost brand-new!"

They walked up the street side by side. Eugenio breathed with pleasure the sweet, slightly rustic perfume which came from Alcibiades. It must be "Christmas Night," and it cost, he knew, almost a hundred milreis a bottle.

"This second year's easy as pie, Genoca. Take today, for instance. A fellow can still get by, not turning his little finger. The third's when the fun begins."

Eugenio nodded. "The really tough thing is getting in, in the first place. After that it's not so bad as they make out."

He thought suddenly of his premedical school days, of the difficulties with which he had had to contend in order to pay his tuition. With no little trouble he had obtained a job as crime reporter on a local newspaper, and night after night he had worked until dawn. How he had hated that job! He used to look enviously after friends who had found steady government employment and were poor but happier than he. One day his mother had said to him:

"That friend of yours, Alcibiades, could fix you up a good job. Isn't his dad a big shot?" Yes, Alcibiades could easily have arranged something for Eugenio; but the poor young man's pride stubbornly refused to allow him to consider so degrading a proposition. He would rather go on grinding forever than humble himself by asking a favor. Above all, Eugenio did not want to be humbled.

Alcibiades was whistling softly "O Biombo Chinês." It was autumn, and Eugenio wondered why the gentle afternoon light caused him to feel somehow fluttery inside, almost as if he were recovering from an illness. The color of the sky was neither even in tone nor brilliant. It looked like ashes sprinkled with faded blue. The shadows of the trees on the sidewalk were almost violet. Their feet as they walked crushed the dry leaves.

"Are you going to the Association meeting today, Genoca?"

Eugenio was going. He wanted to hear Narciso's speech, "If God Exists, Science Will Discover Him." In the Association of Medical Students there were both atheists and Catholics, and they engaged in furious debates over religion. He was inclined to side with the atheists, for he was dazzled by science. He read Darwin and saw in every man an ape. Whenever the city editor had asked him to cover the slum neighborhoods, he had described their inhabitants as a band of gorillas vegetating in the mud, poorly fed, poorly clothed, without sanitation, without happiness, devoid of all save the barest essentials of human life. Of course there was no God. A Divine Spirit would not permit the existence of such squalor, of such miserable, subhuman conditions. The creatures of the slums were beasts, not men. What Artist could be proud of having created them? The editor used to scratch his head and exclaim: "But this stuff is literature, man, it's for the literary section! What I want is plain, honest reporting!"

In anatomy class Professor Mota Leme dissected cadavers and, by demonstrating the perfection of the human body, attempted to prove the existence of God. "See, my friends," he would say in his soft, hissing voice, "only a Superior Intelligence could have created such a perfect mechanism as the human body."

Eugenio would listen with a scornful smile. He thought always of his father, of the dismal poverty of his home, of the gorillas, of his newspaper reports. He reflected on his own strivings and degradation, on life's inequalities, on social injustice. If God existed, then He had forgotten the world, like a writer who voluntarily forgets the book of which he is ashamed. No, God did not exist. Eugenio wanted not to believe in God; he found a certain beauty in atheism.

There came to him, however, moments of doubt, swift flickers of uncertainty, when he was stirred by great beauty or shaken by fear. Sometimes a passage of fine music or a story of self-abnegation would bring him almost to reconciliation with the life he resented, to acceptance, or at least acknowledgment, of his need for God. On stormy nights, when his old affliction returned and his head was giddy with sleep and the ancient, inexplicable terror, he would turn involuntarily to God. Scarcely would the day grow light again, however, scarcely would he see the sun before his calm would return and he would laugh at his fears of the night. But, try as he would, he could not conquer the idea of God, which seemed to slumber inside him, like a distant melody. He read the life of Pasteur and was moved to tears. He could not comprehend how that exceptional man, as his discoveries led him more and more toward materialism, had been drawn ever nearer to God.

Although stories of the great benefactors of humanity had first inspired Eugenio to study medicine, there was a more fundamental reason for his desire to become a doctor. That was his pity for his father in his wretched illness, and his admiration for Dr. Seixas, the physician who attended him. Dr. Seixas, who devoted himself to poor people, was himself a poor man. Already past forty, he had no automobile, possessed not a cent of his own. He lived precariously and had been, since his student days, a constant prey to financial obligations. Dr. Seixas had invented no serum, had discovered no microbe, yet in his own way he was a great benefactor of mankind. He became furious if one of his poor patients spoke to him about money, offended whenever anyone attempted to express gratitude. Eugenio saw great, dramatic beauty in his life of renunciation. He wanted to be a physician like Dr. Seixas. He wanted to cure his father. At least, those had been the ambitions of his premedical school days.

Today. . . Today Eugenio saw the world differently. His job as reporter had placed him in contact with real misery. The poverty of his own family seemed like wealth compared with the destitution which he was forced to witness as he worked in the city's slums, covering stories for his editor. He could not bear to go near those fetid huts, those repugnant people. From a distance he made observations, took notes, and asked swift questions. Then he would hurry back to his desk and complete the report as his fancy dictated. A doctor who wished to devote himself to the poor would be obliged to place his own finger in the festering sores of those people, would have to breathe deeply of the polluted air of their homes, to feel

54

in his own face their pestilent breaths. Eugenio no longer saw beauty in the work of Dr. Seixas.

His friendship with Alcibiades, meanwhile, had opened to him the doors of a new world, a world in which he recognized his own ideal climate. The first time he had visited his friend's home he had been moved almost to tears. How he had loved to sink into the soft easy-chairs! How he had admired the rich inlaid floors, the colorful rugs, the beautiful pictures, the carved furniture that was dark, ponderous, and handsome! Alcibiades had sent for tea with sandwiches and had shown Eugenio rare volumes with luxurious bindings, collections of foreign magazines, *objets d'art* . . . In the unforgettable hour which he had spent in that house, hearing but not understanding the sonnets which Alcibiades read to him in a voice filled with emotion, Eugenio pictured himself for the first time as a wealthy physician, the head of a house like that one. He forgot his father, his mother, Dr. Seixas, the gorillas of the subworld. The atmosphere in which he found himself was subtle and delicate in a way that did not permit the flowering of somber thoughts. How happy Alcibiades must be!

Looking down at his dingy shoes and his three-year-old suit with its sagging knees and its stains, Eugenio had felt his old sense of inferiority return. He had felt more than ever before that Alcibiades' attentions to him had the character of a favor, of charity. What charm or interest could a rich boy, who was fawned on by everyone, who had never had any difficulties in his life, see in Eugenio? And what could he, a poor devil, offer in return to such a creature, to this inhabitant of the best of worlds? Why did Alcibiades invite him to visit his home? Alcibiades had shown his poor classmate everything: his enormous

55

closet full of suits, ties, and hats; the perfumes, lotions, and cosmetics on his dressing table; his books; his typewriter; his collection of rare coins . . . What was the purpose of all this display, if not to torture him? At school there was a great deal of talk about Alcibiades' vanity . . .

But now, walking proudly along the street with Alcibiades, Eugenio could only admire his clothes, his upright carriage and his perfume, could only be flattered by the intimacy of his friendship.

"I want to try to get down to Buenos Aires next vacation," Alcibiades said abruptly. Without changing the tone of his voice, he added: "You know what, I'm trying to fix up a little apartment where I can take a girl I'm trying to make. It'd be damned awkward to take somebody special to one of these common rendezvous, don't you think?" Without waiting for a reply, he went on chattering gayly about his plans.

How frivolous, how vain Alcibiades was! He could speak only to praise himself, to boast of his own prowess. But there was no denying that there was something to him. He had an enviable talent for pleasing women, and his social prestige was enormous.

When the two boys arrived at Praça Marechal Deodoro, Alcibiades squeezed Eugenio's arm.

"Look, there's Castanho!" He motioned with his head in the direction of the opposite sidewalk. "Let's go talk to him."

Eugenio nodded, and they began to cross the street.

Eugenio was excited. Many times at school he had heard the legend of Acelio Castanho, who was about to receive his degree in law. He was one of the most brilliant students who had ever attended the university. Everyone, even the professors, respected his solid scientific and literary knowledge. Articles which he had written were already appearing in the city newspapers, and he was the first person in the state of Rio Grande do Sul to analyze the work of Albert Einstein. The boys went often to him for consultation and advice:

"Castanho, what do you think about Freud?" "Tell me something, Acelio, which of Proust's books should you read first?"

Castanho came from an illustrious family which had in its tradition long lines of counts and barons. He lived in a palatial old house in the upper part of the city, and malicious tongues reported that the Castanho mansion allowed itself the luxury of liveried servants and blue-blooded ghosts. People commented on the rigid moral and mental discipline of Castanho himself, who was chaste in his personal life and thoroughly versed in the classics. He rose early every morning to perform calisthenics and read Byron and Keats for a half-hour, after which he drank a glass of milk and studied the Greek classics. There was talk of a great essay which he was writing on Greek tragedy. Among the students of the institutions of higher learning the name of Castanho was pronounced with respect. Eugenio had always longed to approach him, but he had been restrained not only by unconquerable timidity, but by Castanho's cold, remote attitude. For this reason he felt fiercely excited as he crossed the street.

Alcibiades tapped Acelio Castanho on the shoulder.

"Well, old man, how're you coming along with all your culture?"

With slow dignity, Castanho turned to acknowledge the greeting. He limited himself to a thin-lipped, polished smile and offered his hand graciously. He was a young man of medium height, with an enormous forehead, a pale, serious face, and a marked stoop. He dressed immaculately and with discretion, and he used a cane.

"Do you know Castanho, Genoca? You don't? Well, this is the great Acelio Castanho you've heard so much about. Genoca is in the second year with me."

Awkwardly, Eugenio held out his hand and managed to stammer his name. The pale young man gave him the tips of his cool, delicate fingers.

"How do you do?" he murmured.

Alcibiades took his arm.

"Where are you bound for, Acelio?"

"I'm going to the bookstores." Almost daily visits to the bookstores were for Acelio Castanho a ritual, the adoration of good books a religion.

"Let's all go, then," suggested Alcibiades, and the three young men resumed their walk.

Eugenio felt that he had been abandoned. Alcibiades gave all his attention to the newcomer. Within a few minutes he had become a man of serious interests, preoccupied with politics and culture. Instinctively, Eugenio began to slacken his pace, to fall behind. Like a page . . . Yes, he was only a page. They were the young noblemen, and he was their valet. He lacked only the livery. He derived a strange, bitter pleasure from lowering himself thus.

But Acelio Castanho turned to him with a question:

"Do you like medicine?"

The gates of paradise seemed to have opened. A little flushed and confused, Eugenio answered:

"Ah! Very much."

"Are you interested in general practice or in surgery?"

"I'm not sure yet. Maybe surgery."

Alcibiades interrupted the dialogue.

"Well, Castanho, when are we going to have another

of those magnificent articles you've been turning out?"

Acelio Castanho murmured something about not being in good health, and the little group moved on. Alcibiades asked for a definition of happiness, and Acelio, recalling that morning's selections from Plato, replied with grave simplicity:

"Music and gymnastics."

Music and gymnastics, the Platonic ideal. Acelio began to develop his theme.

Eugenio listened, completely dazzled. Here was he, Eugenio Fontes, walking with the noted Dr. Acelio Castanho and the son of the Secretary of the Interior. Soon they would come to the Rua dos Andradas, and everyone would see him in the company of the famous pair. One part of Eugenio rejoiced and was flattered by the thought of his triumph; but deep inside him there stirred a minute, irreverent self, a tiny imp which laughed and made faces, poking fun at vain Eugenio, at frivolous Alcibiades and professorial Castanho. But then a sensation of glory and importance extinguished the little demon.

Castanho, meanwhile was still in Greece.

"Music and gymnastics, of equal benefit for the body and the mind. I feel, my dear, that I should have been born in ancient Hellas, to love Plato and be one of his disciples. . ."

Suddenly, on the corner just ahead, a familiar figure appeared. Eugenio felt the blood leave his heart. He could recognize that form from any distance, among a thousand. A thin, stooped man, poorly dressed, with a bundle under his arm—his father, poor Angelo. As the old man approached, Eugenio felt a hot, crawling discomfort all through his body. He hoped—how fervently, how desperately he hoped!—that Angelo would cross the street, that he would turn suddenly and walk in the other direction. How embarrassing, how awkward it would be if he should see Eugenio, if he should stop and speak to him! Alcibiades and Castanho would know that he was the son of a poor tailor who went out into the street to deliver suits personally to his customers. They would scorn him even more if they knew. Eugenio glanced swiftly around, looking involuntarily for a means of escape. He could invent a pretext and ask to be excused. He could dash into the door of the next shop . . .

Unaware of Eugenio's crisis, Castanho's calm voice went on: ". . . the Hegelian concept . . ."

He could go into that toy shop and hide until Angelo had passed. He hesitated. Then, when he had resolved at last to flee, he saw that it was too late: Angelo was upon them. The old man saw his son, looked from him to his two companions, and his face broadened in a smile of surprise and joy. He moved servilely to the edge of the sidewalk and removed his hat.

"Good afternoon, Genoca!" Pride shone in his wrinkled face.

Eugenio's face was scarlet. He did not answer, but kept his eyes straight ahead, as if he had neither seen nor heard the greeting. His schoolmates, too, went on talking, for they had not noticed Angelo.

The feeling of happiness, meanwhile, had left Eugenio. Guilt replaced his short-lived exultation. His action had been inhuman. It was unpardonable. Why had he been ashamed of his father? Wasn't he a decent man? Wasn't he a good man? Wasn't he, after all, his own father?

There was still time to repair the wrong that had been done. He could go back, take Angelo's arm, and walk up the street with him. What restrained him? ". . . that

60

passage from the *Banquet*," Castanho was saying. Yes, he might kiss his father's hand and beg his forgiveness—humble himself . . . On he walked, following his friends like an automaton. He looked back. Angelo had disappeared.

As the trio mingled with the crowds which filled the Rua dos Andradas, Eugenio felt a great heaviness in his breast. Castanho and Alcibiades were deeply absorbed in their discussion. They walked arm in arm, drawing gradually away from him. For an instant he lost sight of them in the crowd. He peered around, completely bewildered, like a puppy which had lost its master. Everything unfortunate happened to him! He hated Castanho, he hated Alcibiades, he hated himself. Let them all go to the devil!

At that instant his eyes found Alcibiades, who stood next to Acelio on the edge of the sidewalk, signaling to him. Unhesitatingly, eagerly, Eugenio hurried to join them.

Wagging his little tail with joy, murmured the imp inside him.

That evening when the family assembled around the dinner table, Eugenio could not find the courage to look at his father. All afternoon he had dreaded the meeting at dinnertime. He had considered avoiding it altogether, eating in some downtown restaurant and returning home late, after everyone had gone to bed. As for tomorrow, he had thought, that would have to take care of itself.

But here he was at the table, ill at ease, painfully conscious of his guilt. He noticed that his mother's eyes were red and swollen. She had been crying. Was it because of Ernesto or because of himself?

They ate in silence, Angelo coughing and sighing,

61

lifting his napkin to his mouth, his wife pausing now and again to refill his glass with water. Ernesto crossed his knife and fork abruptly on his plate and pushed it away.

"Don't you want something else?" Dona Alzira asked him. "You didn't eat but such a little bit—"

"I'm not hungry."

The boy's voice was hoarse and tired. Eugenio looked up and saw his brother's dissipated face, his dull eyes, his bitter mouth. In spite of the consciousness of his own guilt, his glance was accusing. For a moment the two boys stared at each other. The first to look away was Ernesto. He played with the corner of the tablecloth, attempting to conceal his feeling.

"Don't forget your drops, Angelo," counseled his wife.

Angelo picked up the medicine dropper and began to let the amber-colored liquid fall slowly into a half-glass of water. "One, two," he counted softly, scarcely moving his lips. "Three." Almost unconsciously, Dona Alzira and Ernesto looked at the medicine dropper and began to accompany him. "Four, five, six." The water was becoming tinged with yellow. "Seven, eight, nine." For a moment there seemed to be a kind of truce. Eugenio looked at his father. His two-day-old beard, already grizzled, made a blue and silvered shadow on his bony, livid cheeks. His face showed weariness and resignation. Under his eyes there were twin pockets of cracked, purple flesh. But the thing which one remembered about poor Angelo was the way he breathed, in cruelly labored, agonizing gasps.

Eugenio pitied his father, and he hated himself. Pity was no fit recognition for all that Angelo had given him. Why was he so ready to criticize, to see only those things which were disagreeable and ugly about his father? Why could he never overcome the near-repulsion which Angelo's physical appearance engendered in him—the sight of his yellow teeth, his unkempt fingernails, his somber, plebeian face, his subservient eyes? Eugenio, thinking of his father, could not escape the powerful supremacy of his mind; in vain he wished that his feeling toward the old man could be guided solely by his heart. He had always admired St. Francis, who had kissed the lepers; yet infinitely simpler accomplishments were beyond his own strength. If only he could learn to accept his people naturally and easily, without having to fight against his own nature! Angelo deserved to be loved. Never had he in any way enforced his authority as a father. "Angelo's a father in a million," his wife used to tell her friends. "The boys just walk all over him, and he never says a word." But it was no use, thought Eugenio. Between himself and his father there lay a deep, broad gulf.

With his mother Eugenio felt more at ease. Could his predilection for her be a form of narcissism, a subtle prolongation of his self-love? Physically he resembled her. In his face one could see her features, remarkably pronounced. Was his love for her only an expression of his own egotism?

Eugenio looked at his mother and saw a woman aged by work and sorrows. She grieved for Ernesto, whose life seemed already past redemption. Her younger son was a drunkard, a tramp who never kept a steady job, who was seen often in the company of vulgar women, who had even been in jail. But in spite of the marks of time and hard work, Dona Alzira conserved vestiges of her former beauty. Her calm eyes never assumed the expression of canine humility which haunted those of her husband. By the same token, however, they never shone with any light of defiance or courage. Hers was a face serene before life;

63

she accepted with imperturbable resignation whatever it brought her. Moments of happiness were met with neither great illusions nor undue excitement, and she greeted small discouragements and griefs without wincing or losing hope. "God is great," she would say. She swept the house, washed the dishes, helped her husband, cooked and did the shopping. There was no illness or catastrophe in the world strong enough to alter the simple routine of her household. They lived in spotless poverty, for which Eugenio was grateful. He was fond of his mother, but he knew that neither fondness nor gratitude could repay all that he owed her.

As he progressed in his studies and his vision of the world broadened, Eugenio felt that, like a leaf caught in an upward current of air, he was rising with increasing swiftness toward some higher level, leaving his family far below, enchained by its rudimentary needs, its solecisms and ignorance, by a life which seemed to him at times purely vegetative. The consciousness of his superiority grew stronger, and he came to feel that he was the victim of an enormous injustice. He looked at the inequalities of the world, and his bitterness grew.

Deep inside him, however, there shone at times a strange light which, in the brief moment of its existence, showed him the ugly magnitude of his pride, his selfishness and conceit. A superior man, he? How? Why? What extraordinary thing had he accomplished? Eugenio's mind buzzed with half-formed ideas. With a feverish desire to acquire wisdom and understanding, he had devoured a half-dozen famous books. . . . What were they, compared to the silent struggle of his parents? What were they, before the truly great saviors and guardians of humanity? He should be humble, compassionate, tolerant . . .

As rapidly as it had been born the mysterious light would vanish, and again Eugenio would feel reality in his flesh, in his bones, in his blood. He would compare Alcibiades' home with his own. He would look up from reading a good book to hear his father's slovenly speech: " 'Member, Alzira, that suit Ribas give me to press?" He would turn from a reproduction of a beautiful painting to see Ernesto reeking with *cachaça*, his father spitting mucus and moaning. He hated poverty. He hated humility. He despised his life.

Angelo lifted the glass to his lips and drank the medicine. With shaking hands Ernesto placed a crushed cigarette in his mouth and began to rummage in his pocket for a match. From across the table his father passed him a burning match. Dona Alzira rose.

"Anybody want anything else?"

Eugenio and Angelo shook their heads. Ernesto lit his cigarette, giving no sign that he had heard. She began to clear the table.

Then the inevitable happened. Eugenio's eyes met his father's. Angelo smiled at his son, not a smile of pardon, but the servile, constrained smile of one who asks it. He asked pardon for having no money, for dressing poorly, for being only a tailor, for being nobody. Eugenio looked away, feeling the hot blood suffuse his face and neck. The sting of Angelo's smile buried itself deep in his consciousness. He thought of a little dog he had had many years before, a poor cur that had been mangy and nearly hairless. It used to lick the hands of those who kicked it.

For the first time that evening Angelo addressed his older son:

"Genoca, aren't you needin' a new suit?"

Eugenio did not dare to look up.

65

"No, father, thank you. My clothes are all right." He writhed. How he longed to break all barriers, to leap from his chair and embrace his father, to beg his forgiveness! A bitter knot rose in his throat.

"I've got a real nice piece of twill over there—"

"No, father, thank you."

Mingled in Angelo's offer there had been affection and timidness. He seemed to wish to compensate with a gift from his own hand his guilt for having bequeathed to his sons no better heritage.

There was an uncomfortable silence. Ernesto smoked, his eyes on the floor. Dona Alzira returned from the kitchen.

"The fire's out, and I need hot water for the dishes. I'm going out to chop some kindling."

Ernesto arose. "I'll go, Mamma." Eugenio felt a strong breath of *cachaça* as his brother spoke.

"All right, Nestinho. Take the hatchet on top of the tank, and be careful not to cut yourself."

As Ernesto left the room, he walked curved over like an old man. He was not twenty years old! Eugenio followed his brother's figure with his eyes, remembering the days when the two of them used to walk to grade school together. Was it nostalgia which he felt? Or was it only the strange emotion which his father's attitude had caused in him?

Angelo toyed with the empty glass. Eugenio rose and began to pace the floor. The house was small and offered no refuge. But he must stay, for he had work to do. He picked up a newspaper and opened it without interest.

"Don't read after you eat. It isn't good for you," his mother advised.

Eugenio folded the paper and put it aside. For the

second time he met his father's eyes. Angelo smiled again, as if to reassure him that he harbored no resentment.

Unbearable! Eugenio leaped to his feet and strode toward the back of the house. "I'm going to take a walk," he said, and went out.

The night was clear and warm, and the little street was deserted. His hands in his pockets, Eugenio began to pace back and forth in front of the house. In the distant sky the glow of the stars was dim and sad. He paused and raised his eyes to look at them. He was filled with nameless anxiety. Hot tears ran down his face. And then, in thought, he embraced his father, kissed his dry forehead, stroked his coarse hair, loved him tenderly.

In the back yard Ernesto was chopping wood. His form was scarcely distinguishable in the darkness. The sounds of the hatchet were dry and rhythmical.

Each stroke buried itself, vibrating, in Eugenio's taut nerves.

The chauffeur pointed outside and shouted to Eugenio over his shoulder, "Dr. Carmo bought that little place from old Tico Rezende!"

Eugenio looked in the direction of his extended finger. The velocity of the car was so great that he could scarcely make out the tip of an orange-colored roof emerging from above a dark grove of trees. There were walls with granite posts, an orchard, a windmill . . .

Eugenio was thinking of his daughter. He could see her growing up, unsheltered against the gossiping tongues of the world. Whispers echoed in his mind. She has neither father nor mother, poor little thing. . . . They found her under a lilac bush, you know. . . . Ah! the illegitimate daughter of that fellow who married . . .

Then he saw himself taking Anamaria by the hand and leading her—leading her—where?

Still holding Anamaria's hand, he saw himself standing before the door of a great house, which he recognized as his father-in-law's mansion. They could not enter.

Olivia was dying. And still life would go on. In spite of everything . . .

The automobile crossed a small bridge.

Chapter 5

Commencement was over. The director's last words were followed by a burst of applause which filled the old theater. As soon as the curtain fell, Eugenio hurried, choking from the stage. He was too warm, and he had a slight headache. A tall, thin, dark man embraced him heartily; it was probably some mistake, for he did not remember the man's face. Eugenio thanked him awkwardly and sought the door, bumping as he did so into a gentleman with a shining, red face, who undid himself in apologies and smiles. He walked perspiring through the hall; his Tuxedo and starched shirt slightly nauseated him. However, as he clutched his diploma in both hands and pushed obstinately, almost blindly, through the crowd that jammed the corridor, he felt pleasantly strong, proud and self-confident. At last he had received his reward for years of hard work and sacrifice, of doubts and costly victories over himself. He felt a wild desire to shout, and it was with an effort that he repressed his elation.

He went into the bar and ordered a drink. From his table he could look into the theater lobby. It was like an aviary swarming with birds (he had a mania for looking at things zoologically), chattering birds. . . . That woman with the tiny head and the hooked nose looked like a hen. Her companion, in a white dress, was a cockatoo. There were larger animals, too. That fat man in the limp trousers, with his back to Eugenio, was an elephant.

Conversations filled the lobby, crisscrossing one another in the air. Even the stone gargoyles on the columns seemed to be speaking, recalling the many graduating classes which had passed through the old theater and had enjoyed moments of triumph like this.

But suddenly a breach seemed to open in the close fabric of conversation. The birds had stopped chattering, sensing the arrival of some larger beast. All eyes were turned toward the stair which led up to the boxes. There was a thunder of applause, and aisles opened up among the crowd. It was the Governor of the state who was coming down, surrounded by his friends. He shook hands with Alcibiades, who bent forward in an exaggerated bow, his mouth open in a grin of idiotic joy. Eugenio felt a twinge of envy and of anger. During the last two years Alcibiades had drawn gradually away from him, seeking other friends. There was already talk about his being slated for Deputy in the State Assembly. It was obvious that the friendship of his more obscure schoolmates would no longer be of interest to him . . .

Eugenio emptied his glass in one swallow. He saw the Governor go out with his top hat in his hand, smiling to right and left. Alcibiades followed him. In the street automobile engines were snorting, brakes were screeching, horns were blowing.

In the midst of the joyous pandemonium, Eugenio began to feel depressed. The day to which he had looked forward for so long had arrived at last. He was *Dr.* Eugenio Fontes. At last he had reached the peak of the mountain. But what did he see on the other side? A nebulous, indistinct panorama. What did he feel? Mingled with his sense of victory there was an unaccountable anxiety, a strange melancholy. He would have liked to forget his worries and celebrate the occasion as the others were doing, to open the rusty gates inside him and let his joy pour out freely. Joy? He was afraid to analyze himself too closely. It would be cruel to discover that the reservoir was dry, or that it contained only the old sorrows and uncertainties, cries of astonishment and doubt, evasions . . .

He must think now of his future. During the past year he had been assisting Dr. Teixeira Torres at operations in the Hospital of the Sacred Heart. It was true that he was practicing, learning, getting experience. But how far that was from his dreams! Many recent graduates had been forced to accept positions outside the profession. Others had risked their fate by hanging out shingles in remote towns or villages of the interior. Of course, nearly all were successful, if one could apply the term "success" to making a few dozen contos, developing a prosperous paunch, and winning local renown as good general practitioners . . .

Eugenio looked at his empty glass. It made him think of Ernesto, who continued to drink insanely. His eyes fell on the diploma lying on the chair, and he thought of his father, who had not lived to see him receive it. Angelo had died the year before of angina pectoris. Dr. Seixas had stayed at his bedside until the last moment. Eugenio could not forget the expression of Angelo's face as he lay in the coffin. His sad, resigned humility seemed to continue even in death. Before his father's body Eugenio had wept tears not only of grief for his loss, but also of remorse.

He peered into the lobby, which was slowly clearing of people. A girl with a bouquet of red roses in her arms was leaning against one of the columns. It was Olivia. He paid for his drink, took his diploma, and walked into the lobby.

"Abandoned?" he asked, half smiling.

The girl by the column stared at him with mock gravity. She glanced down at the roll of parchment under her arm.

"I'm afraid the weight of the diploma leaves me a little speechless."

Olivia was the only girl in his class. He knew that she too had worked to graduate. By assisting in one of the school laboratories she had earned a salary which scarcely sufficed to pay her tuition and living expenses.

"So what now?" said Eugenio, after a moment.

Olivia shrugged her shoulders.

"Life goes on."

"I know. What about us?"

"We go on, too."

"You know what I mean." He pointed to her diploma. "That—"

"—goes into a frame."

He could not help smiling. But it was not her words alone which made him smile. It was rather the amazing dress she wore—that strange, white, vaporous dress, with its high, tight waist and its long, flounced skirt, such as he had never expected to see Olivia wear. He knew her in a skullcap, a simple suit, and low-heeled shoes. Tonight she looked as if she might be posing for a portrait, as she leaned pensively against the white column, her arms full of red roses. He looked at her admiringly.

"You look as if you're going to have a picture made."

She stepped away from the column and began to pirou-ette, like a fashion mannequin.

71

"Do I look chic?"

"Terrific."

Eugenio was genuinely impressed. For the first time he was aware of his classmate's femininity. This was a completely new, different Olivia. He had grown used to thinking of her as a classmate, almost as a boy.

"Do you like the flowers?"

He nodded. "Who sent them to you?"

"My mysterious admirer."

"Oh!"

"Of course, you think I can't have an admirer—"

He shrugged his shoulders. Olivia smiled.

"Well," he said at length, "what are we doing standing here?"

She lowered her eyes coquettishly. "I'm waiting for a gentleman to ask me out in his car . . ."

In her parody on feminine guile Olivia satirized herself rather than the affectation of women in general. Eugenio knew that she harbored no resentment. She considered herself unattractive and let others know in the least dramatic way possible that she did not suffer for it, that she did not hate the world nor consider herself the victim of any injustice. It was her honesty with him and with everyone, her genuine simplicity, which made him enjoy being with her. In women in general he had always found a tendency to resort to blackmail; make-up, flirtation, and fragility were their principal weapons. Olivia, he considered an exception. She did not pretend to be something she was not.

He had met her in his third year of medical school; but only at the end of the fourth had they become good friends. He had suffered on her account when the professor lectured on those portions of the human body which

72

secular convention pronounced taboo. The other students had derived a cruel, libidinous pleasure from searching Olivia's face for her reactions to the nomenclature of the male reproductive system. On such occasions Eugenio's face would become red, and he would look furtively at his classmate, only to find her unperturbed, her eyes very wide, fixed on the professor in the attitude of a child listening to fairy tales. When they dissected cadavers in the morgue she had been subjected to hard tests. Once one of the students had played a cruel trick on her, and the story had spread among the boys. To many it had been a funny anecdote, to others only a poor joke. Eugenio had been revolted. He had felt that he was an ally of Olivia. With almost hostile eyes he watched her being treated badly, for he saw his own drama reenacted in hers. He had few friends in the school; he was an obscure student, and he was poor. He did not, however, seek her friendship openly. He admired her for a while at a distance, but then he forgot her—forgot her for the very reason which had made him want to know her. Olivia was obscure, and she was poor. She had not even the resource of being pretty.

But the Olivia he met in the lobby of the old theater on the night of his graduation was a powerful contradiction of the generally accepted notion that she was not beautiful.

"I have no car," he said, "but if you will accept my arm—"

"With pleasure, my lord."

They left the theater arm in arm. At the edge of the sidewalk they paused, undecided. Near by a single taxi waited. The driver's head appeared at the window.

"Ready, doctor!"

Eugenio dismissed him, and they crossed the street.

They entered the great square and paused at the base of the monument which stood in the center. Olivia looked down at her roses.

"Shall we render homage to the Patriarch?"

"Let's."

They climbed the steps of the monument. The square was deserted. At the foot of the statue they paused again. The Patriarch sat in a great chair, made of the same substance as his body, and he seemed to be meditating gravely. At his feet the dragon Envy was attacking him viciously; but the statue's eyes were oblivious. They stared unwaveringly into the future. Olivia laid the armful of roses down at his feet.

"And the dragon?"

"Oh, of course!"

She picked up a crimson bud and drew it through the mouth of the bronze monster.

"And His Lordship?"

"Oh, I beg His Lordship's pardon!"

She took a second rose from the bouquet and placed it in the buttonhole of Eugenio's Tuxedo.

They sat down on the steps of the monument and looked up at the sky. The theater doors were closing, and the lights of the marquee were going out. Olivia closed her right eye as she placed her diploma over her left like a telescope and leveled it at the sky.

"What do you think they're doing up there on the moon at this hour of the night?"

Eugenio transformed his diploma also into a telescope and pointed it at the moon.

"You know what I see up there? I see a girl and a boy who've just gotten their diplomas and don't know what to do with them."

"Don't be silly. There aren't any diplomas on the moon. Do you know what I see? I can tell from here that the boy never had a shirt with a starched front before in his life, and the girl is wearing a borrowed dress."

Eugenio smiled and pretended to adjust the lens of his telescope.

"Look. His Tuxedo is rented."

It was curious. He would never have thought he could make such a confession to anyone, but he had said it spontaneously to Olivia, without blushing, without any feeling of constraint.

They sat for a moment in silence, Eugenio lit a cigarette. She leaned her head on the dragon's flank.

The shape of her face was long, and its color was pale olive. At first sight it impressed one neither greatly nor little. When he had seen Olivia for the first time, Eugenio had felt inclined to say: "She's not ugly. But pretty? No, she's not pretty, either. . ." But when he had looked more carefully at her black eyes and had seen her face become animated with a life and a strange, mysterious beauty which seemed to arise unexpectedly from within, completely independent of her external features, he had been set to thinking. He had ended by making concessions: "There's something about her . . ." Was it her mouth? No, her mouth was large, and there was nothing extraordinary in its design. Was it her nose? Again the answer was no; it was long and thin. It must be her eyes. Black and serene, they were not distinguished for their vivacity, mobility or for any rare brilliance. They were eyes for which, after some reflection, Eugenio could find only one qualifying adjective: they were *human*. They enveloped warmly the person or the object on which they looked, conveying an impression of unfathomable depth and even

75

greater understanding. They seemed to pierce all things, with a penetration which was neither indiscreet nor aggressive. One could not, however, think of Olivia without recalling immediately the sound of her voice. Even in her manner of speaking she refused to practice deception. Her voice was neither rich with musical inflections nor colored with false sweetness. It was grave and very calm, almost a monotone. And, like her eyes, it had a warm, human quality.

Olivia's classmates, who had derived pleasure at first from playing stupid tricks on her, were won over at length by her unruffled superiority. They began to call her "our little godmother," to confide in her and ask her advice. They came to treat her as a colleague of their own sex, as a pal.

Eugenio looked at Olivia now and wondered how it had taken so long for him to discover that she was more than a schoolmate, that she was an interesting woman.

But suddenly he was looking at the sky again, his eyes wide and vacant, his forehead contracted in deep furrows.

"All joking aside, Olivia, I'd just like to know what we are going to do now."

She looked at him. "Why does the future worry you so much?"

For a moment he did not answer.

"If you only knew, Olivia," he said finally, without taking his eyes from the stars, "if only you knew how I've wanted this day to come! If only you knew how—how proud I am!" He frowned. "And how disappointed—"

"I hope you didn't expect that little piece of parchment to change your life for you—just like *that?*"

"Yes. . . . I guess maybe in a way I did. I thought somehow the new title might add something to me: something in the way of courage, in the way of—of an antidote for a feeling of inadequacy . . ."

Olivia scanned the heavens briefly through her diploma. "Do you believe in astrology?"

"You're joking. But I suppose you can afford to joke. You don't have to worry. You don't know what it's like to be nobody, do you? Always getting stepped on in this damned knock-down-drag-out after money . . . Do you know, Olivia, I used to think I wanted to be like Seixas. I thought it would be quite heroic to do something for the poor—and get along myself, maybe, on charity." He threw away his diploma with a dramatic gesture, letting it roll down the steps.

Olivia smiled, without malice.

"But I hate poverty! I hate being nobody! I want to be someone and have a name, I want to be respected, I want to live!"

He was silent. He regretted having made that theatrical, futile gesture. What was wrong with him? Why couldn't he face reality calmly and intelligently? What made him so bitter?

"Eugenio, go get your diploma."

He got to his feet and walked down five steps to pick up the diploma. Then he went back and sat down beside Olivia.

"The saddest part of all," he said, more calmly, "is that I see now I'm just not cut out for medicine. The day they give me a patient to operate on, I think I'll bolt. I don't know . . . I guess maybe I lack self-confidence."

"Or could it be you're afraid other people have no confidence in you?"

"That must be it. . . . Olivia, how do you know all these things I never told you?"

77

"I know you better than you think."

"Perhaps you do."

"I've been watching you since the second year of school."

"Why?"

"Oh, professional interest."

"I'd like to see my record, doctor."

"Ah! But it's in my private files." She tapped her forehead with her index finger. "My files are in here."

"Trespassing prohibited?"

"To strangers of the service, yes."

"I see. . . . I'm a stranger."

"Who said that?"

Eugenio took a handkerchief from his pocket and mopped his perspiring face and forehead.

"Do you want to know something funny, Olivia? When I'm with you I always want to tell you things."

"I'm afraid that's not much of a compliment. We usually confide in older people."

"Listen, Olivia. Why are you being so ironical tonight?"

"Don't you think irony can be one way of showing that you are deeply affected?"

He was silent.

"Yes," he said slowly, after a moment. "Tonight is different. Maybe years from now we'll remember tonight and wish we could live it over again."

"We'll laugh at the pretty picture we made, you in your Tuxedo and I in my evening dress, as we sat on the steps of the Patriarch's monument, in the empty square . . ."

Eugenio stared meditatively at the tips of his borrowed shoes, as if he could see his thoughts mirrored in the polished leather.

"There are some days we never forget, I guess. I think the day I die I'll still remember one winter afternoon in grade school when I got a terrific booing because my pants were torn. I must have been about nine or ten. . . . And I'll never forget the night when one of my teachers at boarding school shot himself. There was an awful storm, and I woke up afraid I was going to smother to death. The next day they found his body in the ball field. He was the first dead man I ever saw in my life."

He stopped abruptly. He was ashamed to mention other, equally unforgettable moments: the morning when he was fifteen and first became aware of a certain forbidden part of his body as the center of sensations which were at once pleasurable and painful; the afternoon long ago when he had pretended not to see his father.

Presently Olivia looked at her wrist watch. It was midnight.

"Eugenio, your mother must be awake, waiting up to congratulate you."

"You're right." He got up, dusting his trousers with the palms of his hands. "Let's go."

He gave Olivia his hand to help her rise. At the contact of her warm skin he felt a pleasant tremor. As they descended the steps slowly side by side, he felt as never before that he was close to a human being, to someone who *was*, who existed in a profound, integral way, who did not constitute merely a sum of vanities, of attitudes, of desires to appear something she was not.

"Olivia," he said suddenly, "let's always be good friends like this. Somehow when I'm with you things are easier for me. I mean that, Olivia—sincerely."

She looked again at the sky. "It's all very well to make plans on a night like this," she said, after a moment. "But

79

tomorrow will separate us, and you won't even remember the sentimental night when you said you wanted to be friends with a girl named Olivia. I have a feeling, Eugenio, and I'm sorry it's so strong, that you and I are going in completely different directions."

They turned into a deserted street. The melancholy gleam of street lamps brightened its quiet darkness. Eugenio scarcely noticed where he walked, for he was thinking of what Olivia had said. He sensed the truth in her words. Tomorrow they would be separated, because he had chosen a path which would lead him away from her. Only through a brilliant career would he be able to quench his unbearable sensation of inadequacy and defeat. He could not afford to be mediocre. He felt in him the courage to fight. He nourished dreams which must be realized.

"You think I'm wrong, don't you, to worry so much about my career."

"What is a career?"

"Oh! You know what I mean. Do you think I'm wrong?"

"That depends on what you mean by 'wrong.'"

"Olivia, you're impossible tonight!"

With a despairing gesture, Eugenio took a cigarette from his pocket and lit it. His forehead was creased with tiny wrinkles of annoyance, and he closed himself up now in a resentful silence. Olivia smiled and took hold of his arm.

"Don't you see I'm doing everything possible not to fall into the same state of melancholy and hopelessness you're in? Don't you understand that I feel just the way you do, that I ask myself the same questions you ask yourself? Come on, cheer up, Mr. Hyde!"

80

"You're right. I'm a doctor and a brute. Maybe more of a brute than a doctor."

"There's a Dr. Jekyll and a Mr. Hyde in all of us, Eugenio. It may sound like penny philosophizing, but it's true. Mr. Hyde is hopelessly cruel and dangerous. Dr. Jekyll has the tremendous responsibility of controlling him. No one is all good or all bad. Sometimes Mr. Hyde wins, and sometimes, not so often, Dr. Jekyll does. Usually they live as if they were on a seesaw. When one goes up the other comes down. Mr. Hyde is the beast that feels and reacts. Dr. Jekyll is the man who thinks and controls." Olivia sighed. "If the director heard me he'd grab my diploma right out of my hands!"

Eugenio was smiling.

"And do you believe that story of Jekyll and Hyde?"

She looked at him gravely. After a minute she shook her head.

"No."

He threw away his cigarette. Laughing, they turned into another street.

Gradually it grew dark. Frogs croaked in an overgrown pond, and in the faded sky the evening star glimmered delicately.

Eugenio looked at his watch. He felt that he was rolling through some mysterious region outside of time, that perhaps never, never again would he arrive at any earthly destination.

If only he could believe in God, he might pray. Prayer might help a little.

But Olivia was dying, and there could be no God. If God existed, He was brutally cruel. No. No, I am the one who has been cruel . . .

81

"I'm not bad, I'm not bad," he muttered stubbornly, as if to convince himself. There must be in him a good, pure something which was only waiting for an opportunity to dominate. Olivia had been creating in him that opportunity.

"You must accept people," she had told him. "All humanity isn't responsible for the few men who hurt you."

She was right. He lived as one man against the world. He seemed even to derive pleasure from his conflict.

But now, if Olivia should die, he would have to find his way alone. Eunice and his past would be like dead weights around his neck.

But even as he struggled to convince himself, Eugenio knew that his poor flesh would refuse to suffer, that his vacillating will would find no strength to govern it.

Was there still another hour and a half before they would reach the city?

He tossed his head back against the seat. The car glided smoothly over the cement highway.

Chapter 6

Eugenio struggled to overcome his fear. The situation was unbearable. He felt as if his stomach were the focal point of all sensation; just now it was cold and empty, and it nauseated him. It was eleven o'clock, and the battle outside was still raging. From the distance came the sound of gunfire. Only a moment ago a voice had announced in the corridor, "The barracks haven't given up yet."

He stood in the middle of the sterilizing room, fighting desperately to regain his self-control, hoping Sister Isolda, who was at the door, would not perceive his inner exertion, his indecision and dread. The white tile room was making him sick; it gave him an icy sensation of death. He felt as if he were in the enameled cabin of a ship on the high seas. He went to the wash basin, turned on the faucet and began to scrub his hands and forearms with a fierceness which caused his body to tremble. He raised his head and looked at himself in the mirror. He was pale, with a greenish pallor.

"May we bring in the patient, doctor?" asked the nun.

Eugenio nodded. "Didn't they find Dr. Rosa?" He could scarcely control his voice.

If only Dr. Rosa would come, he would have someone with whom to divide the responsibility . . . His mind was filled with misgiving. His nerves betrayed him. The patient had already had two internal hemorrhages. Any fool could see there was no hope for him. They should let him die in his bed! And this stupid revolution . . .

"The telephone at his house doesn't answer," said the nun.

Eugenio began to scrub his nails with the brush.

"Is Dr. Olivia ready?"

"Yes, doctor."

Sister Isolda left the room, and Eugenio stood listening to the gunfire outside. He had never believed that the revolution was possible. He had laughed at the rumors. Now here it was. It might turn into the direst of civil wars. Men were beasts. What must his mother be doing at this hour? There was danger from stray bullets . . . If only he had a drink, perhaps that would calm his nerves. No, he should not drink before an operation. He saw his brother lying senseless in the gutter. He saw his father smiling confidently at him. But the images melted swiftly from his mind, and he was left with only a sensation of dizziness and nausea. He felt as though his stomach were an electric node from which radiated all the fear that consumed his body.

He walked into the operating room with his arms raised. The patient was already strapped to the table. He was a scrawny, livid, middle-aged man. Dr. Teixeira Torres had sent Eugenio an urgent call to take over the case. He himself had an operation to perform immediately at the Metropolitan Hospital—a young army officer who had been wounded severely a few minutes before.

Dr. Teixeira Torres, his face drawn and slightly ashen, his voice shaking almost imperceptibly, had given hasty instructions in the hall: "Ruptured ulcer of the duodenum. Perform a gastroenterostomy. Wasn't it you who assisted me at that operation I did on old Espíndola's wife? Well, the case is identical." He had paused an instant and looked at Eugenio, his lips curved in a barely discernible smile of indulgent sarcasm. "Unless you prefer to do a duodenectomy." He had dashed to his automobile. But before he got in, he had turned and shouted: "Don't get upset if things don't go so well. He may 'leak.' It happens."

Olivia prepared to administer the anesthesia. Sister Isolda watched Eugenio fixedly; he thought he read doubt and mistrust in her impenetrable gray stare.

The silence was terrifying. Outside, the firing had ceased temporarily. Eugenio felt all eyes focused on himself, as though he were on the stage and they were waiting for him to give his finest performance. He looked at the sick man and hated him. He hated him, as if he were to blame for every hideous circumstance of that night—for the ulcer, for the revolution, for the other case which had called Dr. Teixeira Torres away . . .

He placed his hands in the basin of acid alcohol. The

84

smell of the liquid entered his nostrils and rose to his brain, where it was transformed into the image of Ernesto. Eugenio bent his arms and immersed them to the elbows in the cold solution.

A male nurse entered the room and spoke to Olivia in a low voice. "It looks like the barracks are going to give up." He grinned and revealed three shiny gold teeth.

Eugenio turned from the basin, pressed the pedal of the metal container and took out a surgical gown. Linen— laundress . . . There flashed through his mind the vision of his mother washing the linen at the boarding school, her hands drawn from being too long in the water. His father checking the list . . . Why was he reminded so often of these episodes from his childhood?

He pushed his arms through the sleeves of the gown, while a nurse buttoned the back. He put on his mask. Oddly, as though in answer to a prearranged signal, his heart began to beat more rapidly. The decisive moment was near.

Olivia began to administer the anesthetic, and the sweet, sickening odor diffused through the air. Padilha, a fifth-year medical student whom Eugenio did not like, began to arrange the instruments on top of the auxiliary table.

Eugenio approached the patient. He looked around him and saw that his audience was waiting. Padilha seemed to be smiling with the corner of his mouth—a smile of scornful incredulity. Above the patient's face—his skin was almost as white as the mask—Eugenio sensed the friendly presence of Olivia's deep eyes. Only they could help him. For a few seconds he hesitated. Gastroenterostomy. Mentally he reviewed the operation which Dr. Teixeira Torres had performed on old Espíndola's wife, followed the course of his firm, agile hand as it had gripped the bistoury. Then he noticed that his own hands were trembling slightly. Horrible! At each of the several less important operations which he had performed he had had to fight against his nausea and his fear; but things had always turned out well, and he had been rewarded after each ordeal by a sense of relief and a new self-confidence. But this was different. It was night. Outside, madmen, savages were fighting—the firing had begun again! He had been given a corpse to operate on. Everything indicated that the man would not survive the operation. Perhaps he would not even live until it was over.

Eugenio consulted Olivia mutely, with his eyes. She examined the patient's pupillary reflex and nodded her head. The assistant pinched the sick man's skin; there was not the slightest reaction. Eugenio picked up the bistoury. He felt somehow as if he were about to commit a crime, as if at any moment the door would fly open and someone would burst into the room to arrest him and put a substitute in his place, to prevent his going on with the operation.

The firing was growing louder outside. But the silence in the hospital was appalling.

Eugenio made the incision. Curious. . . . When the blood gushed up he felt in a certain way relieved. Somehow, now, he must go on.

The silence in the room continued, broken only by the sharp, dry clicking of the instruments. The nurse, a very tense, red-faced German woman, handed the instruments to the surgeon with the mechanical efficiency of a robot—a robot which had the power of rational thought, which could even read the surgeon's mind and divine which instrument he would require.

Eugenio pricked the peritoneum with the scissors and

began to make the incision. It was then that the thing he had feared began to happen. From the opening there welled a mounting tide of dark and viscous mud, formed of pus, exudates, and feces. For a fraction of a second Eugenio seemed to hesitate. His facial muscles contracted in a mask of repugnance. The mud continued to flow, invading the operative field. One might have said that the poor man's body was no more than a repository in which all the putrid matter in the world had lain concealed. Eugenio raised his eyes to Olivia in a desperate appeal for help. Padilha and the nurse came forward with compresses and swabs.

Dull explosions resounded in the distance. They must be using cannon now. Eugenio imagined the houses of the city in ruins, the city itself destroyed, a grenade striking his own home. He saw his mother lying on the floor, covered with blood. He looked at his gloves, which were soiled with that vile liquid, and he wanted to scream. Men were brutes, men were rotten.

The gunfire continued, punctuated from time to time by a stronger blast. It was not only the patient who was about to die; they would all be destroyed by the bombardment. The heat in the operating room was unbearable. Or was it cold? It must be the smell of the ether that was making him sick.

They had given him a dead man for a patient. He hated Dr. Teixeira Torres. If the patient had been rich, he would have stayed to perform the operation himself, even if it had been only a matter of opening the man's stomach one instant and closing it up the next, in a mere sham operation. There were stores about Dr. Teixeira Torres' professional banditry . . . Or were those stories untrue? Eugenio was an ingrate. The man was friendly to him and tried to help him professionally. Oh, a fine way to help him! Throwing a case like this one into his hands! Only a miracle could save the patient. But miracles didn't happen. In this world there was only the stupidity of men, the unspeakable brutality of life.

"His pulse is almost gone," warned Padilha.

The patient's face and hands were white as paper. His breathing was growing weaker, becoming superficial. Olivia removed the mask.

"His pulse has stopped," the assistant declared, after a few seconds.

Was it triumph, defiance, or censure in Padilha's voice? Eugenio looked at him obliquely.

At that moment the door of the operating room opened. The male nurse came in and whispered something to Sister Isolda. Death seemed to have entered the room with him, for Eugenio experienced a sudden chill—was it a draught or his imagination?—and the patient stopped breathing. Olivia examined the pupils of his eyes. Padilha dropped his wrist and listened to his heart. He looked at Eugenio indifferently.

"Looks like he's kicked off."

Eugenio wanted to slap him. How out of place that slang expression was at a moment when a life was ending, when, outside, many people were dying!

The nurse handed Eugenio the needle and catgut. Her clear blue eyes revealed not the slightest emotion. On her face there was only an infantile expression, as if, instead of handing a surgeon a needle and gut to sew up a corpse, she were asking her older brother to make a dress for her doll.

Eugenio made the suture along one plane only.

Just then he heard a whisper: *He died on the operating*

88

table . . . Someone was saying those words in his mind. Who was it? *He died on the operating table* . . . They were the voices of his colleagues whispering to one another. *He died in Eugenio's hands* . . . The voices were familiar, vaguely hostile.

The operation was over.

"Sister Isolda," said Eugenio, and he wondered at the firmness of his own voice, "please advise his family. Dr. Teixeira Torres told them before that there was no hope."

From where did it come, this sudden calm, this coolness?

Outside, the barrage continued. Padilha and the male nurse were talking loudly, discussing the revolution and laughing. Eugenio's own tortured thoughts obscured all but a few scattered phrases: "A grenade went off on the sidewalk . . . machine-gun fire in the elevator . . . They say the battalion stuck it out . . ."

He pulled off his gloves and tossed them violently into the bucket. He tore off his mask, and suddenly he felt that he was unprotected. Unmasked! The bandit had removed his mask at last . . .

He took off his gown and hurried into the sterilizing room. A voice sounded in the corridor:

"The barracks haven't given up yet."

As he washed his hands in the sink, Eugenio looked up into the mirror and saw Olivia's calm face. He turned, his hands dripping.

"Drink this," she said, and handed him a wineglassful of an amber liquid.

"Cognac?"

She nodded. Eugenio lifted the glass and drained it. While he dried his hands, she placed a cigarette between his lips and lighted it for him.

89

"Shall we go down together?" he asked.

"Let's. Wait a second. I'll be right back."

Five minutes later they descended in the elevator. In the lobby a group of men were talking excitedly.

Olivia and Eugenio went out. How dark the night was! They walked side by side, without speaking. The firing had stopped, and Eugenio felt that his calm was returning. He could not forget the dead man on whom he had operated, but he was resigned. It had been, after all, a hopeless case. He had been a fool to lend himself so readily to that farce.

"Olivia—I'm a failure."

"Because you couldn't bring a dead man back to life?"

He shrugged. "No. . . . Not that. . . . Olivia, you don't know how I have to fight myself, how afraid I am, how unsure. . . . Surgery needs cold blood, and—and I'm just not cold-blooded. When I cut a patient's skin, it's just as if I were cutting my own." He sighed. "Why is it, Olivia, that everything is so different from the way we imagine it when we're little? It's so nice when we hear that Dr. So-and-so saved a man's life and sacrificed himself to humanity. We want to be heroes, too. We look forward to our turn to save lives and make sacrifices. . . . Well, I guess it didn't take so long to see through that. But I thought I could face it, Olivia. I thought it would come to me: the self-confidence, the *sang-froid*, the—maturity—the—I know you understand—something to make me operate on a man with the calm of a child cutting paper dolls. And do you know how I really feel when I operate?"

While he was speaking Olivia took his arm. Now she pressed it more tightly.

"I know. Just the way you'd feel if you were fifteen years old and someone took you into an operating room, showed you an acute abdominal case, handed you a bistoury and said, 'Go to it, little boy!' "

"Yes."

"I think I can tell you almost exactly how you felt today. When Dr. Teixeira Torres turned the case over to you, you were afraid. But you were proud, too. You were afraid, because you had the responsibility of a hopeless case. And you were proud, because Dr. Teixeira Torres trusted you with one of his patients. But the pride disappeared and turned into something almost like terror. Am I right?"

Eugenio stared at her. For a moment he did not answer. "You're right."

"And then what bothered you most was the feeling that the others might think you weren't fit for the responsibility. You thought you could see distrust and ridicule in the way they looked at you—the Sister, the nurse, and your assistant. You yourself thought the situation was beyond your strength, but you couldn't bear for *them* to think so."

It was uncomfortable to be thus discovered. He struggled not to agree with her, not to admit that she was right. But it was no use. Olivia's eyes seemed to see through all things. He did not know why he did not become angry with her. Why was he never irritated by her observations, no matter how direct, how sharp or painful they might be? Why was he never annoyed even when, with her amazing clinical eye, she discovered and probed his deepest wounds?

"Olivia, I don't know how you discover—"

She shook her head. "It must be," she said after a moment, "because I'm a doctor, and medicine is mostly intuition."

He frowned.

91

"Then it's because I'm a doctor and a woman."

"There must be something else."

"Or because, without realizing it, you reveal too much of what you think and feel."

"I don't believe it."

"Then maybe it's because I have lived and have learned how to see."

"You're only twenty-five, Olivia."

"I knew a man once who was sixty and still hadn't learned to know himself."

There was a silence. They turned into another street. A truckful of cheering soldiers raced by.

"This stupid revolution!" muttered Eugenio. "I don't know how people . . ."

He did not finish his sentence. He lit a fresh cigarette. Olivia shrugged her shoulders mildly.

On the opposite sidewalk a drunk was clutching a post, bellowing in Spanish: "Long live the constitutional power! Down with the unitarian savages!" He broke into a nasal, tuneless singing.

Again they heard the booming of guns, far away. Eugenio's skin bristled disagreeably, and the quickened rhythm of his heart betrayed his fear.

They stopped. It was fortunate that they were walking away from the zone where the fighting was taking place. The male nurse had told them that only the barracks of the Seventh Cavalry Battalion was still resisting. The insurrectionists were victorious in all other sectors.

Olivia clung more tightly to Eugenio's arm and pressed close to his side as they hurried across the street. They almost ran, for they were beyond the protection of the houses.

When they reached the opposite sidewalk, they resumed

their normal pace. The roar of the guns began to subside. Eugenio, calmer now, thought again of the man who had died in his hands.

"During almost the whole operation," he said, "all sorts of little things—objects, sounds, smells—made me think of people I used to know and things that happened to me when I was little. Why, do you suppose, are we never free of our childhood? Our whole life, Olivia—the important part of it—seems to be back there, and the rest is only something that ties in."

"There are lots of answers to that in the psychology books." She looked at him oddly. "But I guess everyone finds a different one for himself."

Eugenio tossed his cigarette into the air and exhaled the last bit of smoke. He smiled sadly.

"I'm hopeless, don't you think?"

He shoved his hands deep into his pockets, but Olivia did not withdraw her arm from his. It seemed almost as if she feared that, without her support, he might lose his balance and fall.

When they drew near the house where Olivia stayed, Eugenio began to think of the hours that would follow. He dreaded to leave his friend, for he knew that when he was alone the fear would return and life would again seem cold and empty. His need for happiness and human companionship welled up suddenly inside him, crying to be satisfied.

The turbulent, yet somehow indifferent, October night caused his flesh to prickle. The air was as cold as men, as the cruel men who at that very moment were slaughtering one another. He would go home, where he knew his mother was waiting for him, and he would sit in his room, smoking and thinking. He was alone and unhappy, and his nagging restlessness and dissatisfaction made his life drab and melancholy. He pitied himself; he was a martyr to a great social injustice, which he must overcome by whatever means he could. Only a tiny part of him—so imprecise and weak that at times it disappeared altogether—leveled at himself a criticism not devoid of malice, and was inclined to accept reality with courage and even with humor.

They crossed the little garden. Olivia inserted the key in the lock. She lived with the Falks, a German couple who had no children.

Eugenio held out his hand to say good night. But she looked at her watch.

"It's early. Come on in for a little while."

He hesitated. He excused himself for not going home to his mother, but without conviction. Dona Alzira must be worried. But after all, since it was so early . . .

He went in.

The automobile passed through a tiny village, just as the street lights were beginning to come on. Some mystery seemed to hover in the deserted and poorly lighted little streets, about the old colonial houses with their dark façades. Dogs barked. The automobile passed the lighted doors of a shop, the silhouette of an ancient church. Always there was this suggestion of God, both inside and outside one's thoughts. Why did He not reveal Himself in some more tangible way, in the form of a miracle—the miracle of Olivia's recovery . . . Yes, if Olivia lived, it would be a sign that there was a God.

The car entered the cement highway once more, leaving the little village behind.

Night descended, perfumed with damp herbs. Stars be-

gan to appear more thickly in the dark sky. The wind was warm, like a human breath. Oddly, Eugenio was reminded of the first night he had loved Olivia.

It had happened so unexpectedly. It had seemed so preposterous. He had entered her room after those dreadful hours of the revolution, when his patient had died and he had been haunted by specters of fear and defeat. Like a nurse, she had soothed and comforted him. She had made him lie down on the sofa and had placed his tired head in her lap. He remembered how, for an instant, he had lain in that position, his eyes closed, seeking peace, while Olivia caressed his hair silently. He recalled the sensation he had felt on the nape of his neck, where his skin met the soft firmness of her flesh, under her thin dress. A woman's flesh—Olivia was a woman . . . He had opened his eyes and had seen her calm face. Curious, he had thought, she was beautiful! For a few minutes he had lain very still, gazing at her. Gradually the heat of desire had flooded his body, making it difficult for him to breathe. He had been able to lie still no longer. Brusquely, he had arisen, had sat down beside her on the couch, and he had looked at her in such a way that she had wrinkled her forehead in an uneasy frown.

"Is something wrong?"

He had shaken his head.

How attractive she was! She had warm eyes and a fulllipped, red mouth. He had wanted to kiss her. And why not? She might protest, he had thought; she might be offended . . .

But what did it matter? The end of the world was near. Men were killing themselves. Life was cruel. Some day both of them would be rotting under the ground.

He had seized Olivia's head in both his hands, had kissed

95

her mouth passionately. How silently, how tenderly she had yielded to him!

Frogs croaked mournfully along the edges of the high-way. The headlights of the automobile swept the wide road, swept the dark night.

Chapter 7

It was very late when he left Olivia's room. He felt like a newborn soul, entering a world that was dawning. His life seemed to be in a state of metamorphosis, and he was no longer himself, but only an aerial being without memory, walking in the dawn. Far away, roosters were crowing. The air was cold and penetrating, and it smelled of dew. He did not feel his body. He raised his hand to his cool forehead. On his fingers he smelled Olivia's perfume. He recalled the moments he had held her in his arms. The shock of their revelation had made him a little giddy. He did not want to think. All he wanted now was to sleep, to sleep for a long time, without caring if tomorrow came . . .

When Eugenio arrived home, it was four o'clock. He opened the door noiselessly and tiptoed to his room. He took off his coat and sat down on the bed. There was a muffled sound of footsteps in the hall. He sat listening . . . The door opened, and Dona Alzira appeared, wrapped in a checked shawl.

"Oh, my son! I was so afraid something had happened to you!" She went over to him, bent down and kissed his forehead. "I prayed all the time. When I heard the shooting, I was so scared maybe they'd hit you by mistake."

"Nothing happened, mother."

"What time is it?"

"It must be four—a little after four."

"Did the operation take till now?"

He nodded, avoiding her eyes. He saw so many questions in them . . .

"Why didn't you come home right away? I was so worried! Drink your milk, son." She pointed to the glass of milk and the cookies on the night table. "And you didn't take your overcoat. It's right cold tonight. Do you want me to warm up your milk?"

"No, thank you, mother. I like it better cold."

Her insistence, her solicitude made him uncomfortable. He wished she would leave him alone. He needed to be alone.

"How's the revolution?" In her question there was mingled awe, incomprehension, reproach, and fear.

Eugenio did not answer. Outside, they could hear the thin, far-away sound of gunfire.

"Listen," said Dona Alzira. "They're still fighting." She gave a sigh. "It's awful. It's like the world was going to end."

He lay down on the bed. What did he care about the revolution? His mother began to take off his shoes.

"Do you know who got killed? Dona Gugú's Aluízio."

"Aluízio?"

"The one who was a policeman. They say he got killed by a grenade in the big attack on the general headquarters. Poor Gugú don't know which way to turn. She's just crazy."

Eugenio closed his eyes and saw Aluízio lying in the street with his head open and his brains running out, like the pulp of a rotten fruit squashed on the ground.

97

Dona Alzira sat down at the head of the bed and began to stroke her son's head gently.

"Did everything go all right?" she asked in a hushed voice.

Although he knew to what she was referring, Eugenio merely grunted ill-humoredly, without opening his eyes.

"H'm?"

"How was the operation?"

Oh! Why did she have to ask questions? He wished she would go away. He loved her. Perhaps not so much as she deserved, but he loved her. He knew that she had sacrificed for him, that she had worked to pay for his living, to send him to school. He owed her everything: his life, his doctor's degree, his darned socks, and a million other small things. But he could not bear her persistence in treating him as a child. The milk she brought him every night was a way she had of maintaining the illusion that he was still an infant.

At last, reluctantly, he answered her. "The patient died."

His mother sighed, and her hands lingered as they stroked his hair, as if they wished to be more soothing.

"Don't you worry. Nobody can beat Destiny."

Worse yet, he thought, were her attempts to console him. He needed peace, sleep, oblivion.

"God is great, my son."

There is no God. But Eugenio's protest was timid, and there was an underlying fear in his heart. This dawn, when men were dying, was vaguely sinister. There might be a God, after all. Perhaps Olivia was right. He remembered a talk he had had with her a few days before. "If there is a God, then why hasn't He revealed Himself?" he had asked.

"Because even God needs opportunities," she had answered.

"If there were a God, I'd have found Him long ago."

He recalled Olivia's smile and the calmness of her voice, which had seemed to envelop him totally.

"You atheists want to take God away from us, in order to give us in His place—what? It's like taking bread from a hungry man and giving him a fistful of ashes or sand."

Again he heard his own voice, defying her. "But bread, ashes, and sand are concrete entities. The idea of God is an abstraction."

"You say you believe in success," she had answered calmly. "Well, success is abstract, too, Eugenio."

Olivia—Olivia . . . His eyes closed, Eugenio thought of her. What would become of their friendship after what had happened that night? It was still too early to think clearly. He did not know whether he felt happiness, remorse, astonishment, or disgust at his behavior. The shocking realization of his feeling for her was not altogether disagreeable. He could not escape a sense of victory, in the depths of which, however, there was an element of bitterness. In a single brief, insane moment his lifelong craving for happiness and pleasure, sharpened by the unpleasant scenes in the hospital, seemed to have thrown into focus all the drab, terrifying loneliness of his existence and of the world itself, and he had embraced Olivia as if she alone could save him. They were young and healthy. Had they no right to be happy? That had been a moment of forgetfulness and a moment which he would never forget . . .

Suddenly he was aware of the dreary, spiritless sound of his mother's voice:

"You didn't hear nothing about Ernesto?"

99

It was a timid, reluctant query, mumbled, one felt, after much indecision.

Tonight was a whole world, an eternity which he would never, never forget: the dead man on the operating table; Olivia's kisses; the gunfire and the men tearing one another to bits; the dawn; the turmoil of his thoughts. And now the memory of Ernesto . . .

"Nothing, mother. Nothing."

He had wanted to erase from his mind forever the remembrance of the day he and Ernesto had quarreled. But here it was again; he recalled every detail of it as clearly as if it had been only yesterday. He saw Ernesto slouched at the table, his eyes downcast, fixed on his plate. He saw his mother with her hand over her mouth, her eyes wide with astonishment, and his father huddled in the rocking chair. He saw himself crushing the newspaper in his hands, rage swelling in his breast, choking him.

"In the paper again!" Wrath had altered his voice, distorted his face. "Carousing in the Beco do Império! And his picture, father! Look, mother!" He had held out the police section of the newspaper, *Correio do Povo*. "'Drunk Creates Disturbance in Alley'! His picture and the name Ernesto Fontes—the *whole name!*" He had hurled the paper to the floor and faced his brother wrathfully. "Is it for this that I kill myself studying? Is it for this your mother and father work like slaves? So *you* can wallow in filth, so *you* can get into brawls?" Ernesto had not raised his head. "We do everything that's humanly possible to climb out of this pigsty, and *you* pull us down!" Eugenio had turned to his mother. "If the boys at school ever found out he's my brother, I'd never have the face to go there again!"

Angelo had risen, making an effort to appear indifferent,

and had gone into the kitchen. Dona Alzira had murmured something, in a weak attempt at conciliation. But Eugenio —how precisely, with what perverse gratification he remembered!—had wanted to settle the issue once and for all.

"I want you to know, Ernesto, that one of us in this house is one too many. Either you leave tomorrow, or I'm going to move to a boarding house!"

His whole body had trembled as he sat down. Dona Alzira had wept, and from the kitchen there had come the sound of Angelo's hoarse cough. At last Ernesto had spoken, in a voice which had been scarcely audible.

"I'll go," he had said.

And the next day he disappeared. After that they had heard nothing more from him. In vain Angelo had gone to the newspapers and to the police. A few hours before he had died, he had asked, "Where is our Nestinho?"

Oh, that night! . . . Suddenly, brusquely, Eugenio threw his legs over the side of the bed.

"Laws, Genoca, what is it?"

He sat bolt upright on the edge of the bed, his hands gripping its iron frame, his head sunk deep between his raised shoulders, his eyes staring at the wall.

"What you need is a good sleep, Genoca. Go to sleep, my son. Your father always used to say, 'Sleep is bread.'"

His mother kissed him on the forehead and left the room noiselessly. But she left him in the company of a ghost. *"Sleep is bread," your father always used to say* . . .

Eugenio lit a cigarette. He walked to the window, opened it, and stood looking out. Day was breaking. A sense of mystery prevailed in the world. There must be some meaning in all that had happened that night. The patient who had died in his hands, the woman he had held in his arms, the men who were shooting one another. All that could not have been coincidence.

He stood by the window for a long time, smoking and thinking.

In the little garden below he imagined that he saw his father bending over the largest flower bed, tending his favorite rosebush—"Show Queen"—pulling up the harmful weeds that grew around it, killing the ants. There was the rosebush now, growing vigorously. But Angelo was dead. Eugenio was like the favorite rosebush. Under his father's care he had flourished and bloomed. But he had become ashamed of the gardener. He thought of the afternoon, long ago, when he had walked down the street with Alcibiades and Acelio Castanho . . .

He tossed the cigarette into the garden, closed the window again, and lay down in the bed. His eyelids ached, and his head was light. He thought of Olivia. He saw the skin of the man on whom he had operated, stained brown with iodine, the blood gushing forth. He thought of Aluízio lying on the sidewalk, of Mr. Tearle fallen on his face in the field, in the rain. Ernesto—Olivia—the ruptured ulcer—the firing in the distance . . .

Then a great peace came to him, a great blessing, like a deep, cool lake of calm and freshness—heavy, dreamless sleep.

In the glare of the automobile headlights Eugenio caught a lightning glimpse of a tramp walking along the side of the road.

He was thinking of his brother.

He closed his eyes and saw himself again in the hospital room. It was winter, and the rain was tapping gently on the window panes. The chill, gray morning light gave the faces of people a cadaverous appearance. "Don't worry, mother, I'll look for Nestinho . . ." The hushed echo of his voice fell in his mind. He was again at his mother's bedside, a few hours before she died. How cold her hands had been, and how weak! For his sake. . . . Dr. Seixas had stood at the foot of the bed stroking his beard, gazing at his old friend who was dying. From time to time he had muttered in his harsh voice: "It's nothing, Alzira. Tomorrow you'll be feeling fine. It's nothing." They had done everything possible for her. They had consulted with the best doctors in the city. The only thing which had remained to do had been to make her last hours as comfortable as possible.

Just once her lips had moved. Eugenio had had to bend close to catch the faint whisper: "Nestinho," she had said. "He's so good . . ."

The automobile rolled on. Fireflies glimmered in the dark. They passed fences, trees, the swift, pale outline of a whitewashed house . . .

Tears were rolling down Eugenio's cheeks, and he shook his head from side to side, like a sick child, or a sleeper trying to rid himself of an unpleasant dream. "Don't worry, mother, I'll look for Nestinho . . ." Pronounced at the bedside of a dying woman, his words had seemed to become an oath. What had he actually done to find his brother, if one did not count the weak efforts he had made only to appease his own conscience?

Time had gone by, consumed by his duties at the factory and as a physician, by his accursed social obligations, by his fear of scandal, his desire to conceal from his wife and father-in-law the truth about his brother. Always he had deluded himself with promises. Tomorrow. Later . . . There was always time. One day, timidly, he had told Eunice *about Ernesto, and her only comment had been, "As if you didn't have enough worries of your own!"*

A full moon rose behind the shadowy outline of a hill. Its brilliance was so intense that the stars seemed to go out in the pallid sky.

Eugenio looked at his watch.

We always had dinner now . . . *Ernesto used to sit across from him at the little table. Sometimes he would kick Eugenio in the shins under the table, his little face perfectly serious; only his tiny eyes would laugh, with a poorly simulated gleam of malice.*

"Look at Ernesto, Mamma! He kicked me in the shin!"

And his mother would say, "What's this, Nestinho? Behave yourself!"

Then Eugenio recalled stormy nights at home, when the wind shook the tiles, rattling the doors and windows. Again he heard the rain drumming on the roof, pounding at the windows, and saw flashes of lightning illuminating his old room. Under the covers, united in a tight embrace, he and Ernesto used to lie, rigid with terror, lost in a world of fear and disaster. The thunderbolts might cause the whole sky to fall in, the lightning flashes might tear the houses to bits and burn them up, and the rain might drown the whole world in a second Great Flood. St. Barbara, St. Jerome . . . Our Father, which art in heaven, Hallowed be thy name . . . Genoca, what's that knocking? . . . I don't know. I guess it's my heart. . . . Do you suppose the world's going to end . . . It must be. Pray, pray, Nestinho —Hail Mary, full of Grace . . . *Locked in each other's arms, they used to wait until their Heavenly Father's wrath should subside.*

Nestinho—he's so good . . . *Yes, Ernesto had been good. He used to share with his older brother the sweets and the pennies which people gave him. One day at school he had gotten into a fight with one of his classmates who had made a slurring remark about Genoca. He himself had always received low marks at school; but it was with pride that he used to say, "My brother's the head of his class." With the passing of time the two boys had grown apart. All their parents' care had been lavished on the eldest son. He must go to college and to medical school; he would be a doctor. There had not been enough money to educate the two of them . . .*

Eugenio rubbed his hand across his face. It was Olivia who returned to his thoughts now. No, Olivia was and had always been in his mind. The scene in the hospital, the memory of Ernesto, the images of his childhood, all had a strange transparency through which he never lost sight of Olivia. Olivia herself had a mysterious, ethereal quality, through which he could make out the vague presence of death. Death had no constant form: now it was a pale woman surrounded by four tapers; now it was a white tomb; now, only a decomposing body.

Olivia was dying! Perhaps at this very moment she was dead . . . O God! This trip will never, never end!

Chapter 8

The child was seized by a fresh fit of coughing as Eugenio entered the room. He had thrown the covers off and was tossing in the bed, panting for breath, his body convulsed with pain. His face was purple, and his eyes rolled whitely. His cough was dull and hoarse. When the access had passed, he lay back with his arms and legs flung wide, weakened by his effort, his lips blue, his eyes filled with terror.

Eugenio knew the symptoms. It was advanced laryngeal diphtheria. He took the pulse of the child—a rosy, plump little boy of about five—and listened to his heart. The pulse was fast and extremely weak, and the heart beat irregularly, seeming at times almost to gallop.

"Why didn't you call a doctor right away?"

Immediately Eugenio was aware of the emptiness, the pretension, the futility of his words. He had said them almost as though observing a ritual, perhaps because he had heard another physician say them under similar circumstances. In a novel or a play, one would have expected the doctor to ask that question, with a severe, professional air. Eugenio looked at the child's mother. She was a short, fat woman with a rough, lumpy skin and watery green eyes. In a nervous, disagreeable voice, she broke into a flood of explanations; but he did not listen to her. He looked instead at the little boy, whose face was tinged with a dangerous, cyanotic blue as he tossed fitfully, struggling to breathe. He was a pretty child. His long, curly hair rippled over the pillow, and his little eyes were clear, with a purity which was not diminished even by pain.

"Save our son, doctor!" Eugenio felt on his skin the hot breath of the child's father and saw the drawn expression on the man's face, his frightened eyes and quivering lips. "For the love of God, doctor, I'll give you anything we have!"

At that moment the little boy was shaken by another access. He raised himself up in bed, his little arms flailed the air, and the hollow, racking sound of his coughing filled the room. Then he fell back against the pillow and lay still—almost, it seemed, without breathing. With a scream his mother rushed to his side and began to embrace him desperately.

"Oh! My little boy is dead! Oh, my adorable baby!"

With difficulty her husband pulled her away from the bed. She rose from her knees and stood rigid an instant, staring at Eugenio vacantly. She seemed to be wavering on the fringes of insanity. Her mouth was twisted hideously. He watched her anxiously as her face grew white, her expression glassy. Suddenly, with a dull thud, she fell to the floor.

Unexpectedly, Eugenio felt himself possessed of a cold, lucid composure. He must get the child to the hospital as quickly as possible, must operate immediately. He had not brought a single instrument with him, for he had been overtaken by the child's father in the street.

"Go get a taxi!" he shouted to the man, who knelt at his wife's side, shaking her by the shoulders and calling her name repeatedly. "Quick!" he bellowed.

The fellow scrambled to his feet and stared at Eugenio blankly, as though he had not understood.

"Go get a taxi—hurry!"

As the man ran out of the house, he passed two women and a man at the door, who entered with questioning looks, the women exclaiming, the man on the point of asking a question, which Eugenio cut off.

"Where is the nearest telephone?"

"H-here, next door, doctor. Bu—"

"Put this woman to bed with her head lower than her feet!"

He ran out and knocked at the door of the next house.

"I'm Eugenio Fontes," he said rapidly to the woman who opened it. "I'm a physician. Your neighbor's son isn't well. I'd like to use your telephone. Immediately!"

"Of course, of course, doctor. Come right in—this way please."

Eugenio was amazed at his command of the situation. At any other time he would have knocked at that door humbly as a beggar asking for old clothes.

He called the hospital and asked that everything be gotten ready for the operation.

"Send for Dr. Olivia," he concluded. "I'll be there in ten minutes, at the latest."

When he went out into the street again, a taxi had already drawn up in front of the sick child's home. He went into the house, wrapped the little boy in a blanket, and lifted him in his arms. Suddenly he felt strong, as though at last he had accepted Fate's challenge. He must save the child's life.

In the next room the women were talking loudly, becoming excited. The little boy's mother had not yet recovered consciousness.

"Let's go!" Eugenio called to her husband.

The poor man hesitated.

"Doctor," he ventured timidly, "my—my wife—"

"Leave your wife!" Eugenio snapped, not looking around as he walked to the door. "We've got to save your son!" He dashed out, into the waiting automobile. "To the Sacred Heart Hospital—as fast as you can!"

The child's father got into the car, and it began to move.

Eugenio felt the heat of the little boy's body against his chest. For the first time in his life he found himself in the role of a protector, dominating a situation which was almost heroic. He was happy, for he had entered the battle at last, and he was strong. But he knew that he dared not analyze his feelings too closely, lest his composure, his miraculous new clear-headedness should vanish. He must remain calm; he thought of Olivia. He looked down at the child in his arms and saw that already he looked more dead than alive. The father, who sat beside him, was weeping silently.

With a handkerchief Olivia wiped the perspiration from Eugenio's warm forehead. The tracheotomy was over, and the nurse was busy putting away the instruments. There was a sound of metal ringing against metal, of tables being dragged across the floor. He removed his gloves and took the child's pulse. He seemed to be recovering. His respiration was returning slowly to normal, becoming at first superficial, then deep and perceptible. Gradually his little face was losing its cyanotic lividness. Eugenio watched these changes with moved attention. He had won! He had saved the child's life!

He called Sister Isolda.

"Prepare a room for the boy," he ordered. "We'll be responsible for the charges. Tell Padilha to inoculate him for diphtheria."

He made several other recommendations, and then, after he had removed the surgical gown and put on his coat, he left the room, apparently calm.

But a few minutes later, when Olivia looked for him to go out, she found him in the waiting room, sunk deep in an easy-chair, his face buried in his hands, weeping like a child.

"Shall we have dinner at the Edelweiss?"

"Each fellow pays for himself," was Olivia's condition.

"We'll see about that."

They began to walk arm in arm. A shower had just

fallen, and the air was cool. In the clean sky the gleam of the stars had a liquid purity. It was the hour when shops, garages, and offices were closing. Men and women hurried through the streets, rushing into trolleys and busses. Above the heads of the crowd bright electric signs sparkled.

How good it was to be alive! He had saved a life! Softly Eugenio began to hum an old song he thought he had forgotten long ago. He inhaled with delight the cool air; it was sharp with the scent of burned gasoline. He felt light and buoyant, as though the storm clouds inside him had dissolved in rain and his soul were rinsed clean, were cool and starry as the night.

"Why," he said to Olivia, "do you feel sometimes as if you'd just been born—as if the world were still fresh out of the hands of whoever made it?"

Without waiting for an answer, he squeezed her arm happily and began to hum again. He loved the people who passed in the street and on the sidewalk; he was happy to be a part of that moving forest. He felt suddenly like kissing Olivia. He wanted to embrace her as a comrade, to give her the hearty, passionless kiss which all men, whether friends or strangers, should exchange when they met in the street. It was a sign of solidarity, a symbol of good will—the kiss, after all, which men would exchange naturally if the world were different.

"There seem to be clearings," she said suddenly, as though she had been revolving his question carefully in her mind, "that open up unexpectedly, just so we can get a glimpse of God."

There was a God! Eugenio thought suddenly of his Bible lessons at Columbia Academy. The resurrection of Lazarus—Jairus' daughter . . . Christ was a physician. Christ might be that pure star up there in the sky. Or He might—

Abruptly, with a start which set his heart to bounding, Eugenio felt a sharp tug on his arm, heard the screech of automobile brakes. In a flash he saw his danger and drew back.

"You were almost run over!" Olivia chid him, like a mother reprehending a child.

He looked at the large automobile which had pulled up in front of him. Inside, an attractive, elderly gentleman was smiling tolerantly. On the car door the name V. CINTRA was printed in white letters.

"No harm done," Eugenio remarked as they walked on. "What a good-looking Packard!"

With some difficulty they obtained a table at the Edelweiss, a restaurant with a Tyrolean atmosphere where most of the diners were either Austrian or German. It was full of people eating, drinking, smoking, talking, and singing. A bluish cloud hovered in the air. At the end of the counter, keeping guard over the cash register, which tinkled from time to time, a fat, pimply-faced woman rested her heavy breasts and forearms on the marble slab, watching over her customers with maternal pride.

"What'll we have?" asked Eugenio.

Olivia glanced at the menu absently and handed it over. After some indecision, they agreed at last on eggs, sausages, and beer.

A victrola began to play "The Beautiful Blue Danube." The owner of the restaurant, a short, stocky Austrian with a red nose, a thick neck, and a shaved head, was going from table to table, welcoming his guests. On the top of his head he wore a tiny Alpine hat with a bright feather, which he doffed to every customer in a gay, exaggerated greeting. He winked at his women patrons. His antics were applauded by bursts of laughter. From somewhere in the back of the room came a powerful masculine voice, singing to the music of the victrola. The waiter passed with a tray full of beers.

Eugenio kept time with the waltz rhythm by striking his fork against the edge of his plate.

"Things are looking up," he remarked abruptly, as if Olivia had been able to follow the course of his happy thoughts. "I have a feeling that before the week is over they'll give me that place in the ambulance squad."

"That will be a relief for your pocketbook, won't it?"

"You bet!" In the same breath he added, "I'm so hungry it's driving me crazy!"

"Me too."

Eugenio laughed.

"What made you laugh like that?"

He leaned over the table. "When you were a little girl, didn't you ever hear that routine about 'Me too'? You didn't? Well, listen. Whatever I say, you're supposed to answer, 'Me too.' O.K.? Let's go. I was walking down a road—"

"Me too."

"I met a little bird."

"Me too."

Suddenly he stopped, pretending to be annoyed. "Tch! What a pity! That joke's not for ladies. Lordy, what a memory I have!"

Just then the waiter arrived with a platter of eggs and sausages and two glasses of beer.

"Look at that!" Eugenio exclaimed. "The first one who says a word is a monkey's uncle!"

They ate ravenously, in a silence broken only by

monosyllables or by scattered words. Soon he began to notice that his head was growing lighter, becoming deliciously giddy. And little by little, as he emptied his glass of beer, the world grew clearer for him, life seemed better, and all the people in the restaurant pleasanter and more attractive. How easy everything was! How he would like to be a friend of all those people! He saw Olivia smiling at him across the table.

"Alcohol goes to my head," he apologized. "Waiter, let's have another beer."

"Careful there, doctor. Better take it easy."

"Oh, this is a celebration. I don't always feel like this. You know what they say about making hay while the sun shines. Make it two beers, waiter." He pointed to the owner of the restaurant, who was standing near the victrola, performing amusing tricks for the benefit of his guests. "What does that guy look like to you?"

"A sausage."

"Nope. He looks more like some kind of an animal to me. A seal. I wouldn't be at all surprised if he showed up in a little while with a live fish in his mouth."

The victrola was playing an old German song, and from the loud-speaker came a falsetto voice singing "Ach, du lieber Augustin, Augustin, Augustin." The customers of the Edelweiss began to sing too, in a rasping, tuneless chorus.

Eugenio stared long and soberly into his fresh glass of beer, before he took his first deep swallow from its rim. He licked the white foam from his lips.

"Beginning to taste like soap already," he complained, making a face and pushing the glass away. He began to stare fixedly at the last piece of sausage which remained on the platter.

"Do you know, Olivia—do you know what I'm thinking about now?"

She shook her head.

"I'm thinking about that appendectomy last week."

Olivia laughed. She reached out and drew his glass to her side of the table.

"You've had enough, *senhor*. You're beginning to show it."

But Eugenio was gazing with rapt attention at a rectangular fishbowl which stood on a shelf on the front wall. Tiny gold and blue fish were swimming about in the green water, amid a miniature submarine forest. Eugenio signaled to the waiter, who came promptly.

"I want you to fry me a couple of those fish there—there," he declared uncertainly, jabbing the air with a very rigid forefinger, in the direction of the fishbowl.

The waiter was smiling, exclaiming again and again, "Oh—oh!" very politely, glancing from time to time at Olivia.

"Please bring us two black coffees," she ordered.

After he had drunk the coffee, Eugenio was filled with a sudden, irresistible sleepiness and melancholy. He saw Olivia very hazily, as though he too were a fish, immersed in the dark water of the aquarium.

The victrola began to play a torrential Strauss waltz. A lady of monumental proportions rose suddenly from one of the tables and dragged her husband into the middle of the dance floor, as if she wished to give him a sound public thrashing. The little man straightened up, brushed the ashes from the collar of his coat, and put his arm around his plump spouse. They began to dance, and soon the floor was crowded with furiously waltzing couples.

Eugenio seemed to have recovered from his stupor.

"Want to dance?"

Olivia hesitated. "How are those legs of yours?"

"Oh, all right. Let's dance."

They made their way to the center of the floor, and he drew her to him. They danced out of step, unable to capture the swing of the lively, joyous rhythm. In the midst of the confused mass of heads the feather of the host's Alpine hat bobbed up and down. The woman at the counter was smiling benignly, still at her post by the cash register.

Olivia's hair had a sweet perfume. Eugenio pressed her tightly against his breast. He felt that she belonged to him. He did not want to think, did not want to know what tomorrow might bring. She belonged to him. She had given herself to him unconditionally. Suddenly he bent and kissed her, and for the first time he murmured, "Darling."

But Olivia only retorted coolly, "I'm going to order another black coffee for you, doctor!"

It was eleven o'clock when at last they left the Edelweiss. Eugenio concealed a yawn.

"We'd better drop by the hospital to see how the little boy is getting along," said Olivia.

They took a trolley to the hospital. By now he had lapsed into a profound depression. During the whole trip neither spoke a word.

On the first floor of the quiet hospital, they met Sister Isolda.

"How is our little boy?" Olivia whispered.

"His fever is all gone. He seems to be getting along fine."

As they entered the room the child's mother, who had been sitting beside the bed, rose to her feet, as though she were about to say something. Eugenio, however, motioned her to be quiet.

115

He took the pulse of his young patient and looked tenderly into the rosy, calm little face. And as he passed his hand lightly over the child's head he was reminded of his own brother, Ernesto.

When he left the room the child's mother followed him into the corridor.

"Doctor, I—we—we'd like—" Her voice seemed to stick in her throat, and she began to sob. She seized Eugenio's hand and kissed it fervently.

"Now, now, *Dona*—" he stammered, trying to withdraw his hand. He was embarrassed, and he found it difficult to control his own emotion. He turned pleading eyes to Olivia. He seemed to ask pardon and support.

The woman accompanied them as far as the elevator, trying awkwardly to express her gratitude.

In the lobby downstairs they met Dr. Seixas.

"Look who's here!" Olivia exclaimed delightedly.

Dr. Seixas was a large, aggressive-looking man, with a heavy beard. He did not dress well, and he was the poorest physician they knew.

"Good evening, doctor," said Eugenio.

The older man paused. "Good evening." His voice was thick-toned and harsh, but there was kindliness in his blue eyes.

Olivia took Eugenio's arm.

"Guess what, doctor," she said, in the manner of one describing the latest accomplishment of a precocious child. "Just by the skin of his teeth Eugenio saved a little boy's life today. Tracheotomy. If he had waited five more minutes the child would have died."

Seixas looked at Eugenio from head to foot, incredulously. Then he gave a kind of snort, which might have been interpreted as scorn, praise, or mere acknowledgment. Eugenio felt ill at ease. To him Dr. Seixas was still the big bearded brute of a doctor who used to come to his house when he was a little boy, the outspoken physician who had prescribed physics, bitter-tasting medicine, and fomentations for him long ago.

"Give me a light, you butcher," said Dr. Seixas. "That bitch in second-class Room 17 has a fever again."

He took the matches which Eugenio offered, lit a cigarette, and put the matchbox into his pocket. As he began to smoke, he looked silently at Olivia. Suddenly he spat on the tile floor.

"We doctors save other people," he said abruptly, "but we can't seem to save ourselves." He turned and walked away, without a word of farewell.

When they were again in the street, Eugenio became once more the prey of his bitter reflections.

"Why must I be such a hypocrite, Olivia?" he began fiercely. "Why should I pretend I don't mind being shabby? I don't want to be any Beau Brummell—I only want to keep myself clean and decent! It's no joke feeling down at the heel and having to think at the same time about the bills at the end of the month!" He paused and crooked his right leg against his left, so that it made a figure four. "Look at this shoe. Look at the hole in the bottom. Very romantic!"

Olivia was smiling quietly. In the sky there were stars. Eugenio walked with his head low, his eyes on the toes of his shoes.

"With money at least you can travel and buy things and forget. But when you haven't got money, and you haven't any name either, that's the last straw. And the big dogs who have already made *their* reputations throw their white elephants *our* way—they send *us* the patients who haven't a red cent to pay doctor bills with! And then they try to act protective toward us!"

Olivia took his arm gently.

"When I was twenty," he went on, "I was going to reform the world. And now I'm buried in the Sacred Heart Hospital. A failure today, a little success tomorrow, then more failures. The end of the month, the baker, the butcher—I don't know . . . Why is it that a little while ago I was so happy, and now I'm like this?"

It was a few minutes before Olivia answered him, in her clear, even, soothing voice:

"Why don't you look at the stars, little boy?"

But Eugenio did not look at the sky. He looked instead at Olivia, as if he had not understood what she had said. Sometimes she was so vague and mysterious. But she was made of flesh and blood; she must suffer and have difficulties of her own. Why did she never complain or confide in him? He wanted to ask her questions, but he was afraid. On the other hand, his relationship with her was so pleasant, so comfortable and discreet. . . . There were no scenes, no shows of sentimentality, no unnecessary demonstrations, no settling of accounts.

"I answered Dr. Bellini's letter today," she said, after a moment.

"You did? Did you say you'd go?"

She nodded. "It'll only be for three or four months. Nova Itália must be beautiful." She smiled. "And every now and then we all need to go away somewhere and get our thoughts in shape, don't you think?"

Eugenio shook his head. "I don't know. You're the one who's making the decision. I know I'd be bored to death in a place like Nova Itália. I always thought that business about vineyards and pretty little colonists and the simple life and all the rest of it—was nice enough in poems. Once I went with my fifth-grade class on an excursion through the Italian colonies. We spent a day in each place. You can't imagine what I went through every night when it got dark. In spite of the fact that the whole thing was one long picnic for us."

"Most of us run away from solitude when we're afraid of our thoughts and the things we might remember."

"Maybe so . . ."

"You should know how much good it can do you to go off by yourself sometimes."

Eugenio shrugged his shoulders. The words "by yourself" reminded him oddly of his dread of being buried alive on stormy nights.

"But what the devil does this fellow Bellini want with you?"

Already he was beginning to resent this stranger, who had interfered unwittingly in his affairs. But as soon as he had asked it Eugenio regretted his question. It smacked of jealousy; it was a violation of that tacit law which existed between them, that they should not speak of love, or in any way bring their understanding to a common level.

"I told you he wants me to organize the maternity ward of the hospital he is founding. I'd like you to see the letter he wrote me. He may be a poor doctor, but he certainly has a head for business. He didn't miss a trick in the outline of the contract he sent me. As an organizer our friend Dr. Bellini is a genius."

"When will you go?"

"In two weeks."

"And what if you don't get along with him?"

"I'll come back."

"And then?"

She shrugged. With her hand she made a gesture toward the sky. "The stars are always there."

When they entered her room Olivia flung the windows wide.

"Don't turn on the light," Eugenio begged, sinking down into the soft cushions of the divan. The light of the moon set the room to swimming in a kind of blue radiance.

After she had taken off her hat, she sat down beside him and drew his head down gently to rest in her lap. She began to stroke his hair, and for a brief interval he knew peace and sweet tranquillity, almost sleep.

But the silence, the warmth of Olivia's body, and the perfume which she wore began to conspire together. He opened his eyes and looked up at her. Desire flooded his face, suffusing it with an unmistakable light. Without a word, she bent and kissed him. And once again she gave herself to him, like one who wishes to relieve with a soothing drug the agony of a man who is ill.

Eugenio knew that so long as he lived he would never, never forget that night.

There came to Eugenio a moment of complete forgetfulness, of mist and stupefaction, a warm, sleep-weighted torpor. But his eyes went on staring blankly, and through them he was aware of a smoky haze that was the sky, of a pale glow that was the starlight; on his cheek he felt the cool kiss of the night wind.

Suddenly he awoke, as though someone had shaken him by the shoulders. What had happened? Bewildered, he turned his head, looking from side to side. The automobile sped on. Far away, in the midst of a grove of trees, flashed the swift yellow light of a window. The dim shapes of sleeping oxen hurtled past, black against the dark, passive background of the fields. On the front seat of the car there loomed the chauffeur's impassible back. What had happened? Somewhere, something terrible and irrevocable had happened. Eugenio seemed to feel on his shoulder the warm contact of invisible fingers, shaking him. Yes . . . It was a warning.

He looked at his watch. It was twenty minutes to eight. Mr. Tearle had told him that whenever something important happened it was always either twenty minutes before or twenty minutes after the hour. Something terrible had happened!

He fell weakly against the leather seat. He knew. Olivia had stopped breathing. The mysterious warning could have no other meaning.

How dry his throat had become! How bitter his mouth was! His body ached as though he had been beaten mercilessly. The dull pounding of his heart seemed to echo crazily in his brain. Olivia was dead, yet he would live on with his grief, his remorse, and his cowardice.

He wished he might let the car go on without him, that he might remain behind in the field, at the edge of the road, with his cheeks buried in the fresh, wet grass—asleep, oblivious, only a stone in the road, a leaf fallen from a tree . . . He would escape the dreadful ordeal of seeing Olivia dead. The nurses would not see him weep.

To stay back there on the road, like a blade of grass, like a heap of manure . . . Yes, he was no more than a heap of manure. He was only so much matter. A creature who satisfied his appetites, who had no soul . . . Matter.

He looked out at the sky. How dim the stars had become! Olivia spoke in his memory: Look at the stars. In life there is always hope. *How often she had told him that! There was deep meaning in her words. The stars were symbols of purity, of an unattainable thing which the hands of men had not yet been able to defile. Those who wallowed in filth could be saved if they had eyes to see the stars . . .*

Could there really be hope in the world?

The automobile flew on and on. The first lights of the city began to appear in the distance.

Chapter 9

The male nurse pushed the telephone away and turned to Eugenio.

"Looks like we've got a little work to do, doctor. Some woman's slashed her wrists and is bleeding herself dry."

Eugenio stood up and tossed the magazine, through which he had been thumbing idly, onto the top of the desk.

"Well, what are we waiting for?"

The nurse seized the instrument kit, and the two men hurried out, into the waiting ambulance. The race had begun. The siren howled long and mournfully.

"Suicide?" asked Eugenio, who had climbed into the front seat, next to the driver.

"Accident." The nurse's voice came from the back of the ambulance. "A can opener. It's at that guy Cintra's house."

"Member of the family?"

"Family, my eye! It was the maid. You never catch those rich bitches fooling around trying to open tin cans!"

"Hold your hat, Mr. Mayor, here we come!" exclaimed the driver, shoving his foot down hard on the accelerator, his face spread in a wide grin of delight. The emergency was his party. Before being put in charge of the ambulance, he had been a taxi driver with a love of speeding that kept him constantly at odds with the police department. Now the tables were turned: wherever his ambulance appeared, traffic cops would blow their whistles, other vehicles would stop, and the street would become as free and unobstructed as a race track.

"Yesterday," the driver was saying, "I went with Dr. Tranquedo to pick up a guy who got his arm run over by a train on the Canoas line. Lord, I never saw so much blood! His face was white as a sheet. On the way back I hit a nigger in the road. The poor devil must've been deaf, because he didn't hear when I give out with the siren. It was just *poof!*—and up the old geezer flew. I stopped the car, and we put him in the back and drove right on back to town." He began to whistle furiously, as if he wished to drown out the whine of the siren.

The day was beginning well, thought Eugenio. Already, by nine o'clock in the morning, a woman had slashed her wrist. Next would come the inevitable automobile accident cases. In the lower part of town some girl would be sure to take Lysol because she had been abandoned by her sweetheart, who would probably turn out to be a soldier in the Military Brigade. Blood! Disaster! Death! He felt at times that the city was one enormous hospital. He thought of a striking case he had attended the week before. He had taken the ambulance to pick up the victim of a brawl in one of the city's notorious alleys and had found the man beheaded by a razor. There had been nothing he could do.

123

The ambulance sped on, its siren whining dismally. The driver was whistling. Eugenio felt a vacuum, a twinge of nausea, in his stomach.

"What's the number?" shouted the driver.

"Six-seventy-eight!" answered the nurse.

"Hot tip!"

Eugenio looked out and saw a house with a peaceful garden, dotted with masses of green foliage, with bluish shadows and bright areas of sunlight. He thought immediately of Olivia, who had been in Nova Itália a month. She had written to him only once, saying merely that she was satisfied with her work, and that Dr. Bellini was "the funniest little man in the world."

The driver jerked the ambulance to a stop. "Here we are!"

The gardener was waiting for them at the gate. He took Eugenio and the nurse around to the back door and led them into the house, to a room where a woman was lying on a bed. Blood gushed from a cut on her wrist, and it ran down her hand and dripped from the tips of her fingers into an agate basin. The skin of her face was ashy white, and she bleated like a sick sheep, rolling her eyes from side to side. Someone had tied a strip of cloth tightly around her arm, a few inches above the cut.

"I'm dyin'," she moaned. "Oh, I'm dyin'!"

In a few minutes Eugenio had treated her, had washed his hands, and was drying them, giving instructions simultaneously to a fat, lustrous Negress, who was evidently the cook. He spoke firmly, almost paternally, looking at his audience—the cook, the little mulatto chambermaid, and the old gardener—and deriving from the knowledge of his superior position an agreeable satisfaction. He was surprised to find himself using technical terms, and again he thought of Olivia. He imagined her standing beside him, listening to his words, and he felt suddenly that he was blushing.

"Then they ain't no need to worry?" asked the fat Negress in her oily voice.

"Do as I told you, and everything will be all right. If anything unusual happens, call me."

Scarcely had he finished speaking when he felt in the room a strange, new element, which manifested itself at first by a wave of perfume and by a vague scarlet spot moving in the corner of his eye. He turned his head and saw a blonde girl in a red dressing gown standing near the door. Suddenly confused, he stammered a greeting. Immediately he felt that he had been plunged to the level of the servants. The girl stared at him indifferently. In her eyes there was only a cold curiosity. She looked artificial; the sun gave her bright, straw-colored hair a metallic texture, and she stood very stiffly, as though posing. She was colorful—irritatingly colorful as she stood against the shining, white-enameled door. She was like the bright cover of a magazine.

At last Eugenio ended the uncomfortable silence.

"Everything is all right," he said to the stranger. "The girl is out of danger now." His smile was forced.

The young woman in the scarlet robe continued to stare at him without speaking, and he felt that his own words had returned to slap him in the face. His embarrassment mounted, and he did not know what to do with his hands. Awkwardly, he pulled on his coat.

"Throw out that bloody sheet!" the blonde girl said suddenly to the little mulatto chambermaid. "Throw it in the garbage, or burn it, but get it out of here—quick!" Her face was contracted, filled with disgust. She turned to Eugenio, examined him curiously from head to foot. "You," she said dryly, "come with me."

She turned and walked down the hall, and, after only a second's hesitation, Eugenio followed. He passed both his hands back through his hair and straightened his tie.

"I'll wait for you in the car, doc!" called the nurse.

They crossed the light corridor, Eugenio following close on the heels of the scarlet spot. Like a little dog trotting obediently behind its mistress, he thought. He was annoyed with her and annoyed with himself. Might he not lick her hands? Perhaps he would even bite them—if he did not lack the courage . . . But what the devil did that woman want with him, anyway?

They arrived at last in a cool, dark room, a vast living room, the decoration of which ranged from deep maroon to a pale beige. For a few moments he forgot the girl, as his eyes traveled over the sofa and the comfortable-looking overstuffed chairs, the pictures on the walls—the design of which he could not distinguish clearly but, he guessed, must be strange and modern—the bookstand filled with attractively bound volumes, the enormous, deep-pile rug. He drew a deep breath. If comfort had a special fragrance he knew that he was breathing it now. It was a sweetish, dusty odor that came from polished wood, fine upholstery, and floor wax.

The girl turned to him. She pointed to an easy-chair. "Sit down."

As if he were a servant. It was an order. Eugenio cast a dark look around the room, but he sat down. As he sank into the soft, upholstered depths of the chair, he was rewarded by an unexpected sensation of well-being. For a few seconds he allowed himself to drift on a gentle cloud of luxury and repose. But then his eyes met those of the blonde young woman, fastened unswervingly on his face. How unpleasant it was to be analyzed in this way! Had he no right to relax and be at ease? He straightened up and moved stiffly to the edge of the chair. The girl leaned over the small, round table and opened a cigarette box.

"Do you smoke?" she asked, holding out the silver box.

"No," Eugenio lied. "Thank you." Smoking would only make him feel worse.

She lit a cigarette and began to smoke it, watching him, it seemed, almost maliciously. His discomfort grew. He felt as though fiery ants were crawling through his whole body. *I must be red as a tomato.* He looked away. At the other end of the room now he could make out a hearth built of tiles whose rich color matched that of the upholstery and the rugs. On the mantel there was a black statuette—a nude woman, it seemed, or an athlete. Or was it a Negro?

When he looked at the girl again, he saw that she was serious. There was a thoughtful wrinkle in her forehead.

"What is your opinion of Freud?" she asked suddenly, without warning. The question escaped her lips with a cloud of smoke, but her words did not have its vaporous quality. They were solid and aggressive, and they struck Eugenio violently in the chest, taking his breath away. Her eyes were sarcastic. Indescribable malice gleamed in their burnt-honey depths.

He squirmed.

"What do I think of Freud? Well, I—I—" He laughed awkwardly. "That question—" He took a handkerchief from his pocket and wiped his forehead. He felt that his face must be drenched.

She was still smirking at him, with the corner of her mouth.

"Can it be that you have never heard of Freud? You are a doctor, aren't you?"

"Yes, of course, but—but, you understand . . . Your question was rather unexpected. After all, I don't—"

He stopped abruptly. He must look like an absolute fool. What an ass he was! The girl was teasing him. She was entertaining herself at his expense. She must be one of the rich, spoiled, pseudo-intellectual young women who liked to talk about Freud and sex to show that they were "modern" and had no prejudice. He was letting her make a fool of him. He should have realized it and gone away while there was yet time. He felt like speaking crudely to her, even if his words were cloaked with scientific terms.

He maintained an uneasy silence, shifting nervously in his chair.

"But do you think my question odd? I don't know that you should . . . Would you have preferred that I ask your opinion on Professor Piccard? Or the rate of exchange?" Her face was still serious, but her eyes were laughing hysterically. They glittered behind the bluish curtain of smoke.

Eugenio stood up. "With your permission," he said. "You are making fun of me, and I have work to do." He tried to assume the fatherly attitude of one who tells a naughty child that he has "no time to waste on pranks."

The young woman stepped a little nearer.

"I? Making fun of you? On the contrary, I never spoke more seriously in all my life. What is your name?"

"Eugenio Fontes."

He was aware of her perfume, a warm, sweet fragrance. His uneasiness now was of another nature. Confused thoughts befogged his brain.

128

For a brief instant they stared hostilely at each other. Then she shook her head slowly, tossed her cigarette into the ashtray.

"You are a rare example of a species which is almost extinct."

How she enjoyed turning the spit slowly! Eugenio felt his anger return.

"I don't understand."

"A man who blushes and becomes confused merely because he finds himself alone with a woman he has never met before . . ."

"I beg your pardon—" He wanted to slap her. Or did he want to kiss her?

"And a doctor at that!" Her tone was contemptuous. "Now, if you were only a schoolboy . . ."

Eugenio felt anger swelling in his chest, rising, rising. He knew that if it should break the stout walls of his reserve it might take the form of a brutal epithet. In a lightning flash he envisioned his mother warning little six-year-old Eugenio: *God punishes little boys that say naughty words* . . .

He was seized by an uncontrollable desire to retaliate. This incident was, after all, inconsequential. Soon he would be far away from this place, and certainly he would never see this girl again.

"And what kind of a woman are you?" he lashed out, facing her suddenly, with defiance.

The young woman shook her hair coquettishly and then looked down at her very red, brightly polished fingernails.

"I am a woman," she said calmly, "who likes to provoke reactions. Scientists experiment with frogs and guinea pigs. I prefer to use human beings in my experiments."

He was right. An intellectual snob. What a little idiot she was! A good lesson would not hurt her.

"And you find pleasure in this?"

"Enormous pleasure."

Eugenio shoved his hands into his pockets, remembering the time he had taken part in a play. In spite of knowing his role by heart, he had suffered excruciatingly each time his turn had come to act. He felt now as if he were on the stage again: the hero and the heroine stood face to face, locked head on in a duel of words.

"And of what use are these experiments?"

"One amuses oneself."

"Is that all?"

"Is there anything more important in the world than amusing oneself?"

"There is."

"For example?"

"Considering once in a while, for example, that not everyone can be as well dressed and as well fed as you are—"

"Well!"

Eugenio was carried away by the force of his own words.

"And that in the world there exist not merely human guinea pigs for the amusement of wealthy young ladies, but also men and women who feel, who suffer, who also have a right to be happy—"

He did not finish, for he was embarrassed. This was a melodrama, and he was acting. He was being a melodramatic fool, and the words he had said were only a role he had memorized somewhere. Somewhere . . . Where? When? He certainly did not feel what he had just said. He had repeated words and ideas which had entered his mouth from the air. The poverty and unhappiness of others had no real existence for him; he knew only his own grievances, his own necessities. His words reflected the influence of books and articles he had read, of plays he had seen, words he had heard other people say. They reechoed in his mind like well worn clichés, like a moving picture sound track; and they had no ring of truth. All that really mattered to him just then, he knew, was that he should have his revenge on the little creature who had taunted him.

But he saw that she was smiling.

"Magnificent! At last my guinea pig is reacting! He is moving his little legs and grunting. All right, I have made my diagnosis." She surveyed him critically from head to foot. "You have an inferiority complex."

Eugenio felt his equilibrium leave him. She had placed her finger in his deepest wound. She had stirred in him pain that was almost physical. For an instant he stood before her, uncertain and dizzy. Mutely, he turned, seeking the door. And still without speaking, he moved toward the girl who had injured him.

"Look out, you!" she screamed.

Mechanically, he swerved away.

Then the young woman held toward him her white hand. Between her index and ring fingers there lay a brand-new, carefully folded fifty-milreis note.

"A small tip," she said cruelly. "Divide it with your friend."

A cloud fell suddenly across Eugenio's eyes. All his bitter pent-up fury exploded at last.

"You go to hell," he shouted, "you, your goddam money, Freud, and all your ilk!"

He wheeled and fled blindly from the house.

"We still have a good forty minutes to go," the chauffeur answered.

Eugenio drew his hand wearily across his face. In the last two hours years had been added to his life.

Could not all this agony, all this remorse be signs that some good continued to exist in him?

Involuntarily, he thought of his daughter: of her small, round face; her wide, lively eyes, which seemed to be perpetually amazed at all things; her tiny button nose; her shiny black bangs, that made her look like a little Chinaman. Her features were undeniably his own. He had noticed the surprising likeness the first time he had seen her. All that Anamaria had inherited from Olivia had been an expression of gentle seriousness, a thoughtful serenity, and an indefinable humanness, which had nothing to do with the shape of her face nor her movements, but made itself felt, nevertheless, with a rare, unforgettable power.

Suddenly, the image of his daughter was blotted from his mind by the sound of Eunice's cold, conventional voice: "I want to hear nothing about children—those insatiable, mammiferous little beasts that deform our bodies . . ." That was a stock remark of Eunice's, an expression she was accustomed to using with her friends. Bearing children was an inferior, bourgeois habit, a worthy means of diversion for the proletariat and the middle class. How could an intellectually refined woman subject herself willingly to so brutal, so repugnant and animalistic an ordeal? To become pregnant and remain for nine months in a state of illness, and then to risk dying in childbirth . . . She could never disassociate the idea of childbirth from her horror of being torn limb from limb. Having children was almost the same as committing hara-kiri. The only difference was that there was something romantic about the classical

132

Japanese suicide, while maternity was only a prosaic, slow means of self-destruction.

Old Vicente Cintra always smiled indulgently at her tirades—he too had his youthful whims!—but sometimes he felt the lack of a grandson. At times he even confessed this in his conventional, blasé manner, never losing sight, of course, of the fact that he must not violate his self-chosen role of polished gentleman, which he loved so well.

Now, out of the tumult of Eugenio's thoughts, there arose an elongated, white face with an enormous forehead and feverish eyes. Acelio Castanho was speaking of Plato, reciting for Eunice a few passages from a French translation of the Banquet. How clearly Eugenio heard one sentence from that translation: "Pour enfanter de belles pensées." While Cintra and Filipe discussed business, while Filipe's wife sought Eugenio with impassioned eyes, Castanho read to Eunice passages from Plato. They were united, those two, in spiritual love, "pour enfanter de belles pensées." Beautiful thoughts deformed neither the body nor the mind; on the contrary, they lent to both an eternal harmony. His wife and Acelio Castanho, a handsome pair indeed! They were ideally made for each other! Why hadn't they married? The bases of society were erected on sands of error and incomprehension.

There in the night, in the timeless dusk of the speeding vehicle, Eugenio allowed his thoughts to wander back over the period of his engagement to Eunice.

After their casual meeting when he, a doctor in the Municipal Emergency Aid Corps, had attended an injured servant girl in the Cintra home, Eunice had telephoned several times to invite him to go driving. At first he had refused, thinking she wanted to amuse herself further at his expense. He did not have to lend himself to that

ridiculous farce! But not once had he had sufficient cour-
age to rebuff her altogether. He declined always politely
and indefinitely, and thanked her for her invitations. At
last, one afternoon as he was leaving the hospital, he had
been chagrined to find her parked at the sidewalk, behind
the wheel of a large, olive-colored limousine. He had
greeted her and walked on, but she had called after him:

"Hey! What kind of behavior is that? You aren't afraid
of me, are you?"

He had whirled about, his face crimson, his thoughts in
a tumult.

"Afraid? I?" He had stood very still, clutching his hat
tightly in one hand, and she had smiled, taunting him, her
head tilted to one side. She had the irritating beauty of a
spoiled thing, a fragile look which invited brutal, not
tender, caresses.

"If you will permit me," she had bantered, "I am going
to kidnap you. Your mother won't be angry?"

"Oh!" He had found no words to refuse her, but had
climbed into the car beside her, and they had driven
through the city until nightfall.

She had talked about the twilight and made conversa-
tion about books, had shown herself less cruel and sar-
donic than he had thought her. She had asked him about
himself, had seemed to be genuinely interested in his
affairs.

They had gone to a restaurant for dinner, and he had
scarcely been able to touch his food, knowing the ten-
milreis in his pocket could not pay for the large meal they
had ordered. Eunice had not made things easier for him
by staring at him fixedly while they ate. She had examined
him with an intense, thirsty interest which left him com-
pletely disoriented. In his efforts to devise some means

134

of escape from the difficult situation, he had broken into a cold perspiration. He had looked everywhere for a familiar face, for a friend from whom he could borrow money. There had been no one. And when the meal was over, Eunice had asked for the check and paid it. Eugenio had not dared to look at the waiter who brought her change, but had looked instead all around the room, shifting uneasily in his chair, while the red color which suffused his face had grown increasingly darker. When at last they had left the restaurant, the night air had cooled his hot cheeks and had restored a measure of clarity and composure to his troubled mind.

On the way home, Eunice's car had rolled smoothly over the flagged streets, and Eugenio had sat sullenly at her side, a prisoner of an odd, dim sense of melancholy. Eunice's presence—the presence of a beautiful, well dressed and perfumed woman—was pleasant to him, but it made him even more acutely aware of his own inadequacy. He had asked her to drop him off at the next corner.

"Thank you very much for everything," he had said as he left her. He recalled that he had had to make an effort to seem calm. "But I'm afraid we won't be able to see each other any more, Eunice. Water and oil can't seem to mix, after all." He had realized even as he spoke that his words lacked conviction. "You and I belong to two different worlds. There is nothing for you to gain from my friendship." She had listened carefully, gravely, with a slight frown. "Your own friends can offer you more than I. This must be the last time we see each other. Goodbye, Eunice."

They had shaken hands solemnly. For a moment they had stared at each other. Then Eunice had said simply:

"I like you as you are. I'm sure we can be friends."

That night, after he had left Eunice, he had thought

135

a great deal about her, and about Olivia. If only Olivia had been in the city then, he could have asked her advice. He would have been able to tell her about Eunice, to examine the problem carefully with her. All night he had tossed and turned, remembering the fragrance of Eunice's perfume—it was Mitsouko—and the exquisite childlike frailty of her voice.

The following day he had been surprised to find himself paying greater attention than usual to the set of his necktie, and to his clothing in general. He had even considered buying a new pair of shoes and a hat. And when Eunice had telephoned him at the hospital at noon, he had accepted her invitation immediately. They had gone to a movie. He had not been able to deny the pleasure which he derived from being seen publicly with Eunice. It had been like entering a new world. After the movie, they had gone to a confectioner's shop for ice cream. Her dress had been the same color as the pistachio. She had talked of Verlaine, and, after they had finished the ice cream, she had mentioned Freud. Eugenio had found everything delightful: Eunice, the ice cream, psychoanalysis, life itself. His happiness had been complete when he had reached into his pocket and had drawn out money to pay the check.

How could he possibly remember in detail other days with Eunice, other such pleasant meetings? They blended together in time, mingled inextricably one with another.

Olivia had stayed in Nova Itália a long time. She had written to him only infrequently—inexpressive letters, through which she had managed to convey once again her aversion to any kind of amorous blackmail. Her letters had been as from man to man, from friend to friend.

Eugenio, meanwhile, had experienced bitter moments

of doubt. His affair with Eunice had been flowing along too smoothly. It had been too much like the paradises of his dreams. How would it end? How unequal might marriage with Eunice be? Was it even impossible? They were members of totally different worlds. What if, after all, Eunice should consider what had passed between them as only a game? She was rich and could readily afford lavish experiments with human guinea pigs.

He had met Eunice's father, Vicente Cintra, and her friends. He had felt uncomfortable with them, had imagined his every move to be the target of their sarcasm and scorn. But Eunice had given him no time for pessimistic reflections. It had been obvious that she was rushing him. They had driven daily through the streets in her automobile, discovering on each occasion a new retreat, a different angle from which to look at the city. They had discussed painting and poetry, and soon there had begun to appear in their conversations long intervals of silence. One night, as they watched the lights of the city from the Esplanade of the St. Peter's Church, they had been astonished to find themselves holding hands. For a long time they had stood without speaking, and still without a word they had returned to the car and driven back to the heart of the city. They had parted that night with less emotion than usual. Eugenio had sat up until dawn, smoking cigarette after cigarette. Could he really be in love? And suppose Eunice were in love with him. He had asked himself question after question which he could not answer, or for which he invented replies as false as they were vague and elusive. He had not been able to doubt her beauty, her intelligence, her refinement. Equally indubitable had been his desire for her, the natural desire of a healthy man for a beautiful woman; of course he desired her body as he

137

admired her mind! Could his feeling, then, be mere passion? And where, he had wondered, did Olivia fit into the picture? He had thought tenderly of the friend who had given him freely of herself and had asked no recompense. But did Olivia really love him? Was her feeling for him love or pity? Could not her accidental role of mistress be but a prolongation of her mission as doctor, as nurse?

At last he had gone to bed; but he had not been able to sleep. The same questions had continued to form in his mind. Not once had Olivia left his thoughts. Again he had relived the moment when he had first possessed her. How deeply human her eyes had been! What utter abandon had transformed her face! And yet—not once had she ever hinted, had she said the slightest word which might give him certainty, certainty, certainty . . .

Eunice's perfume had lingered for a long time on his hands. It was at once sweet and wicked. His feeling for Eunice could not be compared with what he felt for Olivia. It was desire of another kind, and in it there was a touch of sadism. For Olivia—he had thought he knew the answer —he felt a tender, sincere affection; for Eunice his desire was a malevolent hunger for possession. Could this be the true answer? How horrible it was not to be able to see clearly in the labyrinth of one's own thoughts!

Later, one of his colleagues at the hospital had teased him casually: "So we're going to come into old Cintra's money, eh, Fontes?"

Eugenio had flushed and walked on without answering, but the remark had rung in his ears interminably. It was absurd that such a silly, casual observation could cut so cruelly into his mind. Old Cintra's money: *Cintra, Textile Manufacturers; Cintra & Company, Rice Growers; the Cintra Real Estate Agency.*

About this time he had been called upon to attend a deplorable case. A messenger had been run down by an automobile and had suffered a fracture at the base of the skull. He lived only eight hours. He was a thin, wasted fellow, the father of five pale, frightened little girls, the husband of a tubercular-looking wife. The seven of them lived in a crowded little house, that was humid and colorless. When the man died the six women had burst into frantic weeping, and Eugenio had waited, his head lowered, for them to subside. The musty smell of the house had mingled with the unpleasant odor of soiled clothes. It had entered his nostrils and poisoned his soul. The messenger had lain still in his bed, his face the color of cider, his crushed head wrapped in bloodstained bandages. A tall, very swarthy man had appeared and called the widow aside to a corner. He had handed her a visiting card that said he was a lawyer; he wanted authorization to file suit against the owner of the car that had killed her husband. The woman had said nothing, had not even moved. She had only wept more violently, her gasping sobs shaking her bony body, while the five little girls, too, had continued to wail.

Eugenio had felt miserable. He had longed for sun and fresh air. He had murmured the first word which came to him and had gone out. He had breathed deeply and gazed at the sky, relieved to see that life went on as before, that men still passed one another in the streets. There had been people as bent and poor as the dead messenger, but expensive automobiles had also passed by, and in the cool shade of their upholstered interiors there had reclined prosperous-looking ladies and gentlemen. On a crowded corner, he had paused abruptly, seized by a swift resolution. He had imagined himself inside one of those luxurious

139

automobiles—Dr. Eugenio Fontes, the son-in-law of Vicente Cintra.

And why not? He did not want to be crushed by life. He had not run after Eunice. Destiny had brought them together, and he had no guilt in the matter.

He had gone home immediately, bathed and changed his clothes, had telephoned Eunice. It had been the first time he had ever called her to make an appointment. The following month they had announced their engagement. Vicente Cintra had congratulated them without enthusiasm. With infinite caution and delicacy he had arranged the "practical details." He would give Eugenio a position in his factory—some simple little thing, signing papers, supervising, you understand. He would also appoint him doctor in a certain union where he had influence.

Olivia had been about to return from Nova Itália. Eugenio had thought it would be best to write to her as soon as possible, telling her everything. He had written her a long letter, which had made him blush as he reread it. He had hesitated before mailing it. But at last he had decided, and he had sighed with relief as he watched it disappear into the mailbox.

Still the automobile sped on. In a miraculous telescoping of time, Eugenio had recalled in a few seconds the period of his engagement to Eunice.

A few years of married life had been enough to show him the mistake he had made. He had married for money. Eunice's beauty, or rather her prettiness, had made things easier and more pleasant for him. She—Eugenio understood now—had let herself be carried away by a romantic desire for adventure. She had acted like any bored heiress who, for the sake of publicity, adopts an orphan from some asylum and poses with the child for newspaper photog-

raphers: "Debutante Adopts Struggling Young Doctor."
Movies, romance, adventure . . .

But always, always, behind his every thought, there was
Olivia. Olivia dead, lying amid four tapers in the hospital
chapel—the chapel in which a wake had been held for the
body of his own mother that rainy winter.

On and on flew the automobile. Was there no end to
this agony? Outside, the stars still shone brightly.

Chapter 10

It was the first opportunity he had had to be alone with
Olivia in her rooms since her return from Nova Itália.

He knew it would be immeasurably easier for him to
talk freely with her if he could not see her face, if the
light were not on. He did not want Olivia to perceive so
clearly his embarrassment, his awkwardness, his misery.

"You won't mind if we leave the light off?" he asked
as she closed the front door.

"Of course not. The moonlight is lovely." She opened
the window and disappeared for a moment into the bedroom.

Eugenio lit a cigarette and sat down in one of the easy-
chairs. He looked at the bit of night sky framed by the
window. He had to look at it carefully, with all his attention, in order to make out the infinitesimal glow of the
stars. A rosebush climbed from the plot in the garden to
the window sill. He could see the silhouette of its topmost
branches and an enormous, white rose, immobile against
the sky. The night air was cool and smelled of honeysuckle.

141

He felt as if he were twelve years old again, leaning at the window of his old home, looking out at the night. The honeysuckle vine which used to grow on the wall of their neighbor's house perfumed the air. There was a full moon, and he was wondering whether there were or were not people living on its white face. He never grew tired of gazing at the pale, luminous disc, with its fine, dark spots. Sometimes he felt that the sweet, delicious fragrance which filled the night air did not come from the honeysuckle vine at all—it was the perfume of the moonlight.

Why was he sad on so beautiful a night? He did not know . . . The odd feeling in his chest seemed to be a yearning for something he could not actually define. Perhaps all he wanted was to cry, or to be able to climb up to the moon. Or was it just that he wanted a blue and yellow ball like the one he had seen in a downtown shop window? The moon was a ball, a white ball. The stars were playing football, and God was the goalkeeper. (Oh, Lordy! God forgive me!) The field in the sky was a good deal bigger than the little one where he and Ernesto played ball with the other boys on their street. Some of the boys had bright sport shirts, real football shoes, and knee pads. He and Nestinho played in their bare feet, and they pricked themselves sometimes on the rosebushes. If God were really and truly good, He would send a ball down from heaven to him and Nestinho. He looked more intently at the moon and, as if the dark spot on its face were God, murmured: "O Lord, Senhor everywhere in the world, please send us a ball to play with. I promise always to be good. Please, dear God, send me a ball!" He sat for a long time at the window, looking up at the moon and waiting for the miracle to happen. God might send the ball down to him in an angel's hands, or He might simply throw it down from up there, making it fall in the garden, on top of the chrysanthemum bed. Eugenio waited. The wind whispered in the trees. God was great, God was good —Mamma said so. What trouble would it be for Him to grant a poor little boy's prayer? All he wanted was a ball. It didn't even have to be a big one; just a little one would do. He was tired of playing with balls made of old stocking feet filled with rags. The minutes went by, and still he waited. His eyes burned from staring at the moon, and his neck ached from holding his head back so long.

"Genoca, come to bed. It's late." That was Mamma's voice.

He got up and went into the bedroom, where Ernesto was already in bed. In a corner, by the table, his father sat sewing. Eugenio looked at him and was afraid. The lamplight made his face so ugly, like a skull . . .

From his bed, Eugenio still saw the moon through the window pane. It was enormous, very round and bright. But God had paid no attention to his prayer. He went to sleep with his young heart embittered, resentful of God's neglect.

Now Eugenio was smoking, lost in his thoughts, his eyes staring blankly out of the window. A stronger breeze shook the white rose, causing it to tremble gently. The slight movement seemed to be a token, a sign from another world, or from some very distant past. He felt a vague chill. He had the odd sensation that someone was calling him, that someone was trying to warn him.

He closed his eyes and saw his father's stooped form walking down the street, carrying a bundle of clothes under his arm. He saw himself at Columbia Academy, looking down at the body of Mr. Tearle, deep among the flowers in the coffin. He heard the gunfire of the fearful night of the revolution, and saw the pale face of the man who had died on the operating table. Other images came to his mind, mixed up, overlapping confusedly. There was Eunice in a scarlet robe—*What do you think of Freud?* Castanho, broad of forehead, sickly—*gymnastics and music* . . . Olivia with an armful of roses . . . Ernesto chopping wood . . .

He opened his eyes. It was impossible that there should be no meaning in all those things. Life was not so cruel that it should have no plan, no purpose.

There was a noise of footsteps in the next room. Olivia was coming back. His heart began to beat faster. The difficult hour, the decisive moment was near. He would have to speak of the letter, if she did not mention it. How much easier it would be for him if she spoke of it first!

Olivia sat down opposite him. He crushed his cigarette out in the ashtray, deliberately lingering longer than was necessary, giving to the simple act an exaggerated importance.

Suddenly he was aware of a sort of torpor, a tremulous need to relax completely, to sink back against the cushions and say nothing. He longed to relax in the gentle peace of this hour that was perfumed with honeysuckle and cleansed with moonlight. He was filled with a sudden dread of talking about Eunice, a terror balanced, none the less, by a warm need of confidence, support, and understanding. He longed to lay his burning head in Olivia's lap, to let her run her hands gently through his hair, while he confided in her his anxiety and doubt, his still irritatingly formless desires.

The silence was agonizing. Brusquely, he leaped to his feet and went to the window. Outside, he saw nothing but his own troubled thoughts. He returned to his chair and sat down with his arms resting on his thighs, his hands locked in front of him, his eyes on the floor. Without looking up, he made an almost desperate effort to speak.

"Did you get my letter?" a voice said at last. But he did not recognize it as his own. Had he actually spoken? His heart beat unsteadily, and he felt that his cheeks were on fire. The silence into which his words disappeared frightened him.

"Yes, Eugenio, I received it."

Suddenly he wanted to throw himself at her feet and confess his guilt like a child. His behavior toward her had been unpardonable. He had betrayed her. He had arranged a marriage for the sake of wealth and position: he was about to sell himself and forsake the only person in the world who really cared what became of him.

"You explained everything in your letter, Eugenio, but you didn't have to. I would have understood. But I was glad you told me."

Her words were like knives cutting him; they hurt just as his father's smile had hurt that night long ago. He looked out of the window and wished fervently that he were far away.

Again he left his chair and went to the window. For an instant he stared unseeingly at the white rose. Then, automatically, he reached out and grasped the stem to break it. A thorn buried itself in his finger. As though he had received an electric shock, he jerked his hand away and raised it instinctively to his mouth. The taste of blood . . . For a few minutes he stood sucking the injured finger. *Take your finger out of your mouth, child!* The teacher was scolding him in front of the whole class . . .

"Eugenio."

At the sound of a living voice pronouncing his name close by, he turned sharply.

"You're just torturing yourself for nothing." Olivia took his arm and led him gently away from the window. "Come here. I'm going to make us some tea."

He wanted to take her in his arms and kiss her again and again, to beg her forgiveness. Or should he take his hat and go away forever—and never come back again?

He allowed Olivia to lead him to the sofa, to make him sit down. He could think of nothing else to do. Her understanding, her acceptance of the situation only made his need for confession the more desperate, only heightened his desire to explain and justify himself, to weave with words a cloak to conceal his embarrassment and shame.

Olivia set a kettle of water to boil on the kitchen stove and returned to the living room. In her absence Eugenio had lit another cigarette. She sat down on the arm of the sofa and placed her hand on his shoulder.

"What is her name?"

"Eunice. Eunice Cintra."

Again he felt his cheeks grow hot. This was becoming ridiculous. She was treating him like a scatterbrained, frivolous child. In spite of the fact that her understanding made it easier for him to talk with her, he could not overlook the slight to his masculine pride. He had known— how well he had known!—that Olivia would not protest: scenes and emotional displays were foreign to her nature. But such absolute passivity, such calm acceptance, took him completely off his guard. Yes, of course he had been wrong: Olivia was not in love with him. And it was better that she was not. Or was it really better? Somehow, it was disappointing . . . Of course, it would be easier for him if she were not in love with him. But he knew that her feelings toward him could not be purely impersonal. She might be pretending. But if she loved him, why didn't she fight back? Why didn't she make some effort to keep him from marrying Eunice?

"Eunice—Eunice," Olivia was saying. "I know I've heard that name somewhere, but I can't remember . . . But tell me, Eugenio, tell me about her."

What a fool he was! What an ass! What an idiot! Wincing at almost every word, he went over the story of his meeting with Eunice. He told it fragmentarily, inventing facts to hide what was ridiculous and absurd in that unequal union.

When he had finished, Olivia rose.

"I think the water must be boiling. Let me go see."

A few minutes later she reappeared, carrying a tray with two teacups, a pot of tea, a sugar bowl, and a plate of cookies. She set the tray down on the table and began pouring tea into the two cups.

"Sugar?"

"A little. . . . That's fine."

As he began to drink his tea, Eugenio knew that the most difficult moment had passed. Mingled with his relief, however, was a sensation of defeat. His hands were not yet steady, and the rhythm of his heart (with what unbearable sharpness he always felt his heart!) was still abnormally quick.

The moonlight shone full and white across Olivia's face, and he saw that she was beautiful. Her beauty was not aggressive. It lay concealed like a treasure. It was serene, and there was in it something which made him think of eternal and changeless things. Why was he not in love with her? Why couldn't he forget Eunice and his ambition?

"Eugenio, some day, many years from now, you will remember tonight and this room—this very moment. You will remember how you sat there on the sofa drinking your tea, and how I sat here in front of you." She paused. "Funny that I should think of that now . . ."

He shook his head slowly. He felt inexplicably sad. There was in his mood regret and a dim foreboding.

For a few instants there was only the tinkle of their tea-cups against the saucers. But Eugenio, intent on justifying himself, spoke again.

"I don't love her, Olivia. What I wrote you in my letter is true. I'm doing this for my future. You know that. Didn't you tell me that faith is everything? My faith, Olivia, is in my career. I've got to prove to myself that life is not just one long, hellish struggle with no reward at the end of it. I've got to put an end to this—this misery— this merciless routine. I'm sure I can do it. You know what my life has been like . . ."

Her eyes were shining kindly in the blue dusk. Her face was sad and calm.

"I can't stand the idea of being nobody all my life. A few years from now, what will I be? A poor man's doctor, like Seixas, always having bills to pay—or maybe I'll have a nice little desk job in some branch of the civil service . . ."

Again he paused. Olivia was still gazing at him, unmoving and silent.

He had observed that men, when drunk, begin to make speeches they cannot or will not stop. Word follows word, and they wander in endless circles of repetition and re-dundancies, each sentence seeming only to augment their intoxication and prolong the speech. He plunged on.

"A friend of mine used to say that life is like a trans-atlantic voyage. There are two kinds of passengers. Some spend the trip getting ready to go ashore when they reach port, ignoring the parties on board and missing the fun of traveling. Others don't know where they are going, and they have no illusions about their destination. They enjoy the trip as much as possible while it lasts. That's the way I am, Olivia. You know how I have looked and looked for a God. A little while ago I was thinking about one night, fifteen years ago, when I asked God to send me a ball. I waited and waited. I expected a miracle. Just a childish whim, I know; but after that I asked for other things and waited again. For nothing. Finally I tried to content myself with just believing that a God existed. And still nothing! I don't believe in an afterlife, Olivia. I want to have a pleasant trip. And I refuse to travel third class. You see I am attempting to pass on to the first . . ." He found the comparison ignoble and hated himself for having made such an appeal to her. "I know that what I'm about to do can't be considered decent—from a certain point of view." His voice became animated; he seemed to be trying to convince himself. "It all boils down to the old story of the end justifying the means. In a word, Olivia, I'm doing it for my career. I know you understand. I can't go on living like this. And I have my mother to think about . . ."

Abruptly, his self-confidence deserted him. He knew that Olivia saw through his words. The reference to his mother had been invented on the spur of the moment. It was a pretext, an insincere, last-minute recourse. He had never really considered his mother's welfare.

Olivia's eyes, with their curious, unfathomable expression, had never once left his face. He felt that they peered straight into his soul, and he almost hated them. Without knowing why, he felt suddenly rebellious. He was com-

mitting no crime. He was his own master. He had promised Olivia nothing. She had been no virgin when he had
first taken her in his arms. He and she had been good
friends and no more. Tender words and caresses had been
the involuntary products of those intimate moments when
any other gesture or word would have been absurd and incongruous.

He waited, a gleam of defiance in his eyes. But Olivia
only smiled.

"It's all right," she said. "Don't worry, Eugenio. Of
course I understand. Of course I understand!"

Her words disarmed him completely. Immediately there
was reborn in him the desire to stay and forget his troubles
by confiding freely to Olivia. More acute than ever before
was his need to confide in her his apprehensions for the
future, to confess to his friend the constraint he could not
help feeling in an atmosphere that was strange and different from his own. He was haunted by a vague presentiment of future unhappiness. But his eagerness for success
overshadowed and dwarfed every other consideration. He
felt somewhat as he had felt years ago on tortured, sleepless nights when his desperate craving for light and fresh
air had made him care little what they might cost him
later.

From where he sat, Eugenio saw the white rose move
again. It seemed to be telling him goodbye.

"What a coincidence," said Olivia, "that you should
come tonight to take leave of your third-class traveling
companion!"

Uneasy, he did not reply. She shook her head slowly,
still smiling oddly. "Tonight is like a crossroads, Eugenio—"

She broke off suddenly, as if she had thought better of

what she had said or was about to say. It was in a different tone that she asked, "When is the wedding to be?"

Eugenio looked suddenly bored. "I should know!" he exclaimed, as though referring to an event which interested him little. "Three months from now, it seems . . ."

"It seems" was the greatest insincerity of all. The wedding was to be in January, and the date was set. His negligent, disinterested attitude was still a vestige of respect for Olivia.

Reluctantly, he stood up. Olivia, too, rose from her chair. For a moment neither spoke, as they stood, face to face, each searching the eyes of the other.

Her eyes. Those kindly eyes, all-encompassing, soothing . . . A tremor ran through his body. In vain he sought to discern some logical pattern, some definite form in the confused tangle of his feelings. Did he want to go away forever, or did he want to stay forever? Should he stay just tonight? Did he want to marry Eunice, or did he want to continue as before with Olivia? If he did not love Eunice, why then did her presence arouse in him the desire for possession, the desire to subjugate her, to be always at her side? And if he did not love Olivia, why did he find it so difficult to leave her?

Eugenio, as he looked into Olivia's eyes, could not restrain himself. He took her head between his hands and began to stroke her hair. "I—I'm a—a—" he stammered, like a child confessing its naughtiness. His arms went down and encircled her. They drew her close against his body, and he kissed her eyes, her forehead, her cheeks, and her mouth.

He did not leave her that night. In her caresses he seemed to perceive an element of desperation. Never had she given herself to him with such moving abandon, as though she were taking leave not only of him, but of life itself. There

151

occurred to his confused mind the idea of suicide, and it brought to the hours of that night a bitter savor.

When Eugenio departed in the early dawn, it was with the certainty—a certainty which he could define as neither sad nor joyous—that he would return the following day, that he would not find it easy to leave Olivia.

The world seemed very different as the sky grew light. His very soul seemed to have been swallowed up in its chill grayness.

"Eunice," he whispered. "Eunice . . ." The name was as cold as the dawn. He lifted the collar of his coat.

"Olivia . . ." Even that familiar name seemed hollow to him now. It did not have the warmth of the body of the woman he had left only a short while ago.

Both names seemed very remote to him.

"Eugenio . . ." He was also a stranger to himself. The whole world was chill and indifferent. *Toc—toc—toc*, echoed his footsteps in the deserted street.

At the hospital the following afternoon he received a note:

"Am leaving immediately for Nova Itália. This time my visit will be long.

"Always,
"O."

Eugenio hurried to the Falks' home. They told him that Olivia had gone that morning.

The lights of the city grew larger and brighter. Soon they came to the suburbs, and the automobile turned off the highway into a street. Suddenly hope was reborn in Eugenio. What if Olivia were still alive? What if the doctors at the hospital could save her?

"Honorio, hurry!"

They sped past houses, shops with lighted windows, restaurants, walls, trees, people . . .

Olivia was alive! Eugenio imagined that he was kissing the warm lids of her tired eyes, her face, her lips, her hands. What did it matter, the things people might say or think? What did Eunice and her conventions matter? Only Olivia mattered in all the world. She must live. Life would have no more meaning if Olivia should die . . .

He imagined how she would look as she recovered from her illness, weak and smiling, as she leaned on his arm. He saw Anamaria running to meet them, jumping and squealing like a puppy. They would be happy. Life would begin again for them.

"Honorio, hurry! Please . . ."

They passed a lighted trolley car. And as they drew nearer and nearer the heart of the city a dark terror began to grip Eugenio. His anxiety that the trip be over was accompanied by a dread of what he might find at its end.

Twenty minutes of nine, by his watch. Something extraordinary had just happened. Olivia had revived! Olivia could not die! Twenty of nine! Olivia was saved!

"Hurry, Honorio—hurry, hurry . . ." *Perspiration was flowing down Eugenio's face.*

The wheels of the automobile slid smoothly over the trolley-car tracks.

Chapter 11

"So you're getting to be thirty-one, eh, old-timer?"

Filipe Lobo patted Eugenio's shoulder affectionately. Eugenio smiled faintly and looked moodily into his wineglass.

Eunice ordered the maid to serve the ice cream. Dinner was almost over.

Vicente Cintra leaned toward Dora, who was sitting next to him at the table. "And what's wrong with you today, little girl?"

The young woman seemed to awaken suddenly from a dream. Her eyes opened wide in an exaggerated look of surprise. "Wrong? With me?" Her lips curved in a half-smile. She defended herself as if she had been accused of a crime. "Why, there's nothing wrong with me. I feel splendid."

Cintra lighted a cigar and laughed his slow, throaty laugh, shaking his gray head. He blew a small cloud of smoke into the air and turned to his guests with an air of politely concealed boredom.

"After dinner Dora is going to sing for us."

"Oh!" The girl gave a little bounce in her chair. "I can't!"

"Now, now, don't argue, child." Cintra spoke with his teeth very close together, biting into his cigar. "Don't argue . . ." The starched front of his shirt and the collar of his dinner jacket shone. Through the curtain of blue smoke his eyes appeared half closed and teasing, and he laughed again his interminable, enigmatic laugh.

Eugenio looked at his father-in-law. He bore the man no ill will, for he understood the effort he made to render life in that household easier and more pleasant. The Cintras lived in an atmosphere of half-conventional cordiality, somewhat like amateur actors attempting to present a high comedy. Old Vicente Cintra enjoyed his role of retired, patriarchal squire. He was clean-cut and healthy-looking, and he reminded one of the rosy-cheeked, vigorous, smiling old gentlemen who appear in attractively colored advertisements, testifying, "I look like this because I take Such-and-such tonic." He dressed meticulously and kept his nails carefully manicured, and he played golf regularly at his country club.

Dora still held back, looking around the table for support.

"But—but it's been such a long time since I've sung anything—"

"Don't be silly, Dora," her mother intervened. "You're no Lily Pons that we have to coax you."

Just then the maid arrived with the ice cream, and Dora was left in peace. Eugenio broke his *petit four*, thinking of a summer evening he had spent with Olivia at the Edelweiss. She had sat opposite him at the table, eating ice cream and telling him a hilarious story about the opinion of a very famous doctor on plastic surgery. He thought, too, of the notice he had seen in the newspaper that morning:

"Dr. Olivia Miranda has reopened her office for consultation. Hora Building, Third Floor, Room 8."

At the other end of the table, Vicente Cintra was busy modeling a little pig out of bread crumbs, while he talked in a low voice with Dora. The girl was smiling, leaning her elbows on the table, her hands interlaced and pressed against her cheek.

When Eugenio raised his eyes, he met Eunice's censuring, sarcastic glance. She seemed to be saying: "Well, Eugenio! And why that martyred look? Always the wet blanket! Always smiling just to be nice!"

To escape his wife's eyes and end the embarrassment he knew he must be causing her, he turned to Filipe at his side and again broached the subject which had occupied the attention of the men during almost the entire meal.

"You mean to tell me the Mammoth is really growing up?"

Filipe's eyes glinted. "Right up to the clouds," he boomed in his heavy voice. "In a year you'll be drinking champagne on the roof of the tallest building in South America. That's going to be the happiest day of my life!" He knocked the ash from his cigar onto the edge of his plate.

Eugenio, who was half absorbed in his own thoughts, absently watched the ash dissolve in the liquid remains of the ice cream. Where was Olivia? Had she returned to the Falks'?

"Sometimes I think," Filipe continued, "that every man is put in the world to carry out a specific, predetermined job. I believe in predestination."

"You, for instance," Eunice interrupted, with a meaningful smile, "came to give us the Mammoth."

Filipe seemed not to have heard his hostess' sarcastic observation. He was blind, thought Eugenio—or did he actually see further and more clearly than the others, being able to view life, as it were, from the topmost story of his Mammoth?

Filipe passed his enormous hand back through his wavy hair. "It's funny," he said, "I remember one night when I was twenty-nine, and I couldn't sleep. I went to the window of the rooming house where I lived and sat there a long time, looking down at the decrepit little shanties in the lower part of town. I was just a student then. I was putting myself through school, and I didn't have a cent to my name. But I knew that some day I was going to do something great. That was the night I made my resolution. I made up my mind I was going to shut my eyes, put my head down, and push out like a mole. I was going to work for all I was worth and make my dream come true. I had to force my way into life, to do my job and leave some kind of mark in the world to show I'd been there. Or else, so far as I'm concerned, life wouldn't be worth living!"

He crumpled his napkin in his hands and threw it dramatically into the center of the table. There was a brief silence. Still at work on the little bread-crumb pig, Cintra smiled and surveyed the engineer through the veil of cigar smoke.

"I told you once, Filipe, you're taking a risk. It's already too late. The most you can do now is reduce the number of floors. Twenty-five thousand contos . . . I don't know. That much money invested in a good industry—"

"Industry!" sputtered Filipe, straightening up in his chair and wiping the perspiration from his gleaming forehead. "Industry!" He bit his cigar viciously. He was uncomfortable; he had eaten and drunk too much, and his mood would brook no argument. "Well now! Well now! Industry—"

Cintra was smiling calmly as he pressed two tiny green pea eyes into place in the snout of the little pig.

"Look, Filipe. That much capital invested in a factory would employ several thousand men."

Filipe Lobo took a swallow of wine before resuming his defense.

"The hell you say! Think how imposing a thirty-story skyscraper is going to look towering over those miserable

157

little shacks that date back to the horse-and-buggy days! There's something heroic about it—it's more than a building. It's a real city. It's a mon-u-ment! And you try to hand me this stuff about industry! Filthy old factory chimneys dirtying up the town with soot; dark, airtight rooms that breed tuberculosis—"

Cintra brandished his foil. "I'm sure there wouldn't be any dark rooms if you were the one who built the factory, Filipe." He looked triumphantly at his daughter, as though for applause, but Eunice was intent on a discussion of flowers with Filipe's wife. As she talked, her white hands caressed the orchids in the smooth crystal vase in the center of the table.

"The Mammoth," Filipe declared, "has hundreds of windows. Direct light on every floor. Don't tell me! Industry, rot!"

" 'Whatsoever a man soweth, that shall he also reap',"
was his adversary's sententious comment.

"I put all my money—why, I put my last cent in that building," thundered Filipe, gripping the stem of his wineglass fiercely. "And what's more, I've given it every second of my time, every iota of my energy. I fought like a raving maniac trying to convince our illustrious friends, the financiers in this town, that the business was sure. What a waste of breath! I finally had to go to São Paulo to get the capital to build it. What a dump this place is! What a hick town! Still in the hide-your-nest-egg-under-the-mattress stage. A little money in the bank to bring you interest, and the future's all sewed up. Every six months our little would-be capitalist goes up to the window, rubbing his hands, and says to the teller, 'Boy, I want to collect my interest.' What great entrepreneurs! What incomparable financiers!"

Eugenio was amused. Dora was absorbed in watching the evolution of the bread-crumb pig. Isabel was talking with Eunice about ever-blooming roses.

"Of course, they wanted me to build the Mammoth in São Paulo. What a fight that was! I insisted I wanted it here, in my home town, and I finally convinced them. I only want to see the faces of our great businessmen when they see my colossus dominating Porto Alegre, with every room rented. The biggest building in South America! Just think of it: not just Brazil—South A-*mer*-ica!" Suddenly Filipe's tone changed. "But this wine of yours—" He looked from Eugenio to his wineglass. "It's pretty strong, isn't it?"

"Filipe can think of nothing but his skyscraper," said Filipe's wife. "You'd think he was raving-insane."

"Now, Isabel, you don't understand at all. You take care of your charity teas and your benefits. Leave me alone."

Dora laughed. "Now, Seu Cintra here is a sculptor from another world!" She held up the bread piglet for everyone to see. "Frankly, senhor, I think you could make your living doing little things like this."

Isabel smiled. Then her oblique eyes narrowed, and, unnoticed amid the laughter and conversation, she turned on Eugenio a warm, impassioned stare. Swiftly he looked down at the table.

Filipe seemed loath to abandon the discussion. He was quick to take advantage of a brief lull in the general chatter.

"You know," he began, "there are some mighty funny things about life. When I was about twelve, my favorite toy used to be an erector set. I used to build houses and bridges with it. One day I built a skyscraper. My god-father asked me what I called that big building—I can remember just as well as if it were yesterday. I thought about it for a while, and then I told him: 'It's the Mammoth,' I said. I was terrifically impressed in those days by a book I had of pictures of prehistoric animals . . ." The maid was serving coffee. Eugenio lit a cigarette. "Yes, it's funny," Filipe concluded, "how little things that happen to you when you're little sometimes are prophetic."

"Sooner or later," said Eunice abruptly, as if she were hurling a dart, "man realizes his childhood desires . . ."

Here comes Freud, thought Eugenio, foreseeing a dissertation by his wife on psychoanalysis. The topic seemed to him very inappropriate at the end of a dinner party, when all the guests must inevitably be filled with the vague melancholy which accompanies satiated appetites and the vapors of alcohol. Cintra, however, saved the situation by carrying on where Filipe had left off.

"But building a skyscraper a foot high out of colored sticks can hardly be compared with building a real one, with thirty stories."

Isabel allied herself with the offensive. "After he finishes the thirty-story one he's sure to want to make one with forty."

"Yes," Cintra chuckled, "but it isn't just every day you pull such expensive, risky pranks as building another skyscraper."

Dora plucked a flower from the centerpiece and drew it through the buttonhole of Cintra's dinner jacket. She turned casually toward Filipe. "But what is there to do?" she sighed. "Daddy loves his Mammoth much more than he does me."

At first Filipe merely shrugged his shoulders, but then his eyes came to rest more affectionately on his daughter. Eugenio thought he could see two images in Filipe's mind at that moment: a tiny, frail Dora, minute in the shade of an enormous, orange-colored concrete skyscraper.

Eunice rose from the table.

"Shall we go into the music room?"

When everyone else had left the table Filipe detained Eugenio in the dining room, holding him by the arm with a gruff affection.

"What the devil's on your mind, old-timer? You look like you'd lost your best friend in the world. I hate to see anyone looking the way you do. You've got to step out there and fight, man. You can't afford to pull any weak punches in this life." With his clenched fist he gouged the empty air.

Eugenio smiled glumly.

"I know *I* wasn't born to lose this bout." Filipe belched. "You wouldn't have any bicarb, would you? I think I had too much to drink. With me it's everything or nothing, you know. Either I drink one drop and stop right there, or I drink a caseful. I either build a one-story bungalow or a regular skyscraper with thirty floors . . ."

Eugenio shrugged his shoulders. "Everyone is different, of course."

Filipe drank the bicarbonate of soda which the maid brought him, dissolved in a glass of water.

"Well, whatever it is, you've got to fight to win. That's why I admire men like Adolf Hitler and Benito Mussolini. They began with nothing—and look where they are now. Man, when I go to the movies and see those military parades, those masses of disciplined human beings—geometrical—and all that enthusiasm, it makes me tremble all over. Just look." He embraced Eugenio impulsively. "The land was bare and ugly, and then men came and covered it with great monuments . . ."

Eugenio wished fervently that Filipe would go away. He wanted fresh air; he wanted to be alone.

"Who were the men that made history? Alexander! Caesar! Napoleon! Did you ever stop to think what a great life that phony old Corsican had? What a magnificent old war horse he was! How I admire him, how excited I get when I read about him!"

They were walking slowly in the direction of the music room.

"And to think that pretentious idiot Beethoven took his name out of the dedication of the Eroica! That deaf old fool! Just because Napoleon made himself Emperor! That narrow-minded old fuss-budget hadn't the least notion what a magnificent gesture Bonaparte had made . . ."

At the door of the music room, Filipe grasped Eugenio's arm forcefully. "In this life there's no mercy for the losers, my friend. Just think! No mercy for the losers!'

They entered the room.

Vicente Cintra clapped his hands. "Let's have a little quiet now, folks. Dora has promised to sing for us."

The girl sat down at the piano. Eunice switched off the chandelier overhead, turning on in its place a shaded floor lamp that stood near the piano. The large room swam in a soft, dim twilight, broken by a single bright island of azure. It was a sort of artificial moonlight, which reminded Eugenio of a certain night, three years ago. Olivia's room. The lights had been off then, too. He and Olivia had dined at the Edelweiss. It was the day he had saved a little boy from suffocating to death.

Dora struck two chords.

"What will you sing, dear?" asked her mother.

" 'Come to My Arms.' "

"Ah!"

There was an expectant hush. In a clear, soft voice, which quavered slightly, Dora began to sing. Vicente Cintra watched her, still smiling and keeping time to the melody with a discreet, rhythmical motion of his head. Filipe shifted in his chair beside Eugenio, as if he did not find his position comfortable.

It was a languid song. It brought to Eugenio a sadness which seemed irrevocable, and a nostalgia for tender caresses. Was it the wind, or was it the song, that made him feel these things? Was it his longing to see Olivia? *Hora Building, Third Floor, Room 8 . . .*

At his side, Filipe whispered, "That music is disgusting." He jerked his huge, hairy hand, as though seeking vainly to grasp something. "It doesn't say anything. It's weak. It's—it's silly. Sentimental boo-boo-boo for little girls in convent schools! It has no dignity. It makes men effeminate, it softens their will. Outside of Bach and Wagner there's nothing decent in music."

Eugenio nodded vaguely, noticing at the same time that Isabel was again staring insistently at him. Eunice sat very straight in her chair, her hands folded across her lap. She looked like a carved statue that should be labeled "Repose."

Alone on her island of blue light, Dora was singing poignantly. In her voice there was unmistakable sadness. The notes formed by her red lips were long and full, drawn out in trembling modulations, charged with emotion. Kiss me—love me . . . With what fresh sensuality she sang! Give me your lips . . . She raised her eyes, half closed, toward the ceiling, and her breasts quivered. Her hands seemed to caress the ivory keys. I love you madly . . . One felt that she sang to someone who was not on

163

her island, to someone who was far away, lost, perhaps in the sea.

In a sort of half-stupor, Eugenio watched her. He could see her dark, delicate profile, and the blue lights in her straight, black hair. She reminded him of spring. Dora was a personification of Spring. What had brought such an idea to his mind? Why did Dora make him think of the flowering plum and peach trees of the long-ago, perfumed springs at Columbia Academy? Why did she remind him suddenly of Margaret and the plantain trees, of moonlight, his adolescent dreams, the fragrance of the plantain sap, the wind blowing the leaves from the trees? Springtime . . . Oh—Isabel was still watching him! Why must she be so incautious? What if someone noticed . . .

Filipe was grunting impatiently. The music seemed to cause him physical discomfort.

On her blue island, Dora was singing of love. She was sobbing. Moved, Eugenio thought of his wedding day, when little thirteen-year-old Dora had entered the church, wearing a sheer, rose-colored dress and a diadem of flowers in her hair. In her arms she had carried the cushion on which the bethrothed pair were to kneel before the priest. That had happened only yesterday! And now, here was Dora grown up, a woman whose body trembled with passion.

Dora was in love with a poor, rebellious Jewish student. His parents and hers opposed the match and refused to allow them to see each other. Dora and Simão suffered.

Watching the girl's young face, Eugenio felt old and embittered. But her song seemed to tell him there was hope and beauty in the world. He imagined that Olivia was there too, that she was sitting in one of the dark corners of the room. Her large, warm eyes were on him, divining his thoughts, seeing that he was unhappy, that under his new veneer he was still the same uncertain, cynical young man who had yet to discover his place in life.

Dora struck the final chord, and Cintra began to clap enthusiastically. Filipe sighed loudly with relief. The girl left the piano and walked to the window overlooking the terrace. Eugenio thought he saw tears in her eyes.

Eunice turned on the lights, and Isabel, tearing her eyes at last from Eugenio, began with an obvious gesture to arrange her hair.

Suddenly, startlingly, Filipe's deep voice thundered from the depths of his chair toward Vicente Cintra on the other side of the large room.

"How is your milk monopoly, Vicente?"

Isabel burst into laughter. Eunice smiled slyly. Her father reflected an instant before he replied.

"Well, it may not be as romantic and grandiose as the Mammoth, Filipe, but I guess it's a pretty good business. It's shaping up. There are about a dozen numskulls who don't want to come into line."

"Well, give them some heat, man! Don't let them get away with anything!"

Cintra knocked the ash from his cigar. His voice was very gentle. "If I have to, I'll sell milk at five hundred reis a liter. I can bankrupt them . . ." Despite the firm resolution and implied violence of his statement, the smile remained on his lips, and the tone of his voice was soft as a caress.

"That's the spirit!" Filipe was exultant. "That's the spirit! Then we'll have good milk for a good price. Order —order and organization!"

Isabel shook her head. "Good milk at a good price. I don't believe it."

Her husband yawned scornfully. "You know what the price of milk is!"

"Speaking of milk," said Isabel, looking at Eunice, "I'm terrified. I've gained five pounds!"

"Oh?" Eunice feigned interest by raising her eyebrows slightly.

Eugenio got up and walked out to the terrace. He felt the need of fresh air and a glimpse of the night sky; it was mute but filled with memories. He found Dora at the balustrade, gazing soberly out at the great tanks of the hydraulic power plant. From the garden below arose the sweet, thick perfume of gardenias.

At the sound of his footsteps, Dora turned. "Oh!" she exclaimed softly, as she recognized him.

He went to the balustrade and looked over. The far-away tanks looked serene, passionless, and everlasting. *Dr. Olivia Miranda has reopened her office for consultation. Hora Building, Third Floor, Room 8.*

Eugenio took out a cigarette and lighted it.

"It's pretty close in there," he said.

"Yes." Dora did not look at him. Was she trying to hide tears?

From the music room came the sound of someone playing the piano. Debussy? Ravel? It must be Eunice who was playing like that. The stars seemed to beat rhythmically. Eugenio looked closely at Dora. He felt somehow paternal toward her. He wished he could think of something to comfort her, to show his sympathy, his desire to help. He felt that he was capable of great tenderness, but in his household it was tacitly understood that any show of emotion was "vulgar" and displayed lack of breeding. One must be constantly aware of one's dignity. Gentlemen never revealed undue emotion. Certain sentiments were

166

appropriate only for the lower classes. Nothing was more ridiculous than oversentimentality.

Meanwhile, here was the night, clear and perfumed; here was a young girl in the full bloom of youth; here was a man who, at the age of thirty-one, was beginning to discover that he had not yet lived.

He wanted to say something, but feared to violate the delicate understanding which existed between himself and the girl. He was afraid she might read into his interest a desire to interfere in her affairs. The silence grew, and his awkwardness increased.

"Dora," he ventured at last, "there's something wrong . . ."

He felt that he was about to make a fool of himself.

"Something wrong? No, sir—"

"I know, Dora. You needn't be afraid to tell me."

He flushed, for he was thinking of Isabel. What a hypocrite he was! First he made love to Dora's mother; then he came to the girl with offers of paternal advice and friendship. He detested himself.

But it was no longer possible to withdraw.

"I know all about it, Dora. It's Simão, isn't it? Your parents are against it . . ."

For a second she did not move. Then she nodded. Suddenly, swiftly, she whirled about, as if resolved to meet an opponent face to face.

"Do you think it's a crime to be a Jew?"

"Of course not—of course I don't."

"Everyone is talking! Everyone blames me! But I love him, Dr. Eugenio! I love him, and that's all there is to it!"

Eugenio was painfully aware of his inadequacy. "Don't give up, Dora," he said lamely. "Don't give up. Some day,

167

I know, everything will be all right. Some day you and Simão will be happy . . ."

Dora stood with her face raised to his. Tears were streaming down her cheeks, and her lips trembled nervously. Her brimming eyes glistened.

"You aren't happy, either," she said unexpectedly.

Eugenio was startled. "I?" How could she know? "Why do you say that?"

"Don't say I'm wrong. I know. I can see. I have eyes."

It was incredible that this girl should know. It weakened him; it made him feel inferior. With a single stroke she had destroyed his paternal authority. Should he attempt to deny her? Or should he confess the truth?

He looked again at the night sky, at the serenely shining tanks, at the deserted streets. He threw his cigarette over the balustrade and watched it describe a glowing arch through the air, like a falling star, before it came to rest on the grassy lawn below.

"You are mistaken, Dora. I am quite happy."

Facing her, he felt again old and bitter. His life was empty. Empty, while there existed in the world beauty, love, tenderness, and understanding. It was spring in Brazil. Here was a girl on a terrace, in the moonlight. The December night was warm, filled with stars and indefinable desires.

"You can say that, sir, but I know you are not happy."

Was it worth the trouble to deny her? He shrugged his shoulders.

Suddenly a voice called from inside.

"Dora!"

"Coming! Excuse me, sir." She held out her hand, smiling gratefully. "Thank you, sir. I won't forget that you are my friend." She turned and disappeared into the house.

Eugenio sat down on the balustrade. He imagined that Olivia was sitting beside him, wearing the same filmy gown she had worn the night of their graduation from medical school, holding in her arms the bouquet of red roses. Yes, again he was sharing the moon with Olivia, wondering with her about their future.

He sighed. He crossed the terrace and reentered the music room. Isabel and Dora were sitting in one corner, whispering. Eunice was playing "Les Nuages." Her hands, passing lightly over the keyboard, seemed white and airy as clouds.

Eugenio resumed his place in the easy-chair. Isabel began immediately to devour him with her eyes. In his chair beside Cintra, Filipe was engaged in earnest conversation, bending eagerly toward his companion.

"Debussy may be the ideal of spinners and gold and silver smiths, but never of an ambitious builder. What I love is Wagner. When I hear Wagner, I think of enormous mountains full of mist and sun. Or a magnificent building rearing up, defying the clouds."

The red traffic light flashed on, and the automobile came to a sudden stop. Eugenio waited tensely. Then finally the green light reappeared, and the car resumed its long journey.

Eugenio was wildly excited. Olivia was out of danger. There was a God. He had received the signal for which he had been waiting. Life was about to begin again. It would be a pure, simple life, constructed on foundations of truth and sincerity.

What was success? Eugenio knew at last that what he had been seeking was a soul, and a clear mind to comprehend and accept life and men. His blindness was gone.

Olivia's cool hands had touched his eyes, and the insane, evil dreams had vanished.

On and on they sped. In only ten minutes they would be at the door of the hospital.

Again a red light flashed on, and again the car came to a standstill.

With his hand Eugenio wiped away the perspiration which rolled down his face and soaked his collar.

Chapter 12

They met in Eugenio's office every afternoon when all the other offices on the third floor of the Mexico Building were closed.

This afternoon, Isabel arrived out of breath and excited, and her mood affected Eugenio quickly. As she had entered the building she had met Dr. Castanho on his way out. She was perfectly sure he had seen her and had pretended to talk with his chauffeur merely in order to spy on her as she got into the elevator.

Isabel sat in a deep chair and related the episode in a broken, quavering voice. Her eyes were very wide, and with one hand she clutched nervously at her breast. Eugenio smoked in uneasy silence.

"But what is there to get upset about, Isabel? What if he did see you? A hundred people go in and out of that door every day. Isn't this a public building?"

"I guess so . . . But he knows you have an office here."

"I'm not the only man with an office in this building. There are more than twenty other doctors and lawyers here, you know."

170

"Yes, but Castanho knows about us—"

"What!"

"I mean, he knows that Filipe and I are friends with you and Eunice. . . . He's probably guessed something . . ."

As he sat hunched forward in the chair, his arms resting on his thighs and his cigarette burning between two fingers of his right hand, Eugenio was staring at the pattern of the rug. At that moment its intricate design was an exact replica of the multi-hued thoughts which seethed in his brain. The coincidence added to his insecurity and dejection. The night before, he had had a startling dream. Olivia had been lost in a fog, and she had signaled to him to save her. He had wanted to hurry to her rescue, but a mysterious power had held him as though rooted to the ground.

For a long time he did not answer Isabel. At last, reluctantly, she removed her hat and gloves and placed them on top of the desk.

"Sometimes I think—" she began, and stopped instantly. Her hands flew to her eyes, and she began to cry.

Eugenio rose brusquely. He was mortified. Angrily, he crushed his cigarette in the ashtray and looked at Isabel. Where was his courage? Why didn't he tell her plainly that he did not love her? Where was his honesty? Why couldn't he confess that he had become her lover for no other reason than that his sense of inferiority required constant sacrificial offerings, that his vanity must be nourished, his animal passions satiated? Intellectually he and Isabel were as far apart as any two people could possibly be.

He looked at her now, at her trembling hands that pressed a handkerchief to her mouth, at her eyes that were glazed with tears, at her breast that heaved tempestuously. He felt sorry for her. She was human. He made a desperate

171

effort to appear sympathetic, to speak gently, to conceal his irritation and impatience.

"What is it, my dear? Perhaps—perhaps it would be better, Isabel—" From the street came the roar of passing trolleys, the blowing of automobile horns. For a few instants Eugenio struggled with his indecision. With an extreme effort he finished the sentence. "—to end this affair once and for all . . ."

Isabel started. As she turned slowly toward him her hands dropped limply to her sides. Her great, tearfilled black eyes stared blankly, as though she had not caught the meaning of his words.

"End?" she whispered. "Is that all—all you—"

"But, Isabel—"

"Oh! Oh!" she whimpered. "I take chances! I come—I come here—I make every sacrifice . . ." She bit her lip, and tears poured down her face, opening tiny crevices in the surface of her powder. "So," she said quietly, "so—you want us—"

"It's not—it's not that I want it, Isabel . . . But you understand—that sooner or later someone may discover . . . Oh, what a hell of a—"

Isabel was wiping away her tears. She gathered up her handbag and walked to the mirror of the hatrack to re-powder her face and apply fresh lipstick. Eugenio watched the tear-stained face reflected in the mirror and understood the piteous effort she was making not to cry, to seem not to care.

Suddenly the rigid tension of her mask gave way, her face crumpled, and the tears came. Eugenio did not know what to do. He caught her shoulders and drew her to him, kissed the nape of her neck.

"Isabel, my sweet, please . . ." His voice was distraught.

"Don't cry. I didn't want to hurt you, I swear I didn't. Look—"

Swiftly, fiercely, she wheeled and embraced him. She laid her head on his breast. Powerful sobs racked her body. Her frantic trembling in some way reminded him of the motions of love-making, and through his pity he began to feel a vague desire. Coming at such a time, in such a situation, it seemed to him sacrilegious, and he despised himself even more.

"Come, come now, Isabel. Be quiet. . . . Don't cry like that, Isabel . . ."

He smoothed her hair gently, trying to seem fatherly and understanding. He remembered Dora. He thought, too, of Eunice and imagined that she was watching them. The idea brought hot blood to his cheeks. He experienced mingled impulses to torture Isabel, to love her tenderly, to run away.

By degrees her sobs died away, and she raised to his a face that was devastated by suffering. Tears stained her cheeks with fine, dark lines, which curled sinuously downward, like tiny rivers. When one looked at Isabel closely, with all her defects so obvious, so glaring—her tired skin, her badly painted lips, her drooping, wilted eyelids—one saw no beauty in her face. In her eyes there shone no light save that of desire and the terror of a woman who fears to grow old. She embraced him desperately, clinging to him as to a last vestige of youth. In those brief instants Eugenio knew her tragedy. He looked at her half-open, quivering lips and pitied her. He bent and kissed her mouth almost tenderly. He felt her body shake against his own; her lips clung to his frantically, and it seemed that the pressure of her burning hands must crush his head. But his own desire, inhibited by her tragic suffering, had vanished.

He felt strangely as though he were about to commit incest.

Eugenio welcomed his mistress' leave-taking that Saturday as an escape. The recollection of the moments he had spent with her was bitter. Like everything else in his life, this affair had turned out badly. He seemed to live from one failure to the next. He did not get on well with Eunice. He was a stranger in his own house. His feeling of inadequacy accompanied him everywhere. Now this liaison with Isabel, far from developing his self-confidence, far from bringing fullness to his life, only added to his torment and confused him, gave him new motives for remorse, self-censure, and apprehension.

He went to the lavatory, washed his hands and face, dampened his hair and combed it, and surveyed himself in the mirror. You are a beast, Eugenio, he told himself. That was the better part of himself speaking—the part which had remained pure and whole, in spite of his many griefs and failures. A beast . . . Perhaps, some day, he might hope for the miracle of rebirth, of strength to react against dissolution, defeat, cowardice. Perhaps, some day . . .

He picked up his hat and left the office. There were papers to be signed at the factory. Actually, that was the only thing he did at the factory—scribble his name on papers brought to him by other people.

"The factory," he told his chauffeur.

It was four o'clock in the afternoon. The automobile advanced slowly through the riot of vehicles, sounds, and human figures which clogged the street at that hour. Again Eugenio saw Olivia wandering in the fog, signaling to him. What if she were really in trouble? What if she really needed him?

He leaned back against the seat and closed his eyes. He could not rid himself of an inexplicable sense of approaching danger, a feeling that this was the eve of a catastrophe. Some tragedy seemed impending. He foresaw it vaguely, and he was alarmed.

When he reopened his eyes, the automobile was passing through the Park of the Redemption. Children were running and playing along the edge of a lake where ducks floated serenely. The shadows cast by the trees were blue. A heron flew up from the aviary. . . . A sharp cry split the air. . . . Two dogs ran barking behind a yellow ball.

At that moment Eugenio felt more acutely than ever the colorless vacuum of his life. He longed for Olivia. *Hora Building, Third Floor, Room 8 . . .*

Eugenio crossed the inner courtyard of the factory. The great concrete structure seemed to pulsate with the heavy rhythm of the machines. To him their dull throbbing was like the beating of an enormous subterranean heart. It stirred in him a vague anguish, an indefinable fear. It was like the affliction of a man who feels in the ground beneath him the stirring of subhuman creatures which work silently toward his destruction. The thundering of the machines was an enemy sound.

The office that day seemed colder and more commonplace than ever. He sat down at his desk, opened one of the drawers, and rummaged among the papers. Not finding what he sought, he called his secretary. She was a thin, tired-looking girl.

"Good afternoon, Dona Ilsa. Did anyone call?"

"No, senhor, no one."

"Where are those papers that are to go to the Ministry of Labor?"

"They're in the middle drawer, senhor."

"I can't find them." He opened the drawer again and found the papers. "You were right—here they are." He laid them on the desk and took up his pen. He glanced up at the girl who stood before him. "You look pale and tired, Dona Ilsa. Why don't you take a vacation?" Automatically, without looking at the papers, he began to sign them. He felt a brotherly interest in his secretary. She looked like a small, tired bird.

"Your backache—does it still bother you?"

"Sometimes, when I lie down, it does."

"It's probably the way you sit when you type. You must take care of yourself, Dona Ilsa."

The girl smiled, a little embarrassed.

Eugenio wondered at his unprecedented solicitude. He concluded that it must be because he felt sorry for her; he felt sorry for everyone who suffered. For a moment he was quite pleased with his piety. But an implacable little voice inside reminded him that his kindness to his secretary and to the other employees of the factory was only a means of purchasing their complicity, their good will. Everyone, or almost everyone, knew why he was there. They all knew he was only a manikin, a robot that signed papers from the hands of lesser-paid men who really knew what they meant. Everyone knew he was only the husband of the boss's daughter; his benevolence and generosity toward his underlings were obvious bids for, if not their sincere good will, at least their tolerance of his presence among them.

He wrote his name angrily. The pen tore the paper, and a blot spread untidily across the center of the sheet. The secretary came forward with a blotter.

"Thank you."

The telephone rang, and he picked up the receiver.

"Hello! This is Eugenio." He never said "Dr." Eugenio; he feared to sound pretentious, or to offend his fellow workers of lesser rank. "Who? . . . Oh!" His face darkened with annoyance. "Yes. . . . All right. I'll be there."

He placed the receiver on its hook and stood up. In Section Three the plant manager had caught one of his men writing indecent words on the walls of the lavatory. He wanted Eugenio to see with his own eyes what had been done. The culprit was a worker named Galvez, who had already been arrested under the charge of being a Communist agitator. He was dangerous, declared the plant manager; he was a disorderly element.

Eugenio's annoyance was obvious as he strode in the direction of Section Three. His ordeal with Isabel had been more than enough to try his patience. He felt that another such difficult scene was beyond his endurance. He hated to become involved in questions of this sort; having to deal directly with the personnel of the factory was for him the most disagreeable part of his job. How he disliked having to settle their arguments, to advise, reprehend, and punish them!

At the door of Section Three, the plant manager was waiting for him. He was a tall, husky German with a bull neck, a shaved head, and steely blue eyes. Eugenio always felt very small in his presence.

"That goddam filthy pig Galvez!" hissed the plant manager between his teeth. His face was like stone. "Come look at what he did this time!"

"Where is he?"

Just then Galvez appeared at the door of the annex. He had scarcely taken three steps across the cement floor when, as if at the signal of a cruel, invisible stage prompter who had only been waiting for his arrival from behind the wings, something terrifying happened.

"Galvez!" bellowed the German. His harsh, metallic voice rang out above the dull pounding of the machines. Eugenio looked in the direction in which he had shouted.

Horrified, he saw a man's body being lifted high into the air by the huge pulley of one of the machines. There was a sharp scream as the body whirled swiftly on the broad belt. Then, like a rag doll, it was hurled through the air, to fall far away amid the other machines. There was a moment of dismayed silence. Then from all sides came exclamations. The German ran to the control board and threw the main switch. The silence which followed the stopping of the machines chilled Eugenio's blood. The men all ran in one direction.

Soon they returned, carrying the mangled, bleeding body, and placed it at his feet, as if he were the blood-thirsty deity which had required the sacrifice. As he bent over to examine the body, he could scarcely control the trembling of his legs. The worker's skull had been crushed to bits; his features were no longer distinguishable. His body could hardly be recognized as having once been human. On the ground around it a pool of blood was growing swiftly.

Terror choked the men and reduced them to silence. The eyes of the plant manager remained cold. His face was an inhuman mask of stone.

When he was again at his desk, it seemed to Eugenio that he had been away from his office not for twenty minutes, but for twenty years. He was older now, wearier and more cynical. He rested his elbows on the desk, his face in his hands. Fixedly he stared into the inkwell.

178

Through the windows still came the sound of voices in the courtyard.

"Have the machines begin again. . . . We can't hold things up any longer. Time is money . . ."

Money. Why could men never forget money? Time was also blood. Money was made with blood.

Eugenio called his secretary. She came immediately. Her face was pale and frightened.

"Dona Ilsa"—he found it difficult to speak firmly— "please bring me his record."

In a few moments his trembling hands were holding a small yellow filing card. The dead man's name was Toríbio Nogueira. He was thirty-seven years old. He was married, the father of five children. Salary: ten milreis per day. To one corner of the card was attached a photograph of a thin-faced man with sad eyes. Eugenio thought it looked vaguely like his own father, like poor Angelo.

Just then Vicente Cintra came into the office.

"Did you see that?" He dusted the lapel of his coat and straightened his tie. "These men are children, Eugenio. They don't know what they're about. I spend all my time telling them what to do. You've no idea what a nuisance it is."

Eugenio held out the filing card. The older man glanced at it carelessly.

"It's better if you go personally to arrange things with his family. We'll pay the compensation according to the labor laws."

Eugenio nodded. "Must I go today?"

Cintra shrugged his shoulders. "No, I guess you needn't bother right away. But go tomorrow, for sure. The main thing is not to let the thing get cold. Some lawyer is liable to get to the family, and there'd be hell to pay." He laid the filing card on top of the desk. "You can do this little thing for me, Eugenio. Go talk to the man's family. It looks decenter for a member of the firm to go. It shows consideration." He put on his hat. "I have to go to a meeting of the Rice Growers' Union, and then . . ." His voice trailed off indefinitely. In a condescending tone, he added, "You have a knack for things like this, boy."

Eugenio hated being called "boy" by his father-in-law.

At the door, Cintra turned. "Tell them we'll pay for the funeral. So long." The door closed behind him.

You have a knack for things like this. His words rang in Eugenio's ears. He might just as well have said, "You're not good for anything else."

Eugenio stood up. He could not forget that mangled, bleeding body, with its crushed head and twisted limbs. He looked again at the card in his hand. Five children . . . He felt somehow responsible for the murder of those children's father.

He went to the window. The fantastic subterranean heart was still beating, marking off each second as it passed. And each second in turn—it seemed to him—marked one more step in the direction of total destruction, of catastrophe. In Section Three the murderous machine rumbled on, as if nothing had happened. It was made of steel, Eugenio reflected, but it could have the cruelty of men.

He put on his hat and went out. It was growing dark. A deep, imperturbable calm seemed to have settled over the world. Birds were singing in the trees that shaded the avenue in front of the factory. The evening sky was tinged with red. Olivia . . . How he needed her, how he needed her today! He dreaded the moments he must spend with his father-in-law and his wife that evening at the dinner table.

Eunice's father seemed to be preoccupied, for he spoke little during the meal. He referred only summarily to the meeting of the Rice Growers' Union, where his point of view had met with little support. When the after-dinner coffees were served, however, he became more communicative. He fashioned a tiny doll of bread crumbs and told an amusing anecdote about one of his political acquaintances.

Eunice took charge of the conversation, speaking almost continually and directing herself more to her father than to her husband. She talked about the movie she had seen that afternoon, made casual observations about books and mutual acquaintances, mentioned her new resolution to study Greek and psychoanalysis. (It was said that Dr. Stekel was going to give a series of lectures at the Medical Society.) Eugenio strove not to succumb to his depression. He spoke little, and ate even less. Cintra made not the slightest reference to the disaster which had taken place at the factory that afternoon; he was a gentleman.

"Where are you bound for tonight?" he asked, setting a cigar band for a hat on the head of the bread-crumb doll. "I feel like going to the club."

Eugenio said nothing, but Eunice answered her father. "I'm going to hear Acelio's lecture at the Culture Circle." She glanced at Eugenio. "Are you going?" Her tone, Eugenio fancied, implied that naturally he would not go, because he had no interest in such intellectual activities.

He frowned. "If you like, I'll take you."

"You know I can go alone. No one is obliged to put himself out unnecessarily." She smiled politely, to mollify the harshness of her words. A lady never lost her temper . . .

"What is the subject of the lecture?" Eugenio still did not dare to say conclusively that he did not wish to go.

" 'Greek Tragedy and the Modern World.' "

"Oh!"

He lit a cigarette. He was in no mood to listen to words. He needed to be alone that night, or with someone who understood him. Olivia. Olivia . . . Could she be living with the Falks again?

"Well," said Eunice decisively, "you're not going, are you? Daddy will leave me at the Circle when he goes to the club." She rose, smiling maliciously at her husband. "By the way, 'The Flight of Tarzan' is at the Apollo now."

Eugenio blushed crimson and glowered into his coffee cup. Cintra rose from the table, laughing in his customary leisurely way, obviously trying to lessen the sting of his daughter's words.

"Well, come along," he said. "I'm going to the club. By the way, Eugenio," he added, "I put your name up for the Country Club. The initiation fee and the first month are all paid."

"Thank you."

"You're not going, then?"

"No."

"Well . . ."

Eugenio was left alone in the dining room, alone with that odd feeling of insecurity, of having been abandoned, of unsureness and melancholy. He began to think ridiculous things about Castanho. The pale young man would reach the age of sixty without publishing his famous essay on Greek tragedy, which had been blazoned so pompously since his student days. He envisioned Castanho behind the desk in the salon of the Culture Circle, wearing a Greek mantle and a crown of laurels, very pale of face and intellectual-looking, reciting in his too-gentle voice passages from Sophocles. All the while he was changing the mask he wore—and every mask was a reproduction of his own vague, sickly face.

And then, as he sat motionless, staring into his empty coffee cup, Eugenio saw himself pushing through the crowds of visitors in the salon, advancing resolutely in the direction of the dais. In the rapid sequence which followed, he reached out and struck Castanho in the face violently with his clenched fist, causing the wan young intellectual to topple over backward, raising a tumult in the salon.

Eugenio knocked his cigarette ash against the edge of his saucer. Already he was filled with remorse for his imagined belligerence. Why did Acelio Castanho irritate him so? The replies he found were numerous and unsatisfactory. Perhaps his dislike for Castanho arose from the latter's connection with an unpleasant memory of his youth. Perhaps it derived from the profound intellectual admiration which he knew Eunice had for Castanho. It might even be jealousy, for as time went on the silent passion which Castanho felt for her was becoming more and more obvious. He worshiped Eugenio's wife with the stubbornness and methodical fury of which chaste men are capable.

Eugenio left the table and walked to the window. The night was calm; it seemed to bring him an invitation from Olivia. Was she living again with the Falks?

In the house next door children were laughing and shouting. Eugenio thought of the five children of the worker who had been killed by the machine. He must do something for the poor man's family.

Suddenly a disturbing thought came to him. There were

people in the world who needed his help. It was within his power to help someone. Perhaps that was the answer. Perhaps at last he had found something to placate his conscience. He recalled the days when he had been a shabby young doctor in the Emergency Ambulance Corps and had attended the poor. He looked down at the gate of the Cintra mansion and saw himself again as he had climbed out of the ambulance in his rumpled gray suit one day long ago, his bag in his hand. He felt a strange nostalgia for himself as he had been in those days. His suffering had been as great then as now, and his preoccupation with making his career had tormented him; but he had had a measure of independence, had known a certain free spirit of rebellion, while now . . .

The silence in the house depressed him. He picked up a book, opened it absent-mindedly, and began to read. It said nothing. He saw on its pages the face of the worker whom the machine had crushed, and the faces of five thin, sickly children who had lost their childhood.

He picked up the telephone directory. A—B—C—D—E—F. Fabrício—Fagundes—Falcão—Falk. Hans Falk, 5765 . . . No. He would not telephone. He flung the directory away, gathered up his hat, and hurried from the house.

The door opened. Eugenio, his heart pounding, found himself standing before Olivia.

"Eugenio!"

She grasped his hand warmly. For a moment they stood staring at each other. Her face was radiant. His was serious, anxious.

"I knew you were coming," she said at last. "Come in."

She took his hat and closed the door. Eugenio could not think of a single word to say. Taking his arm as she used to do, she led him gently to an easy-chair, like a nurse who guides and supports the first steps of a patient.

As he sat down he looked at Olivia, who had taken her old, familiar place opposite him. Her eyes offered him peace. The room was exactly as it had been three years before, every piece of furniture in its old place.

"It's been so long!" he exclaimed, without realizing he had spoken.

Olivia nodded. She waved her hand in the direction of the window.

"Didn't I always tell you? The stars are really there . . ."

Eugenio let himself be carried away by a deep sense of tranquillity. Oddly, he felt no constraint at having returned. Her presence reassured him.

"Last night I dreamed about you," he said. "You were lost in a fog, and you waved to me. I was afraid. I woke up in a cold sweat."

The fresh night wind blowing in through the open window cooled his face. He felt almost as if its freshness came from Olivia herself.

"But I must confess that I came because—because I need you, Olivia. So many things happened today . . . Not just today. So many things have happened in all these three years . . ." He lowered his eyes from her face and added, without looking at her, "The prodigal son has come back, hasn't he?"

She stood up. "And I'm going to order a fatted calf to be killed. I'll bet the teapot is whistling already. I had just put on water for two cups when you rang. I knew you were coming."

"How could you know?"

She shrugged. "Oh, there are signs . . ."

185

When she had left the room, Eugenio lit a cigarette. He felt perfectly at ease. This was his house. He began to walk slowly about the room, pausing now and again in front of a picture, a piece of furniture, a vase or an *objet d'art*. On a table with a vase of flowers stood a portrait of himself. It had been taken the day of his graduation from medical school. He looked very serious; he was frowning, and his lips were shut in a tight, straight line. He took the picture up in both hands to examine it more closely.

When Olivia came back, he pointed to the vase and the portrait.

"Flowers for the deceased?"

She paused, the tray in her hands. "Don't forget that Christ raised Lazarus!"

He returned the portrait to its place on the table. "That was a long time ago, when Christ was on earth."

Olivia was pouring tea. "What makes you think He isn't still here? We don't have to believe only in the things we see and hear and feel. The worst blind man is the one who doesn't want to see."

Eugenio shook his head. He could not see Christ amid the confusion of his own problems, conflicts, doubts, and crass instincts. If Christ really were still on earth, He had probably adapted Himself like a chameleon to its misery, as a means of self-defense. He wanted to express this idea in words, but he was afraid. But why should he try? He had come home; he and Olivia were going to have tea together as in the old days.

They sat down opposite each other, as they had so often sat three years earlier, and he began to tell her about the disaster which had taken place in the factory that afternoon.

"Is it possible," he concluded, "that all this makes any sense? Do you think it can have any meaning, any purpose? Sometimes I think, Olivia—"

She leaned forward and looked him well in the eyes. In her face there was an expression which he would never forget.

"Thank God," she said. "Thank God you suffered!"

He stared at her uncomprehendingly.

As swiftly as she had spoken, she seemed to regret her words. Her tone resumed its usual calm simplicity.

"How much sugar?"

"That's just right."

She gave him the teacup. "Have a cookie?"

"Thank you."

"Is it good?"

He nodded. "May I dip my cookie in the tea?"

"And lick your fingers, if you want to."

"I only asked because at home I can't do that. We're very—very, you know . . ." He smiled, feeling, however, that he must be blushing. There was an uncomfortable silence. Then Olivia leaned forward again.

"Tell me everything, Eugenio."

"What's the use? I know you've guessed anyway."

She nodded slowly. "And now?"

He shrugged. "That's the question I ask myself every day." He set his teacup down and looked at her gravely, for a long time.

"Olivia," he began at last, imploringly, "I know I have no right to ask you questions. But there's something I've got to know . . . You can't imagine what this means to me now." He paused, uncertain. He saw that she was waiting.

"Do you remember that night—our last night?" She

187

nodded. His face wore an expression of pained anxiety. "Why, Olivia—why did you let me go? Why didn't you try to keep me here? When I left you then I knew I would come back the next day. I knew then that nothing else mattered to me. Why did you go away that night, Olivia? Why did you leave me?"

She touched his hand gently. "When you're alone in a house, Eugenio, and you hear a noise on the ground floor, you think immediately of burglars, and you're afraid. If you don't do down right away and see what it is, you spend the rest of the night worrying. You don't sleep, or you sleep lightly and have nightmares. The best thing to do is to go down and make sure it was only the cat that turned over the chair. Then you can go back to bed and sleep in peace." She paused. "If I had tried to keep you here that night you would have spent the rest of your life wondering and regretting, feeling you might have been much happier in that other world—the one you live in today."

He shook his head. She had not yet told him what he wanted to know.

"Olivia, I said before—that I had no right . . . There are some things I don't understand, that I never understood —that in my egotism I never tried to find out. . . . We never spoke openly, you and I. We purposely avoided discussing certain things. I didn't want to talk about them because it was easier not to—because I was a coward. You— I don't know why you didn't. But—but there's something I want to ask you now, Olivia." With considerable reluctance, he continued: "Olivia, you—did you really love me?"

"Blindly."

The pressure of her hand on his tightened, and Eugenio

saw in her face an expression of such great love that for an instant he faltered. No one had ever looked at him like that. Isabel's feeling for him—how could he compare it? Eunice was a total stranger. This was a woman who truly loved him, who loved him deeply. He felt suddenly as if some missing part of him had been found at last, had been found and joined to the whole.

He lifted Olivia's hands and kissed them tenderly, almost reverently. He looked at them very closely, examining them with great care, as if he wished to make sure they were real, and not the hands of a ghost or of some character from his dream world. He felt Olivia's hand on his hair, stroking it. He was happy, with an overpowering, dizzy, almost suffocating happiness.

But suddenly there appeared, in the midst of his paradise, an alien face. Eunice! There was Cintra, too, laughing his slow, throaty laugh. And Isabel, weeping. He was not yet safe. He leaped to his feet. His face was aflame. He went to the window, and Olivia followed him. He heard her low voice:

"Look at the stars, Eugenio."

Slowly he shook his head. He took her hand, but he did not look at her. He looked out of the window.

"Olivia, if only you know how you help me! I was so lonely . . . I was so desperate! I felt as if I were a—a thing. . . . All I saw were indifferent faces. . . . They didn't look human, Olivia. If only you knew how that hurts! Just sometimes I found something good in me. . . . That's all I had to reassure me—all that's kept me from giving up . . ."

"I know, Eugenio. I knew all the time."

For a moment they stood looking out of the window. The soft night wind breathed in their faces.

"How you must have suffered, Olivia! Three years alone in Nova Itália, without friends, without—"

"Alone?" She smiled. "When you went away that night, Eugenio, you didn't leave me alone."

He turned sharply. Her words had a singular ring. Were they merely rhetorical? Or had they some deeper meaning?

"Do you remember the night you told me we were at a crossroads? I think perhaps tonight, too, may be a crossroads, Eugenio. I think it may be the beginning of something very new and wonderful. Come here . . ."

She drew him gently by the sleeve toward the bedroom. When she turned on the light, the first thing he saw was her bed of green enamel, with its light-colored spread. Beside it stood a white cradle. In the cradle a child was sleeping.

As Eugenio drew near, his heart beat furiously. Trembling, faint, moved almost to tears, he recognized in the sleeping child his own likeness. The fresh, calm face had his features as unequivocally as if he were seeing himself at the age of two. It was almost an exact duplicate of his own infant face in a portrait which he had at home. He turned to Olivia, as though for confirmation.

"You understand," she said, "I couldn't be alone." She smiled. "You know, she has a way of wrinkling her forehead and her nose just the way you do. I call her Anamaria."

Tears sprang to Eugenio's eyes. He stood quite still, dizzy, incapable of the slightest gesture, the slightest word.

They passed through a park where all the benches were full of lovers. Through the trees shone the dim outline of a lake, on whose surface floated a tremulous moon. In a flash, Eugenio relived the night—only a few days ago!—

190

when he had walked under those very trees with Olivia and Anamaria. His new life with them was another honeymoon. The revelation of Anamaria had been as sweet and indescribable as the emotion he had experienced at the age of thirteen, when he had fallen in love for the first time. His reunion with Olivia had changed his life completely. Suddenly he had found reason to believe in life and in himself. He had a daughter, a creature of his own flesh and and blood. A daughter! No, he was not lost!

Every night he went to Olivia. It was with her that he found his peace, regained his courage, received stimulation. How sweet those evenings were! Anamaria sat on her father's knee and played with the toys he brought her. She called him "Daddy." Olivia would sit watching them with her deep eyes, that seemed to encompass them in a great, warm wave of love and protection. Then Anamaria would go to bed, and they would be alone.

One night—Eugenio despised himself as he thought of it—the kiss he had given Olivia on leaving had been warmer and more lingering, and his hands had strayed over her body with an unmistakable gesture. She had only looked at him calmly, without resentment.

"Must we, Eugenio?"

No, no, that was not indispensable. It had been an unconscious thing. He was a fool.

She had kissed him tenderly then. Under the circumstances, physical intimacy could be only a stumbling block, a source of new difficulties, a distraction . . .

What had become of the pleasure they had enjoyed in the old days? Uncertainty and regret beset Eugenio. He knew that to continue as lovers would not only dim both Olivia's vision and his own, but aggravate his peculiar moral depression. Desire only blurred his intellectual per-

*ceptions. When he left Olivia that night, he was thoroughly
ashamed of his behavior.*

*A few days later he returned to her. He had resolved
to break off with Isabel, for his liaison with Filipe's wife
now seemed even more hideous than ever. But the atmosphere of his home did little to foster the realization of his
good intentions. Inexorably, he was a part of that system;
it was difficult to react against something of which he was
so integral a part. There seemed to be no way for him to
be free of Isabel. One Saturday, seeking a pretext for the
break with her, he had not gone to the office; and the
following Monday she had telephoned to the factory. He
had only invented another excuse, had made fresh promises.*

*His new life with Olivia lasted fifteen days. Summer
had arrived, and Eunice was eager to leave for Santa Margarida. She was planning receptions; on the week ends
she would receive friends: Filipe, Isabel, and Dora; His
Honor the Secretary of Education and his wife; the Tax
Commissioner General of the Republic and his family . . .
Old Vicente Cintra, too, would spend his Saturdays and
Sundays at the estate. Eugenio was obligated to join the
party.*

*In the solitude of the country, his remorse had been
born anew. Simultaneously, however, he gained new hope.
He thought of getting a divorce, although he did not yet
have sufficient courage actually to propose such a step.
Olivia had never even remotely insinuated such a thing to
him. She said only that she felt he was older, that suffering
had begun to strengthen, to mold his character. Her great,
expressive eyes, however, told him things he could not
yet understand.*

*Her deeply human, unfathomable eyes. . . . Were they
alive, or were they dead?*

192

The automobile drew up before the door of the hospital, and Eugenio leaped out. His heart was bounding, his throat dry, his body racked by a fierce trembling which left it weak.

He ran into the hall. Deserted. . . . Which room was Olivia's? Sister Isolda, on the second floor, could tell him. The ascent in the worn old elevator seemed interminable. His heart was filled with dread to learn what he knew must be true . . .

The dark corridor of the second floor . . . A white phantom . . . Sister Isolda.

"Good evening, doctor."

Eugenio's eyes searched her face desperately.

In a voice so low he could scarcely hear her words, like one who reveals a darkly guarded secret, she told him:

"Dr. Olivia died at nightfall, in the holy peace of Our Lord. Her body is being watched in the Chapel."

PART TWO

Chapter 13

It was night. The window of Olivia's room was open, and the wind shook the light curtain, so that it waved in the air like a handkerchief signaling. The moonlight was a cool, blue fog. There was no sound.

Eugenio sat with his daughter asleep in his lap. He was thinking of Olivia. One by one the minutes slipped by, and through his mind there passed all the old ghosts in silent procession. They caused him no anxiety or fear. In his heart there was only one great, profound sorrow. He knew that once again he had come to a crossroads. He must choose a new path. He could not follow the old. A return to his old way of life would mean death, and he must live. He must live for Anamaria, for Olivia, for himself. What did it matter, any evil which might come to him now? Only through suffering could he find himself. And then—then might come the calm acceptance that he longed for. Some day, perhaps, he might find God.

Anamaria slept soundly. Her breathing was sweet and regular, and she was smiling. He studied her peaceful face. What mysterious images peopled her dreams?

Life must have a meaning. It seemed to him that he could glimpse a more logical pattern now, the outline of a precise design. Goodness and strength in one's goodness, freedom from violence and unbounded ambition, eyes for the deep beauty of things, the ability to see things as a child who at every instant rediscovers the world . . .

"Life begins every day," Olivia had said. His memory rang with the tones of her voice, and his mind was filled with the image of her face. He felt that he was being watched by invisible eyes, and he trembled. Involuntarily he turned his head, searchingly . . .

There was no sound.

He pressed Anamaria close against him, and felt the warmth of her small body in his own. No matter what happened, he promised himself, nothing could separate him from his daughter. For her sake he must find courage to overcome all obstacles—Eunice, his father-in-law, all of society. He knew that the greatest obstacle lay within himself, inside his own body, in his flesh.

Anamaria's head moved; she muttered something in her sleep, whimpered, and was again quiet. He stroked her hair very gently, not to awaken her.

A door opened. He started. Dona Frieda had come for Anamaria. He stood up, his daughter in his arms. Lingeringly he kissed her forehead. Then he gave the child to her godmother, who carried her silently away to bed.

He turned on the small lamp at the foot of the sofa. By its light he began to read again the letter Olivia had written to him only a few hours before she died. He had found it on top of that very table when he returned from her funeral. On the envelope had been the simple direction, "To Eugenio."

My darling,

Dr. Teixeira Torres thinks the operation should be performed immediately, and in a little while I must go to the hospital. I don't know why, but it has occurred to me that I may die during the operation; and I am writing to you now because it would be unforgivable if I died without

198

telling you some things I know I will never say if I should live.

A while ago the pain was terrible; but they have given me morphine, and I think I am calm enough to write to you. I have to ask myself whether or not I am really calm. I think I am. It must be the hope that things will turn out well that keeps me sane enough to write—the hope that two weeks from now I will be in my room again, with our little girl, and that, half laughing and half crying, I will read this letter over and tear it up. It will seem very silly and strange to me then.

I want to talk about you, Eugenio. Do you remember the afternoon we met on the stairs at medical school? We scarcely knew each other then, and you were confused when you spoke to me. I smiled at you a little awkwardly, and each of us went his way. Of course you forgot me the next minute; but I thought a lot about you. I don't know why I was so sure then that you would be very, very important in my life. Sometimes we have strange premonitions that we can't explain.

Today, my darling, you have everything you dreamed of. You have social position, money, and comfort. But, down deep inside, you still feel like that uncertain, unhappy Eugenio, already half defeated and cynical, who was ashamed of his shabby clothes as he went up the stairs at medical school. You still feel inferior (forgive me for writing to you like this!), you still feel that same emptiness inside you, that same need of something to live for. Just now you are beginning to look back at those days a little nostalgically, with a touch of regret. You have had crises of conscience, haven't you, Eugenio? And there will be even bitterer hours. I can almost love your suffering, because out of it, I know, the new Eugenio will be born.

199

One night you told me you didn't believe in God because in more than twenty years of looking you could not find Him. You must believe that God is revealed in that fact alone. Only think of a Being which exists but is invisible to some, now and again perceptible to others, and marvelously distinct to those who were born with the simplicity of a child, or who acquired it through suffering and experience! Some day, I know, you will find God. A friend of mine who called himself an atheist used to scream at the sky on stormy nights, defying God and trying to provoke a bolt of lightning. God is so powerful that He is present even in the thoughts of people who say they don't believe in Him. I never met an atheist who was serene in his convictions. They are all as busy thinking about God as the firmest believer.

The weakest argument I know against atheism is that it is absolutely sterile and useless. It creates nothing—it leads to nothing at all.

If only you knew what faith I have in you, Eugenio, how sure I am of your final victory!

I leave you Anamaria, and I do not worry. Already I can see the two of you together, the great friends you will be in your new life. Only think, Eugenio—there is in her a great deal of me, but principally she is like you. Her father's name is written on her face. It is a mark of God, Genoca. You must know that. You will live on in Anamaria. It is as if you were given a piece of your own clay to model a new Eugenio.

When I was still in Nova Itália, I read your name several times in connection with your father-in-law's in big business associations, unions, monopolies, and so forth. I thought a great deal about how blindly men throw themselves into the struggle for money. That is the principal reason for the tragedy, the injustice and misunderstanding of the age we live in. Men forget to be human. They sacrifice the best things that life has given them—their understanding of each other. What good will it do to build skyscrapers if there are no human beings to live in them?

There is a Bible, Eugenio, lying on the bookstand near the radio. I would like you to read the Sermon on the Mount. The page is marked. Read especially the passage which says, "Consider the lilies of the field, how they grow; they toil not, neither do they spin: And yet I say unto you, that even Solomon in all his glory was not arrayed like one of these."

Of course we should not take Christ's parables literally and stand back with our mouths open gaping at the sky and waiting for things to fall into our hands. We must work. A world full of idle human beings would not be beautiful. We must give human meaning to the things we build. When ambition for money or success begins to blind us, we should remember to pause and consider the lilies of the field and the birds in the sky.

I don't want you to think that I am advocating a life of inactive meditation and renunciation, or that I think people should live drugged by hope for happiness in "another life." There is an enormous job to be done here on earth. It is a job for strong men, with brave hearts. We cannot sit back idly and watch unscrupulous men build up monopolies, intrigue and war. We must face them. We must conquer this world, not with hate and violence, but with weapons of love and persuasion. Think of Christ's life. He was above everything a man of action, not just a thinker.

When I talk about conquering the world I mean the conquest of a decent life for all people everywhere, the *winning of a worthy, universal peace, and the spirit of cooperation.*

And when I talk about accepting life I do not mean passive resignation to every inequality, evil, stupidity, and misery in the world. I mean acknowledgment of the fact that a fight is necessary, and that it will not be easy, that we must suffer.

We need men of good will. And we need strong men, too—men like your friend, Filipe Lobo, who could be a splendid champion of our cause if his ambition could be reoriented, if his talent and his courage could be directed into channels that are social, not merely egotistical.

I don't know, my darling, but I think I am feverish. This enthusiasm must certainly come from the fever.

I hear a noise. It must be the ambulance coming for me. I just had a chill, and I don't seem to be as brave as I thought I was. Do you see how shaky my handwriting is? Oh, I am human, too, Genoca!—so human that I confess (and I'm blushing a little in spite of my thirty years and my professional dignity) that before I go to the hospital I should like to kiss you again and again.

Anamaria will stay with Dona Frieda. I know that if I die you will come for her here, so that you and she can begin your new life together.

I just read over what I have written. I am trying so hard not to cry. How silly this is! I know everything will turn out well, and in a few weeks I will be burning this letter. Even now it seems melodramatic.

Before I forget: in the bureau drawer there is a bundle of letters that I wrote in Nova Itália expressly "not to send you." Now you can read them all. In them you will find nothing about my past, of which I never told you, and about which you had the delicacy not to ask. I am sorry

*for that. I should like you to know everything about me.
I should like you to see how dark and ugly my life has
been, how I fought and suffered to find peace—the peace
of God.*

*Goodbye, my darling. I have always hated storybook
letters that end pathetically. But let me say,*

Yours for eternity,
OLIVIA.

Eugenio folded the letter very carefully. His eyes were
filled with tears. But he found pleasure in his suffering.
He thought of the years Olivia had spent in Nova Itália.
Not once had she forgotten him. She had loved him selflessly. She had been faithful to him until she died.

Olivia was dead! How hideous to think that at that
very moment her body was decomposing under the
ground! Of what had been a tender and comprehensive,
beautiful and courageous woman there remained only a
repugnant carcass, a heap of rotting flesh swarming with
maggots . . . Eugenio pressed his lips tightly together
and tasted the salt of his tears.

Everything could not end in death. God was not so
cruel that He had given men the capacity to feel and create
beauty and then destined them to total oblivion and decay!

It was ten o'clock. He left the house. The night was
clear, the air warm. As he walked toward the downtown
section of the city he thought of the evenings when he
and Olivia had walked those streets together. On those
nights she had told him much about the life she had already
suffered, and which he did not yet know.

At the square Eugenio paused to look at the enormous
skeleton of the Mammoth. He counted the stories—there
were twenty! There was in the towering black silhouette

of Filipe Lobo's skyscraper something monstrous, something almost supernatural. He lit a cigarette, thinking of Filipe and his vast ambition, of his thirst for the grandiose, his idolatry of the colossal. He thought of Vicente Cintra and his unions, monopolies, and commercial organizations. He thought also of the stars shining high above the skyscrapers and the monopolies, pure and far away.

He walked on. The downtown streets were pandemonium, bright with the flash of shop windows, sparkling with neon signs. People crowded the sidewalks and the middle of the street. He walked aimlessly.

With odd stubbornness a small, colorless voice inside him was whispering over and over again, *And yet I say unto you, that even Solomon in all his glory was not arrayed like one of these.*

Chapter 14

One day Eunice gave a dinner for Túlio Altamira, a much discussed painter from São Paulo who had exhibited his pictures recently in the salon of the Culture Circle, of which she was secretary. Acelio Castanho, whose disapproval of Altamira's work was well known, consented, nevertheless, to attend the party.

"Outside the classic lines," Castanho had written in the *Forum*, "there is no salvation for the art of today. The modern, the rigorously modern, still pays onerous tribute to the classic. There exists, as a sad consequence of Bolshevik propaganda, an art (can it merit the name?) which is primary, infantile, negroid, and deprived of all finesse, of the slightest vestige of good taste or refinement. For these low innovators the supreme refinement is to give the impression that they do not know how to draw. It is said that this represents a search for the ingenuous, for an infantile purity of line. But between those who know plastic form and err deliberately, and those who absolutely do not know how to draw and so embrace the new pseudo-school as a last recourse, there exists an abysmal discrepancy."

The dinner had begun with a discussion by Altamira and Castanho of painting and painters. Old Vicente Cintra, at the head of the table, beamed tolerantly, attempting to insinuate by his comprehensive smile that he was not completely uninitiated in the subject. Filipe crushed his napkin in impatient hands; it was impossible for him to remain silent long. For Filipe there existed only one art worthy of strong men, of truly masculine men, and that was, of course, Architecture, supported by her hand-maiden, Sculpture. Painting, music, and literature were diversions for women and for weak, sickly, or effeminate men. Eunice was smiling, in a mood of unusual gayety, glancing now at Castanho, now at Altamira, sharpening the debate from time to time with brief, provocative observations that were like oil on a bonfire.

Isabel seemed disconsolate; Eugenio avoided her eyes. He knew that he would find in them both censure and interrogation. Why had he not gone to his office last Saturday? Why did he avoid her?

When dinner was over, the guests left the table to take coffee in the living room. Acelio was talking about Michelangelo, and Altamira, sucking an enormous cigar with a sort of anxious hunger, rumbled vaguely, lazily, his acquiescence. He was a stocky, crudely built little man, slovenly of dress, with long, unruly hair. His bloated face, with its fleshy, red lips, the lower of which was prominent and lax, had an immoral look.

"All of you have much to learn from the master, Michelangelo," Castanho was saying.

The two women had gone upstairs to Eunice's room. The painter took advantage of their absence to release a belch which he had held in with difficulty at the table. Castanho's lips curled imperceptibly with repugnance for that sonorous manifestation of bestiality.

"Michelangelo," thundered Filipe, "is great only for having invented the cupola—not for having painted those monkeys in the Sistine Chapel."

Looking very blasé as he pulled at his trousers in order to sit down, Cintra offered his opinion. "Nowadays there are no more great figures in art like Michelangelo, Leonardo da Vinci, and—and so forth." His memory betrayed him.

Altamira, who was at that moment about to sit down, straightened up again. "But of course there, are, Colonel!" he exclaimed. "What about Diego Rivera? Have you never heard of the Mexican genius of mural painting?"

For a moment there was no answer. Eugenio sat in a corner, thinking about Olivia. Never had he felt so strange in his own house as he did that day. He thought of other parties—a dinner for Friedmann, a tea for Bidu Sayão. He had borne all those occasions with a stiff collar, a starched shirt, and a false smile. Now he had to be here again, suffering that disagreeable-looking painter who nursed the thin cigar Cintra had given him, as if it were an infant's pacifier. He limited himself to an occasional smile or nod whenever anyone spoke to him or looked in his direction. The memory of Olivia left in his mind little room for other thoughts. He was filled with nostalgia, with intense melancholy, with a desire to stroke the head of his little daughter and to be alone with his thoughts of Olivia. If only there were some way of escape!

Filipe leaned back in his easy-chair. "I saw some mural paintings by Diego Rivera," he boomed, "when I was in the United States."

"And how did you like them?" asked the painter, his hand outstretched with the cigar between his fingers.

"So-so. Rivera is pedantic like all mestizos."

"Now, now, my good friend, I hope you're not going to tell me a man's race has anything to do with his painting! Tommyrot!"

Eugenio was watching Castanho, who seemed even paler than usual. He wore a dark-colored suit, and his black eyes had a feverish brilliance. The broad expanse of his ivory forehead was broken by a multitude of tiny wrinkles, as he sat thinking, his absent eyes fixed on the ceiling.

When Eunice and Isabel returned to the living room, the men were discussing the Bolshevism of Diego Rivera. There was fire in Acelio Castanho's dark eyes.

"It is incredible," he was saying, "the indifference and complicity of the intellectuals of the so-called conservative class in the face of the Bolshevization of the East." The fire shone only in his eyes; his voice was cold, calculated. "It is regrettable, the disrespect in which tradition is held in that part of the world, the disrespect for all that is beautiful and noble, for the conquest through the centuries of culture, good taste, organized will and discipline."

Eunice was listening to him with interest. Her face was serious.

"Look, for example, at the tremendous elements of degeneration, iconoclasm, subversion—of—of poison in the mural paintings of that Mexican. He has no respect for

God. He gives more spiritual importance to Lenin than he does to Christ. No respect for the Church—"

"Oh, the Church! Bah!" Altamira's shrug was eloquent.

Castanho ignored the interruption. "Never have we sunk so low in the realm of books and painting. There has arisen in recent years a sordid literature which proliferates like mildew and fills the conscience of our youth with green mold. It began with that ignoble book *Jews Without Money*. There is no more respect for grammar, for the traditional methods of the good psychological novel. Today's writers are photographers—despicable photographers who only know how to focus their cameras on filthy scenes of misery and immorality. Those detestable proletarian—that adjective alone nauseates me—proletarian writers discovered a justification for their depraved literary appetites in what they are pleased to pretend is a 'social goal.'"

The painter stirred in his chair. "Look here, Dr.— Dr.—" He did not remember Castanho's name. "Look here—"

Castanho paid no attention. "Pornography, scenes of misery and deprivation, slang, negroid effects—those are the delectable herbs with which our so-called proletarian writers season their creations. They reek from the first page to the last. And each of us is guilty, each of us is responsible for the birth and apparent prosperity of such writers."

Altamira knocked the ash from his cigar. "They are only novels which show us reality—and reality, my dear doctor, is not always *this*." He made a sweeping gesture to include the entire living room.

"And neither is reality only the things we perceive with our eyes, the tips of our fingers, and our noses!"

"I know, doctor, that you are going to speak of the sixth sense." Altamira struggled with another belch, suppressed it, and continued. "But you must not forget, when it comes to the senses, it's five against one—"

Filipe interrupted the dialogue. "I have no time to waste on novels," he declared. "They annoy me. They make me lose my patience. A busy citizen who values his time can't afford to waste it on silly stories." He straightened up and looked triumphantly around the room, as if he were about to make a significant revelation. "And as for *poetry* —don't even mention the word in my presence. It makes me see red. Oh, 'your eyes are this,' 'your mouth is that'— what a lot of bunk!"

Eunice's eyes narrowed. Her smile was spiteful, her casual manner assumed. "Liking or not liking poetry," she said, "is a matter of greater or less permeability to impressions of beauty. Filipe has undoubtedly built so many bridges and skyscrapers that he has developed for himself a hide of concrete."

Cintra gave his everlastingly prolonged, hearty chuckle. Isabel expressed her incomprehension with a pallid smile. And Filipe, dusting from his knees the ashes of his cigar, retorted:

"There you are. True poetry is the poetry of the machine, the stone, the skyscrapers. New York is a poem of stone and concrete." He spread his great arms wide. "Not poetry made of sugary words, but poetry with expressions as tough and sharp as steel—and as flexible!"

"How you would love Verhaeren, Filipe!" exclaimed Eunice. "But then, it's a pity your Americanism has made you forget your French."

Castanho and Altamira were again locked in a heated debate.

"Slowly but surely," Castanho was saying, "Bolshe-vism is undermining our society. The plan is fiendish. It's not only their literature, which they use to prepare the ground for free love, atheism, immorality, and the Communist revolution. It is their movies, too—their amoral films. Scurrilous stories, divorces, nudity, sensuous music, insinuating dances, low-minded humor, drinking excesses, crime, suicide—all that is exploited by the movies. They saturate the public with materialistic filth." Castanho spoke in a monotone, pronouncing each word with perfect clarity, with a cold, didactic enthusiasm.

Eugenio, absorbed in his thoughts, saw himself and Olivia on the night of their graduation, as they sat together on the base of the statue of the Patriarch, staring disconsolately at the stars. How soothing her presence had been, how reassuring, how peaceful . . .

A maid served liqueurs. Altamira drained his glass, and, as if he had drunk enthusiasm, he coiled swiftly and pounced upon his opponent's last words:

"And what is this disorder that the movies portray, if not the reflection of the people's loss of faith in the face of economic and moral collapse?" He rose, licking his lips. His trousers were rumpled, and they sagged pronouncedly at the knees. "Suddenly men saw that everything they had been taught at home and in school about God and the Church and the virtue of recompense in the other life, were lies. They discovered their bodies were full of desires, and to satisfy them all they had to do was to jump over the wall that was called 'convention.' They went insane with joy when they saw the wall was made of smoke and not of bricks and mortar, the way it looked. There was a furious race, and the only ones who stayed behind were the timid and the sick."

He hiccoughed, placed his hand over his chest, and begged the pardon of the ladies.

Acelio Castanho was leaning forward in his chair, his hands folded across his knees. He was shaking his head obstinately.

"Only chastity can raise us above the level of irrational beasts," he said dogmatically. After a pause he added, as though at the behest of his conscience: "The phrase is not mine. It is from a contemporary British thinker."

"Chastity?" laughed Altamira. "At your age, and in these days, you come to me with that nonsense?"

Isabel was staring into her lap. Filipe growled something to Cintra with an air of intense boredom. Eunice was examining the painter intently with her cold eyes.

Eugenio had returned to the reality of the living room and was listening to the conversations around him. In a certain way he found it interesting to attend such discussions from his distant, neutral corner. He did his best to hear them tolerantly; that was half the battle. He made a genuine effort not to dislike Castanho, not to be annoyed by Eunice. It was necessary to look at them compassionately.

Castanho was looking at the untouched glass of liqueur which balanced on the arm of his chair.

"You can laugh," he said to Altamira. "While you and the others smoke your cigars complacently"—he waved his hand to indicate Cintra and Filipe—"the Jews are undermining our social structure, preparing the downfall of our civilization. They have the movies and the press in their hands. They have been preparing their slow, evil revenge for centuries."

As the painter walked back to his chair, he winked at Eugenio. "Look—he still believes in that fairy tale about the Protocols of the Elders of Zion!" He shook his head with a deprecating smile, which implied that he believed the situation hopeless.

"Túlio Altamira," Eunice began, as if she were on a stage and that were her cue, "would you like to do a great favor for me?" She tilted her head lightly to one side; her voice was honeyed. The painter stood immobile, waiting for her request. "Tell us frankly what you really think about all this, about all these isms and conflicting schools of thought."

Altamira laid his dead cigar in the ashtray. "No one can alter the course of the river of History," he said simply, "if you will pardon the commonplace."

"And?" Eunice insisted, demanding a conclusion.

The painter shrugged. "I'm just an ordinary paint-slinger, my dear lady—not a prophet."

Castanho rose impatiently. He faced the painter squarely.

"Well, I'll tell you out and out what *I* think, and let my words fall where they may. I believe in the nobility of birth, in the nobility of human sentiments, and in culture, stoicism, and the gentlemanly virtues."

Altamira was trying awkwardly to relight the cigar. "Words," he mumbled between his teeth. "Pretty words from a man who has never been uncomfortable or wanted for a single thing in all his life . . ."

Castanho slid one long, slender, delicate hand back over his hair and moistened his dry lips.

"I have always prided myself," he said, "on having the integrity not to allow myself to become intoxicated or weakened by any ballyhoo about liberty, equality, and human rights. You can look at nature and see that equality is an impossible idea. I believe in hierarchy, in the division of the classes of society according to the ideal of Plato—the lower composed of peasants, workers, and men of business—"

Altamira looked at Cintra with a knowing smile. Filipe made a face which expressed mingled scorn and disgust.

"—the middle class composed of soldiers, and the elite made up of men of superior mentality—"

"You, for instance," interpolated the painter.

"—by those who have the capacity to acquire scientific knowledge and study philosophy. Those are the able who may become the guardians of the state."

"Plato and his ideas would have fitted in admirably back in the Bronze Age," scoffed Altamira.

Castanho was silent. Perspiration—a discreet, well behaved trickle, Eugenio observed—flowed down his emaciated cheeks. It was Filipe who spoke at last:

"I don't believe in all this tripe about Plato. I'll take Fascism any day. Look at how Mussolini disciplined Italy. And how Hitler put Germany back on her feet. Discipline! Making a nation is like building a house. First, you've got to have a plan—a blueprint. Then, good strong building materials, a solid foundation, balance—"

"And beauty of line," contributed Eunice. "Fascism is beautiful and, dizzy: *'Vivere pericolosamente.'*"

"Phrases," said Altamira.

"Remember," Cintra intervened, "there have been phrases that have overturned governments. A word sometimes moves multitudes." He glanced at his daughter for applause.

Eugenio—it was strange—was thinking of his first important operation. How clearly he heard the sound of the distant gunfire, saw the thin, white-faced patient, Olivia's black, warmly human eyes . . . Suddenly he was chagrined to find that he had been gazing unconsciously into the eyes of Isabel. He flushed and shifted uncomfortably in his chair.

"Out of the confusion of decadent Europe," Filipe was saying, "there rises the great skyscraper of Fascism."

Castanho lifted the still untouched glass of liqueur from the arm of his chair—he neither drank nor smoked—and placed it on the small table in the center of the room.

"It remains to be seen," he said, "whether the foundations of that building will prove solid. I have very serious doubts."

"Fascism is a pompous castle built on sand," said Altamira.

Filipe waved his hand in a formless, sloppy gesture. "I answer only for the skyscrapers that I build with my own hands."

Eugenio thought of the Mammoth, of its enormous skeleton rising in the night, and of Filipe's daughter, Dora. Where was she now? She must be with Simão. Their problem had as yet found no solution. Her parents continued steadfastly to oppose the idea of marriage. Their opposition was formal and theoretical. Busy with his own affairs, Filipe did not think to advise his daughter; neither did he make any move actually to prevent her seeing the boy.

For a few moments the conversation became neutral. Isabel told Eunice about a movie she had seen at the Rex.

Altamira seemed to take pity on Eugenio's silent isolation.

"Well, and how is your practice?" he inquired in a fatherly tone.

"Oh—as usual."

Cintra and Filipe were discussing the food tax. And

while Eunice was saying to the painter, "I especially liked the canvas you called 'Voluptuousness,' because in no other painting the sense of volume . . ." Isabel turned on Eugenio a furtive glance of anguished interrogation.

From the depths of his easy-chair, Eugenio looked and listened in silence. In the back of his mind hovered the ever-present image of Olivia. Through her eyes he was able to see and judge these people, and therefore he was calm. Everything he saw now had the transparency of glass. He had never belonged to Eunice's world at all. He was an intruder, and he must go. Those who had loved him and died needed him. From somewhere beyond this life they must still be watching and trusting him. He could not disappoint them again.

The clamor of a new discussion precipitated him abruptly from the depths of his solitary thoughts.

"But I tell you, the Jew is only the goat!" the painter was insisting. "There always has to be someone to blame for the mistakes! Ever since history began that's been true —in every epoch!"

Cintra gave voice to an opinion he had read in a magazine article: "The Jews are a bad element for a country like ours. They won't spread out into the rural areas. They stick in the cities, opening up little businesses, selling on the installment plan. They upset the structure of our working classes . . ."

"I don't like Jews." Filipe summarized in these conclusive words his manner of facing the problem.

Castanho gazed for a long time at Eunice, a serious expression on his sickly countenance. Without taking his eyes from her face, he said: "But the facts are there. What was that despicable, paranoiac Lenin, if not a Jew. And that insufferable Trotsky? The Jews were the race that made the Russian Revolution. The Jew has no spine." He shook his head nervously, betraying his intolerance. "The Jew is a mollusk. He submits willingly to any miserable situation to get what he wants. He considers himself very much above good and evil."

Altamira's gesture was deprecating.

"Jews are people like anyone else. They have their defects and their virtues."

"My best customers are Jews," Cintra declared more tolerantly.

Castanho glared at him with infinite scorn. "It is incredible, senhor, that you industrialists and businessmen, the pillars of our great conservative class, do not recognize the peril which threatens us all. " 'Good customers,' you say? Well, it will be your willingness to tolerate them, your eagerness for profits, that will be the ruin of your class. The hour is grave, my friend, and you capitalists look only for immediate profit. You forget about the future! Tomorrow, when the revolution is in the street, you members of the conservative class will cringe with fear—you will give up your beloved gold in order not to lose your lives!" He paused. Then, his voice still calm but his eyes blazing, he added: "One thing I can tell you. *I* will fight!" He closed his fingers as though brandishing a foil. "They'll never take *me* alive!"

With a bored air, the painter turned to Castanho.

"Tell me something, doctor. What blessed difference do you think it will make to the revolutionaries whether you are dead or alive?"

There was a hiatus in the conversation, a sudden vacuum, an expectant hush. Castanho seemed about to react violently, but he contained himself. With forced naturalness, he turned toward Eunice. "Did you read that Chesterton I sent you?" He turned his back on Altamira, who leaned back in his chair, speaking to Filipe in his somnolent voice:

"Mr. Lobo, I should enjoy doing a mural on one wall of your—your— What do you call that thing?"

"The Mammoth."

"That's it. Well, I'd like to paint a big mural on one of the walls of the Mammoth." He began to slash the air broadly with one hand, giving the impression that he might be painting with an automatic pistol. "I would call it 'The Red Peril,' and I would paint our good friend Colonel Cintra, sitting in a comfortable chair and smoking a cigar, to represent Capital. You will note that the cigar is really a Zeppelin. Then, one of those little Jews that sell neckties in the street will be the symbol of the Red Peril. With the fingernail of his little finger he will be trying with God-awful patience to scratch the leg of Colonel Cintra's chair, with the wicked intention of breaking it and causing the downfall of Capital. And then there's our good friend Plato over there"—he pointed a finger at Castanho—"who will come galloping up, dressed as Don Quixote, a knight in armor astride the jackass Culture, with his sword drawn to attack the Semitic peril." He laughed.

Filipe was convulsed. "Well," he chortled, "for that I'll give you all the walls of the Mammoth!"

Castanho stood up. Eugenio saw that his hands were shaking. Very erect, very grave, attempting to seem calm, he faced Altamira.

"Now that you try to be sarcastic," he said, "I'll tell you with perfect frankness something which I neither said nor wrote before—not only because I am a gentleman, but because I am capable of pity. You, senhor, are a despicable painter!" His last words were almost hissed.

217

Cintra laid his hand on Castanho's arm.

"Here, here! What's all this?"

"A bad draughtsman," Castanho went on, "a bad colorist—"

Altamira shrugged. "What can you do? I was born stupid."

"You seek in originality, in arbitrary design and the exotic, a refuge from your lack of basic knowledge. And if you find someone who praises you and tolerates you, it's because we live in a country full of backwoodsmen. That's what I wanted to say."

He turned to the two women, pressing an immaculate handkerchief to his brow. "I beg your pardon if I exceeded myself."

Eunice was trying hard to remain calm, to think of some witty remark which might be appropriate under the circumstances.

Suddenly, as if only at that moment he were discovering the presence of Eugenio in his distant corner, Filipe asked in a teasing voice, "And what side are you on, Genoca? Are you for Mussolini or Stalin?"

And Eugenio was astonished to hear his own voice repeating words he had heard on Olivia's lips one night long ago:

"Before Mussolini and Stalin there were the stars, and after they are gone the stars will still shine."

Eunice turned to her husband, her brow wrinkled, her eyes wide with amazement.

Chapter 15

He found himself standing on the sidewalk of a dark street, watching the little girls from the orphan asylum file by. They were pale little creatures, broken and sorrowful, dressed in checked flannel, with heavy cotton stockings covering their poor, thin legs. They went two by two, the youngest in the first ranks, making a stairway which climbed up and disappeared into the night sky. Eugenio watched them with the indefinable sadness which he had always felt for little girls who had no parents. He wanted to stroke their heads, but his legs seemed paralyzed and would not move. He recognized his mother in the nun who led the little girls. Her face was waxen, unmoving, like the face he had seen in the coffin, among the flowers. He wanted to call out to let her know that he was there.

The little girls were marching now and were no longer orphans, but angels. But they did not remain angels, for a wicked hand clipped off their wings with the scissors which poor Angelo had always used to cut his cloth. They were rusty; for many years they had lain under the earth with the tailor's body.

The little girls from the orphan asylum stopped, and Eugenio saw that the first in the long line was his daughter. How sad she looked in her little checked dress and cotton stockings, how she trembled with the cold! She was giving her hand to a companion who was a duplicate of herself, who had her own eyes and features, the same height, and who was called Eugenia. Anamaria and Eugenia, holding hands, shivering with cold and sadness. Poor little girls from the orphan asylum! He wanted to run out to save his daughter and to save himself, for sud-

219

denly he felt that some enormous grief was impending. He wanted to rush toward the line. What sadistic power restrained him? The little girls began to march again, and they disappeared into the gray, cold night.

Eugenio awoke in agony. For a few moments he reviewed the dream in his mind. He turned on the light and looked at the clock by his bedside. It was four o'clock in the morning. Dizzy, he arose, stepped into his slippers, and went to the window. The night was clear and starry. Everything was silent in the next room, where Eunice lay sleeping. Suddenly, with sleep still clouding his brain, he experienced the sensation that he was all alone in the world, that the silence would continue forever. He wanted to scream, to wake someone . . .

He opened the window, and the cool night wind struck his face, his hands, his neck. It was crazy to think of these things. He went into the bathroom, dampened the edge of a towel in cold water and passed it over his face, pressed it against his eyelids firmly.

Abruptly, like a man meeting a ghost or an old and long-feared enemy, he encountered his own image in the mirror. At first, in spite of the intensity of the light, something like a cloud came between his eyes and the glass. Then the cloud dissipated, and Eugenio could see himself with his hair awry and a look of astonishment on his face. He stood looking at himself for some time, as though fascinated. The other Eugenio was asking him questions, demanding explanations. Had all of Olivia's suffering been in vain? Would Anamaria continue her life without a mother, without a father, without protection? What had become of the promises he had made? There was no answer. There was only the cowardice of his poor, weak-willed flesh, which loved comfort and refused to detach itself from the things which gave it pleasure and provided for its well-being.

Eugenio, glancing around the glittering blue and yellow tiled bathroom, was surprised that he was still there, in that house, still the husband of Eunice Cintra, the son-in-law of Vicente Cintra. The last few days he had passed in a dull stupor. He could not see clearly, but he knew that somehow he must extricate himself. But how? When? Where? He could not run away like a criminal. He had to give some explanation. There was the factory. There was his office. And there was Eunice. He owed respect to Eunice. He was ashamed of that indecent patronage.

In order to appease his conscience, he began to make plans for the escape. Mentally he brought the papers in the office up to date, dismantled its equipment, liquidated his personal debts. But he knew that the difficult, the unbearably difficult task would be to explain to Eunice. He knew that the least reaction he might expect from his wife would be an incredulous laugh at his romantic notions of regeneration. He foresaw also his father-in-law's natural reaction. At first he would think it merely a poor joke; but then he would offer a thousand valid and imaginary excuses to delay proceedings: his social position, Eunice's reputation, the publication of the divorce by the newspapers, exploitation of the scandal by his enemies, the stories which malicious tongues would be sure to invent.

Eugenio lit a cigarette and went down to the living room. He opened a book and closed it immediately. He lay down on the sofa, put the cigarette on the edge of the ashtray. He shut his eyes and tried to recapture his lost sleep. Once again he recalled the dream. Anamaria in the line of little girls from the orphan asylum. Yes, that would be her inevitable destiny. She had neither father nor mother. Her mother was dead, and her father might never have been really alive.

The silence persisted, but now was heavier and warmer and darker. Unexpectedly, Eugenio felt the presence of Olivia in the room. It was his heart which perceived her first, and began to beat faster. Olivia was sitting beside him on the sofa. He was frightened, because he knew that she had died; he himself had seen her coffin lowered into the grave. He could scarcely make out her features, as on those nights when he and she had sat silently facing each other in her room, the light off, the moonlight coming in through the window. Fear choked him, and he tried to convince himself that he was dreaming. A little while ago he had had a cigarette in his fingers, and he had put it on the ashtray. If the cigarette were still there, it would be a proof that he was not dreaming. He looked. . . . Vaguely he saw the glow of the ash. Yes. He was awake.

And Olivia was still beside him. She was going to say something. A chill ran through his body. He wanted to be the first to speak, to cry out to her to trust him, that he would not leave Anamaria. For now he understood that Olivia had come back to demand a reckoning of him. "Forgive me!" he was trying to say. "Forgive me!" But his throat could make no sound.

It was then that he saw that the living-room light was still on. He had really been asleep. It had been a nightmare. He had gone to sleep with the book lying on his chest. The cigarette was still burning on the edge of the ashtray.

His face wet with perspiration, he got up and went into the kitchen. He opened the refrigerator, removed a tray from the freezing compartment, and made himself a glass of ice water. He drank thirstily. Then he rubbed a small cube of ice over his forehead, cheeks, and neck.

He went back upstairs, entered the bathroom, undressed, and slowly took a cold shower, hoping that it would wash away the sleep from his body, the somber visions from his mind.

He was on the terrace now, looking at the night with a sensation of freshness in his skin and a great lucidity of thought. Olivia's stars were shining in the sky, and there was a mystery in the world. Could it be that the dead were returning? As a child he had heard of haunted houses. He knew now that there were haunted consciences, too.

The tanks of the hydraulic power plant looked like huge sheets of aluminum. From far away came the sound of roosters crowing.

Suddenly, as if it sprang from the early dawn, as if it fell from the stars, as if it arose from the dew-wet earth, a strange emotion seized Eugenio, enveloped him on all sides, chilled him, made his face contract as though in physical pain and his nails dig into the palms of his hands. It was longing for Olivia and Anamaria mingled with hate for himself, with rage for his impotency.

"Everything depends on me, on me alone," he murmured to himself. "Why haven't I courage?"

The serenity of the hydraulic tanks was broken for an instant now, because Eugenio saw them tremulously through tears.

An urgent necessity to see Anamaria, as if the lives of both depended upon it, made him dress swiftly and leave the house, stealthily as a thief. It was four-thirty. The streets were deserted. Eugenio heard his own footsteps on the sidewalk and remembered other dawns, old emotions. He saw himself again in the saddest hours of his life, and suddenly he asked himself if he would ever find peace, the great inner peace he so desired.

Halfway to his destination it occurred to him that in order to see Anamaria he would have to wake the Falks, and that to wake the Falks at five o'clock in the morning without some urgent reason would be inexcusable. But he did not turn back. He would wait in Olivia's room for the day to grow light. He thought confusedly of staying there forever—of never returning to Cintra's house again.

The Falks' garden looked unreal in the light of the early dawn. Eugenio opened the house door softly and entered on tiptoe.

Time slipped by. Seated under the lighted lamp that stood on the small center table, Eugenio was rereading the letters which Olivia had written to him in Nova Itália, the letters she had never mailed. Each time he read them they revealed something new to him. It was tragic that he was beginning only now to know her. All her kindness, all her profound understanding of life had remained hidden from him. In his selfishness, in his blindness, he had never learned to know her. As a friend, she had inspired and comforted him. As a lover, she had fulfilled as by Providence his physical need. She had asked nothing, had not spoken once of love. It had been convenient for him. He had used her . . .

What could Olivia have seen in me? he asked himself. What could he have done to deserve so much love and dedication—loyalty which continued even in death?

He smoothed the letters tenderly. He opened one which contained a passage that affected him deeply, that caused him indescribable pain:

224

The winter here is terrible, my darling. Today it is raining, and the mist is hiding the mountains. My fingers are stiff, and I feel inclined to melancholy. The people who come into the house bring the mud from the roads on their shoes. I feel terribly depressed. Anamaria's little nose is red, but she doesn't seem to feel the cold, for she wants to take off her wool coat and go out into the yard. Water is dripping from a leak, and the good old lady in whose house we live is humming an ancient Neapolitan song in the kitchen. If it were not for my faith in God, in you, and in our daughter's future, I should be sad now. But I refuse to give in to sadness. The rain and the fog will surely go away tomorrow, and the sun will shine again on the vineyards. I think about you, and as the hours go by you ripen as the grapes do. And do you know? Sometimes I am surprised to find myself thinking about you in almost the same motherly way I think about our Anamaria!

In another letter he read:

Our daughter was two years old yesterday. She already talks and asks questions, and she stands with her little head on one side, thinking of no one knows what. I have to explain to her that she too has a father like the other little girls. She asks questions about the father she has never seen and is already beginning to love. For her, then, you exist in the same way God exists. Your daughter doesn't see you, but she knows that you "are." She feels your existence in me and in a certain way in herself. How can it be that there are still men who do not believe in God? The simple miracle of our existence is a proof that there is a God.

225

Eugenio closed his eyes and saw Olivia and Anamaria on a rainy day in Nova Itália. What must he have been doing when she wrote those words? Panting like a beast in Isabel's arms—or listening indifferently, perhaps, to Eunice's cold voice and Cintra's polished, condescending laugh . . .

In another undated letter Olivia had written:

We must find our happiness through the happiness of other people. I am not trying to preach asceticism or holiness, not praising mere sacrifice and renunciation. That would not be true to human nature. It would be an escape from life. The important thing, the thing I look for, is to take life by the shoulders and press it against me, to kiss its face. Life is not the atmosphere you live in. Studied manners, conventional phrases, too much comfort, expensive perfumes and worry about money are only an ugly counterfeit. Do you see any sense in looking for the poetry of living outside life itself?

Eugenio had never lived. He had been like a dead man walking among the living.

The most important day of my life was the one when I remembered all my mistakes and found that the time had come to look for a new way to be useful to other people, to give a new direction to my dealings with men. What had I done, more than satisfy my own desires, my own egotism? Should I be considered good simply because I did not rob, because I did not kill, because I did not commit assault? Goodness should not be a passive virtue. On the day that I found God I found peace, and at the same time I realized that in a way there would never be any peace for me again. I discovered that inner peace is won only at the expense of outward peace. I had to do something for other people. The world is full of suffering, of calls for help. What had I done up to that time to lessen that suffering, to answer those calls? All around me I saw unhappy people who were waiting for nothing more than one supporting hand to save them. And God had given me two hands!

I thought of all this one night when I could not sleep. When day came I felt that I too had been born again. I was a different person.

Eugenio got up and went to open the window. The sky was growing light.

Chapter 16

As he was about to leave the house, Anamaria caught the tail of his coat.

"Why you goin' away, Daddy? Why you goin' away?"

She stood on the tips of her toes, her head tilted back, her eyes very wide and serious, her lips pursed, and one hand opened, palm upward. Her little body was one animated question mark.

Eugenio squatted on his heels and took her into his arms.

"Daddy has to go to work."

"Why you has to go to work, Daddy?" Her fat, dimpled little hands clung to his cheeks.

"You stay here and be real quiet with Dona Frieda, and Daddy'll be right back. Look—I'll bring you a dolly. Would you like that?"

She nodded her head slowly three times. Her face was still perfectly serious. He looked at her for a long time without speaking.

"Daddy—where's Mommy?"

"Do you want me to bring you a doll-baby or a doggy?" His voice was guarded.

"I want Mommy."

"Mommy's coming right away."

"Where did she go?"

"She went for a walk."

"Why didn't she take me?"

"Little girls should stay at home and be very quiet."

He pressed her against his breast and kissed her hair, her forehead, and her hands. Then he stood up.

"Daddy's coming back soon. All right?"

He went down into the garden. As he closed the gate, he turned and saw Anamaria standing in the doorway, waving to him.

"Goodbye, my little girl!"

Suddenly, as if she had just remembered something, she called to him:

"Daddy, why don't you come sleep with us?"

All the way from the Falks' house to the heart of the city, the childish voice followed Eugenio. *Daddy, why don't you come sleep with us?*

The sun was bright that morning, and the sky was a fresh, pure blue. It's today or never, he told himself. *Today or never, today or never . . .*

Looking up, he saw the immense hulk of the Mammoth looming over the roofs of the city. He paused, as he always did, to stare at it. The sight of the great building caused an odd flicker of terror in his heart.

Eugenio walked on, thinking of Isabel. Her telephone calls were insistent now, and he saw that it was going to be difficult to be rid of her. It was odd how, suddenly, things were changing. More than ever before he realized the horrible gratuitousness of his relationship with her. He was a traitor to Filipe, to Dora, to Olivia, and to himself. He must finish everything once and for all.

When he arrived home, he found Eunice reading in the living room.

"Good evening."

"Good evening." She did not look up from her book.

Eugenio stopped in front of his wife. He had feared this moment, and now he found himself as cool and composed as if he were about to perform an operation. Before putting on his mask and gloves he was always gripped with fear; his hands would tremble, his heart would pound, his throat would be dry, his stomach nauseated. From the moment he took up the bistoury, however, he began to feel the return of his calm. It was a painful calm, through which he could discern his tensed nerves, ready at any moment to snap and fall slack.

He looked at Eunice and tried to vanquish the humility which she deliberately or inadvertently caused him to feel in her presence.

"What is it?" she asked indifferently.

His heart sank, and for a fraction of a second he seemed ready to weaken. Firmly, he stifled the feeling. Hundreds of times he had thought of what he would say when this moment should arrive, had prepared the speech and collected his arguments. Now he did not know how to begin.

"There's a very important subject I want to discuss with you, Eunice. When may I see you about it?" Instantly he was aware of the cowardice in his involuntary attempt to postpone the ordeal.

"We can talk now, can't we?" She closed her book, first marking with exquisite care the page she had been reading.

At a loss for something to do with his hands, Eugenio shoved them into his coat pockets.

"Eunice," he began uncertainly. He stopped. Then, suddenly, he was surprised to hear himself saying things about which he had not thought before.

"It seems incredible that after more than three years of married life you and I feel no intimacy, no frankness with each other—"

"You think I'm to blame for that?"

He shook his head. "The fault is all mine. I should have known that oil and water can't mix. I should have understood that you—well, that it was a mistake, this—this marriage."

"The realization seems to have come a little late," she said, shrugging her shoulders and reopening the book.

"No, Eunice—no, it's not too late. I want to tell you something I should have had the courage to tell you long ago. I have never felt any more than an intruder in this house."

"That's your own fault."

"Why do you say that?"

"Instead of eyes in your head, Eugenio, you seem to have two convex, or concave—I don't know what they are! —two mirrors that distort everything they reflect. You never see people as they really are. You never really understand the things they say to you. That's your everlasting inferiority complex!"

He was disarmed. Things had taken an unexpected turn, and he was losing ground. He retaliated, but without any real impetus.

"And *you* can never see anything except through the 'scientific method'—through your cursed psychoanalysis! You should talk about the way *I* look at things! You have two books in those eyesockets of yours, Eunice—a thousand books!"

His wife smiled. She took a cigarette from a chromium box which stood on a table near the sofa. As she lit the cigarette, Eugenio could see that her fingers shook a little.

"I tried hard to cure you, Eugenio. I thought of everything. I even resorted to trying to humiliate you. It didn't help." She shrugged. "I admit that I failed."

Eugenio swung one leg nervously.

"About all you can do now is throw the dead guinea pig away—isn't that it? Well, what's preventing you? Pity?"

Their eyes met briefly, and for an instant they stared at each other without blinking. Eugenio was the first to look away. He sat down, because he had to do or say something.

"Pity, rubbish! You always have the idea that people want to make a fool of you, that they want to humiliate you deliberately. You come to me now, for instance, like a sacrificed lamb, like a martyr. As if *you* were the only hurt person in this whole unpleasant affair!" The cigarette burned, forgotten, between her fingers. "You forget, of course, that I too am a creature of flesh and blood. There is a limit to my patience, also, and I believe I too have a right to a little peace and—and happiness. Do you think it wasn't difficult for me to bear your suspicious moods, your depressions, your—your exaggerated sensitivity?" She seemed to be inebriated by her own words. "You were never more than a misanthrope, Eugenio, a killjoy, a—an egotist!"

He listened to her silently, avoiding her eyes. At last she seemed to have regained control of her emotion; lifting the cigarette to her lips, she added, more calmly: "If I seem to have exalted myself, it is your fault. You think I'm not human. Perhaps the trouble with me is that I take this thing called 'good breeding' too seriously. There are certain indelicate sentiments that a well bred person is careful to avoid. It is a matter of education—a feeling which, if not inherited, is acquired through association with cultured people. I don't know if you understand me—"

Eugenio felt her last words like a whiplash.

"I understand perfectly, Eunice. You and I have nothing in common. You are a lady. You are well bred and refined. I am an ordinary man."

She shrugged again and looked down at her book, but he knew that she was not seeing the words printed on the page.

"You may interpret what I have just said any way you like," she said at last. "But there is one thing you can be sure of: it was you who forced me to say it."

He stood up. He felt strangely relieved. Now he could tell her everything.

"Good. That makes it easier for me to make my confession to you."

"Oh? There is still a confession to be made?"

"There is," he said sharply, almost angrily. "It's that I was enough of a heel to marry you without being in love with you—just because of your money."

Tiny, vertical lines sprang up in Eunice's brow; her eyes narrowed, and her lips twitched nervously.

232

"I was poor, and I hated poverty. This marriage—" The words stuck in his throat. "This marriage was an opportunity for me to get ahead in my career, for—"

He stopped. His collar was choking him. Eunice bit her lips. Her book had slid, unnoticed, from her knees. The silence between them was electric.

"Do you think you are telling me something I don't already know?" she said finally. "Do you think you can hurt my pride with this—this—what you call a 'confession'?" Her smile was contemptuous. She gathered up the fallen book and placed her cigarette in the ashtray. "Now —now let me tell you why I married you. I did it half to satisfy a whim—and half out of plain, unadulterated pity. And it was also out of pity that I tried to cure you of your very unfortunate sense of inferiority. It was an act of charity, pure and simple. You must admit that the job of playing husband to a rich girl was certainly more advantageous to you than that of being a doctor in the city ambulance squad. I felt quite pious for having given you such a splendid opportunity!"

She smiled, victorious.

"Wait!" said Eugenio. "Wait! There is something else." He flushed. "There has been another woman—"

"Oh!" She laughed sarcastically. "There is *always* 'another woman'! *Every* man has 'another woman'—every little store clerk!"

"—a woman who made me see the terrible mistake I had made—who gave me courage to correct it and make plans for a decenter life."

"Fiddlesticks!"

"It's the truth. She died two weeks ago. But I am only beginning to live now."

Soberly, Eunice searched his face.

233

"I have a child by her."

"A child?"

He sat down again. He fell limply, heavily into the chair, as if he had arrived at the limit of his endurance. The silence was unbearable. Eunice toyed with her book.

Suddenly he was surprised to hear her whisper, as if she were speaking to herself:

"The lamentable part of it is that the two of us should have come to this." Her cheeks twitched nervously.

Gently, almost like a man dictating a will from his deathbed, Eugenio spoke.

"I'm leaving today, Eunice. I'll arrange the details later with your father. I'm taking only what belongs to me—my personal things. I'd like you to bring suit for the divorce. It would look better for you to do it. You can allege incompatibility or anything you like."

He rose and left the room.

Chapter 17

When Eugenio had finished telling his story, Dr. Seixas merely stroked his coarse, heavy beard and stared at his friend with his childlike blue eyes.

"Pretty good bedtime story," he observed dryly, after several moments.

"And the queerest part of it is that now, even to me, everything seems like just that—a kind of fairy tale. I don't think I'll ever know how I had the nerve to leave that house."

Seixas left the chair where he had been sitting in Eugenio's new office—two of the cheaper rooms in a modest building.

"You'll need plenty of nerve from now on."

He began to pace back and forth across the room, examining the pictures on the wall, pausing a moment before a glass case in which surgical instruments were arranged.

"You don't think I am wrong, do you?" Eugenio asked suddenly.

The old doctor shrugged his shoulders. He did not turn around.

"You're thirty-one years old. You ought to know what you're doing."

Eugenio was a little disappointed. He considered Dr. Seixas as a kind of ally, and had counted on the old man's enthusiastic applause and encouragement, if only in the form of good-humored ribbing. Satan himself, thought Eugenio, might not understand that funny old toad!

"There was no other way it could have turned out—"

"Of course! Of course!" Seixas was impatient. "I'm not saying it could have. You're young. Me, I'm getting along in years. They say the damnedest heretics, when they die, make up with the Church. Maybe I'm already fixing to worship the golden calf and sell my soul for thirty pieces of silver." He gave a short, rasping laugh. "But who in hell would ever want to buy this bunged-up old soul of mine?"

He lit a cigarette. His eyes were pensive.

"Genoca, you'll find out money is pretty damned important in this life. Sometimes I think I've been a jackass, living the way I always have—not so much for my own sake because, after all, everyone has a right to do as he damned pleases with the carcass God gave him. But any time now I'm liable to kick off. So what? Nothing very valuable lost to the world. But what about my old woman and my daughter? I never could keep up any insurance, and what I did manage to keep up for a while finally went the way of all the rest. Savings? Don't even mention savings to me! Yes, Seu Genoca, money is pretty blamed important!"

Something froze inside Eugenio. He felt empty and helpless. It was as though he had just witnessed the fall of an ancient, beloved idol.

"And if you had it to do over again?" he asked. "Would you have the courage to do it differently—to live some other way?"

Seixas was putting on his hat. "How should I know! I've got to be going. Be happy."

"Come around again, doctor."

"Oh, I'll be around, all right. Tomorrow I'm sending you one of these fellows that haven't even got a hole to curl up and die in. Just so you'll be getting used to them." At the door he turned, his hand on the knob. "The high priesthood of medicine," he exclaimed, "the great high priesthood!" He laughed shortly. "Priesthood, my eye! It may be for a bare dozen lunatics like that stupid, sentimental friend of yours. Give me a light."

Eugenio hastened to give him the box of matches. After Seixas had relighted his cigarette, he went on:

"For lots of men the medical profession isn't anything more than a sales counter. All that matters is the money that goes over the counter. Didn't you read in the paper the other day? A bunch of doctors in some city in the United States got together and pretended to operate on a millionaire widow. They cooked up some fancy ailment, plunked the poor beggar onto an operating table, opened up her belly, and shut it again without touching a gut.

Then bingo! The woman died. The bill came to half a million or something like it. Gangsters! All because of money." He sucked his homemade straw cigarette. "Seu Eugenio, remember what I tell you. Money's a disgusting thing, and a decent guy's no slave to it."

He opened the door and slammed it behind him like a clap of thunder.

The office was crowded that afternoon. The majority of his patients, Eugenio reflected as he took notes for the file cabinet he was organizing, were store clerks, civil employees, poor students, and prostitutes. Almost invariably, they entered the office timidly and were able to tell their stories only with great difficulty; or, like the mother who came to him with a child that had swallowed a pin, they would break into an interminable, nervous torrent of explanations.

He was surprised to find himself taking more than a mere professional interest in his patients, to learn that he was genuinely concerned for their welfare. It was pleasant to have someone come to him for assistance, to know that somone had need of his services. The hours of that afternoon flew by almost unnoticed, and it was twilight when the last patient left. He was a store clerk who suffered stomach pains and had an almost hysterical dread of cancer.

"Then it isn't—what I thought it was, doctor?"

"You needn't worry." Eugenio felt as if he were master of the destiny of all creatures. "Your case is not at all serious. Just remember to come back here for your injections. They won't cost you anything."

"Thank you—thank you, doctor. May God in heaven bless you!"

At seven o'clock he left the office. He felt clean inside, and a curious new freedom seemed to stir in his breast. What strong and varied emotions he had experienced in the ten days of his new life! It had been hard to rid himself of the chains which bound him to the old life. He had had had a difficult session with his father-in-law.

Old Vicente Cintra had come to him with persuasive arguments. If they would just let things ride for a while as they were and wait—say, a year? Time was often the cure prescribed for ills of this nature . . . Or mightn't it be a good idea for the young couple to take a trip to Buenos Aires, or maybe to Europe? This business of a divorce in the prejudiced, bourgeois world we live in . . . "Think it over, Eugenio—you're a sensible young man."

"It's no use," Eugenio told him. "I've made up my mind."

Defeated, Cintra limited himself to a polite, resigned shrug and wave of the hand; he was a gentleman through and through. All that remained now was to discuss the details of the separation. A lawyer would take care of the friendly divorce, and the young people's immediate circle of friends would be notified discreetly. Incompatibility.

Eugenio made it clear that he would take with him only what was strictly his own—clothes, objects of personal use, books. He would keep only what money he had earned professionally. He would leave the automobile and his responsibilities at the factory. From the latter he did not want a cent.

When he heard this last condition, Cintra could not contain his amazement: "But you must be absolutely insane!"

Now Eugenio was walking along the crowded sidewalks toward his room. Absolutely insane, indeed! He had never

238

been so sane in all his life. How clearly he was beginning to see! What undreamed-of perspectives he was discovering! He did not expect his new life to be without its trials; he looked ahead to bitter, difficult days. But what did it matter? Anything that might happen to him would be nothing, compared with all that Olivia had suffered for his sake, compared with the obscure, sad life of his father, the uncomplaining sacrifices of his mother.

As he walked, he looked with strange pleasure at the faces of the people he passed. They must all have dramas of their own—problems both moral and material, joys great and small. They were people like himself. They were living!

"Life begins every day" was the phrase which echoed again and again through his mind as he walked from the office to his home.

Eugenio took his meals with the Falks.

Dona Frieda was a tall, heavy woman with graying blond hair, gray eyes, and a crooked nose. She had, as Dr. Seixas put it, the look of a "retired Valkyrie." When Olivia was still in her fifth year of medicine, Dona Frieda had become seriously ill, and Olivia had taken care of her zealously. By the time the big German woman recovered, she had fallen in love with the girl. She had insisted on taking her into her home and had soon come to consider her a member of the family. She had given Olivia rooms of her own and complete freedom to come and go as she pleased.

Hans Falk was the perfect prototype of the fine old German exploited by caricature. Lover of his pipe, his sausage, and his beer, he was fat, with a shiny bald head. The nape of his neck was always clean-shaven and very red, and his somnolent eyes had a playful twinkle. He had been born in Munich and had come to Brazil at the age of twenty-five. Now he was fifty-five, and often at night as he smoked the long pottery pipe decorated with scenes of Bavaria, he would sigh for the good old days of the *Vaterland,* for the old Germany that was so different from the Third Reich, of which he read somber things in the newspapers.

The Falks' dining room was simply furnished and tidy, and it had a warm air of domesticity. A number of large, glazed clay mugs with colored figures and symbolical inscriptions were displayed in a walnut cupboard. On the walls were several lithographs of German cities cut from old magazines and framed by Hans himself, a portrait of Bismarck and another of Hindenburg. The window curtains were made of cotton flour sacks with tiny, yellow flowers. They were also the work of Hans, who, whenever someone commented on them, would make a dissertation on economy in the home, in support of the thesis, "Necessity is the mother of Invention."

Old Hans was melancholy that night. He had just returned from his club, where he had had a violent argument with a compatriot of Nazi sympathies.

"The devil!" he exclaimed. "So a fella can't be let alone even when he's outside Germany! What have I got to do with Hitler?"

"And why do you go to the club?" asked his wife.

Hans bent across his plate and speared a sausage with his fork. Eugenio looked at Anamaria, who sat opposite him at the table, a bib around her neck. She was pounding her spoon against her plate, chanting:

"I want a wienie! I want a wienie!" She was pointing at the plate of sausages.

"Little girls can't eat wienies," Dona Frieda admonished her. "Come, eat your potato soup like a good girl."

Eugenio looked sadly at the fourth place at the table, the place which had been Olivia's. Her plate was still there, with her silver, her glass, and the napkin on which was embroidered the initial O. Dona Frieda always said: "Olivia's place must stay. It makes it seem like she was still with us."

If only Olivia were still with them, their happiness would be complete. It would be easier for him to go on with his new work; Anamaria would have her "Mommy;" all of life would be brighter and more smiling.

Dinner over, Hans retired to the rocking chair, which he himself had made, and lit his pipe. The maid began to take the dishes from the table. Dona Frieda gave Anamaria a picture book.

Eugenio went into the living room that had been Olivia's. Now it belonged to him. Everything in it was exactly as it had been when she was alive.

But could one say that Olivia was really dead? Eugenio felt that she lived in the very words he spoke, and in Anamaria's eyes. He felt her presence in the longing which the Falks evinced for the departed member of their household, in the aspect and fragrance of this room. She lived, above all, in the letters she had left him.

Yes, in a certain way Olivia was alive. The memory of her accompanied him everywhere.

He was distressed, however, to find that this subjective, spiritual manner of existence did not suffice for him. Was he, perhaps, too grossly materialistic? There were moments —such as this one of quiet and solitude—when he longed to have Olivia close beside him, to touch her with his hand and feel her skin against his own, to breathe the perfume of her hair, to hear the deep, resonant tones of her voice. His hours of solitude were his hours of greatest danger. In the morning there were the sun and his patients' calls, the sounds of the house and the street. These were things to occupy his mind. In the afternoon there was the office, with its endless file of patients and the surprises which they brought him. There was also the strange, new pleasure he was beginning to feel as he met life for the first time and engaged in battle in the open.

But at night, in the quiet of his room, he dreaded the return of his old fear. Then he would think apprehensively of the future and would recall the comfort and luxury of his old life.

He sat down on the sofa. He stroked the upholstery in a vague, physical desire for feminine companionship. In the minutes which went by, he thought of Eunice, of Filipe, of Isabel, of others he had known when he had been "old Cintra's son-in-law." Life in that other world had not ceased when he had left it. It was still flowing along pleasantly, easily, free of annoying jolts and friction. If only God had not given him a conscience!

God. Was there really a God? Perhaps there was, and one day He would reveal Himself with the gift of eternal peace, of perfect detachment from things material.

"Genoca!" That was Dona Frieda's voice. Her efforts to be more familiar with her guest were touching. "Anamaria says she won't go to sleep without her Daddy."

Eugenio entered the Falks' bedroom. Anamaria was lying in the large double bed, nursing a pacifier. She had acquired the habit of going to sleep holding her father's ear. When she saw him, she began to whimper.

"Daddy, I want your ear."

He lay down beside her, being careful not to let his

shoes soil the bedclothes. The room was in shadow. Anamaria seized the lobe of her father's ear.

"Daddy's going to buy you a little donkey."

"Why, Daddy?"

"So you can go to sleep holding his ear."

"I don't need a little donkey, Daddy. I have your ear."

He felt the child's warm breath on his cheek. Anamaria
smelled of milk and bananas.

"Da'y?" she said winking. When she said "Da'y" in
that sleepy, dragging voice, instead of "Daddy," Eugenio
knew the sandman had already begun to fill her eyes with
sand.

"What is it, sweetheart?"

"Tell me a story."

"Oh! Daddy doesn't know any. It's time for his little
girl to go to sleep."

"Tell me, Daddy—tell me about the piggy."

"All right. Once there was a piggy." Eugenio was
whispering softly. "The piggy went into the woods." He
stopped, seeing that her eyes were closed.

"And then what happened?" she mumbled drowsily.

"Ah! In the woods there was a doggy. The doggy bit
the little pig." There was another pause. It was the story
he told every night. He never finished it, for sleep would
invariably lure away his small audience too soon, with
promises, no doubt, of the more attractive stories of dream-
land. "And the cow . . ."

"The cow went *Moo-oo*," his daughter continued hope-
fully.

There was a silence. The minutes dragged by, and
Eugenio's thoughts began to wander. When he had made
certain that Anamaria was asleep, he got up cautiously
and tiptoed from the room.

That night he read through Olivia's letters again:

Have you ever thought, Eugenio, of the great social importance of doctors, and of the enormous work that remains to be done in the field of hygiene?

Sometimes I ask myself whether each one of us, in spending too much time on himself, isn't specifically to blame for a share of the misery and grief in the world. I am consoled a little by the thought that some day, not too far in the future, one of us will begin serious work.

In a letter dated May 5th he found the following passage:

When I first learned to know you, Eugenio, I saw that you were a person who loved life but did not live it completely, who had the potentialities of a wonderful human being but was not yet truly human. From what you told me about yourself, I felt that you had been humiliated, that your heart had been disfigured and warped, and that you were used to looking at life suspiciously and even resentfully.

In a letter which she had written early in the winter, Olivia spoke of Cintra, of his monopolies and other enterprises:

Life the way some men live it is not human, Genoca. Running after money for its own sake is a way of escaping from life. And one who looks for peace and happiness through money is something like the monkey in the children's story. They gave him a little milk in a pan, and in order to keep up the illusion that it was always full, the monkey boiled the milk till it foamed up and overflowed.

244

Of course, there are rich people who know how to put their money to good uses. And praise of poverty is stupid. The world was made for everyone to have a decent place in it. Nothing can better illustrate the egotistical nature of some people than the fable of the ant and the grasshopper. The grasshopper, it seems, had read the Sermon on the Mount and wanted to imitate the lilies of the field. She spent the whole summer singing, while the ants worked and worked. The ants were like so many people, including your friend Filipe Lobo, who live blindly, thinking only of money, forgetting they are mortal, that they might be enjoying such things as the sun and the fields and the grasshoppers. The ideal world, my darling, would be one in which grasshoppers and ants lived intelligently, in harmony.

These are things I have thought about and never wanted to tell you, because I hoped you would come to feel them for yourself. The only worth-while experiences are the ones we live through ourselves. All this may be just a dream of mine. But then, my darling, dreaming is human, too.

Eugenio folded the letters carefully and put them away. He stood up. It was only nine o'clock.

Just as he was about to remove a book from the bookcase, the telephone rang. It was an urgent call. He seized his hat and hurried into the street.

Chapter 18

"I don't understand, Eugenio, I don't understand. I've gone almost crazy thinking about it."

Isabel's eyes were searching his face anxiously. The wrinkle between her brows denoted the effort she was making to solve the enigma.

"When Filipe told me you two were going to get a divorce, I nearly fainted. I think I must have shown it. I thought they had discovered that we—that— I don't know what went through my mind when he told me!"

Eugenio was staring intently into the glass of port wine he had ordered only so that they might occupy the table for a few minutes. They were in the rear of a tearoom, which at that hour was almost deserted. He had been reluctant to make the appointment, but Isabel had been so insistent, had telephoned so repeatedly that he decided it would be best to see her and end the affair neatly. For a long time he stared, unmoving, into the wineglass.

"Tell me what's wrong," she pleaded.

He looked up. Her insistence did not make him angry. He was very sorry for Isabel. Through his pity he looked with loathing on the other Eugenio, who had been so cynical, vain, and sensual as to become the lover of his friend's wife.

"There's nothing wrong, Isabel. It's only that I couldn't see before, and now I can. You and I can't go on like that any more. It's horrible."

"All I want to know is why—why now, after all this time, you've so suddenly come to see it's 'horrible.' Before, you never—"

"I said I was blind before."

She shook her head nervously. Her eyes had the strain-

246

ing, troubled look of one who tries vainly to see through a mist.

"But I still can't understand. I just can't understand. For so many months we . . . And only now . . . Please, Eugenio, tell me the truth!"

"I told you the truth."

Isabel's hand shook as she lifted her glass.

"Then why did you and Eunice separate?" Her head was thrust forward almost aggressively, like a bridge player showing his trump card. Eugenio looked away.

"That—that's a long story."

"You're not being sincere with me."

His tone changed abruptly. "Think of your husband, Isabel. Think of your daughter."

"So that's what you say now?"

"No. . . . I only have the courage to think of it now."

"Why don't you have the courage to tell me you're tired of me?" Her voice was guarded, almost hoarse. "Don't think I'm here to ask you to come back—I have more pride than that. All I want is an explanation, a—"

She stopped suddenly, and her eyes took on a liquid brilliance. When he lifted the glass once more to his lips, Eugenio felt exactly as if he were watching a whimpering child forced by the threats of an older person to swallow a bitter medicine.

"Look, Isabel," he said gently. "Stop and think a minute. Don't you see we have made a mistake and there's still time to avoid the serious consequences? Your daughter is young. It would be rather painful for her if—"

He hesitated before formulating the disagreeable hypothesis. He wanted to speak also of Filipe, to remind Isabel that she might still win back his affection. But he foresaw how ludicrous his words would sound. They

247

would be like a sermon. In the light of all that had happened, they would be grotesque.

He lit a cigarette. Isabel was sipping her cocktail, her eyes fixed with a stunned expression on her lover's face. What a helpless creature she was! She had no ideals, nothing to believe in. Her education had been mediocre, and he knew that she never opened a book. She was content merely with leafing through magazines; she was particularly fond of fashion magazines.

Filipe had told him about his engagement to Isabel. Their courtship had been like a storybook idyl. During the first years of their marriage, they had struggled side by side. He had been poor and ambitious, had just received his degree in engineering and was trying to get a foothold in the world. Together they had known bitter, trying hours. Filipe had worked tirelessly, had made slow progress and risen gradually. Better days had come at last. Dora was born, and they had celebrated their tenth anniversary in a comfortable home, with a brilliant party attended by many guests. As Filipe prospered socially and financially, the relations of the Lobos in the higher social brackets of the city had broadened. They had made a trip to the United States, and Filipe had returned to Brazil full of plans, obsessed with American manias for rationalization and organization, intoxicated with the colossal. His name and his picture had appeared in the newspapers of Porto Alegre, in interviews in which he had revealed his impressions of North America and had formulated grandiose schemes for projects he meant to undertake in Brazil.

Meanwhile, Madame Lobo gave receptions and took part in the activities of various charitable organizations. Madame Lobo was a lady of the city's first society, and Dr. Lobo was going to build the tallest skyscraper in South

America. Dr. Lobo worked fifteen hours a day. He was vastly ambitious, and he had no time to enjoy life. He forgot his wife and daughter; the Mammoth demanded all his paternal attentions. The task of erecting those thirty stories was almost like constructing an empire. Madame Lobo watched the approach of her fortieth birthday with fearful eyes. Her teas and garden parties and works of charity could not appease the indefinable longing which tormented her. . . . Then one day, in the Cintra home, a lingering pressure of hands, a warmer, longer exchange of glances . . .

Eugenio thought of all these things now as he looked at Isabel. How well he understood! With what amazing clarity he saw now!

Isabel set her glass on the table. With some reluctance, she asked:

"Then—then there really isn't someone else?"

For a fraction of a second Eugenio hesitated. To tell her the truth would only complicate the situation, hurt her more. She would not believe him; for her, Olivia could be no more than a myth. He shook his head.

"You can be sure there isn't."

"Then—it's all over."

"It's all over."

There was a moment of silence. Then Isabel rose. Eugenio, too, stood up. They looked at each other briefly across the table.

"Goodbye."

They shook hands.

"Goodbye."

Eugenio paid for the drinks and left the tearoom. At the first news stand he found he bought a paper and opened it to the want-ad section. There he found the announcement for which he had paid: "Wanted: Information concerning the whereabouts of Ernesto Fontes." A description of Ernesto followed. "Anyone having such information, please notify Dr. Eugenio Fontes, Rua Da Paz, 675. Reward." He had had the same announcement read over the local radio stations. He had to find Ernesto.

He looked at his watch. It was two o'clock, and he was due at the office. He boarded a trolley. He could not forget the expression on Isabel's face. She suffered, no doubt, from wounded pride, from having been abandoned, perhaps—who knew?—from regret. He had been the cause of all that!

The waiting room of his office was already filled. Eugenio took off his jacket and shrugged into his starched white coat. He washed his hands and told his receptionist to send in the patients in order. The long file began.

That afternoon it was particularly dreary. There were three men and two women with venereal diseases. Their faces were yellow and worn, marred by the consciousness of their shame. All were young, except one man, who seemed to be about fifty. Painfully embarrassed, he confessed that he was married and had several children; he didn't know how it was possible that—that . . .

While he treated them medically and cheered them with reassuring words, Eugenio thought of the frailty, the perishableness of human flesh. The smell of iodoform filled the air, and as it entered his nostrils it brought him a sense of disease and irremediable sordidness. That night he would need stars, many stars, to convince him there was still hope in the world.

His fifth patient was a thin girl with frightened eyes. She was brought into the office by her father, a man named

Anaurelino Mendonça, who demanded to know whether she was still a virgin. He treated her brutally and swore at her. She was crying.

"You're not helping the situation by treating her like that," Eugenio told him.

"But she's no account, doctor. She didn't have to act like a tramp, did she? like an ordinary prostitute? She had everything she needed at home, doctor. There wasn't anything she didn't have. She's enough to rile a priest, this no-account little—little—! I wish she'd died when she had typhus!"

The examination was brief. Eugenio looked for a long time at the girl's father, dreading to tell him.

"Well? Is she, or isn't she?"

Eugenio shook his head. "She isn't. It happened recently."

The girl burst into violent weeping. The father, his face very red, stammered, "Why, that brazen little—" His rage choked him.

Eugenio felt sorry for the girl. "How old is she?"

Neither was able to reply. The girl sobbed heart-brokenly, covering her face with her hands. Her father snorted, eyeing her darkly. After a moment, he regained control of himself.

"I'd like a certificate, doctor."

Eugenio sat down at his desk. He asked the girl's name and her age.

"Aurora," said her father. "She's fifteen. Aurora Mendonça. I'm ashamed to have her even use my name, that no-good, trashy little—that little hussy!" He too began to weep, and as the tears slithered down his sunburned face, he wiped them away with his coat sleeve.

Aurora, thought Eugenio. Dawn. Such a fresh, lovely

name—the early morning, a rose-colored sky . . . He thought of Anamaria. One day she too would be a woman. A chill ran through his body.

He rose and handed the man his certfiicate.

"What'll I do, doctor?" the man asked humbly, almost pleadingly. "What'll I do with this girl at home in the state she's in?" He sighed deeply. A tear hung trembling, ready to drop, from the end of his nose. "He's married, that low-down— If I ever get hold of him, I'll—I'll kill him!" His thick fingers shook as they gripped the certificate.

"Will you do something for me?" Eugenio asked.

The man nodded.

"Don't mistreat your daughter. Think, think now what I tell you. She's only fifteen years old. She's only a child."

"A *child?* A child does things like that?" The man stared incredulously. "And the little bitch has the nerve to say he didn't force her!"

Eugenio shrugged. "However it happened, that's not important now. If you're rough with her, you'll only make things worse. We all make mistakes. And remember—you may be just as much to blame for what happened as she is—maybe even more."

"*Me? Me* more to blame than this—this little— You tell me that?" The man's eyes revealed both astonishment and disgust.

When his last patient had gone, Eugenio opened the window and breathed deeply of the cool afternoon air. He was happy, for at last he had begun to take life by the shoulders and kiss its face. His embrace was a sacrifice: he offered it still with repugnance, with inward revulsion and a weakness that came from his fear. There was in it, however, a strange element of fascination, and he knew that one day he would bestow it even with love, with love for this same life, which, in spite of its incoherence, sordidness, and brutality—or perhaps because of them—was beautiful.

By the time he arrived home that night, he had begun to notice his fatigue, to feel somewhat depressed. He took a leisurely bath and changed his clothes before he went into the dining room.

When he bent to kiss Anamaria, he was received with a complaint:

"You didn't bring my vi'lin, Daddy!"

Swiftly he remembered that, the night before, she had requested a violin like the one she had seen a man playing in the street.

"Oh! . . . Daddy forgot."

The little girl's lips drew together in disappointment, and a cloud of sadness crossed her small face.

Dona Frieda, to whom Eugenio was no longer a guest, began just then to scold her husband. Hans had spent the afternoon drinking and gambling with friends as Bohemian as himself. A fine thing! While he loafed, his competitors were in the streets, taking advantage of good opportunities, doing business. Not only that, but at the end of the month there would be a bill from the tavern! Outrageous! In the midst of her harangue, which was becoming more and more spirited, Dona Frieda began to speak German. Every now and then Hans would look up from his plate and wink at Eugenio.

Anamaria was gazing disconsolately at her father, muttering, "My vi'lin—my vi'lin . . ."

Eugenio felt uncomfortable, for he was thinking of a night many years ago when he had sat at table, seeking to avoid his father's eyes. For a brief second he thought he saw in the face of his daughter poor Angelo's eyes, looking at him with the same humble appeal.

"My vi'lin—"

Dona Frieda left her husband in peace for a moment and turned to reproach Anamaria. "Be quiet now, or your Daddy'll be angry."

The little girl tilted her head to one side and looked at her father questioningly.

"Really, Daddy?"

Eugenio frowned and nodded solemnly. This time it was Olivia whom he saw mirrored in Anamaria's eyes; they seemed to shine with a warm, human light of tolerance. How strange it was, how disturbing, that the dead should revisit him so constantly!

"I don't need a vi'lin now, do I?" said Anamaria. "Daddy'll bring my vi'lin tomorrow."

Eugenio bent and kissed the tips of her small fingers.

About ten o'clock that night he was called to attend a patient in the lower part of the city. By twenty minutes of eleven he was on his way home again on foot. As he passed the Mammoth, he paused. It was amazing, the fascination which the big building had for him. It seemed to be linked intimately to his personal life, to his problems, to Olivia's letters. Each time he passed he stopped to look at it, and always he saw that Filipe's skyscraper was growing taller. He looked at it now, reaching up arrogantly toward the stars—lifted, he thought, not by the lyric desire to be near them, but by the proud intention to dominate them.

Eugenio raised the brim of his hat and tilted his head back to see the highest floor of the building. For a few moments he stood without moving, one hand in his pocket, the other holding his bag.

Suddenly, he heard a familiar voice speak his name.

"There's Dr. Eugenio!"

He looked around. On one of the benches in the square, directly opposite the Mammoth, sat Dora and Simão.

"I didn't see you," he said, as he walked toward them.

"We've been sitting here talking," Dora explained.

Without raising his head, Simão muttered, "Neither of us has said a word for the last half-hour."

Eugenio looked down at them and said nothing. The bench was sheltered by a tree, and the pattern of its leaves fell over Dora's neck in a moving lacework of shadow. She wore a white dress, and her tiny black straw hat, with its brim turned back, made her face seem touchingly childlike.

Simão sat with his head low, his hands folded, and his body inclined so that his arms rested on his thighs. He seemed to be staring at the tips of his shoes. His thoughts must be far away, Eugenio judged, for he knew the boy well. Doubtless, he was pondering not merely his own troubles, but those of his people as well, and those—who could say?—of all humanity.

"Why don't you sit down a little while, doctor?"

In Dora's voice Eugenio thought he caught a plea for assistance. He knew that her invitation was sincere; her eyes were beseeching.

"Well, I'm not sleepy," he said, taking off his hat and sitting down beside her. "I was just on my way home from seeing a patient." There was no reply. "A pretty serious case." His companions remained silent. Simão lit a cigarette and offered one to Eugenio.

"No, thank you."

The Mammoth resembled the thorax of a gigantic skeleton. Through its symmetrical concrete ribs Eugenio could see the stars. Trolley cars and automobiles passed in the street, but the number of pedestrians abroad at that hour was small.

"What's on your mind, Simão?" he inquired professionally. He could not refrain from applauding himself inwardly; his kindly words sounded, he thought, as if he sincerely wished to be of assistance.

Simão merely shrugged his shoulders. Dora, however, could not contain herself.

"At school today one of his professors said something against the Jews, and he left the class. There was a big fuss about it, and he may be suspended."

"I know the dean, Simão. If you want me to—"

The boy cut him off sharply. "What do I care if they kick me out? What earthly difference can it make if Simão Kantermann gets his degree in medicine or sells furniture on the installment plan? I don't care about myself. What hurts me is the unfairness of the way they hate Jews. We're people just like anybody else!"

His words, scarcely above a whisper, reverberated in Eugenio's mind as if the boy had screamed desperately.

"How can men be so blind, so cruel!" he murmured, shaking his head. Inside him a voice whispered, *You too were blind and cruel.*

Dora was toying with her black leather purse. Her eyes were fixed anxiously on Simão.

"A Jew is being born in Brazil this very minute," the boy said, "and already there has fallen on his head the curse of his people. Why? Why are we still Jews? We wouldn't still be Jews if the Christians didn't hate us. They hunt us down, they torture us . . . Yes, we have

256

a tradition! But it would have died centuries ago if they didn't hate us—hate us unreasonably—if we didn't always have to be defending ourselves. Defending ourselves! We never went out of our way to hurt anyone!"

He threw away his cigarette, straightened up, and looked at Eugenio. His face was long and handsome, with dark, somber eyes.

"History begins, full of my people's screams of agony. They were denied the right to a land of their own. Right down through the centuries they've had to live like hunted animals. They fed the fires of the Inquisition, they died under the sword of the Crusades and in the pogroms of Russia, Poland, and Rumania. I suppose you read about the concentration camps in Germany today? There you'll see thousands of Jews getting their reward for their sacrifices in the trenches of the World War. They were German soldiers then—they were defending the country that renounces them, that exiles them today. And, in spite of all that, we haven't learned yet to hate!"

Unmoving, the Mammoth seemed to be listening. Eugenio looked at a rainbow-colored star which shone directly above the last story of the building. A cool wind played in the foliage of the trees, making the shadows dance across Dora's face, arms, and breast.

"We're too meek for them—that's why we suffer! That's our great glory before God and our worst sin in men's eyes. We've given the world great writers, philosophers, politicians, and scientists, and no matter what they did for humanity, they were still Jews. Was that because they wanted to be? No. It was because the world wouldn't let them be anything else. The Christians hate us, yet we gave them their Christ of love and forgiveness. Forgiveness! Ha!" His dry laugh was like a sob.

Eugenio and Dora said nothing.

"We were a race of shepherds—that you can read in the Bible—and they turned us into an army of clever little merchants. Because they wouldn't let us own land! For two thousand years we have been exiled, despised, accused, ridiculed, and massacred. If we had been a weak people, we should have disappeared—or we should have taken to rooting in the slime like pigs. But no—we go on giving the world great scholars, philosophers, musicians, and writers! You hear lots of people say Jews are dangerous for the very reason that we breed so many superior men. Is it right, I ask you, is it decent, is it logical to want to destroy a people merely because it is intelligent?"

"Listen, Simão, your professor's prejudice is an isolated case. In Brazil, fortunately, there is no racial prejudice. Look, for instance, at the Negroes in Brazil. I think that you—"

"Do you think I'm not human enough and not Jew enough to feel in my own body and brain the suffering of the bodies and brains of the Jews in Germany and Rumania and Russia—and—and everywhere in the world?"

Dora gripped Simão's arm. "Don't talk like that! Dr. Eugenio is your friend!"

"Look at me, doctor," Simão went on, more calmly. "I'm not Orthodox. I don't support the old tradition. I consider myself as good a Brazilian as you. But sometimes I ask myself questions like this: whether the real reason that I renounced my parents' faith wasn't maybe that I was afraid—that I wanted to escape the humiliating mark of Jew . . . And whether, if I do go on being a Jew in my blood and bones, I shouldn't be a man anyway, a human being with the right to love and possess a woman of any faith or blood, to breathe this air and live like other people?

Those are the times I go into a kind of rage—the times when I want to be Jewish, fanatically Jewish, to face the hatred that persecutes my people. If I like to be with Christians, it's not because they're Christians, but because they are human beings, like me. But still, all the time, I'm haunted by the awful certainty that no matter what I do, no matter how I try, I'll never stop being a Jew, because they—because other people will never let me be anything else. Sooner or later I know they'll fling in my face the cursed name of Jew!"

Suddenly he was on his feet, facing Eugenio.

"And why should 'Jew' be a cursed name? Why should it be an insult, something to be ashamed of? They say we murdered Christ, but yes, the Christians burned Joan of Arc, their saint!"

"Don't talk so loudly," Dora pleaded.

"They say the capitalists that make the world miserable are Jews; but it so happens they're not Jews but just capitalists, which is a class without any race or nationality. They say we are antinationalists; but during the War thousands of Jewish soldiers gave their lifeblood in trenches under the flags of Russia and Germany and England! And while this 'race without a country' was being torn to bits on the battlefields, the capitalists—who kept the fire burning, selling arms and munitions to both sides—were partners among themselves and passed over all the frontiers and flags!"

"Incredible," murmured Engenio, and immediately he cursed his stupidity for having uttered so inexpressive, so useless a word.

Dora was watching Simão with eyes full of love, pity, and fear. The boy sat down again. It was a few minutes before he continued.

"This is called a rock," he said, kicking a flagstone in the sidewalk, "and over there is a house. A cat is a cat. And we are obliged always to be Jews, just so we can be humiliated and despised for it. The thing that hurts is the unfairness! But I feel proud when I see that through it all, in spite of everything, my people have kept themselves basically whole and pure. The day the Jew stops having a 'moral reason' for his existence, he'll lose his identity as a Jew. There aren't twenty million Jews in the world, and the other billions of human beings could easily have eliminated the 'cursed race' from the face of the earth, if it weren't for that 'moral reason.' "

" 'Love thy neighbor as thyself,' " Eugenio said lamely, wondering what Olivia would have said if she had been there.

"Oh, yes! Oh, yes indeed!" Simão interrupted him. "Confiscate thy neighbor's property and burn him to death! Do you think Christ would approve of the persecution of the Jews? Or can't Jews be considered 'neighbors' like other people?"

There was no answer. The three persons on the little bench stared up at the Mammoth in silence.

"What about you two?" said Eugenio, after a few minutes.

Dora shrugged her shoulders. Simão waved his hand in a hopeless gesture.

"No answer."

He looked at Dora passionately, wrathfully. "I don't know why I love her! She's no more than a beautiful piece of flesh. Her head is empty. Everything I've just said is no more than a fairy tale to Dora. She doesn't understand. She hasn't the slightest notion that the problem exists. To her, after all, Turks and Russians and Poles and Jews are all one big happy family, with no friction, no individual consciousness—"

He seized Dora's chin, and his eyes glittered. "But I love her!" He frowned, and his lips were a hard, straight line. "Like a madman. I know she belongs to another world, a world that's as different from mine as night from day. From the minute I discovered I loved her, I knew I was done for—that I'd never have any peace of mind again."

Again there was the heavy silence. The Mammoth was still listening. Above it, the stars shone purely.

"What do you intend to do?" Eugenio asked.

Simão shrugged. "Look at us. My parents are against our getting married because Dora isn't Jewish, and Dora's parents won't hear of me because I'm a Jew. We could go ahead and get married without their consent. That's easy to say, but where would we get money to live on? I haven't a cent, and even if I got a good job we'd never be happy, because Dora is used to luxury, to expensive dresses and a car and perfumes. And even if her father finally gave up and accepted me, what would happen? Sooner or later would come the inevitable—someone in Dora's world would throw the cursed name of 'Jew' in my face. Our children would be despised by both Jews and Christians. You see what a one-way street it is? And the saddest part of all is that I can't live without this girl." Again he looked at Dora with a strange expression.

Eugenio pitied them; but pity, he rejoiced, was not all he felt for Dora and Simão. He regarded them almost as he would a younger brother and sister; he loved them. He loved them because they were young and unhappy, because they were in trouble, and because he knew that, had she been in his place, Olivia would have loved them.

"It's unbelievable," he said, "that things apparently so small, obstacles apparently so easy to remove, sometimes have the power to ruin a life, or two lives, or a thousand."

Dora and Simão looked at each other tenderly. They seemed to have forgotten that he was there.

"Do you think it would help," asked Eugenio, "to talk with Filipe? I can't believe he wouldn't understand. After all, he used to be young, too. He fell in love and married."

Simão grimaced pessimistically.

"The great engineer Filipe Lobo understands only creatures that are made of stone and concrete!" He nodded in the direction of the Mammoth, and the three lapsed once more into silence. as they sat looking up at the huge building.

Chapter 19

There were, however, dark days in Eugenio's new life. Difficulties seemed to arise out of nowhere, and suddenly once again he would be stunned to find himself facing the other Eugenio, the vacillating jellyfish, the coward.

One morning he found himself alone at dawn, awaiting the arrival of death in a poor home in the outskirts of the city. The patient's heart was growing steadily weaker, and his breathing was almost imperceptible. Sleep made Eugenio's thought hazy, his body limp. He knew there was nothing more for him to do, but he could not leave the poor man to die alone. The minutes dragged by slowly; at four o'clock he gave the dying man an injection of morphine. Day was breaking, and the poor man was still alive, his eyes glazed, his face coldly impassive. One might have said the fine thread of life remaining in his skinny body had withdrawn to his small, dull eyes, which were beginning to take on a glassy brilliance. His wife watched Eugenio's every move, whimpering, "If we was jest rich, they'd save Manoel."

Eugenio felt as if his aching head were on fire. In desperation he went to the window and flung it open.

"Won't that be bad for him, doctor?"

Eugenio did not reply. On his tired cheeks he felt the cool breath of the morning wind. He looked at the lights of the city and thought of the room that had been his at the Cintra home. In other days he would have been sleeping peacefully at this hour; he would have awakened later to find his Packard waiting to take him to the factory to sign the papers his secretary would bring him; in the afternoon he would have had Isabel in his arms. On the Cintras' table there was fine crystal, exquisite wines, delectable foods . . .

He raised his hand to his forehead, recalling as he did so a phrase from one of Olivia's letters: "Goodness is not a passive virtue." How easy it was to do wrong, and how many hundreds of times easier it was to be indifferent! The cycle of life went on, and in the end everything resolved itself in death, silence, and defeat. Who could guarantee him that Olivia on the "other side" had found her God, and not merely void and decay?

His thoughts were interrupted by the woman's scream. "Doctor! He's rattling!" Eugenio ran to the patient's side and saw that death, at last, had come.

"Do something, doctor! Do something! For God's sake, save my man!"

The sick man was gasping for breath, his eyes were losing their luster, and from his half-opened mouth there issued a horrible rattling sound.

263

The woman lighted a candle and attempted to place it in her husband's hands. It fell and set the bedsheet on fire, and Eugenio hastened to stifle the growing flames with a blanket. The woman, who had thrown herself on the floor, was rolling from side to side, moaning:

"It's a sign, it's a sign! He goin' to hell! Oh, my God, my God . . . It's punishment!"

With difficulty Eugenio succeeded in giving her an injection of ether, and in a few seconds she lay still on the floor. When he rose to examine his patient, the man was dead.

He called in the neighbors and wrote out the death certificate. Then, saying he would return, he picked up his hat and bag and hurried from the house.

The following day he confided his doubts to Dr. Seixas.

"What I can't understand, and what I never asked Olivia, is why her God, if He is good and merciful, lets there be so much misery and suffering in the world. All it takes is some little, incidental thing to throw you off completely. That story I told you a little while ago, for instance. The woman went to put a candle in her husband's hand just as he was dying; the candle fell and set the bedclothes on fire. And there I was trying to put out the fire, while the poor devil died and his wife rolled on the floor screaming. It doesn't even sound true to me now when I tell it."

Seixas shrugged. From his lower lip there hung a burned-out cigarette stub.

"I gave up trying to figure it out long ago," he said. "The best thing to do is not to think too much. And don't ask questions. Why should you want to think and ask questions, anyway? When I get hurt, I do everything I can to keep from touching the sore spot. But you seem to be the kind of guy who likes to dig around in his sores . . ."

Their conversation shifted without further comment to talk of patients and doctors, to speculation about life and about God.

"There are some pretty funny things," mumbled Seixas as he held a match to a fresh cigarette. "Whenever we save a patient, they like to say, 'Next to God, doctor, I owe my life to you.' All right, so we don't count. I admit there's got to be somebody a damn sight bigger than we are to keep this rat-race going. But when a patient dies, why do they always forget about their God and blame us?" He snorted impatiently, turned, and left the room.

That day the newspapers announced the trip Eunice and her father were planning to make to Europe. They would go first to Rio de Janeiro, and would sail from there on board the *Neptunia*. According to the article, the well known industrialist was making the voyage for business and pleasure.

Eugenio folded the paper and began to think, somewhat dejectedly, about Eunice. He had in many ways brought only annoyance and difficulty into her life. Even if she should come to love someone else, she would always, in a certain way, be chained to him. Yes, as she herself had said, it was lamentable that things should have come to such a pass!

He was still thinking of Eunice as he walked to the office that afternoon. She was frivolous, snobbish, and sarcastic. But what, after all, could one expect of a girl who had been brought up by a widowed father who wished no more for her than to see her educated and admired? Actually, she could not be blamed for her shortcomings.

No one could be blamed for anything in this world; all people were blind. He thought of Dora and Simão, remembering that the evening before he had seen Isabel at a distance, passing in an automobile. His thoughts returned to Eunice, to the few pleasant memories he had of his wife. Their honeymoon had been strangely delightful; it had brought many exciting revelations. How they had deluded themselves in those days!

It was almost two o'clock when he passed the Mammoth. The builders were working frantically, and he paused an instant to watch them.

Suddenly a car drew alongside the curb, and Filipe Lobo jumped out.

"Man alive!" he exclaimed. "Where in the devil have you been hiding out?" He seized Eugenio's hand and pumped it vigorously.

The last time Eugenio had seen Filipe had been a few days after his break with Eunice, when the engineer had come to him, hoping to effect a reconciliation.

"Where are you heading for?"

"I was just on my way to the office."

Filipe took his arm. "The patients can wait. If they were in Sparta they'd be thrown down the mountain pass. Come on, let's go up to the top of the Mammoth. Have you been up yet? You haven't? Well, senhor, come and see a magnificent sight."

Eugenio allowed himself to be pulled along. They crossed the street and entered the front door of the Mammoth. Filipe dragged him into the freight elevator.

"I'm taking you up to the highest spot in the city!"

Inside the elevator, he scrutinized Eugenio from head to foot. "What the devil have you been doing with yourself?"

Eugenio made a vague gesture with his hand. "Oh, working a little."

Filipe lit a cigar and exhaled an enormous cloud of smoke. With mock seriousness, he caught at the lapel of Eugenio's coat.

"A man like you ought to be shoved off the top floor here and smashed to pieces on the sidewalk. You know what I mean, don't you?"

Eugenio nodded, smiling. He found it difficult to follow what Filipe was saying, for, as the car rose, he was beginning to feel dizzy. The square far below seemed to be part of a toy city. Trolley cars looked like crawling worms.

The wind was blowing strongly when they arrived at the top floor. Eugenio held fast to his hat brim.

"Come here." Filipe extended a hand to help him along a plank which stretched between two concrete beams.

Eugenio looked around dizzily. From this height they could see the whole city, the river with its tiny islands, and the mountains.

"Isn't it magnificent?" said Filipe.

Workmen were passing to and fro with wheelbarrows full of cement. They emptied the cement onto a network of narrow steel rods, which seemed to make up the symmetrical nervous system of the monster.

"How long will it take to finish this thing?" Eugenio asked.

"In ten months, at the most, we'll all be drinking champagne on the roof of the Mammoth," Filipe shouted, as if he wanted the wind to carry the news throughout the whole world.

Eugenio looked down at the city. It seemed very flat and quiet, cluttered with light and dark roofs, cut by streets, dotted with groves of trees and spots of sun and shadow, brilliantly illumined here and there by sudden, blinding flashes of sunlight. It was absurd, incomprehensible, moving. On the top of a little hill the cemetery shone whitely.

Eugenio trembled when Filipe squeezed his arm.

"Just look at that scene, man," said the engineer, extending his other arm in a sweeping arc. "What a feeling of victory you have up here!"

An airplane crossed the river, flying in the direction of the mountains.

"Just look at that plane and think of this skyscraper and all the other great buildings and everything else man has built here and in other parts of the world." He tightened his grip on Eugenio's arm. "You know, old man, if everyone thought the way you do, the world would still be a wilderness."

"It takes a little of everything to make a world," Eugenio retorted, recalling a favorite saying of one of his old teachers at Columbia Academy.

"Yes, of course. You mean there have to be doctors and builders, lawyers and shoemakers, tailors and poets. I agree with you. But I'm talking about the way we feel life. Do you remember that day when I tried to make you see what a crazy thing you had done?"

Eugenio nodded.

"I wanted you to open your eyes. You're young, you have a terrific life ahead of you, you could do wonderful things with old Cintra's money. Only a weak man cares what people say. And, after all, what are people, anyway? Look—down there are the people!" He pointed far below to the tiny, dim shapes moving about on the streets and sidewalks. "The people don't think. They have no will.

Words are words. Rock is rock. So! You came to me ranting like an idiot. You had no fire in you. You talked some kind of rot about blindness and lack of character. You said you had been dead and now you wanted to live. Now, I want you to take a look and tell me if you don't think this is life. Not so long ago there was a two-by-four colonial shanty on this piece of ground. Today there's a thirty-story skyscraper on its way up to heaven. Terrific, isn't it?"

"I'd be the last man to say it wasn't. I admire you and what you're doing, Filipe. But I think—I think—"

Filipe was defiant. "All right, tell me frankly. What do you think?"

Eugenio thought a moment before he answered. "We are men, Filipe," he said at length, "but we live almost like machines. This anxiousness for progress, to make money and build things, makes people forget to be human. Did you ever think of that? Well—I guess your life is none of my business."

In the river far below a white sail was moving upstream of a tiny, rocky island.

Filipe laughed. " 'Human,' he says! That's good! I suppose you think there's someone more human than I am?" He struck his chest and bit into his cigar fiercely. "I'm ambitious; I'm an all-around fellow; I can appreciate a good-looking woman as well as the next one; every month I contribute 300 milreis to charity; I'm vain as hell, and I have my little vices—I'll eat my hat if that's not being human!"

"You don't understand me, Filipe," said Engenio, shaking his head slowly. He was looking for an opportunity to bring up the subject of Dora and Simão.

"Look, my friend," Filipe continued. "There's nothing

more human under the sun than to want to enjoy life. The world was made for the go-getters, for the people who jump out of bed early in the morning and have the guts to go ahead and get things done. You sentimental idiots that go around preaching about 'humanity'—you're the very ones who aren't human. Well, I guess you're human, but you're kind of saints. The trouble with you is, you're sick, and the world doesn't need sick people. Sick people get in the way of healthy people. If I weren't building this thing here, if I were just any little clerk in an office or a store, you know how I'd feel? I'd feel dead—dead as a doornail!"

He took off his hat, and the wind blew his hair. Eugenio's eyes watched the progress of the little sailboat on the river.

"I know of only one thing you can really bank on as true in this life. And that's that the strong fellow swallows the weak, and for the weak there's only one hope. That's to make himself strong and get into the fight. Do you know why I admire Mussolini and consider the iron arm of Fascism the ideal regime? Because Mussolini's not the kind to put up with any of your saintly blah-de-blah. Look at what he did for Ethiopia. Your sweet Williams whimpered behind their hankies and felt for the poor, massacred niggers. But men of my temperament thought about the magnificent highways Mussolini would give them—the buildings and the plantations he'd build in that wilderness. The massacre lasted a matter of months, but those buildings, those highways—all the benefits of Italian civilization —will last forever!"

The little sailboat was heading now toward one bank of the river.

"Forever," said Eugenio. "Forever. Have you ever

thought what good the Mammoth will be to you after you're dead?"

"A strong man never thinks about an afterlife," snapped Filipe. "He can feel that God exists, though. God is a great builder; of course He understands the smaller builders of the universe."

Again Eugenio was aware of that odd sensation of fear and giddiness, like weird background music for the engineer's words. The wind was whistling softly. The elevators came and went. From time to time a man shouted an order or made some comment.

Filipe stood with his legs wide apart, his coat unbuttoned, his hands on his hips. He was looking around the roof, asking questions of the workers, giving them instructions.

"The Mammoth," he said, turning to Eugenio, "will take care of twenty-four hundred and fifty men. Tomorrow it will be beautifying our capital. It will be the pride of Brazil, a city within a city. Tell me, now—is it or isn't it wonderful?"

"Oh," said Eugenio, "I have nothing against the Mammoth. Why should I? All I'm trying to say is that the Mammoth isn't everything—'everything,' you understand? After you've finished this one, Filipe, you'll want to build another; then another and still another, always at the same furious pace. There's something I wonder if you've ever thought about, Filipe."

"What is that?"

"Do you ever think about your daughter—about Dora? I've often wondered which means more to you, Filipe— Dora or the Mammoth."

The engineer laughed. "Well, well, Eugenio! Two such different things! That's a pretty childish question."

"It's usually the questions children ask that upset us most."

"But what in the world made you think about that? Dora has everything she wants. She has a home and clothes, her own car—she has perfumes, lots of friends. You know, old man, she's past the age of being carried in her mother's arms. And you can't afford to spoil children too much. You don't dare give in to them in every little thing."

"Don't try to change the subject, Filipe. You know what I mean."

"You mean that forward little Jew?"

"I mean Simão."

"Well, all I know is, some day I'm going to put an end to this monkey business. I can't afford to waste time on kids' crazy notions. If he keeps after me, I'll let loose with a few swift kicks you-know-where." He tossed his cigar high in the air, watching the curve it made as it fell to the street below.

"Swift kicks won't solve anything."

"Jews are cowards."

"Well, for cowards you'll have to admit they're pretty persevering."

Filipe shrugged. "I don't like Jews." His words were conclusive.

" 'Jew' is just a word, Filipe. You've got to realize Jews are people like anybody else."

"Mean, treacherous people—"

"I said they are people, and everyone knows there are both good and bad people."

Filipe laid his hand on Eugenio's shoulder. "Look, my friend, do you want to know something? That fellow will never marry my daughter, and I don't want to hear any more about it."

"It's not a matter of hearing or not hearing any more about it, Filipe. It's a good deal bigger than that. Dora is in love with him."

Filipe looked at Eugenio suspiciously. "This is beginning to smell like a sermon, my friend—a specially prepared sermon. There's just one thing I want to ask you, Eugenio. Live your own life any way you want to, but I'll thank you to let mine alone. Don't go putting any of your ideas into my daughter's head. I'm her father, after all, and entitled, I think, to a little paternal authority—"

"Authority—that's another word."

"I don't know what you're talking about! When it comes to some things I could mention, you're not so all-fired insistent." Filipe looked around. "Do you want to see what authority really is? Listen." He shouted to one of the workmen. "Maneco, go down to the cafeteria and get me a pack of Astoria cigarettes."

He tossed the man a coin. The fellow caught it in the air, made an almost servile gesture of compliance, and went down in the elevator. Filipe turned to Eugenio. "That's authority. I command, and he obeys. I'm the boss, and he's the employee."

"You forget he's still a man and can say No."

"Yes, and if he did he'd be out of a job today."

"The world is big. There'd be other work for him."

Filipe threw up his hands in resignation. "That I can't deny."

A few minutes later they went down together in the elevator. As he left Eugenio, Filipe asked, "Don't speak to me again about Dora, you hear?"

Eugenio looked at him. "I promise. But I want you to make me a promise, too."

"What's that?"

273

"Think about what I asked you—about Dora and the Mammoth."

"Nonsense!"

Filipe's tone was light, but as Eugenio walked away he thought it strange that his friend had not offered to take him to the office in his car.

That day Eugenio heard the latest versions of his break with Eunice. Some people said that he had caught his wife in Filipe's arms. Others vowed that he had found her making love to Acelio Castanho. Old Cintra had given his son-in-law 200 contos to keep the story quiet, to allege merely incompatibility. Still others inclined to spicier versions. The truth, they said, was that Eugenio was sexually impotent, and Eunice had agreed to a friendly settlement out of pity, so that the true reason should not be known.

Eugenio merely smiled at the malicious rumors. When he was alone, however, he wondered how he could listen to those stories with such cool detachment. If they had told him such infamous tales in other days, his reaction might have been actually violent. He would have suffered physical pain and lapsed into a state of anguished prostration which would have lasted for days.

Men were inherently evil, he concluded. But then he corrected himself: There were extremely evil men in the world. Weren't the actual miseries of life enough—those miseries whose unforgettable victims he met each day in his own office—without the additional misfortunes created by such men? Some persons, it seemed, were depraved; they gained a perverted sort of enjoyment from creating misfortune.

He thought of something Olivia had written in one of

274

her letters: "I remember once you compared life to a transatlantic passage, and you asked yourself, Am I having a pleasant journey? The more human question would have been, Genoca, Am I being a good traveling companion?" Truly, men in general were bad traveling companions. In spite of the breadth and uncertainty of the sea, in spite of the frailness of the boat, the peril of storm and lightning, they persisted stubbornly in quarreling among themselves, in making enemies of one another. How much more sensible it would be to unite in self-defense, to exchange courtesies, and so make the voyage pleasanter for all!"

While the hypodermic needle was boiling and his patient, a scrawny, sallow youth, waited with his coat off and one shirt sleeve rolled up, Eugenio arrived once again at the same conclusion. Courtesy could make the world a better place. If men would only be civil toward one another, they might alleviate much of the harshness and brutality of life.

Eugenio looked at his patient's skinny arm, but all he saw were the images of his own thoughts. The alcohol flame went out, and he picked up the needle with tongs.

That night he read again one of the last letters which Olivia had written to him from Nova Itália:

I have made a wonderful new friend, Eugenio—an old Italian named Dr. Candia. He must be about sixty years old, and he is the oddest old fellow! He has lived in Brazil for eight years, and he owns a beautiful farm with an orchard here in Nova Itália. From my windows I can see his property. Dr. Candia lives alone and runs away from people, but he is very fond of animals. I like him immensely. He is a tall, strong man, with a rosy complexion, and his gray mustache droops down over the corners of his mouth and makes him look like somebody's kind old grandfather. He is a great walker and does all his own shopping, going down to the village and walking from shop to shop with a basket on his arm. He and I talk about everything under the sun. He is an atheist, a skeptic, and a cynic, but perfectly adorable! I have to admit I am nearly always thrown off balance by the questions he asks me—those odd, unexpected questions he asks with a smile as he strokes his mustache and stares at me with his amazingly blue eyes. A few weeks ago I was talking to him about pacifism, and he said to me, "Colonel Tinoco is the big political boss in this part of the country. Well and good. Colonel Tinoco is also a very unscrupulous man. Now, tell me something, Dona Olivia. If he sent one of his henchmen to kill Anamaria, and you were there, what would you do? Would you stick to your ideals of nonviolence? Would you still love Colonel Tinoco as your God commands?"

Of course I couldn't answer him, and I had to counter with another question. "Isn't it a little silly to be calling up out-of-the-way possibilities like that? Suppose a comet struck the earth suddenly? Or what if the law of gravity failed?"

But Dr. Candia just shook his head, and he was still smiling. "Confess that life is horrible," he said to me. "And confess, too, that the possibility of Colonel Tinoco's ordering your little girl to be killed is a good deal less remote than that a comet might hit the earth."

Isn't he an impossible old fellow? But I like him tremendously. He brought me a basket of ripe raspberries to make up for what he called the unpleasantness he had caused me with his skeptical and embarrassing questions.

Yesterday he came again and brought me a basket of

276

grapes and apples. He brought a newspaper, too, and he opened it to show me half a dozen news items he had marked with a red pencil—robberies, larceny, war, assault, blackmail, hideous cruelties. Like a schoolmaster, he said to me, "The world is full of bold, bad egotists, Dona Olivia, and they don't bother to choose the methods they use to get the things they want. All right. What decisive steps do you, with your philosophy of love, tolerance, and good will, propose to take to rid the world of the influence of unscrupulous politicians and greedy exploiters, of all the evils that beset it? Unscrupulous men use violence. What will you pacifists use? Will you cross your arms and stand transfixed in the contemplation of God?"

"Of course not!" I told him. I invited him to sit down, and then I took a pencil and a piece of paper and showed him there is nothing vague, nothing passive or fatalistic, about my plan of campaign.

First, I wrote, we must gather together all the good men who believe in peaceful methods and determine the task for each one. Every one, from the humblest worker to the greatest intellectual, can help us.

Love and persuasion must be our weapons.

We must avoid using violence of any kind, but we must know how to deal serenely with the violence that will be used against us.

We must mobilize all our moral forces and use them in the war against war and all social evils.

We must see to it that disinterested men with healthy minds—men who see clearly—take the high posts in government and become our leaders.

We must educate children. We must try from kindergarten to give them a social conscience. We must give our greatest and most efficient aid to childhood.

In order to boycott all the influences of vice and corruption, we must exploit to the full every device of modern propaganda warfare—books, the movies, the theater, the press, and the radio. And we must not forget that the example set by the individual himself is a powerful weapon of propaganda.

We must be ready to make sacrifices. We must never run away.

We must fill the country with schools, hospitals, and clinics.

Gradually we must attain the socialization of medicine.

When Dr. Candia had read my outline, he only smiled again and shook his head, very slowly. Finally he told me I was very young—imagine!—and that I did not know the world. "Your ideas are only a dream," he told me. "Force will always win out. It's no use to look for any logic at all in this ugly mess they call life."

I came back at him then. I told him of course I didn't believe we could make the world perfect, but that I did have absolute confidence that a few dozen years of re-education could bring about an appreciable betterment of the situation. Not only that, I said, but I was sure we could obtain some very appreciable immediate *results.*

"All right," he told me, quite pleasantly. "Then keep your beautiful illusion. It will bring you comfort." Before he went away, he gave me a handsome bunch of grapes, two apples, and a kiss on my forehead.

Eugenio returned the letter to its place in the drawer and looked at the photograph of Olivia which stood under the lamp. He stretched himself out on the sofa, his eyes fixed on the photograph, and in this position he went to sleep.

278

In the middle of the night he awoke, imagining in his dizzy, half-dreaming state that he was back in the old days. He had held Olivia in his arms that night; outside, it was growing light, and he must go. His mother must be waiting up for him. She must be worried . . .

Chapter 20

One morning Simão rushed into Eugenio's office with an urgent summons to come to the bedside of his father, who had suffered a fresh attack of angina pectoris. A taxi took them to Mendel Kantermann's house, a tiny, humid dwelling with only one door and two windows. The moment he entered, Eugenio detected in the air the poverty in which Simão's people lived.

Mendel lay curled up on his side in the old double bed, moaning. His face was pale, and except for his heavy breathing, he did not move. In his eyes Eugenio recognized an expression which was now familiar to him. It was the fear of death.

At the foot of the bed stood Simão's mother, her head bowed, her hands folded, and in her eyes the look of a martyr. She seemed, as she watched her husband's face, to be praying already for his departed soul. She was a short, rotund woman, with Mongolian features and the eyes of a sacrificial lamb. She said nothing, but only sighed from time to time. She was the living image of discouragement and grief.

Eugenio broke an ampoule of amyl nitrite and lifted it to the old man's nostrils, so that he might breathe it deeply. Then he gave him an injection of barbital.

Minutes dragged by, while Eugenio checked and re-checked the patient's pulse. His wife continued to stand withdrawn in her silence of grief.

Mendel Kantermann was breathing more deeply now. He was almost sixty years old, and he had a gray beard and very white, flaccid skin. His eyes were a sad, opaque blue. Eugenio patted his shoulder affectionately.

"The worst is over," he said jovially.

Mendel smiled weakly and looked at his wife. Eugenio took out his note pad and fountain pen and scribbled a prescription.

"Have this filled," he said to Simão, as he tore off the top sheet. He handed it to the boy. "There are directions here for giving him the medicine. I'll drop by again to-night, after the office is closed."

When Eugenio stood up to go, his patient's eyes begged him to stay. In a thin, grating voice, Mendel was mum-bling something unintelligible.

"Don't be afraid," Eugenio said to calm him. "I'll be back." He patted his shoulder once more and followed Simão into the dining room. He looked at his wrist watch; it was ten minutes after eight.

"Where can I wash my hands?" he asked.

"Mamma!" the boy called. "Bring Dr. Eugenio a pan of water and a towel!"

A moment later the woman appeared with the articles her son had requested. She walked with tiny steps, holding the basin with painful, sad precaution, as though she car-ried in her arms the corpse of a child.

Eugenio was advising Simão about the patient's diet and other necessary attentions. Did he smoke? Did he drink? Did he indulge in any violent exercise? He needed a great deal of rest—absolute rest.

The woman set the basin and towel on the table and left the room. Simão's eyes followed her, and when she had gone he said in a low voice:

"She has only one breast."

Eugenio was lathering his hands with soap. "Cancer?"

Simão shook his head sadly. "If only it had been! Cancer is nature's cruelty. Mamma knows what men's cruelty can be like." He sighed deeply. "In 1906 there was a wave of pogroms in Russia. A Cossack cut off her breast with his sword."

Eugenio frowned. The ugly story sounded like fiction—extravagant fiction. The only thing that occurred to him to say was: "Well . . . At least she is alive, and the injury does not endanger her life. If it were cancer—"

Simão stiffened, as if he had been struck in the face.

"*Alive?* Do you call *this* life?"

Eugenio was drying his hands. He knew where these words might lead the conversation. Simão seemed to derive a morbid satisfaction from picking the scabs from his wounds. It would be best to change the subject.

"How is Dora?"

Scarcely had Eugenio spoken the words when he knew that he had entered through another gate onto the same dangerous terrain.

"She's all right . . ." Simão answered vaguely. "Do you know?" he asked with greater animation. "One day I brought Dora here. I wanted her to see with her own eyes what my parents and the house I live in are like. I showed her everything."

He took Eugenio's arm and drew him toward his bedroom. It was a tiny, musty-smelling cubicle in which there was scarcely room for the dilapidated iron bed and a rickety table from which the varnish had long disappeared.

Books—greasy paper-bound volumes bought in the second-hand store—were piled in the corners, under the bed and table and on the window sill.

"Look," said Simão. "I showed Dora this. I didn't try to hide anything. She met my father and mother, she saw what they're like. Creatures from another world . . . I wanted her to see how my people have nothing in common with hers." He was silent.

"Why did you do that?"

"Out of love for the truth, and so she can never say I deceived her."

"Was that the only reason?"

The boy shrugged his shoulders. "Maybe because of some kind of sickly pleasure I get out of torturing her . . . Human beings have very mysterious souls . . ."

"As if she were to blame for belonging to another class . . ."

They returned to the dining room, and Eugenio closed his bag, ready to leave. As he was about to go, Simão stepped in front of him almost aggressively, blocking his way.

"Doctor," he said emphatically, "don't think I asked you to come because I don't want to pay. I want to."

Eugenio smiled. "But no one has said anything about money."

"*I* am saying something about money. I want you to send me a bill."

"And if I don't feel like sending it?"

Simão did not answer immediately. Then he smiled disdainfully. "Charity?"

Eugenio picked up his hat. He was uncomfortable. "According to current usage," he said, trying not to sound sententious, "the man who practices charity exalts himself, and the man who receives it is humbled. No, not charity."

"Pity, then?" Simão seemed to desire an argument at any cost.

"No, not pity either. You can call it whatever you want to: good will, brotherly love, solidarity—" He was walking toward the door.

"But still," insisted Simão, following him, "still, it's a form of egotism."

It was the failing of his people, Eugenio thought, this mania for argument, this pleasure derived from putting on a deep-sea diver's suit and going to the depths of things. But some lakes were shallow. He thought of a Charlie Chaplin movie he had seen. The hero had put on a bathing suit, struck an elegant pose and leaped into the pool, dreaming of a graceful swan dive. The pool, however, had contained only six inches of water, and poor Charlie had stuck fast at the bottom, with his feet waving in the air and his head buried in the mud.

"So, must we torment ourselves with words?"

Simão was calmer. He seemed to perceive that Eugenio had no desire to appear patronizing.

"But you make your living by medicine. You must earn money."

"My needs are small. I can live on very little. I have only one ambition now—" He stopped, and it seemed that he paused on the brink of a confession. Simão was waiting.

"Well," Eugenio broke off suddenly, "have the prescription filled right away, and don't let the old fellow get out of hand. My regards to your mother. So long!"

When he arrived home, Eugenio found Dr. Seixas sitting in Dona Frieda's dining room, with Anamaria on his knees. With her chubby hands buried in the old doctor's beard, the little girl was chanting:

"Looky at Santy Claus! Looky at Santy Claus!"

Seixas laughed harshly and gutturally and shook his legs, bouncing the child up and down as if she were astride a galloping horse.

"Let go my beard, you little witch!"

"Good morning!"

Seixas did not answer Eugenio's greeting.

"Whose little toad-face is this?" asked Eugenio, pinching Anamaria's cheeks.

"Granddaddy's," she replied and pulled the old man's beard.

Without warning, Seixas jumped up from the chair and set the little girl on the floor. "Seu Genoca," he exclaimed, "I've got another headache for you. You and I have a little butchering to do over in the Holy Family Hospital."

"When?"

"Today. Now."

"Stomach?"

"That's it."

They took a taxi, and Seixas told Eugenio the history of the case. Their patient was a poverty-stricken widow, the mother of five children, who had been his laundress for some time. She lived in a section of the city called the Colonia Africana.

"She's a skinny, broken-down old mulatto, but we'll try to save her. What for, I don't know."

"Will she take the operative shot?"

"Huh! . . . Sometimes these skinny ones will surprise you!"

After a moment, he spoke again. "Seu Genoca, do you think the day will ever come when these poor devils that

284

can't pay for hospital care will get decent medical attention?" He stroked his beard impatiently.

Eugenio leaned back against the upholstered seat of the automobile. "Some day," he said, "maybe medicine will be socialized."

"For our great grandchildren, maybe!" the old man snorted.

"A big emergency hospital with top-notch ambulance service, the best equipment, lots of doctors . . ." Eugenio seemed to be describing scenes from a wonderful dream.

He was satisfied with himself. It was no longer difficult for him to speak the language of humanity. He rejoiced to see that he was no longer so preoccupied with his own affairs, that he was living more outside himself.

Seixas chewed his cigarette thoughtfully, gazing out at the street.

"And when medicine is socialized," Eugenio continued, "only men with real ability will follow the medical profession. We will see doctors with the spirit of doctors."

"Huh! A couple of lunatics dreaming with their eyes open in a taxi!"

"Who knows? Men have accomplished harder things than that."

Seixas spat through the open window. "Man is a stupid animal. Stupid and aimless."

"But you like him anyway. Come on—admit it!"

"Well . . . I guess maybe I'm like the shameless woman who loves only the man who beats her. Just a typical old fool." He threw his cigarette away. Suddenly, he leaned forward and shouted to the driver:

"Hey, boy! Get a move on with this rattletrap, will you?"

The operation lasted twenty-five minutes. Eugenio felt particularly happy. He operated with enthusiasm and was amused at the occasional witty remarks of Seixas, who assisted him.

He seemed to be cutting the flesh of a mummy. The woman's skin was like ancient parchment.

"Ten days from now she'll be at the creek again rubbing clothes," Seixas prophesied, as they took her from the operating table. "They're some tough animals!" he added, to conceal his emotion.

"I have another surprise for you," said the old doctor, when they were again in the corridor.

"Is it good?"

"Good and bad. There's a patient here who's an old friend of yours."

Eugenio's heart skipped a beat, for the first thought which came to his mind was of Ernesto. He wanted to ask the patient's name, but he was afraid.

"Here," said Seixas, pausing in front of a door.

They entered a vast room, in which there were a dozen beds in a row. The pestilent odor of sweaty bodies, phenol and dirty clothes hovered in the air. In the beds there lay or sat thin, sallow, unshaven men. Men? They seemed rather to belong to another branch of the animal kingdom —an intermediary species between man and ape. In some of their faces only the eyes showed any life. That must be the fever. In others the eyes also had begun to die. Some moaned. Others, who were beginning to convalesce, started to smile pallidly, horribly, with their yellow teeth.

Seixas paused before one of the beds. "Know him?" he asked Eugenio.

Eugenio was moved. The sick man indicated by Seixas' hairy hand was a bald little fellow, with a silvered beard and tiny, lively eyes. He had a curious air of superiority, and one could see immediately that if, for some strange reason, it had been necessary to elect a chief of that sub-human community, all of the votes would have been cast for the dignified little man who sat there, stiffly ensconced among the hard pillows, with their rough, greasy pillowcases.

"Florismart," murmured Eugenio. He went to the bed and grasped the hand of the little man, who showed his tiny, decayed teeth in a broad smile. "But what's this, Florismart?"

Florismart gestured mildly with his child's hand and spoke in a voice that was weak yet dignified. "Life has its reverses."

Eugenio sat down beside him, trying desperately to keep his face from revealing his repugnance at the stench which arose from the sick man and his bed.

"I didn't know you were ill. How are you getting along?"

"I'm fine—perfectly fine," Florismart answered in a slow, deliberate voice, as if he were a chief of state answering his minister's inquiries about his health. "And how are you, doctor?"

"Don't call me 'doctor,' Florismart."

"Well, give every man his due, they say." He straightened the bedcovers and buttoned the top of his nightshirt. "I heard about your parents' death." He arranged his face in a careful mask of compunction. "That's life, Genoca. Can I call you Genoca? That's good. Sometimes life can be like a stepmother."

Seixas came to take Florismart's pulse. He looked at the little man half threateningly, half teasingly. "Well, Florismart, when are you planning to kick the bucket?"

Florismart grinned. "I have been conferring with Death," he said with dignity, "but I'm sorry to say that as yet we have been unable to reach a decision."

"That's right. You'll outsmart her."

The little fellow beamed with pride. "Well, I never lacked for a smooth tongue. Everybody says that." He looked up at Seixas with a serious, professional air. "Look, doctor, I'd appreciate your doing everything you can to get me out of this hospital as soon as possible. I have several cases waiting. You heard about Ribas, didn't you—that rich old devil that just died? Well, I'm going to look after his will." His hand cut the air with an exceedingly mild gesture. "The fee and all that have already been arranged. This one will set me up for life."

When Seixas asked Eugenio to go, Florismart caught his friend's hand tightly in his own.

"Genoca," he whispered confidently, his little eyes glowing with eager excitement. "Genoca, who was Florismart?"

Instantly Eugenio was transported to his paternal home, and he saw himself at the age of nine, standing before "Dr." Florismart in his stiff collar, his flecked coat, and his baggy, clownlike trousers.

Deeply moved, he answered, "He was one of the Twelve Peers of France."

A nostalgic light appeared in the eyes of the little man. "The good old days," he murmured, squeezing Eugenio's hand more tightly and looking up at the ceiling. "The good old days! But they'll come back. They have to come back!"

In the corridor, as they were about to reach the head of the stairs, Seixas told Eugenio that Florismart would live only a few days. In answer to his friend's questioning look,

288

he explained, "The poor fellow's heart isn't worth a plugged nickel."

The following week Florismart died. When a new day again brought light to that sad room, all its subhuman occupants except one continued to moan or smile their cadaverous smiles. Only Florismart was not there, for death had surprised him as he slept. In death as in life, his face conserved its great dignity. Eugenio offered to pay for his burial and bought him a modest grave.

As he was returning from the cemetery after the burial, Eugenio could not help thinking of his own loved ones who had died. In the sunlight of the Indian summer evening there was a sweet ripeness, and the air was soft and tinged with blue. Life seemed good to him, and he felt that at last he was beginning to glimpse his long-sought peace. Even death no longer frightened him, and his thirst for success seemed to have died. He longed only for human affection, kindness, and gentle words. But he knew that this moment of reconciliation would pass, that in the air and light and sun of tomorrow the face of things would wear some new element of strangeness and hostility. Again he would weaken and become discouraged. A thousand times he would be put to the test. But Olivia would help him through the crises, and such precious moments as this would surely return.

When he arrived home, Anamaria, who had been playing in the garden, ran to meet him and threw her arms around his neck.

"What did you bring Anamaria?"

"A kiss."

"Oh, I don't want a kiss!"

Eugenio bent and gave her a resounding kiss on the cheek, then lifted her in his arms and looked at her closely.

She was still fresh from her bath, and her skin had a mild, ingenuous fragrance of toilet soap. He looked for a long time at her round, serious face, with its lustrous, damp, black bang, marveling at the depth of his love for the small creature who had entered his life like a miracle. Olivia had been right; Anamaria was a sign from God.

He carried her into the house in his arms.

He was met at the door by an excited, beaming Dona Frieda, who could scarcely remain still long enough to tell him about her little goddaughter's latest exploit. She hopped up and down, pressing her hands together as though in prayer, and her face was crimson from her exertion. "Come see! Just come see what that adorable baby did! Just come see!"

She dragged Eugenio to the pantry. There, beside a blue enameled table, she knelt. Inside a shoebox a tiny gray cat with black spots lay curled, one of its paws tied in a strip of white cloth.

"Just look!" said Dona Frieda, looking from the cat to Eugenio. "Kitty hurt his little leg, and, without anybody saying a thing, Anamaria went right away and put water on it and tied it up with a little bandage. She was so quiet and so cute that I thought she was being naughty, and I tiptoed up behind her to see. Imagine! 'Ach,' I said, 'what are you doing?' 'Oh, Godmother,' she said, 'I'm curing Kitty.' What a little darling!"

Anamaria clung to her father's cheeks with both hands. "Poor Kitty said: 'You can give me the injection. It won't hurt.'"

Eugenio looked at his daughter very sternly. "What a little story-teller! Kitty can't talk!"

"Yes, he can."

"No, Kitty can't talk."

"Then why did you tell me about Puss in Boots that talked?"

Defeated, Eugenio could not argue. He covered her small face with kisses.

In the bathroom, Hans Falk was singing an old drinking song. Outside it was growing dark.

Eugenio spent the evening leafing through Olivia's photograph album.

He saw her as she had been at the age of eleven, with long hair and frightened eyes, wearing a little white dress whose sadly fallen waistline was accented by a ribbon that might have been blue. Under the photograph there was a date—1918. There was another picture of her at fifteen, in a white blouse with a dark cap and skirt. With mixed emotions, he examined the two photographs, studying their details, searching for a resemblance to the Olivia he had known.

He turned with misty eyes to other pages of the album. He found a group of related snapshots, which seemed to make up a series. One scene showed five girls with their arms around one another, Olivia in the middle. There was a picnic scene, and a photograph of Olivia reading a book under a tree, dated 1921. In another she was climbing a fence. In still another she stood in the foreground, smiling. Eugenio examined this last photograph carefully. He felt an ill defined jealousy for the thoughts Olivia might have been thinking when that picture was taken. At whom was she smiling? Why was she smiling? What did she think, what did she do in those days? Who was that boy with the handsome, oval face, slanting eyes, and petulant mouth in the picture on the next page?

That photograph had been a mystery to Eugenio from

the first time he had seen it. Under it had been written a name and two dates: "Carlos, 1921–1923." For the hundredth time he paused to conjecture about the picture of the stranger. Olivia had no brothers. She had never spoken of anyone named Carlos. Why had she put such a picture in her album? Examining it more closely, he saw again that its gleaming surface was broken in many places, as though it had been crushed by a passionate hand. He could not escape a stabbing twinge of jealousy, for he suspected that this Carlos was in some way linked to the dark part of Olivia's past. Yes, it was not impossible that he was the man who had first held Olivia in his arms . . .

Still holding the album, Eugenio leaned his head back against the upholstery of his chair. How Olivia must have loved that Carlos to give herself to him! Hateful visions rose before his eyes. He tried to banish them and found that he could not. He saw Olivia as she must have been at eighteen, saw her tremble with pleasure in Carlos' arms; he even heard confusedly the tender words she must have whispered then.

It was unbearable! He did not recognize Olivia, his true Olivia, in the girl he saw in his thoughts. Again he looked at the mysterious photograph and was surprised to find himself hating a man he had never known.

Recently he had experienced a sickly, morose curiosity about Olivia's past. He had written letters to several people in the village of São Martinho, asking if any relatives of the family of Orlando Miranda were still living, requesting information about a girl named Olivia Miranda who had studied in the capital, who had received her degree in medicine, and so on. Weeks later he had received two letters, almost at the same time. The writer of the first, a man who claimed to be one of the oldest inhabitants of the village, said that he had not the slightest idea who Orlando Miranda might be. Could not Dr. Eugenio be mistaken? Might he not be referring to Colonel Orlandino Moreira? The author of the second letter wrote that he had known a girl named Olivia who had gone to the capital to study and had drowned to death during the celebration of the *Centenário*. Disappointed, Eugenio had torn up the letters.

It was incredible that, in a village as small as São Martinho, Olivia's family was unknown. Could they have lived in some other village? No, that was not possible; Eugenio remembered with perfect clarity the many times Olivia had spoken to him of São Martinho. She had told him about things that had happened there, the way it looked, about the historical fountain where Giuseppi Garibaldi and his horse had drunk water, the house where Bento Gonçalves had spent a night . . . Eugenio could remember one day in particular, when he and Olivia had been in an especially good mood. Just as they were leaving the Hospital of the Sacred Heart, after Olivia had performed a minor operation, he had exclaimed with mock reverence, "Let the multitudes make way for the pride of São Martinho!"

As he closed the album, he felt that he would die of old age without unraveling Olivia's secrets. In all his life he had never known a person so human in her appearance, bearing, words, and aims. Yet her detachment and lack of egotism gave her a character that was more than human. She had had no living relatives. She had spoken rarely or never of her past. She had torn up all documents which might contain memories of those days. Only these photographs could tell him anything at all.

At the hospital Olivia's name was no longer mentioned.

Within a few years, Dr. Teixeira Torres, Sister Isolda, and the other nurses and attendants would forget her completely. To the people to whom she had given medical attention Olivia had never told her name or made confessions. Even the Falks, who were so fond of her, had known her only three years, a period broken by frequent absences. Between the old German couple and their young boarder there had never been any exchange of confidences. Anamaria had almost completely forgotten her mother. Eugenio and her godparents told the little girl stories about Olivia, about her kindness and love. They pointed to the place where she had sat at the table and told Anamaria that up in heaven Mother was smiling down at her darling little girl. But Eugenio knew that in Anamaria's infant mind the image of Olivia was growing dimmer and dimmer.

He looked around the room. He felt Olivia's presence there, in the furniture and every object, in the fragrance of the air. She was present in her letters, in the light of the stars that shone through the window, and in the heart and flesh of Anamaria.

But in a little while, Eugenio realized painfully Olivia would be only a symbol for them all, a name without a body, a face without distinguishable features.

He went to bed, deeply shaken by these reflections. That night he dreamed that Olivia herself had been no more than a dream in his life.

Chapter 21

At the beginning of that winter Eugenio was surprised to note that his practice was growing by leaps and bounds. The news of his break with Eunice, which had become known chiefly in middle-class circles, seemed to have given him prestige. That a man should leave the comfortable position of husband of a rich girl to return to the life of an ordinary consulting physician at five milreis per visit was something rare, almost miraculous. Legends grew up around the name of Dr. Eugenio. The poor came to him because they knew he would treat them for nothing. Boys and young men preferred to entrust him with the solution of their sexual difficulties or the cure of shameful diseases because "you know, he's young and understands these things." Seixas had heard from one of his patients that her neighbor had advised her to go to Eugenio "because he's such a nice young man, so—so—I don't know—I mean, he makes you feel confident right away." Eugenio's ideas about socialized medicine brought him a vast clientele of workers and sympathizers of socialism, who came with the confiding, friendly air of one who says, "You are one of us."

And it was through these first friends and admirers whom he won in his new life that Eugenio acquired also his first enemies and critics.

One day Seixas came into his office unexpectedly.

"Dr. Eugenio Fontes is becoming important," he announced. "They're beginning to gossip about him."

"Who is?" Eugenio was sitting at his desk, making notes on a filing card.

"Who! Why, your honorable and distinguished colleagues. Who else?"

"Oh, of course. What are they accusing me of?"

Seixas sat down on the edge of the desk and began to play with a paper cutter.

"Well, for one thing, they say you're a communist."

Eugenio smiled. He got up to replace the filing card in its drawer in the steel cabinet. "Words again! Communist, socialist, fascist—they throw names around as if they had some special hitting power of their own, apart from whatever they may stand for." He slammed the cabinet drawer shut with a bang and turned to face Seixas. "What else do they say?"

"Oh, that you want socialized medicine because you've got the mentality of a public clerk."

Eugenio sat down again at his desk. He leaned back in the chair and crossed his arms.

"And that you were kicked out of Cintra & Company because of a fraud."

Eugenio could not keep his annoyance, his surprise, and a touch of anger from showing in his face.

"Who said that?"

His companion shrugged. "You know as well as I do there's never anyone who *said* it. Along comes some friendly cuss that sidles up to you and says someone told him that a certain So-and-so was going around *saying*— and after all is said and done nobody *said* anything. But there's the story, and it sticks."

Eugenio looked at his watch. He rose and took off his white coat, then went to wash his hands in the lavatory.

"It doesn't seem—" he began.

"Don't let it bother you. It's a sign you're coming up in the world."

"I don't give a hang about coming up in the world. I don't want to be a successful doctor the way most people think of successful doctors. And all I ask is to be left alone!"

He was hurt, but it was only a scratch. Such pain brought him an odd gratification. He felt that suffering was a very necessary part of his new life.

"What do you want? A man who's afraid of getting wet shouldn't go out in the rain."

Eugenio put on his coat and picked up his hat. "Let's go."

When they were in the street, Seixas asked about Anamaria.

"How's my little granddaughter?"

"Oh, she's fine! Yesterday she asked about her 'big ol' granddaddy with the beard.'"

The old man's enormous mustache hid his pleasure. "What a wonderful child she is, Genoca! There's something about her . . ." He shook his head slowly. His eyes expressed his fondness and longing for the little girl. Suddenly he added: "You needn't be so proud. She takes more after Olivia than she does you."

Eugenio imagined that Olivia was walking beside him. He longed ardently, painfully, for her physical presence. It was frightening to have her come to him thus only impalpably. There were moments when he could not recall her image at all, but only her ideas. At such times he would wonder whether Olivia had really ever been more than an abstraction, an idea.

Seixas pressed his arm. They stopped.

"Just look at that thing."

They were standing in front of the Mammoth. Eugenio looked up at the tall building. The speed of its growth was almost terrifying. The two men stood for a moment without moving.

"What's that big thing for, anyway?" exclaimed Seixas. "This stupid craze for imitating everything foreign, just because it's foreign—it's uncivilized. Think what could be done with all that money, Genoca!"

"Build a big hospital, for instance."

"Every one of these they build pushes rents up a little higher." He cleared his throat noisily. "Have you seen that maniac?"

"You mean Filipe? Last time I talked with him was over a month ago."

"Have you seen Dora?"

"Oh, she's around. Always with the boy."

Seixas gave a snort which expressed his displeasure and concern.

"One of these days she'll be pregnant."

"Oh, I don't think—"

"You don't think!" Seixas was impatient. "What do you want them to do? They're young. They're in love, and they run around loose. They can't get married. The girl's father has no time to look after her, and her mother is a bitch. A bitch, did I say? Bitches at least are good for something—they feed their puppies, and they can be good watchdogs. What do you want those kids to do? Ever since the world began, it's been the same."

"Isn't there something we can do?"

Seixas glared hostilely at Eugenio.

"We?" He spat his cigarette butt into the gutter. "Why, we can't even keep our own pants up!"

Shortly thereafter Eugenio was called to attend a case which was startlingly picturesque. Summoned to the home of a veteran public servant, he was received at the door by the man's wife.

"Oh, doctor!" she greeted him anxiously. "I called you to see my husband. Come in. I'll take your hat. Right this way."

She led him into a modest living room, where a skinny, pimply-faced girl sat on a divan, holding hands with a pale, emaciated boy. Eugenio greeted them discreetly with a nod of his head, and his hostess introduced them summarily.

"My daughter and my future son-in-law."

"How do you do?" said Eugenio.

The girl merely nodded her peroxide blond head; the boy muttered some curt acknowledgment.

"Sit down, doctor. There's a chair." The woman had an unpleasantly harsh manner of speaking, and her gray-green eyes did not inspire confidence.

Eugenio sat down. The engaged couple stared at him fixedly, and the woman began her story.

"My husband's a clerk in the Treasury, doctor. He always was a easy-going kind of a man, and he never was real sick. But now, all of a sudden, something's wrong with my poor Trajano! Two days ago was when we first noticed the difference in him. Ain't that right, Jandira?" Her daughter nodded. "That's right. Trajano's not feeling so good, I think to myself. Why, just yesterday he goes off and locks hisself in his room, and stays in there a hour. And you know what he's doing all that time? Well, let me tell you. He's packing his suitcase. He packed up everything, doctor. 'What are you packing for, Trajano?' says I. Him, not a word. He goes to the little desk and writes something. Then he gets up and shows me the paper. 'Look, Ernestina'—I'm Ernestina—'I owe this much to Almeida, and this much to the tailor. Garcia at the office owes me forty-five milreis, and my insurance policy's

299

in the top drawer.' 'But what's this, Trajano?' says I. Him, not a blessed word, and real serious-looking. The first thing that comes to me is he's going to kill hisself. So I begin to watch him, without saying anything. So finally this morning, Trajano sends for Jandira and Ricardo—that's my son—and when he sees us all here in the room he says, just like this: 'Look, I want you to take care of everything for me, because I'm going away.' 'Where are you going, Trajano?' I ask him. 'I'm going to give myself up to the director of the insane asylum,' he says. 'I'm crazy,' he says. 'The only thing I ask is for them to put me in the first-class ward, and I don't want you to forget to pay every month.' Just imagine, doctor, how we felt. Ricardo didn't give a hoot, that no-account little fool. But Jandira was so nervous—you can't imagine. It's a good thing Licurgo here came—Licurgo's her fiancé—and said we ought to call a doctor." The woman paused and laid her hand, outstretched, over her heaving bosom.

"Where is your husband?"

"In his room, lying down. He says tomorrow morning he's going to the crazy house. You can just imagine the state I'm in. Poor Trajano, always so easy-going, and now, all of a sudden, this thing! Please, doctor, go in and see what's wrong."

In the bedroom Eugenio found a short, bald man with a pleasant face and a tranquil air.

"Good evening, Seu Trajano," he said, as if he were greeting an old friend.

The little man sat down on the edge of the bed, adjusted his pince-nez and examined Eugenio carefully, as though wishing to determine whether he knew him.

"Good evening," he said at length, and motioned to a chair at the foot of the bed. "Please sit down."

Eugenio sat down. "I've come to find out what's wrong with you, Seu Trajano."

"Wrong? Why, nothing."

"They tell me you're going to the insane asylum."

The old man nodded gently. "Yes, senhor, that's where I'm going." His tone was humble, mild.

Eugenio assumed a paternal attitude. "But that's impossible, Seu Trajano. How can a sane, healthy man like you think of going to an asylum?"

"That's just it. I'm not a sane, healthy man. I'm crazy. You're the doctor that Ernestina called, aren't you? Well, I tell you, I'm crazy. And I didn't get that way just today. I've always been crazy."

Eugenio smiled and drew his chair nearer to the bed. He placed his hand on the old man's knee. "Come," he coaxed. "Tell me about it."

A smile of derision animated the old man's face for an instant.

"I'm sixty years old, young fellow, and I've always tried to be as decent as I could. Of public service alone I've got thirty-five years to my credit, I want you to know. I might at least be the boss of my section by now. I might, but I'm not. Younger men passed me long ago. They passed me, and today they're earning twice what I do. But that's nothing. I never stayed home from work unless I was really sick. I never took a bribe, because I think a man that serves the public should take care of everyone as he comes. And what did I get out of all that? Not one blessed thing. It was the lazy ones they promoted, and I stayed behind.

"Here in my own house I'm never right. I try to be a good husband, and a good father. But who could ever say that anyone ever pays any attention to me? They

301

blame me because I don't make much money, because I never get a raise, because I don't take hold of my boss's nose and tell him off. They say I ought to get a hustle on, that I'm no-account and a tramp and I don't know what all. At breakfast and dinner it's enough to make me want to curl up and die, the way they hint—you know, So-and-so says that So-and-so . . . Mrs. Whosit has a refrigerator, Cicrano just bought a new car, somebody's daughter has this or that kind of a new dress. It's real Hades! They give themselves airs and run up my bills. They get me into hot water with my creditors, and I'm the one that has to make the excuses. They embarrass me in front of guests. No one ever remembers that I go around with my pants shiny in the seat, that I work like a dog, that I have no vices, that—that—that—"

He paused and sighed gently.

"Well," he said, more calmly, "so now we have the case of Jandira. Jandira's an ugly girl, and she's poor besides. You must have seen her. There wasn't any way to find her a husband. One day that sack of bones, Licurgo, showed up. He's a declared tubercular. I was against it. You understand, the boy's no good. He's sick, and he doesn't make much. They'll get married, and tomorrow he'll give Jandira t.b. The children will be wrecks before they're born, and goodbye, Aunty!—misery's knocking at their door. But they nearly beat me over the head when I said I wouldn't hear to the marriage. Well—that's nothing. I talk with my friends about things. They think one way, and I think another. They think the world is for the smart ones and the cheats. I think that first of all a fellow should be decent. We never think the same way on anything. They call me a dope. They borrow money from me and never pay it back, and when I complain about

302

some rotten deal they pull they laugh in my face and say I'm old-fashioned. One day I was reading in the newspaper about all the craziness in the world—about frauds and robberies and all kinds of low-down tricks—and I began to wonder if, after all, maybe I wasn't the crazy one. Thieves never get caught; they come up in the world. Worthless swindlers live like lords and have credit everywhere. That's the way it is. I'm crazy. Stark, raving crazy, young fellow!"

He crossed his arms, tilted his head to one side, and looked at Eugenio questioningly. "How is it that here I am sixty years old and only finding all this out now? Just one more proof that insanity is a pretty fierce ailment." He sighed placidly. "I thought up a plan then that I'm carrying out completely now, to the last detail. I packed my things and left all my papers in order. And now I'm going to the insane asylum. I hope maybe I'll find some people there who will understand me. Maybe in the crazy house I'll have a little authority some day. Maybe I'll find somebody there who'll pay some attention to me, who'll agree with what I think."

Eugenio shook his head, smiling. He patted the old man's knee. "Seu Trajano, they called me in to look after you, but I can't."

"Why?" asked the old man. There was infinite sweetness in his voice and eyes.

"Because I'm crazy, too."

The veteran clerk jumped to his feet. "You're making fun of me!" he shouted. "What I said is serious, young man, very serious—the most serious thing I ever said in my life!"

"I know, I know—"

"You think you'll keep me from doing what I want to?

303

Well, you're very much mistaken." He was exalting himself, waving his arms wildly. "I do what I want to because I want to—because I want to, you hear?" He struck his chest. "I'm a defeated old man. I've been sacrificed and humiliated. My wife doesn't listen to me, my daughter doesn't listen to me"—he stressed each complaint by striking the forefinger of his right hand against the fingers of his left—"my boss doesn't listen to me, nobody listens to me! I am a zero on the left side of the decimal point. But in this worn-out old body—you hear?—in this tired old carcass the one in command is me! I'll do what I blamed please with it. It's my revenge. I'm going to the asylum, I'm going to the asylum, I'm going to the asylum!"

The little man was trembling all over, and in his eyes there was a strange glitter. Eugenio smiled no longer. Frowning, he struggled with his own perplexity. He did not know whether the man was a comedian, an actor, a lunatic, or a combination of all three.

One Sunday morning Eugenio went to Seixas' home to invite him out for a walk. He found him still in bed. While he waited for his friend to get dressed, Eugenio talked with his wife. She was a tall, thin woman, bent and quiescent.

"Poor Seixas," she said in her gentle, scarcely audible voice. "He had an awful night. He had a call along about dawn, and when he came back he had a terrible cough." She tugged at the sleeve of Eugenio's coat, as though she wished to confide in him. "Make—make him take a teaspoon of syrup," she pleaded. "Please."

"Your husband is worse than any child, Dona Quinota. You know yourself that he doesn't believe in doctors or taking medicine."

The woman frowned, so that her nose wrinkled. She looked as if she were trying to convince a reluctant child. "But you'll make him take a little, won't you?"

At that moment Seixas' daughter, an exceedingly unattractive girl in her thirties, entered with a tray, on which there were two steaming cups of coffee and a plateful of cookies.

"Have some cookies," said Dona Quinota. "I made them."

In the bathroom Seixas was moving about noisily. There were the tinkling of glass, the thumping of wood, bumps, snorts, snuffles, squeaks, the gurgle of water. A monkey turned loose in the bathroom would not have made a greater racket.

While he sipped his coffee and nibbled at the cookies, Eugenio looked about the room. On a table in the middle of the room stood a vase filled with fresh, brilliant flowers. They contrasted sharply with the gray dreariness of the old room.

"I'll bet you're wondering about those flowers," said Seixas, entering the room suddenly, still struggling with the sleeve of his coat. "I'm not much for that kind of frippery; Quinota isn't just crazy about flowers, either. I'll tell you how they got there."

His wife gave him a cup of coffee, which he drank hastily, without sitting down. Then he pushed Eugenio toward the door. The morning was cold and misty.

"Those flowers are on the table in the living room because there's a man in this town who doesn't want to be forgotten after he dies."

Eugenio looked at his friend, uncomprehending.

"Every Saturday a little kid comes with a nice bouquet of flowers for my wife, from Dr. Ilya Dubov."

"That Russian Jewish doctor Teixeira Torres operated on last week?"

"That's the one. I kid Quinota about the flowers. I tell her the Russian wants to court her." He laughed. "Not long ago I took her to the hospital, and Dubov said to her, 'Look, Dona Quinota.' He has a funny way of speaking, he pronounces words kind of gingerly, as if he was afraid of biting them. 'Look, Dona Quinota,' he said. 'The flowers I send you aren't gifts. I just lend them to you. When I die, I want you to take a nice bouquet to my grave every Saturday. All right? That's a sacred duty I'm giving you.'" Seixas stroked his beard, and a low, hoarse laugh rumbled from his throat. "Just think, Genoca. The poor fellow can't stand the idea of being forgotten after he dies. He's all alone in the world. No wife, no children, no friends. He just dies, and that's that—no one will ever think of him again. As if the poor devil had never lived, in the first place. But he certainly is crazy about life, in spite of the rough going-over she's given him. You should hear him talk! A few nights ago I sat up late with him. I gave him a good shot of morphine to calm him, and it sure loosened up his tongue."

Seixas stopped to light a cigarette.

"Well, Dr. Ilya Dubov was born in Odessa. He got his degree in medicine when he was just a kid. Then he inherited a little fortune and was pretty happy with his practice. He married a beautiful girl, the kind that makes everyone stare when she walks down the street or comes into a room. Poor Dubov is ugly as hell. Have you ever seen him? Well, you should. Try to imagine a swelled-up, gray old ape with a mustache like a broom. I don't imagine he was much prettier at twenty than he is now, at fifty-two. Whatever the girl could have seen in him, I don't know. Women are apt to get some mighty funny ideas sometimes."

"She must have been hard up, and Dubov had money and a good position."

"Well, anyway, they got married. He showed me her picture. What a woman, Seu Genoca! One of those beauties that would drive a saint to drink."

"What a woman she *is*—or was?"

Seixas shrugged. "She was. . . . She must be pretty dried up by now. That is, if the worms haven't already had a good meal off her. But here comes the interesting part of the story. They got married, and Dubov lived for a year like he was in heaven. I wish you could have seen his face when he told me about it. He just melted all over. His eyes filled up, and his toothless mouth trembled so much he almost swallowed his whiskers."

They crossed the street. When they reached the opposite sidewalk, Seixas continued: "Then there was the war, and Dubov went to the front as a captain in the medical corps. That was where he got his first taste of wormwood and gall." Seixas chuckled inwardly, and his eyes twinkled with impish glee. "He told me all about the battles, and he shook his fists back and forth, puffing his cheeks out and going—very seriously—'Boom! Boom!' Well, anyway, when the Revolution broke out, Dubov was on furlough in St. Petersburg. By some miracle he was able to get away with his wife. They took two suitcases, with her jewelry and some money, and went to Vienna. Dubov made some good contacts with a bunch of famous doctors, went through the hospitals and I don't know what else. It wasn't long before that devil of a man had got himself established, had a name, a big practice and money. His wife made a sensation wherever they went. You can imagine—a beautiful woman on the arm of an orangutan. But life in Vienna after the war was no picnic. There was a lot of poverty, a lot of sadness, a lot of tension. Dubov's wife all of a sudden went into a fit of depression. She got sadder and sadder and began to lose weight. Poor Dubov was desperate. He called in the best doctors in Vienna, but no one could tell what was wrong with her. I think even Freud came into the picture."

They rounded the first corner and began to walk in the direction of the river.

"Where are we going?"

"How would you like to walk along the water front?" Eugenio suggested.

The old man nodded.

"That's how things were going when one day Madame Dubov was leafing through a French magazine and saw a picture of an officer of the Foreign Legion leaning against a palm tree or something. That was the last straw. She started to cry. 'But what is wrong, my little jewel?' asked Dubov. 'I'm homesick for the desert,' she sobbed. 'But you never saw the desert, my little jewel!' (I wish you could have seen Dubov when he told me this part.) And the little jewel confessed that ever since she had been a little girl she had wanted to see a real, live Legionnaire. She wanted to go to Morocco! She wanted to because she wanted to, and that was all there was to it. Poor Dubov—you could have knocked him over with a feather. But he told her, all right, they would go, hoping all the time the fool notion would go away. Not on your life! From that minute on there wasn't anything in this world could get the idea out of her head. And in the end they packed their bags and sailed for Morocco."

"And Madame Dubov realizes her dream. She meets her

real, live Legionnaire and sees he's just a bearded, sweaty, rough, smelly—"

"Who's telling this? Madame Dubov scores new triumphs in Morocco. She makes a sensation in the hotels, in the cafés, in the theaters. Poor Dubov satisfies her every whim. And one day, as they get up from their table in a café, Madame Dubov drops her gloves. Her husband, heavy as lead and clumsy, bends down moaning and groaning to pick them up. But he's too late! Quick as lightning, an officer of the Foreign Legion jumps out of his chair, picks up the gloves, and gives them to Madame Dubov. He clicks his heels, bows, and smiles."

"Romance!"

"Stop spoiling my story. Madame Dubov thanks him, smiles politely, and goes out on the arm of her husband. A couple of days later, as Dubov is returning from the hospital or somewhere, he finds his wife and the same officer drinking tea together on the hotel terrace. He gets all upset. His wife stands up and introduces them. 'Lieutenant So-and-so, Dr. Dubov,' et cetera. 'How do you do?' Well, let's see. I don't remember very well what happened then. I've got one hell of a memory. Oh! Dubov spends a few days very busy in the hospitals and in conferences, and then one afternoon he has a visit. It's the lieutenant of the Foreign Legion, who seems to be nervous. So you can get a better idea of what went on, you've got to realize that Dubov is the most delicate little fellow in the world, all full of hand-kissings, flowery talk, bows, and that kind of thing. The lieutenant comes in clicking his heels and says, fast enough to singe your eyelashes, 'Dr. Dubov, I have the honor to advise you that I am in love with your wife.' Well, Dubov is completely tongue-tied. But he pulls himself together and gets out, 'But, my dear

Lieutenant, my dear Lieutenant—' That's all he can go. The lieutenant stands in front of him, very pale and stiff. He looks like a challenge to a duel. Dubov collapses in a chair. 'C'est dommage!' he says. 'C'est dommage! Je—je—' I don't remember what he said. But to make a long story short, the officer was going to Paris on a furlough. He went, and he took Dubov's wife with him. She left a letter for her husband, begging his pardon and saying she was going to follow the only man she had ever loved in her whole life. Imagine!"

"Make a good newspaper serial," murmured Eugenio.

"Well, it's for you to see. Dubov nearly went crazy. He went to Paris, too. He searched high and low and finally found out the runaways were staying in a hotel on the Place de la Concorde. He wasn't sure whether to go after them there or not. He was afraid. He hung around for days. He heard that his wife and her lover were living in one big, all-out binge, that they were drunk all the time on champagne, and that they practically lived in night clubs and theaters." Seixas paused briefly, spat his cigarette butt far away, and continued: "Do you know what all this came to? Get ready for a shock, and don't call me a liar. Because Madame Dubov ran away to South America with a lousy-rich perfume manufacturer, and the lieutenant shot himself."

The old man watched Eugenio's face eagerly for the effect of his dramatic pronouncement.

"Incredible."

"Isn't it crazy? Imagine how Dubov felt. There he was stranded in Paris without the heart to do anything. He took to his bed and stayed there for weeks, only half conscious, running a high fever and delirious. As soon as he was on his feet again and had the strength, he started to hunt for his wife. He couldn't live without her. He found out the perfume manufacturer was in Brazil, so he raked up the last little bit of money he had and sailed for Rio. When he got there, the country hit him between the eyes. He'd never seen so much sky, so much sun, so much greenness. But the perfume manufacturer and Madame Dubov had gone on to Argentina. Dubov didn't have another nickel to his name. Things really looked tough. He tried to practice, but he couldn't even make enough to buy cigarettes. He ended up finally with a job as ship's doctor on board a Lloyd steamship. It was going to Porto Alegre, and Porto Alegre was in the direction of Buenos Aires. The poor man had an idea maybe he'd find his wife."

They had reached the water front. The river was tranquil. The two men paused to stare at the black hulk of a ship at anchor.

"For a couple of years Dubov went back and forth on one of those ships; but finally he got tired and came ashore. He went into the interior. He was poor as the devil, and he was getting old. If he hadn't found some friends, he'd have starved to death. But after a while, things began to pick up. After all, Dubov was a good doctor. His practice began to grow, he made a little bit of money and came back to Porto Alegre. He kept getting better off all the time, and today he has a pretty good roll under the mattress."

"How many years has it been since his wife ran away?"

"Almost twenty."

"Does he still remember her?"

Seixas nodded. "And there he is now in the hospital. It's the fourth operation he's had. Bladder. This time he won't escape. Just look at how life is! Dr. Ilya Dubov was born in Odessa. He went to Morocco, and that was the end of him. Now the poor devil's going to leave his carcass in Porto Alegre."

There was a brief silence. Then the two friends began to speak impersonally of travel.

A fortnight later, Dr. Dubov died, leaving all the money he possessed—one hundred and twenty contos—to the School of Israel, under the condition that it be used to erect a new building, on the portico of which should appear the full name of the giver in clearly visible letters.

Seixas and Eugenio went to see him buried. Arriving unexpectedly in the little mausoleum of the Jewish cemetery, they witnessed a grotesque scene. At the moment when they entered, the corpse, completely nude except for an improvised turban on its head, was standing upright, supported by the two men who were washing it. According to the Hebrew rite, the dead man could not enter the presence of Jehovah without some kind of covering for his head, which might harbor impure thoughts.

It was an unexpected and shocking sight. Dr. Dubov, with his gray-tinged, bloated features, his coarse, stiff mustache and odd white turban, reminded one of portraits of Rembrandt in his years of senility. There he stood, unarmed, defenseless, in his ridiculous nudity, while the two mournful-looking men washed his body, joking with each other in Yiddish.

"Just look at what a poor man is subjected to after he dies!" murmured Seixas. With mingled irony and pity, he exclaimed, "Lord, what an ugly Indian!"

Eugenio returned from the cemetery enriched by his experience. How often his own life had seemed to him lacking in event and color! He compared it now with the adventure and suffering of Ilya Dubov, who in spite

312

of everything had loved to live. To him it had been unbearable to think that he might be totally forgotten by the world he loved. Knowing he could not overcome physical death, he had wanted at least a guarantee, however pallid, that his name should not be erased completely from the lives and minds of men. Dona Quinota would take flowers to his grave each week for a long time. His name on the portico of the new building of the School of Israel would be for indifferent men a reminder that there had lived in the world a certain Dr. Ilya Dubov, native of Odessa.

Days went by before Eugenio could forget the sight of Dr. Dubov's nude corpse standing upright, its head wrapped in the improvised turban, its stomach hanging flaccidly, its arms and legs exaggeratedly thin—the end of a life of suffering, love, and adventure.

And the memory of that sight was blended in his mind with the words from one of Olivia's letters: "We must always remember that we weren't consulted about coming into this world, and that we shan't be consulted when we have to go. That is the real measure of our material importance on earth. It must bring us consolation, not despair."

One Saturday afternoon after the office was closed, Eugenio sat examining his file cabinet. Each card was much more than a collection of names, physical characteristics, and symptoms, it was also the drama of a human life. As he reread each card, he recalled the story behind the hasty notes he had scribbled on its yellow surface. Some of the stories were almost unbelievable; they were more like the wild inventions of a writer of fiction than like palpable, visible, audible reality. So many people had passed before his eyes in a nudity or seminudity which was now physical, now moral, or, not rarely, both physical and moral, that Eugenio was struck overwhelmingly by the notion that an invisible and capricious impresario had undertaken—who knew for what mysterious reason!—to parade before him the entire cast of minor characters which made up all of life.

In the days when he had been an ambulance doctor and assistant to Dr. Teixeira Torres at the Sacred Heart Hospital, Eugenio had seen real suffering, pitiful physical and mental injuries. But he had averted his eyes from the unpleasant sight, had tried to forget as soon as possible what he had seen. He had attended his patients like one who fulfills a distasteful obligation. He had never succeeded in penetrating their intimate lives. As an ambulance doctor he had given only first aid, leaning for support as much as possible on the nurses. As Dr. Teixeira Torres' assistant at the hospital he had never felt the weight of any responsibility; and very seldom had he been placed in a position in which it was necessary to make decisions for himself. For almost two years he had practiced medicine with no more than a superficial interest in his work. And always he had been tormented by the persistent consciousness of his failure to become adapted to his work, by his apparent lack of inclination toward the medical profession.

The three years he had spent in Cintra's home had been like a sponge dipped in perfume with which he erased from his mind the disagreeable memories of the hospital and the ambulance corps. He had equipped an office—very white and clean and useless—to appease his own conscience, to convince himself and others that he still had a liberal profession, that he was still Dr. Eugenio Fontes, physician,

and not merely "that boy who married Cintra's daughter."
There had come to that office a very clean, elegant, and
vague-tongued clientele—men and women who were careful not to suffer from shameful or indiscreet maladies.
Famous doctors invited him to assist them at operations;
and those invitations, he knew, he owed to the social
prestige of his father-in-law.

But now, at last, Eugenio felt that he was becoming
a real doctor. He cared for his patients with genuine solicitude, having at times to force himself to be delicate, or
not to cringe before creatures whose physical aspect or
nature of illness disgusted or horrified him. And slowly
he began to lose his old dread of failure, the feeling that
people lacked confidence in him. Because of the unre-
strained confidence of those who came to him he was
acquiring, day by day, confidence in himself.

He lived now in close contact with human suffering.
He knew the intimate lives of his patients and was invited
to give opinions and advice on subjects which often
escaped the diagnosis and even the knowledge of an ordinary doctor. He met surprise after surprise; each day
brought him new revelations, unknown and even unsus-
pected aspects of life. And Eugenio, who had thought
egotistically, uncomprehendingly, that through his own
suffering he had plumbed nearly all the dramatic possibilities of life, was surprised to discover new forms of
suffering, unknown fountains of affliction and unrest,
complications which arose suddenly to blind and disorient,
incurable disease, lives irrevocably destroyed, consciences
corroded by insanity. He seemed to be rediscovering life.
His horizons expanded breathtakingly. Sometimes, as he
stood before a soul, a life, an ordinary person of prosaic
and little inspiring appearance, he would pause, fearful,

like a diver who, before preparing to leave the board, asks himself what great depths may be hidden under the apparently innocent surface of the lake, what great secrets may sleep in its murky depths.

Many of his patients were apparently normal people who confessed depraved sexual appetites. Husbands and wives, some cynical, others ingenuous, still others constrained and reluctant, told him the secrets of their alcoves. Ashamed, miserable young men came to show him the marks purchased love had left on their bodies. The strangest psychoses were revealed to him through the most varied and complex cases. He felt small before the abounding drama of life. As a man he wanted to understand, to be useful, to comfort, to give aid. As a doctor he wanted to prescribe the remedy which would cure or relieve pain. In the great majority of cases, however, he was impotent; he could only stand with folded arms before a crossroads from which forked a thousand roads. Which should he take?

His work was intense, and his moments of respite became each day rarer. He scarcely had time to scan briefly treatises on medicine. How interesting it would be, he thought, in view of these cases which came to him, to practice psychoanalysis! His reading in this branch of medicine was superficial and inferior, and he was disheartened by the thought of plunging into a more thorough study.

"A poor man's doctor is like a woman of the streets—he does everything," Seixas used to say with his bitter humor each time Eugenio manifested a desire to devote himself to some specialty.

Days went by, and the long parade continued to file by. The cowering, sick creatures who came to Eugenio's office to exhibit their wounds began in his eyes to be the expression of a cruel warning. A voice seemed to whisper to him constantly: *The flesh is weak, and it decays. You also will decay.*

"Send in the next patient, Dona Amelia," he would say to his assistant, as each patient was leaving the office.

There were men who suffered the horrible pain of incurable diseases, who dragged themselves through a miserable existence of suffering and deformation. Some were so disfigured by disease that they had begun to lose their human semblance. One could not say that they lived; theirs was a sordid, lusterless imitation of living. Nevertheless, in spite of everything, they feared death hysterically; they clung to the world, wanting above all else to live.

There entered the white, cold-looking office well dressed, perfumed ladies and gentlemen of dignified, sometimes even haughty, bearing. Scarcly, however, would the closing door shut them in with the doctor before something inside them would break, would fold, would soften. Their features would relax, there would be sudden or slow modifications of the masks they wore, and confessions would be made spontaneously or come forth painfully, bit by bit, in answer to the doctor's questions. Desperate conflicts would come to light—dramas, often, in which the piteous and the laughable walked side by side. Eugenio was reminded frequently of the sermons Dr. Parker used to preach in the chapel at Columbia Academy. The good man would pound with his clenched fist on the pulpit and blast his audience: "I know you well! You are like whitened sepulchers without, but within you are filled with corruption and decay!"

Eugenio's first reaction before that procession of physical and moral distress which filed daily through his office had been a mixture of revulsion and terror. Life was ignoble and fearsome, and his first impulse had been to flee from its disagreeableness. He longed for other times which had been more tranquil, longed each day for the hour when his work would be done and he could leave the office. But gradually, as the tide of days and men ebbed and flowed, he came to accept their sufferings and their dramas and through them to lose the fear and repugnance which he himself had felt for life. It was a matter of habit, he concluded. He thought constantly of something Olivia had said after she and Eugenio had assisted Dr. Teixeira Torres in an operation at the Sacred Heart Hospital: "Only life teaches us to live, Genoca. First we must see what there is about life that is sordid and ugly, so that later we can discover what there is in it that is beautiful and good."

Sometimes the ugly dance that was performed day after day in Eugenio's office around the themes of love, greed, envy, hate, jealousy, sensuality, and all depraved human appetites—the hideous ballet in which the dancers appeared with their flesh half eaten away—led him to dishearteningly materialistic conclusions. There could be no meaning in all that. Death was total, absolute decay, the end.

From further observation of people and facts, however, he came to the conclusion that what he saw, what he could feel, smell, and hear, was not all. There was something indefinable which existed beyond the material world. He did not know precisely what it was; he had only a vague, misty idea of its nature. Could it spring merely from his desire to believe that in some part of the universe Olivia still lived? Or could it be his reluctance to accept the irrevocable oblivion of death?

He found men and women who were resigned, full of

goodness, faith, comprehension and self-denial. Among the pitiful, dolorous stories he found acts of beauty and courage. And always there was the mystery. The mystery was everywhere, even in the most obvious and apparently simple things.

He thought frequently of Olivia. She was dead. Was it possible that her gentleness and goodness, her tolerance, courage, and unconquerable faith, had decayed with her flesh?

No. There was in the world an immense harmony. He sensed somehow that ultimately all the misery and the conflict would be dissolved in the great universal harmony. Life was good.

But with the sensitivity of mortal flesh Eugenio found it difficult to resign himself to the inevitable, irrevocable facts of human suffering and unhappiness. Could they really be inevitable and irrevocable? Might not men of genius and good will discover one day a means of employing all the conquests of the human mind to lessen the ills of humanity? Perhaps, someday, there might be bread for everyone, health for everyone, work for everyone . . .

Was it worth the effort? Granted that it was, and that human bodies were so consumed by incurable disease, how might the great reaction be initiated? Should it be a reaction of the mind—a reaction of faith? There again he encountered something which seemed apart from the material world. He had seen faith work miracles; he had heard of a man who had been born blind and dumb and had learned to read and write so that his life had taken on usefulness and meaning. He had read also about a paralytic whom faith had transformed into a man of amazing vitality.

These thoughts left him somehow giddy. He knew that

he would never be able to arrive at truth. At the most he could only glimpse small truths.

There were days when he was so busy that he had no time to think. The money he earned was generally little, but this, far from discouraging him, was a stimulus. In the past he had paid too great tribute to vanity and greed. He must cleanse himself of old errors.

Frequently he was called out in the middle of the night. One early dawn, a man came to take him to his little daughter, who was gravely ill. It was raining, and the wind was icy. On the way the man apologized profusely for having gotten the doctor out of bed at that hour. But the case was urgent. A taxi left the two men on a dingy little street in the outskirts of the city, in front of a wooden house, which appeared to be almost submerged in the depths of a swampy terrain. Eugenio felt in his feet the dampness of the ground, and the rain which beat in his face was thin and cold. To go out into the street at such a time was unpleasant, he thought; but to live permanently in such a damp, unhealthful place would be a thousand times more disagreeable. This thought consoled him and led him to formulate still others as he walked along through the mud and water. Beside him, the little man was muttering words to which he paid no attention. There was much to be done in the world. A better life must be provided for such people as these. It could not be done with revolutions, for violence generates violence, and its fruits are dangerous. Men were too preoccupied with words; they were forever revolving fruitlessly around words and overlooking the important, basic facts. But the facts always remained.

At the bedside of the little patient, Eugenio struggled with death until sunrise. When it was again light and the rain had stopped, the sky was washed clean and the child was out of danger.

Eugenio set out for home on foot. He would take the trolley a few blocks away. He splashed, ankle-deep, in the puddles of water. Frogs croaked in an overgrown pond near by, and a startled little bird with ruffled feathers chirped sadly as it sat on the twig of a tree. He whistled as he walked. He thought of his childhood, when he had walked to school on early winter mornings, Ernesto's hand clinging tightly to his own—a younger, frailer hand, which clung to his as though for protection.

Eugenio whistled lustily. He was happy because he had saved the little girl's life. He had taken one more step in the direction of saving his own.

Chapter 22

"Send in the next patient, Dona Amelia," said Engenio, as he sat down at his desk to make a notation.

Almost immediately there was the sound of the inner door closing and the soft tread of feet. He looked up and was surprised to see standing before him, motionless and silent as if condemned and awaiting final sentence, Dora and Simão. The girl was extraordinarily pale and crest-fallen. Simão scarcely concealed his agitation. Eugenio felt a strange foreboding. He rose, making an effort to speak naturally.

"What miracle brings you two here? Nothing wrong, I hope?" He extended both arms and grasped for an instant two limp, cold hands.

"Let's sit down," he suggested.

Dora sat down. The trembling of her hands was marked, and by the irregular rise and fall of her breast one could make out the rhythm of her heart.

Simão did not move, but stood crushing his felt hat in both hands, as if he wished to tear it to bits. He stared at Eugenio with an odd expression that seemed almost defiant. His voice was strained.

"It's better—better to tell you right away." He sighed deeply several times. "Dora is pregnant."

Eugenio opened his mouth slightly, but no word came. He held his breath. Dora covered her face with her hands and broke into convulsive weeping.

"Are you sure?"

"Almost absolutely."

There was a tense, heavy silence. It was filled with indecision. Simão looked at Eugenio, and Eugenio looked at Dora.

"Leave the room for a minute," he said curtly to Simão.

The boy hesitated, as if he had not understood.

"Leave the room," Eugenio repeated impatiently. Then he added, more gently, "I want to examine her."

Simão went out. When he returned a few minutes later, he found Dora standing at the window, even paler than she had been when he left her. Eugenio was waiting for him in the middle of the room.

"Well?"

Eugenio nodded. "There is no question. She's been pregnant three months." He tugged angrily at his rubber gloves, walked to the lavatory and began to wash his hands. Dora and Simão exchanged looks of stunned dismay.

Eugenio was thinking of little thirteen-year-old Dora as she had entered the church on his wedding day. She had worn a rose-colored dress and short socks, and there had been a garland of silk flowers on her hair. The thing that was happening now was brutal; it was unreasonably cruel.

He turned to face them, drying his hands. Simão looked at him pleadingly.

"You're the only one who can help us," the boy stammered. "Please help us."

Eugenio threw the towel down and walked to his desk. He sat down in the swivel chair, picked up the paper cutter, and began to tap its bone shaft against the palm of his left hand. He must regain his calm, must organize his thoughts. He must discover some way out. The great, immediate obstacle would be Dora's parents. Filipe would be furious when he learned what had happened. He was capable of doing something violent. And there was society —the famous society to which the Lobos belonged. It was a den of wolves ready to pounce upon them and devour them. If the news of Dora's pregnancy reached their ears, they would have an extraordinary titbit of a rare and exquisite savor.

"Well?" he said at last. He looked at Simão.

The boy went to the desk and grasped its edge in both hands. He leaned forward; his voice was almost a whisper.

"Everything depends on you."

Eugenio's eyes reflected doubt and near-incomprehension. He did not want to understand. The idea was in itself too brutal, too hideous. He refused to let himself think of what he knew the boy was insinuating. No. No, that was not possible.

"Have you thought what can happen if this child is born?" asked Simão. "Dora's father hates me. She lives in a society that doesn't understand certain things. I— I'm a Jew. For her to give herself, before marriage, to a Christian would be shame enough for them. But to give herself to a *Jew*—that's criminal!" The boy was trembling all over, and his voice was gradually becoming hoarse, almost inaudible. "Think, doctor—Dora's father might do something violent. I'm not afraid. I'm thinking of what can happen to Dora. I was to blame for everything. It was up to me to see clearly and avoid what happened. I'm a pig!" He struck his chest savagely. "Because I was weak she's the one who is going to suffer!"

Eugenio was trying desperately to remain calm. The tapping of the paper cutter against his palm had a quicker, sharper rhythm.

For interminable minutes no one spoke. At the window, Dora was biting her lip, staring unwinkingly down at the street. One might have guessed that outside a heartrending scene was taking place, a tragedy whose dark fascination was so great that she could not take her eyes from it; always she would continue to see and to suffer. Suffering disfigured her face, destroying its childlike freshness.

Eugenio stood up. He made Dora sit down on the couch. Then he went to Simão and patted him on the shoulder.

"Don't worry," he said. "Sit down there by Dora."

Without a word, the boy did as he was told. Eugenio leaned back against the desk.

"There are no two ways out," he said. "The only thing to do is to tell Filipe everything." Simão made a gesture of protest. "Wait a minute, Simão. Listen first to what I'm going to say. After all, Dora's father is a human being like the rest of us. I know he'll understand. In a month or two Dora won't be able to hide her condition any longer. Everyone will notice. I'll take the responsibility of telling Filipe. I'll suggest that he send Dora to the country, to a sanitarium in some little town in the interior—"

324

Simão stood up. His tone was belligerent. "Such a solution would undoubtedly be very comfortable for you! But think what will happen to Dora! Think what the life of the child will be, if it's born! Besides being the child of a Jew, it will be a—a—" He panted, ready to pronounce the offensive word.

"Shut up!" Eugenio exploded. "You don't know what you're saying!"

Simão sank back against the couch. He covered his face in his hands. Timidly, Dora tried to comfort him, passing her fingers gently through his dark, wavy hair. When she looked at Eugenio, he saw in her face both a plea and an apology.

There was a long silence. Eugenio lit a cigarette, thrust his hands into his trousers pockets and began to pace back and forth. If only Seixas were there, he could suggest some way out. He was a man of experience. He knew the world.

Simão straightened up. "Excuse me, doctor. You understand how I feel. I haven't slept for two nights." He was calmer now. All his despair was apparent in the way he dragged out each word, in the weariness of his eyes, in the myriad tiny lines of his forehead. He leaned his head back against the couch, seeming to lapse into a speechless prostration.

Eugenio looked at Dora.

"Think, Dora. Of course your mother will understand. It will be easier than you imagine."

The girl's lips quivered, so that she could scarcely pronounce the words. "M-Mamma never cared about me . . . I know she'd never understand. I know, I know! She never told me anything, she never explained anything to me . . ." Tears came again to her eyes. "Mother doesn't

325

love me. You'll see. They only quarrel, they only scold when I do something wrong . . ."

"But, it's not—" Eugenio began.

As if with fresh hope, Simão got resolutely to his feet. He seemed to have come to a decision. He walked across the room to Eugenio. "I was beginning to weaken already," he said firmly, and shook his head. "But I have thought a lot—a lot about this thing. And there's only one answer."

Eugenio waited.

"Abortion."

Eugenio shook his head. "Don't count on me."

"You're the only friend we have."

"It's no use. I wouldn't do that to any woman under the circumstances—and much less to Dora."

Simão folded his arms. He had passed from indecision to desperation, from desperation to utter despair, then once again to determination. Now he was sarcastic. He stepped forward contentiously, his face twisted in a scornful half-smile.

"Oh! Professional honor, is that it? The sacred priest-hood of medicine. What! *I? I* perform an abortion? Oh, *never!*" He unfolded his arms brusquely, his eyes blazing, and it was as if he were assaulting Eugenio. "If it's money you want, tell me!" Simão was shouting. "I'll rob, I'll kill, I'll sell my soul, I'll do anything—but I'll get money to pay for your precious conscience!"

"Don't be melodramatic," Eugenio said quietly.

Simão seized Eugenio's shoulders and shook him fiercely, as though to awaken him. "All I'm asking you to do is something many doctors do every day. I know it's simple. Please—please think about it. Just a few minutes and every-thing would be over. Dora would be spared the humilia-tion—" He was still shaking Eugenio. "For the love of

326

God—for the love of your God! The child would never be happy. We have no right to bring into the world a child we know will suffer. I'm to blame—I know. I'm ready to go to jail, to die of shame, to go to hell! But please do this—do it for Dora!"

Eugenio was shaking his head stubbornly. Simão loosened his fierce grip on his shoulders and wiped away the perspiration that was flowing down his face.

"Coward!"

Eugenio winced as if he had been struck on a wound that was scarcely healed. But he controlled himself. He went to Dora and took her hand.

"Think now, Dora. Don't you think it would be better to make up your mind it must be done, to let the child be born? Just think, Dora—your child. I know your father will agree to the marriage now. Just think of your baby, Dora. What woman doesn't want to have a child of her own?" (There crossed his mind the vision of Eunice: "Those mammiferous little beasts that deform our bodies . . .") "Do you know Anamaria, Dora? Wouldn't you like to have a little girl like her?"

Simão laughed sharply. He was standing behind Eugenio.

"He has the nerve to mention his daughter! Ha! That's funny! The daughter he never even saw until she was three years old! The child he caused to be conceived in a moment of egotism and brutishness, like me—" Eugenio felt as if he had been knifed suddenly from behind. "The daughter that someone else bore, that someone else brought up quietly while he, the great moralist—"

Eugenio stiffened.

"Shut up!" he shouted hoarsely.

He stepped toward Simão menacingly. The boy did not flinch. Dora gave a weak little scream that was almost like a whisper. Eugenio stopped in his tracks. Something—a thought or an invisible hand—held him back. He sighed deeply, as if in sighing he wished to expel all his sudden, unexpected, uncalled-for wrath. He passed his hand back over his hair and sat down again at the desk. For a long time he merely sat, staring first at Dora, then at Simão. At last, in a voice altered by emotion, he said:

"We're not getting anywhere like this, are we? Well, let's see if we can't look at things a little more calmly. I'm not angry with you, Simão. I can't be, for two reasons. First, because what you said about me is true. Second, in your situation, everything is excusable."

Again Dora and Simão were on their feet in front of him, anxious, expectant.

"I'm going to call Filipe. I'm going to tell him everything and ask him to come for Dora." Eugenio spoke quietly, resolutely. He picked up the telephone. "Hello. Dona Amelia, connect me immediately with Dr. Filipe Lobo. Immediately, do you hear?"

For a few moments Simão stood immobilized by indecision. Then, suddenly, the tension broke.

"Don't do that, doctor! For the love of God, don't do that!"

Dora was trembling, clinging to the boy's arm.

"Hello! Dr. Eugenio speaking. I'd like to talk immediately with Dr. Filipe." There was a pause. Eugenio frowned. "Impossible? But it's absolutely urgent." There was another pause. "Fifteen minutes! But that will be too late! Hello! Hello!"

Simão jumped forward suddenly and broke the connection. "Think what you're doing! Give us a chance!"

Eugenio placed the receiver on its cradle. His head was beginning to ache, and his tongue was dry. The per-

328

spiration which stood out on his brow was cold and disagreeable.

"Filipe couldn't come to the phone. He's having an
important conference."

Simão's lips twisted derisively. "You see? He has no
time for his daughter. Business, business, business! He and
his skyscraper! You and your professional conscience! As
long as the Mammoth grows and your conscience is at
peace, what does it matter how other people suffer,
whether they're humiliated or whether they're happy?
That's it! I know!"

For a moment no one spoke. Eugenio stared hopelessly
at a blank sheet of paper which lay on his desk.

"Well?" Simão said at last. "Our problem can be solved
today—right now. It all depends on you. Just a little kindness on your part. Think how much misery could be
avoided—"

Eugenio was shaking his head stubbornly. "No. Don't
count on me."

Simão sighed with an air of finality. He put on his hat
and took Dora's arm.

"All right. We went to a friend when we were in
trouble, and he didn't want to help us. Now we'll go look
for some stranger."

Eugenio stared at him questioningly.

"There's sure to be an abortionist or some doctor who'll
do for us what you don't want to." Taking Dora's arm,
Simão moved toward the door.

The moment was critical for Eugenio. Should he let
them go, and free himself of the responsibility? Dora
might lose her life at the hands of some unscrupulous
abortionist, some irresponsible charlatan. He could not
permit—

He leaped to his feet. With long strides he placed himself squarely between the couple and the door.

"You can go," he told Simão. "But Dora stays."

The girl looked uncertainly at Simão.

"She's coming with me."

"I won't let her. I'm taking her to her father."

There was a silence pregnant with hesitancy and tension. All three were breathing heavily.

"Come on, Dora." Simão's hand was on the doorknob.

Eugenio saw that if he wished to keep them from going, he would have to use force. Had he a right? Should he use violence to keep them there? Perhaps Simão would not carry out his threat. There was still time to get in touch with Filipe, so that he might intervene . . .

Simão opened the door and pushed Dora before him, into the hall. Eugenio looked away.

"Send in the next patient."

Minutes went by, and patients came and went. Eugenio attended them distractedly. He was worried. Where had Dora and Simão gone? He should not have let them go . . . If only he had used force to keep them there . . . He was strong; he would have been able to restrain Simão with relative ease in case the boy had resisted him. His obligation as Filipe's friend . . . Obligation? Friend? Always words! The doubt, the uncertainty . . . Why had these unpleasant things been laid at his door?

A half-hour went by. With difficulty Eugenio concentrated on what he was saying to his patients. He imagined Dora in a thousand situations—in the hands of a certain abortionist he knew, in the office of a doctor whose scruples he suspected. He saw her taking drugs, dying, dead . . . Oh, why had he not had more courage? But Eugenio hated violence; before resorting to it he would have had to use violence on himself. Or was he only a coward? Perhaps . . . But no, indecision does not always have its roots in fear.

However it was, he decided he must notify Filipe.

He put on his coat and picked up his hat. He excused himself to the patients who sat in the waiting room and hurried into the street and into a waiting taxi. He gave the driver the address of Filipe's office.

"He's still busy," one of the secretaries informed him.

"But I tell you, it's urgent!"

The man looked at his watch. "Just be patient. He'll only be five more minutes, at the most."

A few minutes later the door of the private office opened, and two middle-aged men appeared, followed by Filipe. "Then it's all settled?" Filipe was saying. There was a confused exchange of words of agreement, cordiality, and farewell.

Filipe spied Eugenio and waved to him amicably. "Hello there, old man! Wait inside there. I'll be right with you."

While he accompanied the two men to the elevator Eugenio went into the office. He was nervous. His heart was beating wildly, and his tongue was dry and bitter-tasting. How should he go about telling Filipe the unpleasant news? What would his friend's reaction be? A thousand times he wished he had not become involved in the disagreeable situation.

Filipe's face was radiant when he entered the office. He shut the door and embraced Eugenio.

"My boy, I have just executed a master stroke! I have just pulled myself out of one hell of a hole. I can take it easy the rest of the day. But look here! What kind of a face is this? Is somebody dead?"

Eugenio did not know how to begin. Filipe offered him a cigar, which he refused.

"Well? Well, come on—out with it!"

It would be better to tell him immediately, without preliminaries.

"Something very serious has happened, Filipe. To Dora." He still did not have courage to speak the whole truth.

Filipe held his breath, frowning.

"The car?" he muttered. "Tell me, man!"

Eugenio shook his head.

"Dora is pregnant."

Filipe was stupefied. He stared blankly at Eugenio. "What! Dora—my daugh— But—that's impossible!"

"Unfortunately, it is true. I—I examined her myself," Eugenio added reluctantly, flushing slightly.

He told Filipe all that had happened. Dora's father, as he listened, sank back limply in his chair; but his stunned prostration was short-lived.

"That goddam little Jew!" He broke a pencil in his big hands. "And you! Why didn't you do something to keep them from leaving your office?"

"I tried to call you, Filipe. They told me you were busy."

"You should have used force! You should have beat the hell out of that goddam Jew! And now? Where are they now?" He picked up the telephone and asked to be connected with his home.

"Hello! Hello! What the devil! Hello! It's Filipe. Has Dora come in?" There was a pause. "No? Not since morning?" He banged the receiver down furiously. He glared at Eugenio.

"As a doctor and as a man," he muttered between his

332

clenched teeth, "you are responsible for whatever happens to—to my daughter." He towered toward Eugenio, trembling with rage. "If at least you had been man enough to prevent that bastard from taking Dora out of your office, you—you—" He hesitated before he spat out the word Eugenio had feared most. "You coward!"

Eugenio felt the hot blood flow to his head. His face contracted suddenly in a mask of fury.

"And you—you, Filipe Lobo, are a rotten, contemptible fool!"

Astonished at Eugenio's unexpected reaction, Filipe's wrath abated somewhat. But once the barriers of timidity and convention were broken Eugenio's words spilled over in a torrent.

"Yes! As a doctor and as a man—you hear?—I hold you and only you responsible for what is happening now and for what—and for what is going to happen—" He was panting; his face was crimson, and his hands shook. "Dora is right. You care more for your Mammoth than you ever did for her. You left her completely to look out for your stupid skyscraper—because you're a conceited ass, because you're an exhibitionist, because you're an inhuman monster! See now if your fool skyscraper and all your money and your fame can make up for the harm that's done! See if—" Emotion choked him.

Filipe had turned away. On his face, for the first time, Eugenio saw a look of suffering, of fear, of intense and utter misery.

He was amazed at what he had said and at the strength and the courage he had shown in saying it. Silently he turned and left the office, crossed the waiting room to the hall, and hurried down the stairs without waiting for the elevator.

333

The rest of the afternoon they spent looking for Dora. Filipe called in the chief of police, who was his friend, and Eugenio went to Seixas, to tell him what had happened and to beg his help in finding Dora. He and the old doctor took a taxi and a telephone book, and together they visited every abortionist and doubtful physician in the city. Nightfall found them weary and anxious. They had discovered not the slightest clue. They had gone to Simão's home and had found the elderly Kantermanns uneasy, for the boy had not slept the night before, had left the house early that morning, and had not yet returned. Seixas entered the first drugstore they came to and telephoned Filipe's home. He spoke with Isabel, who told him that until that moment nothing had been learned.

When Seixas came back to the taxi he found Eugenio in a deplorable frame of mind.

"Hey! Cheer up! A body'd think you were the one who's pregnant."

Eugenio did not reply. His mind was filled with but one thought. He could have averted the tragedy. He had been a coward.

"I could have prevented this."

Seixas looked at him obliquely. "I didn't know you were God."

"Just the courage to give him a couple of good punches —that was all I had to do . . . I could have kept her in my office. I could have called her father."

Seixas shrugged his shoulders. "Her father would have come and given the poor kid a couple of good, hard wallops—and for the boy a couple of bullets in the head. He would have cussed like a sailor and talked himself blue in the face about his honor and his good name, about his being *the* great Dr. Filipe. And you can bet your bottom

334

dollar he would have used his good name and his money to get another doctor—without batting an eyelash, and for a handsome fee—to perform the abortion you very honestly didn't want to do. Don't be a fool. Stop worrying. By the way, where are we headed for now?"

"Don't ask me."

"Let's go home. The only thing we can do now is wait. Why don't you have dinner with me? All we have to do is put a little more water on the beans."

"I'm not hungry."

Seixas gave the driver Eugenio's address, and the automobile began to move again.

"It doesn't seem true," said Eugenio, "that you can't live without using force. . . . If I were made differently —if I were hot-tempered and impulsive, for instance, Dora would be safe at home now."

"Safe? At home? How do you know? Look at the possibilities. Dora may have had the abortion and be getting along fine. Or let's say she hasn't had it yet, and Filipe finds her. He might even accept the situation and decide to wait for the child to be born. And how can we be sure Dora wouldn't die in childbirth? I told you once not to worry. Don't go poking around in a cut just because it begins to hurt and bleed a little. Think about something else. Wait. Be patient."

He left Eugenio at the door of his home and promised to notify him personally or by telephone of any developments which might take place during the night.

In his home, Eugenio was able to find some release. Anamaria greeted him by clasping her arms tightly about his legs and plying him with her customary questions.

"What did you bring Anamaria? Where is my present, Daddy?"

335

Eugenio took her in his arms. More and more he was growing to identify himself with that tiny creature. He kissed her forehead and hair, and he thought immediately of Dora. Anamaria would grow up, would become a young woman, like Filipe's daughter. The world was evil, and all things seemed to indicate it was growing worse as time went by. He must be strong and clear-eyed in order to direct his daughter wisely. He sat down, placed Anamaria on his knees, and took up the portrait of Olivia.

"Who is this, sweetheart?"

"Mamma."

"And where is Mamma?"

"In heaven."

"Who told you so?"

"Godmother Frieda."

"And who else lives up in heaven?"

"God," she replied, very seriously, and on her plump, round little face was an expression that was Olivia's.

God. . . . If only he could believe as Olivia had believed! It would be easier for him now . . .

At dinnertime the Falks were in a good mood. Hans had made an excellent deal that afternoon. Dona Frieda was humming, and Anamaria was pounding her spoon joyously against her plate. Old Hans told an anecdote about his youth in Hamburg. Eugenio nibbled at his food. They had not yet risen from the table when the telephone rang. His heart skipped a beat. He rose swiftly and ran to pick up the receiver.

"Hello! Who? . . . Oh!"

He turned to Hans. "Seu Falk, it's for you." He handed the receiver to the little man. The rhythm of his breathing had altered perceptibly.

After Anamaria had gone to sleep Eugenio sat up reading the evening papers; but it was hard to focus his attention on what he read. He reviewed instead the disagreeable events of the afternoon. Seen through the short interval of time and space, they took on a slightly melodramatic coloring. He recalled every detail with perfect clarity.

It was almost ten o'clock when Seixas burst into the living room, his hat on his head. Panting, he sank down on the sofa and looked at Eugenio. His voice was low, infinitely weary.

"This life is really a—a—" He swore profoundly, and his eyes were wet. "Wouldn't you know it?"

Eugenio waited. He could not have said a single word; he seemed to have been rendered mute by his presentiment.

"The worst is always what happens. Anunciata—that bitch—did the abortion. There was a hemorrhage. When she saw how things were, she asked Rezende for help. Rezende didn't want to take the responsibility. She called Dora's father."

He was silent. He stood up, tossed his hat onto the table, combed his fingers through his coarse, gray hair.

"There wasn't anything she could do. Dora died just as it was getting dark. Give me a cigarette."

He held out his hairy hand to Eugenio. It was shaking.

Eugenio had no heart to go see Dora's body. He spent a sleepless night, tormented by his own feverish thoughts.

The afternoon of the following day Seixas told him the funeral had been crowded. Filipe and his wife were completely overcome. Isabel had fainted when they had brought out the coffin.

"And Simão?"

Seixas made a vague gesture. "I was at his house today. The old folks are pretty upset. He hasn't shown up yet."

337

After a moment the old man spoke again, and his voice was unusually gentle.

"Dora was so pretty in the coffin, Genoca. She looked like she was asleep. She was just a baby . . ." He sighed dejectedly and began to roll a cigarette. "Quinota sent a bunch of flowers that was really pretty—some she got for Dr. Ilya." He smiled, moistening the edges of the paper with the tip of his tongue. "This time, Seu Genoca, I guess the old Russian got cheated."

Chapter 23

The end of that winter was particularly somber for Eugenio. Dora's death had opened old wounds, and they were bleeding again.

He was no longer tormented by the sense of guilt in the girl's death, by the thought that one gesture on his part could have averted the disaster; he felt rather, and with painful acuteness, the futility of all gestures. His mother had been right. No one could outwit Destiny. Life rolled on, drawing men irresistibly toward the mad indulgence of their desires. He recalled having heard one of his patients say: "I'm no fool, doctor. I get as much out of life as I can. Conscience? That's silly. The world is wide open for the man who hasn't got a conscience." There were days when the faces of people and things seemed colder and more hostile than ever to him. At such times inspiration and joy disappeared from the world and, worst of all, Olivia herself seemed to have disappeared from his life. He fought against his pessimism and doubt, feeling that to give in to them would be to betray Olivia.

One afternoon he left the office in a particularly morbid frame of mind. It was raining, and the chill dampness of the streets, with its irremediable sadness, penetrated to the marrow of his bones. The sky was ashen, and men skulked by, tightly buttoned up. The hour was not like the end of a day, but like the end of the world. Eugenio's thoughts were bitter. That morning an old patient of his had died. The priest was still standing at the foot of the bed, administering extreme unction, when the loud voices of the dying man's three sons were heard in the dining room, in heated argument over the partition of their inheritance, for the administration of which no will had been left. They did not seem to be brothers; at that moment they were no more than enemies. Greed disfigured their faces. They looked like demons, like famished beasts.

Everywhere, thought Eugenio, there was parsimony and envy, avarice and hate, pettiness and malice. How could there be hope for mankind?

At that moment he felt that Olivia was dead. It must be the coldness, the dismal gray sky, the chill rain, the sadness of the paving stones and of the people who passed that made him think like that, for he knew Olivia could not die.

He walked with his hands buried deep in the pockets of his raincoat. He thought of Seixas. His old friend's life was beset by creditors, and he suffered from chronic bronchitis. Weary and ill, he dragged his enormous frame about his office, about the homes of his patients, about the streets, grumbling to himself, coughing, cursing, and prophesying that he would not survive the winter.

As he crossed the street Eugenio spied a metal placard which read "London Tailoring," and in his mind there appeared simultaneously the image of his father bent over his work, thin, infinitely patient, forlorn. He saw his mother crossing the room with a stack of dishes in her arms, Ernesto chopping wood in the back yard. How strange those memories seemed now! They seemed to belong to another life—voices, gestures, and people from a world that had vanished.

He felt, as he arrived home, the need for human companionship. His cold solitude was difficult to bear. In the dining room Hans Falk was smoking his pipe and reading a German-language newspaper; Dona Frieda sat with her knitting at the foot of the table.

Anamaria ran to meet her father. Eugenio took her in his arms and hugged her against his chest. The child clutched at his face with both hands.

"Daddy, I want to sleep in your room. I'm a big girl now."

"In my room?" he marveled. "But you don't want to leave Dona Frieda all alone, do you, sweetheart?"

"Godmother sleeps with Godfather."

The Falks burst into laughter.

"And do you really want to sleep in your Daddy's room?"

Anamaria shrugged her little shoulders, wrinkled her nose, and tilted her head to one side in astonishment.

"Aren't I your little girl?"

Again, as always, he found himself at a loss for an argument, and he gave her a sonorous kiss of capitulation.

That night Anamaria's bed was placed next to that of her father, and at seven o'clock Eugenio had to lie down beside her, so that she could go to sleep holding his ear. He looked at the delicate, serene little face, and Olivia's voice whispered in his mind: "You will live on in Anamaria. It is just as if you were given a piece of your own clay to model a new Eugenio." He could not weaken now; he could not disappoint Olivia.

When Anamaria had fallen asleep, he rose softly and tip-toed from the room. The atmosphere of the room which had belonged to Olivia choked him. He wanted to go out-side, to go to a movie or to a café, to a place where there was noise, the sound of human voices, so that he could be sure men had not perished from the earth. He put on his raincoat and galoshes.

"I'm going out, Dona Frieda," he called into the dining room. "If anyone calls, say I'll be back at ten."

He put on his hat and went out. The rain was still fall-ing, a thin, cold drizzle.

The Teatro São Pedro advertised a comedy. Almost without thinking what he was doing, Eugenio bought a ticket and entered the warm, delicately scented lobby. Too many lights and eyes made him vaguely uncomfortable. Fortunately, his seat was at the far end of one row, where he would not be in the way of anyone wishing to enter the row.

As he sat down, he glanced over the orchestra and the lower boxes. He started. In one of the boxes nearest the stage Eunice sat with her father. She was dressed in black, and she looked very white and blonde—almost platinum blonde. Eugenio looked away. He was upset. His first im-pulse was to jump up and run out of the theater, but a swift reflection convinced him of the senselessness of such an action. Yes, he thought, his heart still pounding, why not stay? Eunice meant nothing to him. They were like strangers. They belonged to separate worlds. He was aware, nevertheless, that he was blushing. He shifted un-easily in his seat, scarcely daring to look around. There must be other people who knew him in the theater. They

341

would be sure to see him there, and they would talk. But what did he care? Had he committed some crime? He remembered the insinuating, vicious rumors that had arisen when his divorce from Eunice had been made public. Unconsciously he moved a leg. The man in the seat in front of him turned around and stared significantly. With a jolt, Eugenio realized he had hit the man's chair. If only the lights would go out! If only the curtain would rise!

After a few minutes the lights dimmed appreciably and the orchestra began to play. Eugenio stole a furtive glance at Eunice's box. Cintra was bending over his daughter. In the rear of the box another man was standing. It was Castanho; his dark eyes gleamed in his long, pale face. Essay on Greek tragedy . . . He bent to say something to Eunice, and she smiled. Eugenio watched them cautiously. *Pour enfanter de belles pensées* . . . Cintra was shaking his head, displaying his white teeth. Dairy monopoly . . . *You have a knack for things like this, boy* . . . Suddenly Eugenio was calm, with the proud calmness of the man who knows he has not erred in his decision. Yes, he was proud of his solitude. He did not belong to the world of the Cintras and the Castanhos. He was strong, he was his own master.

He looked at the stage. The musical overture came to an end with a series of flourishes on the drums, followed by three evenly spaced booms, and the curtain rose. The other drama had begun, thought Eugenio. Which was the more false? he asked himself some minutes later, when the plot of the comedy had begun to take shape and the individual characters of the cast were beginning to be delineated through actions and dialogue. Which of the two dramas was the more conventional—the one on the stage, or the one in which Eunice was the principal figure? He imagined how Eunice would look on the stage, in a pair of silk pajamas, sitting with her legs crossed Oriental-fashion on a divan, reading a book and smoking a cigarette through an amber holder held elegantly between her white fingers.

A burst of laughter from the audience summoned him to reality. He began to concentrate his attention on what was happening on the stage. It was a run-of-the-mill comedy with poor dialogue, full of puns and trite plays on words.

Suddenly, he was seized by a desperate longing to take part in the general gayety, to laugh with his neighbors and forget Eunice and Cintra and Castanho, to forget his past, the rain and the cold outside, Dora's death, the inherent evil of mankind, the incongruity of life. But he could not forget. He was condemned by his memories to a life apart, a life of isolation. He was compelled by his memories to suffer. He wished he could exchange places with the fat old man at his side, who shook heartily as he laughed, his face deeply creased with mirth, his heavy jowls quivering like gelatin, his round shoulders rising and falling.

When the curtain fell and the lights came on, Eugenio left the orchestra. In the lobby he paused, remembering his graduation day. Right there, beside that column, he had found Olivia with her arms full of red roses.

He lit a cigarette. Should he stay for the rest of the performance? He hesitated. No, he resolved, he would go now.

He left the theater and crossed the street in the direction of the square. A thin, steady drizzle was falling. He paused to look at the monument on which he and Olivia had sat that night, weighed down by their diplomas. The

343

dragon was just as it had been then, crawling up the first step, one claw raised, its teeth bared. Its bronze back gleamed.

He walked on, thinking now of Eunice. It was hard to believe that he had lived with her three years, in the same house, as man and wife. She was a total stranger now. As if he had never spoken the slightest word to her . . .

Suddenly he was surprised to find himself whistling a merry tune. It was good to feel strong. There was something pleasant in being alone.

When he came to the Mammoth, he stopped. He felt as ill at ease as if he had come face to face with a man who knew his darkest secret. He looked at the bench where he had sat one night talking with Dora and Simão. Now he was alone. Alone with the bench and the Mammoth and the emptiness and the rain.

At home Dona Frieda was waiting for him when he opened the door.

"Somebody called from Seu Travis' house, Genoca. The little boy has a bad fever."

"Was it long ago?"

"Just this minute."

Eugenio nodded. He turned and went out again.

The rain was falling harder now, but even that did not matter. He knew the hour was not far off when once again he would know perfect calm, acceptance, great peace.

September ushered in the Brazilian springtime with strong, wintry winds and heavy showers. But one morning in October Anamaria and old Hans Falk filled the house with resounding gayety, and Eugenio was awakened by his little daughter bounding up and down on his bed.

344

"Looky at the sun!" she shrieked. "Looky at the sun! Look at the pretty sun, Daddy!"

The next minute he was out of bed, hearing the excited voice of Hans Falk, who was shouting from the yard.

"Come see, Frieda! Do come see how beautiful!"

Eugenio flung open the window and leaned out. Hans was pointing to the rear of the yard, where his favorite tree, a peach, was covered with pink bloom. It was the tree on which the childless old man lavished paternal affection.

"Look, Genoca!" he called, his face very red as he looked up at the window. "See how beautiful it is!"

The sky was a clear, luminous blue. The breeze smelled of sap and flowers.

Eugenio went into the street that morning in love with the world. The number of patients who came to his office in the afternoon was greater than usual.

At nightfall Seixas found his friend at his desk, smiling to himself, reading a small, yellow card.

"Well! What hit you? What's that you're reading?"

"This is wonderful!" Eugenio exclaimed as he looked up. "You really do learn something every day!"

Seixas sat down, brushing the cigarette ashes from his vest. "When you're my age you'll find there isn't anything new in the world."

Eugenio was going through his files. "Do you know," he said, "I've been finding right here in real life, in flesh and blood, some of my old friends in books."

"You don't say." There was little enthusiasm in Seixas' voice. He rolled a cigarette with an air of intense boredom.

"Faust, for instance." Eugenio picked up one of the cards. "Right here he is. He won't be coming back, because I was lucky enough to be able to straighten him out. I took down his real name and age and a couple of notes,

345

just for my own information." He put the card back in its place and took out another. "And here's Hamlet. And yesterday I talked to Pygmalion." He leaned back in his chair and looked at Seixas, who was moistening the edge of the cigarette paper with his tongue, his blue eyes fixed in a vacant, alien stare, "Do you know the story of Pygmalion?"

The old man felt in his pocket for a matchbox. "I'm not interested in fairy tales."

"Well, I know you've heard the story of Faust."

"That old geezer that couldn't manage his own drawers, the one that fell in love with Margaret? Sure."

"You get A-plus. Well, I've been working with all those old fellows. Sure, they come in dressed the way we do, and they have different names. But really, underneath, they're the same old storybook characters we've always known."

Seixas took a long draw from his cigarette and exhaled the smoke uninterestedly. But Eugenio, with determination began to tell his story.

Faust had entered Eugenio's office in the person of a tiny old man with bow-legs and a bald head, who came scraping and bowing and pleaded as he gave his name that what he was about to say be kept secret. He was a widower, sixty-eight years old, and within a few months he was going to remarry. He wanted—he wanted . . . He winked at Eugenio. "You know, doctor, I'm not exactly a boy any more . . ."

Eugenio studied the old man's features. His face was like a faun's.

"How old is your fiancée?"

"Eighteen. She's a cashier in Sloper's, and what a little

346

doll!" He kissed the tips of his fingers ecstatically. "You can't imagine, doctor."

Eugenio was pensive. "You're not afraid?" he said cautiously, after a moment.

"Afraid? Of what?"

"The difference in your ages."

The old fellow leaned forward and slapped Eugenio's knee. "Life is short, doctor, and every fellow ought to get the most out of it he can. She's willing, and I can tell you I'm not the man to throw away a little gift from heaven. No siree, I'm no dumbbell!" His dim little eyes glistened.

"So you want to be young again—"

"That's it, doctor. Even if it's just for a couple of years —or even one. As a matter of fact, I'd be happy with six months. Prescribe something for me, doctor, give me some kind of a diet. The money doesn't matter." He paused, and his face became clouded. "For that I could even sell my own soul."

Hamlet had come to Eugenio in the guise of a tall, skinny, sad-eyed bookkeeper. He was not yet thirty years old, but his life was one prolonged state of depression. He ate little, slept poorly, and brooded constantly. He could not bear to be with people; he did not know how to make friends, and he had no faith in anything. He told Eugenio that his life had been a failure because of constant doubt and inability to make decisions. Recently he had been haunted by the idea of suicide, but, because of his doubt and uncertainty, he had been unable to carry it out.

Eugenio listened with his arms folded, patiently and attentively. The bookkeeper did not look at him; he kept his enormous, dark eyes fixed on the linoleum floor and

347

spoke in a colorless monotone, as though reciting a speech he had memorized.

"What is life, anyway, doctor? Life—life . . . You know . . . It isn't worth the effort . . . Sometimes I think, Well, you're born, you suffer all your life, and what for? No one is really sincere. All men are egotists. Women too. Sometimes you fall in love and make an ass of yourself, and what for? For one of these painted, false little she-devils the worms'll eat after she dies and turn into a skeleton like any cook. You heard that little verse about the two skeletons that were talking under the ground. The poor one sat up and said to the aristocrat, 'Where are your ancestors in that pile of white bones?' The aristocrat didn't know. We're all the same when we die. And what is death? Maybe it's a dreamless sleep. Or maybe life is a dream about death . . ."

His unusual hands, which were strikingly long, thin, white, and hairy, were nervously clutching a book with a beige cover. With some difficulty Eugenio made out the title: *Problems in Accounting.*

Eugenio's Pygmalion was a moneylender named Ramão Rosa. He was a middle-aged man, and lived in a melancholy, rose-colored house near Ponte do Riacho. His wife had run away with a sergeant of the Military Brigade, and in desperation he had taken the creosote his unfaithful wife had bought a few days earlier to put on a tooth that had been troubling her. Ramão Rosa left a letter for the police, asking that no one be blamed for his death—he was a reader of the serials in the *Correio do Povo*—and bequeathing all his earthly possessions to the charitable works of the Belém Sanitarium. Arriving in time, Eugenio was able in a few seconds to put him out of danger. And the next day Ramão Rosa, crestfallen and sad as he lay in his big double bed, his lips and mouth badly burned, told Eugenio his story.

"Imagine, doctor, the ingratitude. I found Mimi in an alley. She was a streetwalker, doctor—a soldier's girl. I liked her—so young, you know, and already gone . . . Just imagine, she was only fourteen." He sighed deeply. "I brought the poor little tyke home and had her cleaned up—my neighbor there can tell you about it. I got her some decent clothes—nice underwear and silk stockings, shoes and everything. She couldn't read or write, doctor. She didn't even know which letter was A. I'll have you know I taught her—Lordy, I was patient! but I taught her to read. I educated her: 'Mimi, don't eat with your knife; Mimi, take your hand away from your nose; Mimi, don't laugh like that, it's ugly; Mimi, don't do this; Mimi, don't do that.' Well, doctor, I'm not bragging, but I turned that little alley rat into a lady as good as any of these in high society. If you'd seen her after a year, you'd never have recognized her. She looked like a good girl, from a good family." He paused. "Will you have a little shot of *cachaça* with honey, doctor? It's the best kind. No? Well, I educated that kid, and then I fell in love with her and gave her the best proof of it a man can give a woman. I married her. I really married her, doctor, it was a real wedding, with a license and a priest and a justice and everything. Well, to make a long story short, I took Mimi out the of the gutter and fixed up a decent life for both of us—Aunty Mariana here'll bear me out." He sighed again and clutched the bedcovers tensely. "Well, that little devil left me for a sergeant in the Brigade." He looked at Eugenio as though for assistance and explanation of a phenomenon he did not understand. Then he added, philo-

349

sophically: "It was the stuff she was made of, doctor. She had bad blood."

Eugenio rose from his desk. Seixas had listened to his recital without showing any sign either of enthusiasm or of interest. Presently the old man said:

"Life has a little of everything. It's like a little market with completely stocked booths. Speaking of markets, how was your practice today?"

"Like a mad house. I'm done in."

Eugenio sat down on the desk facing his friend. "You know, I'm dead tired, but I'm happy." He looked over Seixas' head, in the direction of the window, and his glance was lost in the distance. "You know, Olivia was right. Happiness is the feeling you get at times like this, between one tiring job and the next, when you can talk with a friend or play with your children or read a good book. To see anything, you need contrast. How could I really appreciate an hour with Anamaria if I hadn't spent hours here first, curing other people's sickness and trying to work out a solution of my own problems?"

Seixas moved restlessly in his chair. "Unh-huh. You want contrast. A kind of Turkish bath. Steam cabinets, then—*sssst!* ice water."

"Well, you can call it whatever you want to. What's wrong with us is that we've made comfort and pleasure the sole objects of living. You know, now, for the first time in my life, I'm beginning to feel as if I amount to something, because now I can look back at all that and not care."

Seixas was shaking his head. "Mighty pretty, mighty pretty. You wait till you're as old as I am."

Eugenio seemed not to have heard him. "Look at the harm it does people not to have some kind of ideal they

350

can work for. If they don't have that, then there's only one object, and that is to have a good time. And you can buy a good time. You know better than anyone how hard it is to make money honestly. Life is so short; and, youth being even shorter, no one cares much how they get their money. That's why they call this the century of gangsterism. Anything goes—the rawest kind of low deals and immorality."

Seixas shook his head vigorously, as if to loosen from his brain the clinging mist of incomprehension. He dusted his trousers, which were covered with cigarette ashes, and got slowly to his feet.

"I'm leaving you because today you've turned to philosophizing. I'm a simple man, and I don't like to think about things."

"Wait, I'll go with you."

When they reached the street Eugenio asked Seixas whether he had had any news of Simão.

"I've seen him to talk to. The poor kid is completely shot. He's not worth a hoot any more. I offered to give him a few shots of strychnine."

"What about Filipe?"

"I talked to him, too. I asked him not to pick on the boy. Told him he'd only make things worse that way, that he'd wind up with everyone knowing the truth about Dora. But, just the same, I'm still afraid they'll run into each other some day."

For a long time Eugenio and Seixas walked along, side by side in silence. It was growing dark, and the street lights were already on.

At last Eugenio broke the long silence. "Aren't you afraid Simão might do something crazy?"

The old doctor shook his head. "Hell, no! He's gotten

through the worst of it already. He'll forget. Time's a good cure for anything."

Yes, thought Eugenio, time was a good cure for anything. Soon Dora would disappear from the lives of Filipe, Isabel, and Simão, just as Olivia herself had disappeared from his own.

It was sad but inevitable. And in her deep way Olivia herself had expressed its truth when she had said, "Life begins every day." The world, thought Eugenio, would be unbearable if man had a good memory.

Chapter 24

It was New Year's Eve, and Hans Falk was watching his cuckoo clock anxiously, for it was only ten minutes to midnight. Dona Frieda was arranging plates of sandwiches and croquettes on the table. The radio was flooding the little room with the resounding strains of a march.

Hans went to the pantry to refill his empty mug from the beer barrel. He had been drinking since dinnertime, and his cheeks were very red, his eyes brilliant.

From the window, Eugenio could see the gigantic form of the Mammoth towering over the city, every window illuminated. More than three hundred squares of light were cut out brightly in its black face. Two powerful searchlights on its roof swept the sky with their narrow, pallid shafts.

The music stopped, and the announcer began to speak. "This is Station PRH-2. In a few minutes we will transmit to all the Americas the New Year's Eve ceremony of the dedication of the Mammoth, the superb skyscraper

352

erected by the firm of Lobo & Company, Limited. This gigantic structure, the pride of Brazilian engineering genius, is the tallest building in Latin America and was designed by the noted engineer-architect, Dr. Filipe Lobo, who personally supervised its construction. We are honored to have with us tonight His Excellency, the Governor of the State of Rio Grande do Sul, who will officiate at the inauguration ceremony. Our microphones are installed in the grand salon on the thirtieth floor of the Mammoth, where there are gathered tonight many high-ranking authorities of our municipal, state, and federal governments, as well as representatives of the leading organizations of our capital and many other distinguished personages. Ladies and gentlemen, the spectacle before me is dazzling. On the stroke of midnight His Excellency the Governor will begin the dedication speech, at the conclusion of which there will be a grand display of fireworks from the roof of this monumental edifice. It is now only a few minutes before midnight. While we are waiting to usher in the New Year, let us hear a bit of music."

From the loud-speaker the rippling strains of a waltz flowed into the room. Dona Frieda began to dance happily across the floor, carrying in one hand a plate of hazelnuts, walnuts, and almonds and in the other a basket of raisins. Hans kept time with the music by swinging his clay mug rhythmically from side to side.

"Heavenly days!" exclaimed Dona Frieda, as she looked at the generously laden table. "Do you suppose there'll be enough?" The Falks were expecting friends to drop in after midnight.

"I have my beer, and I'm happy," declared Hans, winking one eye and licking the foam from his upper lip.

Dona Frieda ate a croquette and made a little pirouette,

humming to herself. Hans rose on his toes, lunged forward, and slapped his wife's back side. *"Prosit!"* he shouted.

"Hans! Behave yourself!" she laughed.

Without setting down his mug, Hans put one arm around her waist, and they began to dance. They were as excited as two children.

"Heavens! Hans! Let me go get things ready!"

She freed herself of his embrace and ran into the kitchen. Hans turned up his enormous mug and drained it.

At the window, Eugenio was still watching the Mammoth, fascinated. The great building was a part of his life, a kind of omnipresent divinity, for no matter where he might be in the city, he always saw its gray form rising toward the sky. He never saw the Mammoth without seeing also visions of Filipe, Isabel, Dora, and Simão. The huge creature of cement and steel was for him a constant, tangible reminder of many things.

The hands of the clock were nearing twelve. Dona Frieda and her husband sat opposite each other at the table, exchanging glances of great and silent expectancy. Something momentous, something extraordinary was about to happen. They seemed to be awaiting a supernatural revelation.

Eugenio too was excited. A vague anxiety, oddly not unpleasant, had possessed him since nightfall. Soon the New Year would begin. Soon the Mammoth would be dedicated. In vain he tried to convince himself that, in spite of these two facts, life would not change. He began to envy the simple, lighthearted gayety of the Falks. He wanted, like them, to dance, without either care for the present or memory of the past. But he could only lean at the window sill and watch the Mammoth. There was striking beauty in that enormous, rigid thing. But in its cornerstone, he thought, there was a body. The Mammoth had been erected over the body of Dora. Was Filipe happy that night?

He looked at the stars, and they reminded him of Olivia. The searchlights of the Mammoth moved from side to side, like the fiery eyes of a monster looking for stars to devour. From the river there came the sound of a motor launch. In the intervals when the radio music stopped, the roar of traffic in the crowded streets below echoed dully in his ears.

He wondered what Filipe would be thinking when the Governor dedicated his building, at the moment which should be, as he himself had said, the proudest and happiest of his life. If only Filipe could be made to see his mistake, to do something to correct it, Dora's tragic death would not have been for nothing. Eugenio thought also of Isabel, whom he had seen two months earlier as she passed in an automobile, thinner now and older, her face and her dress in deepest mourning.

Suddenly he was jolted from his reverie by the loud voice of Hans Falk.

"It's midnight!" he shouted, rushing to embrace his wife. They stood tightly clasped in the center of the room, kissing each other frantically.

From the city a clamor arose. There were gunshots, the blowing of factory and steamboat whistles, the honking of automobile horns, the ringing of bells, human screams, music.

Suddenly Eugenio was enveloped in Dona Frieda's hearty embrace, and he received on each cheek a resounding kiss.

"May God bring you happiness, Genoca—you and Anamaria and all of us!"

Hans, as he hugged Eugenio, began to weep and mutter incongruous things about Germany and life. The sounds of the merry-makers grew louder. The strident voice of the radio announcer was raised against a deafening, tangled background of human voices.

Dona Frieda went to get Anamaria, who came rubbing her startled eyes.

"Hug Daddy, Mamma Frieda's little sweetheart."

Eugenio took Aanamaria in his arms. He pressed her against his chest and kissed her tenderly. She was not yet awake, and she did not quite understand. She blinked her eyes, pursing her lips and shaking her tousled head.

Dona Frieda filled a glass with white wine and handed it to Eugenio.

"To Anamaria's health."

Eugenio drained the glass.

Hans rose unsteadily from his chair and went to stand before the portrait of Hindenburg.

"To dear old Germany!" he shouted, and drank the last drop of beer in his mug. He began to sing a draggy, monotonous old German song.

From the loud-speaker came the voice of His Excellency the Governor. Anamaria had returned to the arms of Dona Frieda, who gave her a small glass of *guaraná*.

Eugenio resumed his post at the window. From the roof of the Mammoth spewed great geysers of colored fire. The monster was spitting fire at heaven. They were a rare sight, those shining stars and spirals, circular flowers and garlands. Rockets traced long scratches of gold straight up against the black sky; then they burst, letting fall a shower of sulphurous green, blue, red and yellow stars. A phantasmagorial radiance crowned the head of the Mammoth.

At Eugenio's side, Hans, Dona Frieda, and Anamaria were also watching.

"How beautiful!" murmured Dona Frieda.

Anamaria was frightened and began to cry. Eugenio stroked her head gently.

"Don't be afraid, sweetheart."

"That hurts, Daddy. I'm afraid."

"It won't hurt you. Daddy won't let it."

Yes, he must protect Anamaria, now and always. He looked back at the Mammoth with defiance.

At twenty minutes past midnight, Seixas arrived. He received the embraces of his friends without enthusiam. He accepted a glass of wine, nibbled a croquette, and looked long on the sleeping form of Anamaria on the sofa.

"Let's make a toast," proposed Dona Frieda.

Hans walked unsteadily to his wife's side. "Viva!"

Dona Frieda filled Eugenio's glass and her own.

"Whom shall we toast?"

"Life," suggested Eugenio.

Seixas grimaced wryly. "You won't see me drinking to that bitch. I've broken off with her for good."

"Stop trying to kid us," said Eugenio. "You know you're in love with her."

Seixas shrugged his shoulders. "Let's drink to Anamaria. Of all of us she's the only one there's any hope for."

There was a clinking of glasses, and the four drank up.

With the arrival of the guests Hans and Frieda had been expecting, Eugenio invited Seixas to go out with him. The night was mild and clear.

"Where shall we go?" asked Eugenio.

"Let's just walk." After a moment the old doctor added, "I haven't done much of anything else all my life anyway."

Eugenio offered him a cigarette.

"You're pessimistic tonight."

"Do you want me to go around giving off fireworks? I'll be sixty-one this year. There's nothing so gay about that."

They walked a few yards in silence.

"It's funny," Eugenio said at last. "It's funny, and it's silly, how every New Year you make plans—how, just because it's New Year, you begin to think about the past and philosophize."

"Well, it never cost any money to make plans."

"Maybe it's because it gives you a boost—inspires you to go on."

"And deceives you."

The street was filled with the noise and movement of many people. Cafés and restaurants swarmed with merry crowds. Groups of men and women stood in knots on street corners, talking loudly, gesticulating, and singing. Trolley cars were overflowing, and automobiles passed, filled with turbulent passengers who waved and shouted.

A gray ambulance flew by at top speed, whining steadily and mournfully.

"Some drunk, you can bet," Seixas remarked. "In a coma."

This observation was an opening for Eugenio.

"Sometimes I think," he said, "that the medical profession can have a much more important function than the majority of people give it credit for. I think, since most human beings are sick mentally, the job of improving conditions in the world might well be up to the doctors. Think what can happen when a man with an inferiority complex becomes a dictator. Look at what can happen when some police chief in the interior goes berserk. Look at a lot of the men in power all over the world, men who have the masses at their disposal. If those men were perfectly healthy there wouldn't be any wars, governments wouldn't commit wholesale atrocities—"

"You and your fool philosophizing! I don't know what's got into you lately. You're getting to be worse than—worse than—I don't know what!"

"Just think what wonderful rulers doctors would make! No one else works so close to life, to the people. No one else knows better than the doctors what the people really need."

"Yes," Seixas broke in harshly. "But did you ever notice that in nine cases out of ten, when a doctor gets to be a politician, that's the end of him as a medical man? Politicians! Politicking gangsters! Just take a look around you." He shook his head repeatedly. "What a funny kind of an animal man is, anyway! Conceited, vindictive, intolerant, thoughtless, and principally lacking in memory. He forgets everything except what concerns his stomach, his sex, and his vanity."

As if he had not heard his friend's pessimistic outburst, Eugenio continued:

"And if *all* kinds of specialists and experts—scientists, physicians, writers, economists—would work together, according to a well thought-out plan, they could really accomplish something for the world. Of course you can't make the world perfect. But wanting to put an end to the senseless paradoxes of the century we live in isn't so crazy. Hunger in an age of overproduction, too much work for some, and nothing for others—and this is the 'Machine Age'!—disease and ill health in an era in which medicine has made such enormous progress . . ."

Seixas was smoking thoughtfully. He looked at Eugenio out of the tail of his eye. "Tell me something, my naïve

359

young friend. Do you really think you're going to save the world?"

"Well, it's funny how I think about these things now. A few years ago I'd never have believed something Olivia said once would have such an effect on me. She said, 'Consider the lilies of the field, how they grow; they toil not, neither do they spin: And yet I say unto you, that even Solomon in all his glory was not arrayed like one of these.'"

"Uh-huh, have faith in the Virgin Mary and don't go running to see what's going to happen to you!"

Eugenio smiled. They were crossing a street. As they reached the opposite sidewalk he continued:

"It all boils down to one thing—that men should respect each other and be willing to work for their common good. All the elements are there, but the difficult thing so far has been to reach an understanding. No one wants to take the first step."

They passed a night club with brilliantly lighted windows. From inside came the sounds of jazz music and human voices. Eugenio threw his cigarette away.

"It would be enough if everyone would just live up to what Christ preached in the Sermon on the Mount. The Sermon on the Mount is a condemnation of war, covetousness, and violence; it praises love, tolerance, patience, and peace."

"Sure, sure. Sounds fine. But you'll learn that making a plan like that work out in real life can be something else again. Don't fool yourself. Filipe, for instance, could tell you that without covetousness there'd be no competition, and that without competition there'd be no progress."

"Progress is a means, not an end," said Eugenio vigorously. "Progress is a means to comfort, well-being, and

360

happiness. But a man shouldn't want all those things just for himself and his own family. He should want them for everyone."

"I suppose you think that's human nature? Take a good look around you and tell me whether you think men have or haven't always behaved like a pack of wolves. Remember human egotism, remember instinct, and tell me if all this craziness you're talking isn't just a pipe dream."

They turned into a street that was not crowded.

"There are two kinds of cruelty," said Eugenio. "There's the kind of cruelty men commit out of blindness, for lack of understanding, and there's the kind of cruelty men commit because they enjoy it. There is a remedy for both. In the first case the answer is education. For the second it's the sanitarium. That's why I tell you there's a great task for the doctors and the teachers."

Seixas' gesture was impatient. "And what makes you think doctors and teachers don't need education and sanitariums?"

"Well, whatever name you want to give them, there's no denying the world would be better off if there were a handful of good, intelligent, strong men who were willing to make the experiment."

Eugenio wondered at his own enthusiasm. His arguments came to him easily, and his words were fluent. There must be something unusual about this night . . .

"Goodness and strength are almost never bedfellows," said Seixas after a moment. "The good, wise man hates violence; but the only way to make men who don't have any sense listen to you is to use force. You've got to use strait-jackets on lunatics. Look, you yourself are against using violence. Men with common sense are an insignificant minority. What does that leave us?"

For a long time they walked in silence, their footsteps echoing sadly in the deserted street.

"Take war, for instance," said Seixas. "From the strictly humanitarian point of view, war is barbarous. Ask any man. Ask him, 'Do you want war?' 'No,' he'll tell you, 'I don't.' 'And what about you?' you ask the next one. 'No,' he says, 'I don't want war either.' No one wants war. But just the same, war comes. It's the same with everything else. Anything is easy to say. But in life, Seu Genoca, you keep butting up against stone walls."

"I insist the answer is reeducation. A revolution may change a system of government, but it can't change human nature."

"All right, then! So you do agree that man is really a beast held in leash to a certain extent by religion, law, and a thousand other tiny little things invented by a group of men with utilitarian aims?"

"Dr. Seixas! I don't recognize you!"

"Must be the wine. Let's talk about something more serious. Is Ulysses' son any better?"

"Yes. I gave him some more insulin."

The old man snorted approvingly. They turned a corner, and Eugenio saw that unintentionally they were walking in the direction of the Mammoth.

"Take our case, for instance," began Seixas, returning unconsciously to the subject he wished to avoid. "What are we? Nothing. What can we do? Very little. How can we expect to save the world, if we can't even save our own selves? Look how hard it is to keep peace in a little family. Look at the fight a poor schoolteacher has to put up to keep order in a class of thirty students. And you talk about saving the world!"

"So then we must shut ourselves up inside our egotistical

shells and confine our meditations to our own tiny spheres?"

"You know what they say about our being 'pawns of Fate,' don't you?"

"Whatever we are, I believe Fate can be improved upon."

Seixas broke into a loud guffaw. "You can't fool me! What a time little Genoca is having, trying to believe there isn't any bogey man!" He coughed painfully. "Who could be an optimist with a cough like this? And a stack of unpaid notes in the bank? And a neurotic daughter at home? And sixty years of a ruined life gone by?"

They were approaching the Mammoth. Eugenio wanted to run away from it; at every corner he tried to redirect their footsteps. But always, inexplicably, they drew nearer to Filipe's skyscraper.

They walked for a time beside a long wall, where someone had scrawled a crude legend of hate.

"Look at that," said Seixas. "It's a whole lot easier to get people to follow you by waving a red flag at them than it is if you wave a white flag. There's more drive in an emotion like hate. Hate is masculine, and love is feminine. You can get men to go to war a whole lot quicker than you can get them to pray."

"What about Gandhi?"

"That's a different story. The Hindus are dealing with Englishmen, and Englishmen will sacrifice a lot to keep up their reputation for being 'gentlemen.' That obsession of theirs is the only thing that saves England from so many of the scrapes she gets into on account of her imperialistic skulduggery."

Eugenio reflected for a moment.

"That's it," he said after a while. "The spirit of being

363

a gentleman could do it. If every man would be courteous to every other man—"

"That's a dream. Hate and egotism are natural. Courtesy is something men have to be taught."

"All right. Let's go back then to the need for reeducation."

Seixas stopped abruptly and gripped Eugenio's arm. "You mentioned Jesus Christ. If one man's opinion means anything, I don't believe in this business of taking a slap on one cheek and then turning the other, and I don't believe many other people do either. If anyone hit me, I'd give him a black eye."

"So?"

"So I'd feel better. I'd go up to the man, and I'd say, 'Let Grampa see where it hurts.' I'd put a piece of raw meat or some arnica on his eye, whichever he needed. Yes, Genoca, you're dreaming."

"A dream isn't a dream any more when someone carries it out."

"Life is life. And make-believe is make-believe. You're in your thirties, and you can still dream. Listen to what I'm going to tell you, and think it over when you get to be fifty. I'll be dead and in my grave by then, so I won't be able to hear what you think. Not that it'll matter. Listen. Take a walk alone some night like this and say to yourself, 'Seixas, you were a rat, but you were absolutely right.' And maybe, somewhere, I'll be listening."

They had arrived in front of the Mammoth, where a small crowd was gathered. Eugenio and Seixas stood side by side on the edge of the sidewalk, gazing up silently at the brightly lighted building.

"There's no doubt about it. That thing is pretty," murmured Seixas.

Eugenio nodded. "I get chills whenever I look at it, the way I do when I pass a battalion and they give a roll on the drums. Or when I hear a beautiful speech. The kind of thing that makes a man go to war and kill, and tear other men to bits. I ask myself now, How much of that is natural, and how much is the result of defective education?"

"Don't ask me any more questions!" the old doctor exploded.

Eugenio smiled. "I guess I'm worse than Simão today, trying to get to the bottom of things."

There was a long silence. With slow, deliberate fingers, Seixas rolled a cigarette.

"Don't take what I say seriously," he said, striking a match. "You may be right. What the hell! I guess if I didn't believe in life I'd have shot myself long ago. It's just that sometimes you get fed up. Don't pay any attention to a broken-down old goat like me. When Quinota hugged me at midnight tonight she cried, poor thing. I didn't ask her why. After all, she's right. She's borne up pretty well all these years. She's seen some pretty tough sledding. And she's been a first-class buddy through everything." He sighed and took a draught from his cigarette. "Thirty years ago, on a night like this one, I made her some promises. I was going to change my life, I was going to make a pile of money and buy a house and a car . . . What the hell! Just the same as ever. Sometimes I figure I got a damned raw deal." He eyed his cigarette. "Grampappy sure is bitter tonight. Let's get out of here. This place is like Hades itself."

They walked slowly away, across the square. They walked together in silence, each withdrawn in his own thoughts.

At the end of that summer, Eugenio received news which filled him with a profound, strange peace. Eunice and Castanho were scheduled to sail for Uruguay, where they would be married. "Pour enfanter de belles pensées," Eugenio reflected. Yes, now Eunice and Acelio would be able to spend whole days discussing literature and litterateurs. When they awoke each morning they could read to each other selections from the classic English and French writers. At lunch they would have Plato, and at five o'clock tea, the moderns. They would dine with the surrealists, and, naturally, they would sleep with Freud. Eugenio considered these things without malice, with a shade of compassion.

On that early April morning he sang as he left his bath. He was happy, at peace with the world and with himself, and he did not want to analyze his feelings.

At the breakfast table he opened the morning paper and turned as always to the "want ads," where every Thursday and Sunday a small notice appeared, requesting information concerning the whereabouts of Ernesto Fontes. He had to find his brother. A mysterious intuition told him Ernesto was still alive and not far away.

On the last page of the paper he found a picture of Filipe at his desk, in front of two telephones, a dictaphone, and a stack of papers. Next to it was a four-column article with a showy headline: "Builder of Mammoth Engaged in New and Spectacular Undertaking." The writer of the article praised Dr. Filipe Lobo extravagantly, his physical appearance, and the atmosphere in which he worked. The words "dynamic" and "formidable" appeared again and again. Dr. Filipe Lobo revealed his newest plans. His company had acquired a vast tract of land on the bank of the Guaíba, where in the near future he planned to build the most modern and luxurious resort villa in all Latin America. It would have a large casino in an original interpretation of the Spanish mission style, in a setting of . . . Specific data followed; there were figures and details.

As Eugenio folded the paper, his thoughts were of Filipe's daughter. How cruel that Dora should be dead on so beautiful a day!

He swallowed the last drop of coffee in his cup, got up from the table, and went to the window. The morning sun was cool, tinged with the rich, old-gold light of a gentle sun. A fine lavender mist hovered in the air, softening the outlines of things and giving them a faintly dissolved appearance. The city, enveloped in the sun-threaded mist, was like a child's bright toy wrapped in cellophane.

No one could do wrong on a day like this, thought Eugenio, accepting the moment wholly. He longed for human companionship, and he thought of his daughter, then of Olivia. A shade of remorse darkened the light surface of his happiness. Recently he had had little time to think of Olivia. The cares and complexities of his new life, his intensive and unscheduled work, took every precious moment which he might spend with her, rereading her letters, recalling things she had said and done.

He turned from the window and, as was his custom in the morning, picked up a text on medicine. He read a few pages, but his mind wandered from their printed surface, out into the sunlight. The sweetness of the autumn morning haunted him. How beautiful the streets must be in the light of that ripe, friendly sun! He imagined how its beams must be playing over the leaves of the trees in the park, with their cool shadows, bluish and smelling of dew. He thought of the ducks swimming on the lake, of Anamaria throwing bread crumbs for them to catch. He closed the book brusquely and returned it to the shelf. Again he went to stand at the window. He could see the Mammoth, smoky in the mist. Its concrete façade was accented with tiny, symmetrical areas of pale color—printed signs and plaques with the names of doctors, dentists, engineers, lawyers, modistes, offices, organizations.

If at that moment, Eugenio reflected, an inhabitant of Mars should land suddenly on the earth, how astonished he would be that on a day so bland, so magnificently beautiful, with a sun so golden, the majority of men were indoors, in offices, shops, factories . . . And if the hypothetical visitor should ask one of them, "Man, why do you work so hard when the sun is shining?" he would receive the singular reply, "To make a living." To make a living . . . Life was there outdoors, offering herself with miraculous gratuity to all men. But men were too blind even to notice that she was there. With all the conquests of their superior intelligence, they had not discovered a means of working less and living more. They struggled through life and neither loved nor recognized one another. Competition transformed them into enemies. Many centuries ago they had crucified a prophet who had tried to show them they were brothers.

Oliyia's words echoed in his mind: "We must not forget to be a little like the grasshoppers." How strange! Already he could no longer remember precisely the sound of her voice.

"Dona Frieda!" he called.

"Ye-es!" came her jovial reply from the back of the house.

"Would you mind getting Anamaria ready for a walk in the park?"

In the kitchen, Anamaria, who had been playing in the sink, began to dance up and down and squeal delightedly.

"Don't forget the bread for the ducks!" Eugenio added.

Whistling like a schoolboy, he went to his room and took off his robe. He put on a tie and coat and picked up his hat.

A few minutes later, Anamaria arrived, filled with excitement. She was dressed in blue. In the middle of the room she paused, caught the hem of her dress, and pirouetted coquettishly.

"Look, Daddy, don't I look pretty?"

In his daughter Eugenio saw Olivia on the night of their graduation, in the lobby of the Teatro São Pedro. He saw the filmy gown she had worn, the armful of red roses, the parody she had made on feminine coquetry . . .

Yes, he resolved, in the park he would think about Olivia. He would think and think about Olivia . . .

He knelt to embrace Anamaria and kiss her cheek, but she pushed him away, whimpering as her little brow wrinkled in an expression of annoyance:

"Oh, Daddy, you'll muss my curls!"

Eugenio looked at her happily. Life was good. He wished that this light, shining moment might never end. But he knew how fragile it was, how fragile . . . He did not want to analyze it, for he sensed in the recesses of his mind a concealed darkness which might at any moment— which must not be allowed to come to the surface.

"Do you want to feed the ducks?" he asked Anamaria, shaking her gently. "Do you want to take a walk in the park?"

She clapped her hands and jumped up and down. "Oh, yes! Let's go! Let's go feed the ducks! Oh, goody, goody!"

But Eugenio's eyes had suddenly become grave. Anamaria knit one small eyebrow and tilted her head to one side.

"Daddy—Daddy, what's wrong?"

He did not answer. He was thinking of the little girl he had attended the night before. She had been thin and dirty, and her eyes had been sad. Her clothes had been rags, and she had looked undernourished and hungry. He had seen that if she were not removed from the filthy house in which she lived, if she did not receive proper medical care, she would undoubtedly become tubercular. There were in the city, in the state, in the nation thousands of children like her . . .

Eugenio got up. He put on his hat abstractedly.

No, it was not enough that he should be happy, that he should have a rosy-cheeked, happy, well dressed and well fed Anamaria at his side. What of some project to give other children adequate food and clothing, proper hygiene, instruction, medical and dental care, summer camps, opportunities for recreation, for happiness . . . It was a great plan. Seixas would help him. The old doctor loved children and young people. He considered adults and the aged as irrevocably lost.

"But no one is lost," said Olivia in his memory. Yes, it was sad: he had completely forgotten the sound of her voice. But he knew that Olivia was alive; he was almost obsessed by the odd notion that she had made an appointment to meet him in the shade of the trees in the park. They would talk about themselves and other people, while Anamaria threw crumbs to the ducks on the lake . . .

Anamaria pulled at the sleeve of his coat frantically.

"Daddy! Daddy! Da-a-addy!"

Eugenio looked down at her, his mind still far away. "H'm?"

"Let's go right away, Daddy. The ducks are hungry."

"Ah!"

He bent and took her hand, and side by side they set out for the park, to feed the ducks on the lake, in the sunlight.